BEING INES

A novel by

Eva Lauder

Copyright © Eva Lauder 2022

The moral right of Eva Lauder to be identified as the creator of this work has been asserted in accordance with the Copyright, Designs and Patents Act 1988

All rights reserved. No part of this publication may be reproduced, distributed, or transmitted in any form or by any means, including photocopying, recording, or other electronic or mechanical methods, without the prior written permission of the publisher, except in the case of brief quotations embodied in critical reviews and certain other noncommercial uses permitted by copyright law. For permission requests, write to the publisher: info@evalauder.com

Published and printed in the United Kingdom
ISBN 978-1-3999-2418-4

A CIP catalogue record for this book is available from the British Library

Published by Ethica Publishing©
Formatted by Rae Davennor in collaboration with Stardust Book Services

This novel's story and characters are fictitious. Certain long-standing institutions, brands, places and transport systems are mentioned, but the characters involved are wholly imaginary. The author is providing this book and its contents on an "as is" basis and makes no representations or warranties of any kind with respect to this book or its contents. The author disclaims all such representations and warranties, including but not limited to warranties of healthcare for a particular purpose. In addition, the author assumes no responsibility for errors, inaccuracies, omissions, or any other inconsistencies herein.

The content of this book is for informational purposes only and is not intended to diagnose, treat, cure, or prevent any condition or disease. You understand that this book is not intended as a substitute for consultation with a licensed practitioner. Please consult with your physician or healthcare specialist regarding the suggestions in this book. The use of this book implies your acceptance of this disclaimer.

evalauder.com

London Borough of Enfield	
91200000804750	
Askews & Holts	10-Jan-2024
AF ROM	
ENWINC	

To my kids, nothing is impossible. To my friends and family, thank you.

Table of Contents

Chapter 1	1
Chapter 2	15
Chapter 3	35
Chapter 4	57
Chapter 5	75
Chapter 6	97
Chapter 7	123
Chapter 8	149
Chapter 9	171
Chapter 10	189
Chapter 11	215
Chapter 12	225
Chapter 13	239
Chapter 14	259
Chapter 15	271
Chapter 16	299
Chapter 17	307
Chapter 18	313
Chapter 19	321

Chapter 20	333
Chapter 21	341
Chapter 22	355
Chapter 23	359
Chapter 24	363
Chapter 25	369
Acknowledgements	375
About the Author	377

Chapter 1

In the hope that she would see the silhouette of Dylan, her asshat of a boyfriend, sauntering across the tree-lined square at any moment, Ines realised that she hadn't left the kitchen, all night. Hating herself that bit more for checking the phone again—on the off chance that there was a missed call from him, the image of her partying on a beach with friends stared back, a bleak reminder of the life she once had before they met.

The clock flickered to 03:37 and Ines resigned herself to the fact that she was heading for yet another night on her own. Stubbing out the cigarette, she squeezed it against the odorous pile in the glass ashtray swiped from Fordhams, during a raucous night out celebrating her best friend Sally's much anticipated divorce. Sealing the contents into a ziplock bag before tossing it into the bin, the young woman watched the pewter grey lid shut with a gentle click before she turned and left the kitchen.

Wriggling under the covers until the soft cotton duvet shrouded her petite frame she took one last glance at her phone; a small part of her still clung on to the vain hope that maybe he would send news of his whereabouts.

Exhausted, her shaky fingers switched the device off, her mind, replaying memories of better and carefree days, as she watched the screen spiral into blackness…

Three years ago, when she'd been handed the property details by the estate agent on a chilly spring morning, Ines knew it would be love at first viewing. Looking across at the elegant white Georgian facade in all its impressive grandeur, Montague Square was in full bloom; the cherry blossom sighing in harmony with the tulips, the chatter between walkers receding into the distance. Clouds of vapour trailed her words. 'It's beautiful.'

Standing beside his smitten client, the estate agent Luke Benoit was used to the reactions of house-hunters whereupon they lay eyes on the stunning properties shown to them. Hearing his soft French lilt as he uttered the words, 'Shall we go in?' Ines' guard was well and truly weakened. He could have asked her to "Pass the cleaning bucket," and it would have still had the same effect on her!

Gawking at the beautiful high ceiling and cornices, a fantasy began to unfurl of how happy she'd be living in such a stunning home, dinner parties and fresh croissants and coffee from the artisanal café across the square, on lazy Sunday mornings. Living la dolce vita!

Interrupting her thoughts, the agent continued with his polished sales pitch. 'The kitchen is of exquisite quality, designed by Butler and Wright.'

Running her hand across the smooth opaque worktop, the surface felt cool against her skin. With a shrewd glint in his eyes, Luke watched his client's every move. Pretty, he thought. Yes, this lady was very pretty. Her elfin face was unconventional, but it suited her. An imperceptible show of approval, Luke strode across the kitchen for a closer inspection of the ceramic hob — a ruse for a distraction, creating a respectable distance between him and Ines.

Blowing dark curls out of the corner of her mouth, Ines was able to assess the agent for the first time: high cheekbones accentuated by chestnut hair falling around his face, and eyes the colour of artichokes... *artichokes?* Of all the colours nature can offer, Ines could only liken the agent's eyes to artichokes! Feeling the blood rush to her face, Ines sensed her cheeks turning a shade that reflected the colour of her crimson coat, spurring the decision that now was not the time to assess the gorgeous guy standing opposite her. With a deft manoeuvre, she found herself at the tall sash window overlooking the square, having developed a fascination with the magnolia tree in the distance. Perceiving this as an indicator that she needed a little personal space before they continued the tour, the estate agent took measured steps towards the door. His discretion had not gone unnoticed.

FWITTT!!

Looking buoyant for slapping Ines' bottom, Dylan stood by and watched on with a wicked grin. Irritated and upset at his audacity, she brushed a freckled hand away from the curve of her hip as if he had been a very unwelcome louse. She was emotional and suffering from sleep deprivation. Rubbing tired eyes that stung with the effort of peeling them open, her face crumpled in disdain on seeing the time. Half-past-six! A grand total of two hours sleep. This terrible sleep pattern was playing havoc with her body clock, as well as the dark purple smudges developing under her eyes. Desperate for a decent night's sleep, she was well aware that she was now becoming an insomniac, thanks to Dylan.

Sliding off the bed with the willingness of a crotchety old lady and heading for the kitchen, it was hardly worth leaving it in the first place.

Lolling against the kitchen counter, brushing dark auburn curls away, Dylan grinned behind bright and incredulous eyes. 'What's your problem?'

'My problem? Are you for real?' Spinning round to face him, Ines had begun spooning fresh coffee with vigour, into the coffee machine for a much-needed morning pick-me-up. Leaning forward to turn it on, she shook her thick mane, adopting the "tousled bed hair look" she had seen in a magazine feature about what men find sexy in a woman.

Observing with irksome amusement, Dylan moved his testy girlfriend away from the close proximity of the knife block (he wasn't taking chances) and draped a sinewy arm over her shoulder, leaning in for a tentative kiss on pursed lips, the smell of stale beer and cigarettes on his breath, repulsive. Spurning Dylan's advances, Ines muttered her disgust. 'Where have you been these last two days?'

Looking through narrow eyes, Dylan scrunched his face. 'Since when do I answer to you?'

Turning back to the coffee machine and switching the button off with a lofty flick, Ines made a show of removing her cup and taking a sip, choosing not to answer him.

Perched on the same acrylic bar stool she had sat on only a couple of hours ago, the discontented young woman lit a cigarette, its tip glimmering as she drew in a long inhale. Blowing out a steady stream of smoke up into the air, she took her time to reply.

'It's funny how light can affect your judgement and decisions. Last night I sat in this exact place staring out of the window, hoping to see you making your way back home. I was ready to end it. I still am, if I'm honest. Where do we go from here? Do you have any idea?' If she was honest, Ines didn't even know the answer. Swivelling back and forth on the stool, engaged in her thoughts, Ines refused to face Dylan. Piqued, her jaw was set, emphasising the definition of her bone structure 'You can't blame it on your job. It's just an excuse. You can, however, blame it on your complete disregard for me and our relationship.'

For once, Ines wasn't the hysterical wreck she usually became in response to Dylan's misdemeanours. Had she become so immune to his selfishness and womanising, that it no longer stirred despair within her? Sighing louder than she intended, she took a final drag on the cigarette, flicking it with precision into the ashtray. Cradling the glazed cup, Ines found that rolling it between her small hands had a cathartic effect—plus it prevented her from wrapping them around Dylan's throat.

Locked in their own thoughts, the mood felt oppressive. Contemplating the rabbit hole of conflicting emotions, she found herself being dragged into, Ines knew that somehow things had to change… but how and when? She'd think about it another day. Right now, work responsibilities were calling her and she had to get ready.

Dismissing the sudden giddiness as being the result of getting up too quick and a rush of blood to her head, Ines made her way to the bathroom, walking with the rigidity of a tin soldier. The cold and fatigue started having this impact on her body on a regular basis over the last few months. Perplexed at this unpleasant manifestation, she reasoned that it was probably stress related.

Standing at the kitchen door, Dylan watched the solitary figure disappear into the bathroom. 'Erm yeah, when your spoiled highness has had her shower, can she at least have the frigging decency to tell me where we go from here? I've got people to see and work to go to!'

Pushing the bathroom door with a determined tap, Ines demonstrated to the imperious boyfriend what she thought of his demand, with a one finger salute. It was a minor triumph, but for her it was a huge deal. On this occasion, she stood strong. 'Morning love.' The voice was always cheerful, never threatening or leering. Ryan was homeless, and despite his hardship, he always had a smile and a truly admirable air of positivity about him.

'Hello, you. Are you managing to keep warm and dry in this horrible weather?'

Smirking, Ryan sat up, pulling his legs out from inside his sleeping bag and showed Ines his new joggers. 'Kind of. Some buggers knicked my tent and clothes yesterday, so I've raised enough money to buy me some new threads.' Nodding at his ensemble, he continued. 'I'm a few quid away from buying a tent as well.'

Shaking her head, Ines huffed her exasperation. 'I can't believe the asshats that are out there. Who the hell would do a thing like that?'

Ryan's small mouth twisted up in one corner, suggesting that he was used to this. But he wasn't. Ines could see that. He was far from okay.

Surrendering to the enticing aroma of warm food, Ines deliberated the options ahead. *Hmmmm, I think today's a sausage and egg toasted baguette day.* Reaching in to grab one, a voice close behind startled her into almost dropping the brown paper bag.

'Too many of those can be lethal. You want more wiggle than wobble on those cheeks,' teased Luke, the Estate Agent, who had become a good friend to Ines over the years.

'Ha! Thanks for your concern, funny boy, but it's not for me.'

Chuckling with self-approval, continued. 'Don't lie.'

The muscles in her shoulders tightened at Luke's repartee. Sensing her discontent, he lent a consoling arm around the sullen young woman and kissed her on the cheek.

'Hey, I'm only joking.' Somehow, in the three years they had known each other, Luke always made her feel secure although he did drive her insane at times. She felt a warmth that she never experienced with Dylan.

Moving across to the self-serve beverages, Luke ushered Ines in the same direction. Reaching for a wooden stirrer as he poured brown sugar into his macchiato, Luke felt distinctly apathetic in what he was about to ask, but he felt the need to know. 'So, where's Dildo?'

Ignoring the disparaging nickname he has for Dylan, Ines began dipping a mint teabag in and out of her cup, lost in her own thoughts. Watching with cheerful adoration and fighting the urge to come out with a double entendre, Luke broke into a childish snigger.

Ruffled, she peered up at him. 'What? What is going through that peanut butter brain of yours?' Taking the teabag out of the cup and dropping it into the litter basket, it landed with a satisfying squishy "plop". Luke regarded her with a lopsided smile. Ignoring the puerility, Ines jostled him along. He being six-foot-three and she a mere five-foot-one, it was always a matter of great amusement for everyone who saw them together, especially when she was cross with him. Whatever the reason for her complaint, it was hard to stay peeved at him for long, no matter how determined she was to stay that way.

'So?'

'He's away on business. He left this morning for Manchester.' Not believing it herself either, she redirected the subject with the expertise of a politician— it's surprising she didn't get a cricked- neck. 'You shouldn't take sugar in your coffee, it's not good for you.'

'I need a little brown sugar in my life. It's good for my soul.' Sparkling with mischief, Luke took pleasure in embarrassing Ines.

Dropping her gaze when their eyes met, she lay her hand on her stomach hoping to allay the topsy-turvy churning. 'Well, we all need a little sugar in our lives, but yes, it is recommended that brown is better for you.'

This had been a reference to his recent dalliances with a flight attendant who had a conflicting love affair with too much makeup and very revealing clothes. So conflicted were the two, that she wore both at the same time, all the time. Happy with her retort, Ines's heart did a little victory dance as she turned on her tiny kitten heels and made way to leave. Dutifully, Luke followed suit.

'I got you these.' Offering the paper bag to Ryan, Ines took pleasure in seeing the smile on his lovely face. And he did have a lovely face. Shaped like a heart with a dusting of tiny freckles under deep-set hazel eyes and an unruly mop of fine rose-blond hair, he resembled a member of a rock band. Leaning down, aware that her skirt fluttering in the wind could flip up, Ines held the hem down against the backs of her legs, ensuring her modesty remained intact. Reaching further into where Ryan was huddled, a mouth-watering whiff drifted through the air as she passed the bag across.

'Sausage and egg in a toasted baguette, a large tea and some chocolate… and please take this to get yourself a tent.'

Taking hold of the bag and the twenty pound note she had squeezed into his weather beaten palm, Ryan's grip on Ines' hand tightened with overwhelming gratitude as he looked into her dark, almond eyes. 'Thank you.' Ryan tapped his chest with his free hand. 'You're always so kind to me.'

'It's nothing, honestly. I wish I could do more.'

Straightening back up, with a broad smile, she bade him goodbye and turned to find Luke still standing in the doorway having watched the whole scene unfold before him. Ines never ceased to amaze him, although he drew the line at her taste in boyfriends. Smiling back at her, Luke nodded towards the direction of the station, a gesture signifying that they should leave.

In comfortable silence, Ines and Luke walked down the street towards the estate agents' where he was the manager, and she would then disappear down the steps of the underground and begin her commute to Smythe & Co, a large department store in the heart of the West End, where she worked as a buyer.

The wind had picked up, and the morning air had become chilly. She could feel her legs becoming as leaden as the clouds above. Struggling to walk in a straight line, Ines staggered towards the ground. Snapping out two long arms, Luke had prevented a stupendous fall. His words puffed in ambiguous tones. 'How many times have I told you to stay off the rum before work? If you're going to stack it, at least do it in the comfort of your own home.' Wide eyed and open-mouthed Ines struggled to find her voice.

Having her friend make light of the situation was what she needed. He knew how to deal with her, even when she was having moments of low mood.

'I know right? I've a reputation to uphold, my secret life of a lush could be scuppered.'

Dringgg dringgg

'Someone's calling you. Give me your tea so you can answer it,' he offered.

Struggling to hold her cup in one hand and the lemon drizzle flapjack lodged between clenched teeth, Ines hedged herself a bet that the caller would hang up just as she managed to retrieve the phone from the abyss of her oversized handbag. 'I'm fine…I can manage,' came the muffled reply. Luke looked on, fascinated at her obstinacy and the chaos that she leaves in her wake.

Trying to juggle a cup and a crumbling flapjack wedged in her mouth, whilst trying (and failing) to look elegant, it was inevitable that this was not going to end well. Thrusting her cup and tilting her chin, Ines was now squealing in desperation. 'Take my flapjack!'

With military efficiency he took both, allowing Ines to spin her bucket of a bag from her hip to find the offending phone.

Dringgg, dringgg

'For crying out loud, I'm trying!! Grrr, where's my phone!?' Rummaging with desperation through her bag, and now resorting to emptying out some of its contents, Ines finally grabbed a hold of the shrilling phone as though it were a prized sporting trophy. Silence. The caller hung up!

Her eyes on Luke, Ines couldn't help but think he resembled a cup holder (albeit a very dapper one) carrying the hot beverages… one with remnants of a flapjack placed precariously atop the lid.

Dipping his eyes in the direction of the red lined interior of her bag, Luke broke into a wry smile. 'See those two pockets? I believe one is for a mobile and the other for stuff that you need to access quickly. From my understanding, they're very useful.'

Ines glared at him from where she had been crouching, the contents, in a heap on the pavement. 'I actually don't know why I even talk to you.' Hands clawed like an arcade grabber machine, she snatched the items, and without giving any attention, dumped them back into her bag. 'Missed call from Zara,' she sighed.

Still in a tizzy with the events of the last twenty minutes, Ines needed to sit down. Her head spinning and her body weak, she began to make headway for the bench near the station. Bumping shoulders with waves of commuters hell-bent on not being late, bustled past. 'I don't feel well, Luke. I need to sit down and rest before I get on the train.'

With a protective arm around her, Luke guided Ines across the busy street. Urging her to sit down, he lowered himself alongside Ines.

'Shall I call work and tell them that you'll be late because you're too dumb to even contemplate what an inside pocket of a bucket size bag is made for?' He patted Ines's knobbly knee. 'And that when you discovered what its actual purpose is, you promptly passed out at such a revelation. Hmmm?' Luke squeezed her knee for good measure.

'Very funny.'

Considering the phone, Ines chewed her lip. As if he could read her mind, with the skill of a pickpocket, Luke swiped the phone out of Ines' grip and dropped it into the pocket of her bag. Although she watched on agape, she concurred that her friend should take matters into his own hands. Passing the cup, Luke nodded as he watched her take a sip from the fuchsia pink cup. 'Pink to make the boys wink, heh?'

Smiling at the new expression Luke had picked up after meeting a young woman wearing a pink top, Ines swallowed the hot tea, screwing up her eyes and grimacing like a child. Watching as people began to pick up their pace at the first sign of rain, she turned to face Luke who was looking ahead, deep in thought. With lackadaisical effort, Ines broke the lull. 'You're going to be late opening up. You should go…'

Beep beep!

The high-pitched sound resonated from inside Luke's suit jacket. '…and answer that.'

With a deft manoeuvre he removed his phone from the purple lined pocket. 'See how fast I was when I pulled that out?' Declaring this with a cockiness that only he could get away with, the bonhomie was short lived. The smile on his face melted like the last snow of winter when his eyes fell upon the name of the caller blinking back at him.

'A talent like that could be a game changer when it comes to closing the deal on a potential bedding partner,' came Ines' sardonic response.

Beeep beep!

In her mind, if the ringtone was humanised, she could sense the caller's desperation. Rolling his eyes, Luke muttered. 'Pffffff, what does she want at this time of the morning?' he groaned.

Judging by his reaction, it was more than likely his clingier than cling film girlfriend, Courtney. 'You should answer it,' encouraged Ines.

As thoughts of Dylan whirled around her head, Ines had become lost in her own melancholy: Somehow, without even realising it was happening, she had become an ambivalent half-wit. She knew her boyfriend was a self-entered schmuck but felt trapped in the belief that she would never get anyone better than him. She was a shapeless mess who nobody would ever fancy or want. In the two years they'd been together, Ines had gone from a confident, vivacious young woman to a sceptical introvert, lacking self-belief.

Ines' negative thoughts were swept aside at the sound of Luke's irritated voice in the background.

'Are you serious? Couldn't you have waited until tonight, and we could have discussed this properly?' Luke was positively peeved. 'No, I said it's a possibility. POSSIBILITY. P-O-double ESSSS-I-B…' He was flushed with anger. Uh oh. 'I'm not being patronising, Courtney, I'm being pragmatic.'

With that, he hung up and slipped the phone back into his pocket. Shaking his head, he reached into Ines's bag and pulled out a box of menthol cigarettes. Popping one into his mouth, with a deft flick of the spark wheel, he lit it and took a long, indulgent drag. Checking the time, Luke calculated how long he had to spare, taking into consideration the time to walk to work, open up and get the day's schedule in order for the team. He hated this part of the day as much as he hated saying goodbye to Ines. Wonderful Ines, who had no idea of her true worth or beauty. Making a quick mental calculation, he had eight minutes to sit with her before they had to go their separate ways.

'Well?' she prompted playfully.

Shaking his head in frustration, Luke took another drag of the cigarette, and leant forward, propping his chin over a dark olive knuckle. 'She's made an appointment to view an apartment in Notting Hill,' he breathed with an air of reluctance. 'She made it yesterday, without consulting me first. It's at 3 pm today.'

Sweeping a cursory look, Ines felt it was better to say nothing and instead, forage through her bag for mints, fearful of exposing an iota of her feelings for Luke. Wordless, her distracted friend accepted the sweet. Savouring the sensation as it prickled his taste buds, he looked at his watch again. They had three minutes before going their separate ways.

'But I thought you liked her.'

Rubbing the whiskers along his jaw with a free hand, Luke looked into the distance as though the answer could be found there; 'I like coffee, but it doesn't mean I'd buy a coffee plantation.' Letting out a soft growl, revealing his umbrage more than what was intended, Luke crushed the cigarette beneath an ox-blood leather brogue. 'It's just moving too fast.'

'She could just be afraid to lose you,' reasoned Ines, trying to sound sympathetic.

Exasperated, Luke leant back. 'You've got Dildo who disappears for days without so much as a message and I've got Courtney who has to be with me twenty-four seven.'

Aware of time ticking away, Ines made to stand up and head for the underground. 'Come on, we'll both be late if we don't get our shimmy on. Let's meet after work if you can get away.'

Luke nodded his approval. 'Okay, cool. I'll message you later. And yeah, I can get away. I'm not a pet.' Feeling recharged, Ines turned on her heels and began to walk in the direction of Earl's Court station. Feeling better and more positive, she reached out and rubbed his arm. 'Go, have a nice day and don't stress. What will be, will be.' Lifting an expectant face, Luke leant in to kiss her goodbye. 'Bonne journée, ma belle,' Luke uttered.

'À bientôt,' waved Ines, as they parted. Waving back with a boyish smile, Luke continued with his walk to work.

Chapter 2

The sparkling glass doors slid open onto the lobby of Ines' workplace. She never took for granted how lucky she was to be working as a senior buyer for Smythe & Co. at such a young age, and she would often gaze up in admiration of the company signage, with its simple classic logo, eponymous with style and trends. 'Morning, Miss Garcia,' crooned the voice from behind the reception desk.

'Morning, Michael,' she beamed. 'How are you this morning?' 'I'm not bad, thanks. Spring seems to have lost its way but as always you fill the dullest days with rays of sunshine.' A smile as broad as his face crept into the creases of his eyes. Reddening at the compliment, Ines smiled to herself. The simplest appraisal was like a much hankered after hug.

'Well, we've only just left winter. Maybe give it a chance, eh?' reasoned Ines as she continued walking to the elevator.

Sitting at her desk, Ines booted up the computer and began to look through the list of things she had to do for the day:- Meeting at 11:00 a.m with Bridget Nyman, the Head of Buying.

She considered rescheduling, but in her experience, it was better to just get it over with rather than prolonging the tortuous experience. Sighing her discontent, she tapped her pen on the desk to the rhythm of the song she was humming, pondering legitimate excuses that could get her out of the meeting. Owing to Bridget's Nordic stature and personality, Ines found herself unable to warm to her boss. They were polar opposites in every way possible. Bridget was like an exquisite marble statue with hair the colour of pearls and eyes of cornflower blue. Her personality, Ines found, was as opaque as her skin. She was model material without a doubt. Ines, on the other hand, who always felt like the dumpy, unglamorous sidekick in a comedy duo, the Costello to the Abbott, was petite and curvy with tourmaline brown eyes and a warm demeanour.

Ping. Ping. Ping.

Three texts from Zara— or "Me Me" as Luke called her in secret, came through at once. Ines jabbed the glowing home button. Three consecutive messages creating one very short sentence for added effect: -Call me-when you can-need to talk xx

Oh the drama, it's all too much, thought Ines, her fingers flying across the touchscreen keyboard. Checking it didn't "sound" as it looked, she clicked "send".

Feeling accomplished and ready for work, Ines began to look at the analytics of the recent week's takings for the women's wear department. Without even looking up from the screen in front of her, she was well aware that the buying assistants were looking over at her, no doubt talking tripe and creating elaborate stories stemming from something very insignificant. It's how they functioned through the day— a small compensation for not being able to stand at the school gates with all the Lycra-clad gym mummies and gossiping about non-Lycra-clad gym mummies.

Ines examined all the data before her, working through each recent purchase and what order was next in line to be placed. It was the cusp of spring 2019, but she was thinking of the autumn/winter 2019 collection. What would be trending and what to purchase, to ensure successful commercial yield with little profit loss.

Massaging the bridge of her freckled nose she looked down at her phone and realised that her meeting with Bridget was in half an hour. Had she been so engrossed in her work? Taking a deep breath she pushed back her chair, enjoying the feeling as it glided away on its chrome castors, refraining from squealing "Wheee!" Her flask of lemon and ginger water was almost finished. Feeling self-righteous, Ines thought that a well-deserved trip to the coffee machine for an espresso and some chocolate was very much in order. Sauntering past the buying assistants, she could feel their eyes boring into her. Smiling straight at them, Ines couldn't help but think of the Pendle Witches. Reaching for her cup, she programmed the machine to double espresso mode. The lack of sleep was taking its toll and beginning to affect her physical and emotional well-being.

'Oh hiiii, Ines,' drawled Echo, one of the assistant buyers. She was named Echo as a result of being born during the Echo Boomer generation. She also revelled in the fact that Echo was, in Ancient Greek mythology a mountain nymph cursed by Hera, so that she would never speak again other than to repeat someone's last words. She had fallen in love with Narcissus, but her infatuation was unrequited. Following Narcissus' death, Echo had faded away and all that was left was the sound of her voice repeating last words spoken by someone. This Echo, however, was here for the foreseeable future, talking about her sideline work as a "life coach"— a Vlogger on YouTube. She was a self-proclaimed "Yummy Mummy" who wanted women to feel empowered. What she doesn't tell her viewers, however, was that she has a Thai housekeeper who cooks, cleans, does the grocery shopping and deals with Balthasar and Titus, her two little boys. Ines wouldn't be surprised if the housekeeper was also fulfilling her husband Conrad's conjugal rights. This cheered Ines up every time she looked at Echo wittering on about her #blessedlife.

'Hello, Echo. Are you and Martha up to speed with the deadline for next week's store promotion?' Ines pressed the start button and listened as the machine gurgled and belched into life.

Nettled by Ines's lack of interest in small talk, she confirmed that yes indeed, they were up to speed.

'Good. When the story board is ready, can you leave it on my desk so that I can authorise it please?' Ines mustered the broadest smile possible, looking over at the rest of the small group, who were by now, surveying everything.

'Yes, of course. We're halfway through. The rest of the team are deciding on directions for the visual merchandisers,' came Echo's hurried reply.

'Excellent, thank you, Echo.' With a curt nod and a flourishing departure, Ines returned to her desk with the coffee, recapping on the conversation. A sense of self-loathing grappled at her conscience; her amenable character was waning, and Ines was well aware of the changes which were now affecting her everyday life and it was something only she could resolve.

Looking up from the screen, Ines gazed across the open-plan office where the buying assistants were huddled around their desks discussing "moods", slapping magazine cuttings, quick illustrations and visuals on a large board, all the while whispering their thoughts amongst each other.

Ping!

Zara. Her timing was incredible. *Now what?*

-Can you talk?

-No, I'll call you later. Have a meeting to go to x Whoosh. Message sent.

Buzz!

'Ines, Bridget is ready to see you,' a cheery voice called down the phone.

'Thanks, Marie.'

Replacing the receiver, she gathered the printouts to discuss analytics with her boss.

Waving through the frosted window, it appeared that Bridget was in an upbeat mood.

'Morning Ines, please, sit down. Can I get you something to eat or drink?'

Remembering that she never did eat her chocolate with the espresso, and aware of the strong coffee taste in her mouth, Ines promptly accepted.

'Can I have a peppermint tea, please?' Looking over at the Patisserie Lydia box with its pretty pink ribbon hanging loose, she realised how hungry she felt. 'And an almond croissant please,' smiling into the box of delights.

Dylan, being a fitness fanatic, had always been quick to criticise or comment on Ines's curves and her refusal to torment herself about not having abs and a thigh gap. Her lack of interest in looking honed and living by the hallowed guidelines of social media, rendered her open to his snarky jibes. Ines wasn't overweight in the slightest, and nor had she any intention of starving herself. However, regardless of how happy she was with her shape, Dylan often made her feel that she was a bulging lump. Being told;

'you know babe, you'd be perfect if your hips were smaller,' had become an unwelcome ear-worm that often wriggled from within.

Shutting down that memory, Ines grasped the warm pastry and took an indulgent bite, almond paste oozing out the sides. Bridget followed, and for a minute, there was silence as both women luxuriated in their pastries.

Brushing her hands clear of crumbs and wiping them with a pink embellished napkin, the older woman began to speak, gingerly taking a sip of her matcha tea. 'So, what are the figures saying?' …

***

Noticing it was lunchtime, Ines gathered her bag and phone, making a conscious effort to place it in the inside pocket, as per Luke's advice. She could see him now, standing before her, looking pleased with himself.

Lunch was a solitary event for Ines. In an occupation that involves talking to people, this was the only opportunity she had to catch her breath and regain some form of sanity. Having made her way to Violets, the eatery every employee of Smythe & Co. headed for, Ines was not feeling hungry after devouring half of the patisserie box during the meeting. Standing in front of the hot food cabinet and staring at the options, Ines decided with indifference on a broth. Grabbing a tall cup of the liquid lunch and a carton of coconut water, she paid before heading to the eating area where she could sit amongst others who also wanted peace and quiet.

Opting for a corner and removing herself from queuing customers and chatter, Ines gave the tacky rubber wood table a quick spritz of sanitiser with disapproving strokes before taking a seat. Deliberating whether anyone would notice if she took off her shoes, she decided it would be okay to slide her petite feet out, as long as she was discreet. Wiggling her liberated toes was a lovely feeling.

Distracted with reading the newspaper, Ines took a large gulp of the steaming broth. A searing fire pit tore through the roof of her mouth. Wincing her way in the course of the ordeal, hot coals flushed down her throat. Conscious that her nose was mutating into a fierce red beacon and her eyes watering, the calamitous young woman knew that this was not a great look to be sporting. Gasping short, sharp intakes of breath, desperate for the sensation to vanish, she blew her streaming nose into a napkin with such gusto her brain was sure to follow.

Beseeching her Guardian Angel of Calamity that nobody from work was present, Ines was relieved to see, albeit through blurred vision, that apart from the barista who had looked on with twisted amusement, diners seemed oblivious. Phew. Concluding that it would be wise to allow the soup to cool down, she moved the tall cup away from her clumsy reach, noticing the 'WARNING: CONTAINS HOT LIQUID' label. Twit. Ines's scatty ways never ceased to impress her— or anyone else for that matter.

Yanking her bag with zeal she plopped it into her lap and delved deep. Rummaging, the heady scent of vanilla and amber floated into the air, a stark reminder of what happens if you don't close the lid on your perfume bottle. Baring a string of perfect teeth beneath a jubilant smile, her hands curled over the phone. *Aha! Gotcha.* Where's Luke when she wants to gloat?

Lowering her head, Ines saw that she'd missed calls from Zara, Sally and Luke. Nothing from Dylan. Feeling optimistic that her boyfriend had at least deigned to send her a message, her stomach flipped when her eyes caught sight of Luke's surprise texts…but— oh look, Dylan had sent one too! Opening this message first, eager eyes studied the words he'd taken the time to write in his busy schedule!

-You ok babe? Hope all's good. Business trip's boring but people up here are cool. Have to stay in Manchester two more days to seal the deal. See you soon. Ciao x

'Seal the deal. Ciao.' Ines shook her head. Dylan's promotion from Sales Manager to Regional Operations Manager for a pharmaceutical company turned him into an even bigger nob than he already was, according to Luke and her brother, Marco.

Not wanting to sound disappointed or bitter, Ines replied with a genial:-

-Hey, yes all is good, thanks. At least everyone is nice there.

See you when you get back xx

Luke's messages were short and sweet:-

-Hello, how's your day going? Are you feeling better? Half an hour later:-

-I assume you're doing important buying stuff like looking at male models in underwear ;)

Ten minutes afterwards…

-So, Miss Garcia, do you still want to meet after work?

Smiling to herself Ines began to type her reply. Of course she still wanted to meet after work. She'd been looking forward to it all day.

-Oi, Mr Benoit. How's YOUR day going? I'm feeling better, thank you. No male models in underwear I'm sad to say. Yes, of course I want to still meet after work. Shall we say 6 pm at Fordhams?

Message sent, delivered and read.

-Perfect, see you later. Ciao ;D

'Cheeky sausage,' muttered Ines. 'Ciao' was in reference to Dylan's

Being Ines

pretentious diction.

-See you x

Now to call Sally. Thankful that her friend was easy going, Ines enjoyed her quick catch-up call to slag off Dylan, discuss Sally's current man drought and deliberate whether it's possible for your virginity to grow back. It was always a pleasure to speak to Sally. They bounced off each other and had a bond like sisters. Zara, on the other hand, was also a good friend but the dynamics could be very unequal at times. Although she had a heart of gold, it was often very one-sided when it came to chatting. Speed dialling her friend's number, Ines changed her seating position in preparation for a long conversation, while she drank her broth. Ringing for what seemed like an eternity, Zara answered.

'Bloody hell, you took your time. You're always stuck to your phone,' laughed Ines.

'Ooh I know but I'm playing hard to get. Nick's been showing signs of interest.' Zara was almost singing. Nick. Nick the Prick. The investment banker. Great. 'Right, I need your advice. I have a plan,' announced Zara in a conspiratorial tone, as she began to divulge her idea. She prattled on for a little while and all Ines could do was sit there in silence, gobsmacked by her friend's absurdity.

'So?' Zara said after a few minutes. 'What do you think?'

Not sure whether Zara had lost the plot, Ines took a moment to process the proposal. Placing the lid back on the empty cup, she pushed it away. 'Do you not think that this is borderline obsession? Is it even legal?'

Squealing, Zara continued to hatch her plan whilst Ines listened with lukewarm interest. '…and then I'll ask Sal.'

Wait, what? Zara's sordid plan involved dear, sweet Sally?!

'You can't be doing that. Sally shouldn't be dragged into your madcap ideas,' protested Ines. The line went silent. A pang of guilt from Zara perhaps? 'Are you still there?'

'Yup, sorry. I'm just thinking about what you said while I was texting Coco Beauty. I'm going for lip fillers and a top up.' Judging by the long, drawn-out reply, Ines could tell that Zara was now focused on her reflection on selfie mode.

With a jaded air to her words, Ines broke the silence. 'I don't think that using our friend as honey-bait for Nick is fair on her. If you don't trust him, then don't date him. It's quite simple, but you can't bring others into it. It's your look out and nobody else's. Maybe if you're that set on doing this, why don't you hire someone?' Tracing the broth stains down the side of the cup with a fingernail, she coughed her conclusion.

Feeling slighted by Ines's response, Zara sulked down the line. Ines knew what her friend would be doing because it's what she always did. Pout. 'Fine. I'll work something out myself. It was just an idea.' Zara conceded. 'Anyway, how are you? Is Dylan still being a dickhead? What about your health?'

Caught off guard by Zara's question, Ines found herself scrambling for a plausible reply. 'Oh you know Dylan, busy as usual. He's in Manchester on business, at the moment.'

'Is he now?'

Ines chose to ignore Zara's sly dig. 'Yep, he is. He's travelling a lot now that he's been promoted.' Feeling Zara's seething disapproval, Ines continued. 'So, at the moment we're like passing ships in the night while he gets used to the role.' Feeling obligated to fill the silence, Ines changed the subject. 'I had a wobbly moment earlier this morning but thank goodness Luke was with me to help.'

'Lovely Luke,' swooned Zara. 'Well, I'm glad he was there for you which says more for your man. As long as you feel better now that's the main thing.' Sympathy didn't come naturally to Zara, Ines knew this. But she also knew that the conversation was about to be redirected back to Zara. 'So, I'll send you a photo when I'm done. I might even get my eyelashes permed. I'm going to confront old age kicking and screaming. Sod growing old with grace.'

'You're 27 years old!'

'Even more reason to look after myself. Ooh, have to go, Nick's messaged me again!'

'Another X-rated pic?' predicted Ines.

Giggling like a naughty school-girl, Zara needn't say anything more. 'Gotta go. Love you, Ini Panini ! Speak soon darling, byeee.' And just like that, she disappeared like a cosmic genie into the telecommunications ether.

Checking the time, Ines was relieved to see that her working day was done. It also signalled that it wouldn't be long before she would be sharing some time with Luke, bouncing witticisms off each other and indulging in relaxed conversation. These meetings occasioned themselves as a welcome relief from her personal strife. Thinking about their rapport consumed her with exhilaration. Cheerfully swiping her coat off the hook, she made her way towards the lifts.

Breezing past the small cluster of buying assistants, Ines knew full well that every step, every sway of her hips was being scrutinised. Watching Echo in an exaggerated response to Martha's hushed dialogue was like witnessing a sexually frustrated woman in a bar vying for the attention of a potential shag, knocking back a glass of sweet Prosecco, and laughing for all to hear. Shuddering at the scenario, Ines continued sashaying down the aisle, passing the inquisitive group and the gregarious merchandising team.

'Have a good evening, Ines,' called out Stevie, the head of the merchandising team. Quietly strong and confident, Stevie remained humble about his endearing qualities and good looks, which made him desirable to most of the staff in the office.

'Bye Stevie, you too. See you tomorrow!' Ines flashed a huge smile at him, and followed with a deliberate turn towards the huddle of women, their eyes fixed in her direction. Unable to resist obstructing their view of Stevie, Ines's smiling mouth transformed into a knowing smirk. Watching them struggle to appear unaffected always tickled her; it somehow gave her a sense of warped satisfaction, leaving these women with the look of having bitten into a rotten apple.

Stepping out onto the street, Ines looked at the clock tower across the plaza.

Hmmm quarter-past-five. I've got loads of time. I could pop to Violets. Unable to determine what she should do, Ines launched a mental calculation of distance and timing needed to reach the bar. Her brain felt it was going to explode. Furrowing her brow with the effort, she came to her own conclusion. 'Sod it, I'll get to Knightsbridge— at least I'll be in the area.' Happy with her idea and giving herself a congratulatory pat on the back for being so decisive, Ines made her way down the imposing escalators at Bond Street tube station, headed for the Central line.

Standing on Knightsbridge, Ines could see Harvey Nichols in the distance. Tempted by the allure of another purchase, she opted with reluctance not to enter the divine realm for fashionistas for a spot of browsing, positive that her magpie tendencies and all her self-control would be left at the shiny, sparkling doors. Instead, she would go for a meander down Sloane Street.

The street was a bustling hive of eager tourists, laden with boutique bags bearing the world-renowned logos of Harrods and a plethora of haute-couture designers. In the throng of what seemed like a siege of denim jeans and trainers, Ines caught a glimpse of a pair of beautiful black tall stilettos exposing the trademark red sole of Louboutin. The owner, whose legs were as long as her stride, negotiated the cracks and obstacles on the pavement with expert ease, and disappeared into the crowd, her golden mane, shimmering in the weakening sunlight. Watching this ethereal vision, an overwhelming sense of insecurity grabbed her like an invisible cloak of broken glass. Catching her reflection in the windows of the double-decker bus edging forward in the slow-moving traffic, the image looking back at her didn't do much to allay her anxiety. All she could see were deep jowls, dark hollow eyes and a short stumpy body. How can a pair of long legs in skinny jeans with red bottomed heels on their feet stir such self-deprecation? Vexed at how morose she felt, Ines turned away from the bus and decided that she may as well head to Fordhams and get a seat somewhere discreet where she could chat with Luke. Her self-doubt would be brushed away. He always made her feel better.

Unusual for the time of year, the evening was mild, even though it had rained at sporadic intervals during the day. Watching the offending bus trundle ahead, its wheels sloshing through small puddles, Ines began to make her way across the busy road, weaving between prestigious cars humming in the congestion, the tail of her beige mac sweeping and swirling in the springtime breeze, as she edged ahead.

Taking a jaunty step over the kerb, Ines took quick confident strides, her Jimmy Choo kitten heels click clacking on the dull, grey pavement towards the bar, she was half an hour away from Luke's company!

Entering Fordhams was always a mission of personal accomplishment for Ines. The entrance was a set of imposing double oak doors, a fastidious written black logo descending along each frosted glass inlay. The burly doorman standing ramrod in his black suit, with a meticulous shaped goatee, reminded Ines of a Lego man. His eyes flickered as he scanned her from head to toe before deciding that she could go in.

Nodding in approval, his well-oiled head glistened under the lights of the doorway and watched on as Ines made her way in, smiling as she walked past.

The entrance to the bar was a long runway, lined with dim lighting and not for the partially sighted. Her fast walking had abated to an idle pace, the music getting louder as she grew ever closer to the main area. The Bauhaus style bar was a welcome sight, as was the handsome bar tender. Watching him creating cocktails and interacting with the two coquettish girls sitting in front of him, it was an impressive performance worthy of an Oscar nomination. Approaching the vacant bar stool, with the stealth of a gazelle, Ines climbed up with ease, and made herself comfortable as she gave the girls a tight little smile.

'I'll be with you in a minute,' the bartender winked.

Raising her hands in a 'no problem' gesture, Ines delved into her cavernous handbag, retrieving her mobile with ease from the designated pocket. Luke would feel righteous that his advice proved to be of great benefit today.

Looking down at the floor, Ines noticed that the crossed legs donning stilettos beside her, bore red soles. Frowning, curiosity got the better of her as she cast a discreet sideways glance. Ines's suspicion wasn't unfounded. The cascading blonde hair, the long legs shrink wrapped in denim and the winged eyeliner was unmistakable. It was her! Red Sole Girl, with her friend.

Taking advantage of being incognito, Ines was at liberty to eavesdrop while she waited for Luke to arrive. Maybe she could seek out a private table later— she was early after all. Ines loved to people-watch and listen to the various conversations around her. Marco called it being nosy.

Enveloping a hand around the thick, solid tumbler of dark rum and enjoying the sounds of Ibiza lounge music, Ines took a tiny sip of the amber liquid and decided that up close, Red Sole Girl was not all she had perceived her to be.

'So, are you gonna call him or not?' squawked Annie, the wide- eyed excitable friend; her lash extensions looking more drag queen than sex siren as she looked on. Stirring her cocktail with the mixer, the Red Sole Girl raised two slender shoulders.

'Well, that's not a bloody answer!'

Admiring herself in the mirrored wall behind the bar, the Red Sole Girl watched her reflection, pouting her filled lips as she sipped through a straw. The Red Sole Girl gave the answer careful consideration.

'Are you talking about Dylan?'

'Well yeah, Jenna, *who* else is determined to get into your size 6 Agent P panties?'

Hearing Dylan's name made Ines's heart skip a beat. Swallowing hard and reasoning with her thoughts, Ines concluded that Dylan wasn't an unusual name, and they may be referring to a Dillon, not a Dylan and not her Dylan. This, however, didn't stop her from listening in. 'Well,' Jenna, drew out her words. 'We've been messaging each other while he's been away and it's getting hotter. He's already asked me to send nudes.' By now, Jenna had shuffled her bottom closer to the edge of her stool, leaning towards her eager listener. 'So, he started it by sending me a pic.' Miming an indicator of how well-endowed Dylan/Dillon is, she revelled at the excitement on her friend's face. Jenna's delight was infectious. 'Oh. My.God!' Clapping in euphoric glee, Annie looked as though she was going to combust. 'And? Did you send one back?'

Just like a cat that's got the cream, Jenna's face broke into a crooked smile. 'Of course I did. He's seen enough to keep him busy until he gets back from Manchester. *Then*, we'll meet up again, but this time I don't think we'll be so restrained. I can't play hard to get any longer, he's driving me wild.'

Like sunburned gravel, Ines' mouth began to dry up, her heart rising to her throat. She took a swift mouthful of her drink. Like an addict who can't quit she remained on her stool, not daring to move.

'When's he back?'

'Tomorrow afternoon, so we're meeting when I've finished work.'

Feeling confident that it wasn't her Dylan they were talking about, Ines' anxiety began to ease; after all, he wasn't going to be back in London for a couple of days or more.

Alerted by the words 'Earl's Court', Ines reeled her thoughts back to reality. Inching closer to her excitable neighbours, her world began to fall apart as she heard the conversation unravel like twine, right before her.

'He's got a flat in Montague Square…'

I believe you'll find it's my flat…IF it is him.

Being Ines

'But it's being renovated, so he's staying at The Selby in Marble Arch. I won't lie, I am excited about seeing him tomorrow.' Swooning, Jenna fanned her face with a tanned hand.

'Try and get a photo,' suggested, Annie, who by now was fit to burst at the thrilling idea. Slapping her rounded thighs in delight, she felt the moment necessitated another round of cocktails. Leaning her large silicone bosom over the bar to attract the bar tender, Annie began to giggle as she ordered their drinks. 'Can I have a Screaming Orgasm and a Leg Spreader please?'

Ooff. Enough said.

Ines' legs weakened more-so than they had been all day, and she felt sick. Sick and giddy enough to pass out from the overwhelming anxiety pumping through her body. The man they were talking about was too familiar to be a coincidence. How many good looking, fit- bodied Dylans living in Montague Square were there hanging around? Feeling like a rabbit caught in headlights, Ines looked around, desperately searching for an answer on what she should do next. The world appeared to be moving in slow motion. What to do, what to do? Should she burst into a furious tirade of abusive accusations at Jenna? Stay calm and think it through? Or go to the loos and cry? A metal blade sliced at her thumping heart, threatening to wrench it out. Never had she needed Luke by her side more than she did right now.

'Well, hello there hottie,' leered Annie.

Inquisitive, Jenna spun around to see what had rudely distracted her friend from the incessant prattle about her new stud. Realising why Annie had suddenly steered her attention from their conversation, a hush descended upon the two women. Heavily lined eyes and canopied eyelids were all a flitter as both girls watched on in appreciative unison. Annie's vulgar tones rang through Ines' ears like stone grinding against stone. 'Christ, he's fit. Seriously, can anyone really be that gorgeous?'

The two amorous young women preened themselves as they looked at their reflection in the mirror behind the bar. 'You're a taken woman,' her shameless friend pointed out. 'You don't need to check yourself.'

'I've not even had sex with Dylan yet, so I can do what I want.' Pondering for a moment, Annie's face lit up as her face broke into a mischievous snicker. 'We can always share, I won't tell.'

Pleased with the idea, Annie fluttered her eyelashes for good measure. 'We're friends, right? Sharing is caring.'

Ines felt like she was going to be violently ill.

'Oh my God, oh my God. Oh.My.God, he's coming our way!' flapped the half-witted friend. 'Pretend we haven't noticed him.' Apprehension welled inside Ines, her stomach, a mass of clenched knots. Hanging her head low in utter despair, unable to fathom what it was that she should do, she had never felt this desolate.

Turmoil weighed heavy on her shoulders, so much so, that as anxiety gripped like ivy, Ines, who had been engrossed in weaving her hands, hadn't noticed somebody was standing close behind. Two strong arms wrapped themselves around her small waist and a pair of hands clasped themselves upon her stomach. Her woes were suddenly lifted when she heard a whisper in her ear. 'Honey I'm home.'

The wan face he was greeted by was tainted with anguish behind a forced smile. Luke's expression had transformed from cheeky rogue to grave concern as his eyes searched Ines in an attempt to decipher what had happened to upset her so. No matter, he had seen enough to know that being here right now was not helping the situation. Making a snap decision, he grabbed her coat and bag, taking a masterful hold of a clammy hand into his and made a swift manoeuvre through the throng of drinkers, steering her to safety.

The two vixens had remained open-mouthed during the entire spectacle, watching agog as it unfolded before their eyes … how the gorgeous guy, loaded with worry for the petite mixed-race girl, led her away, as though she were precious cargo. Jenna couldn't help but let out an audible gasp. 'Wow. Just wow. If I had a man who could treat me like I was the only thing that mattered in his world…'

Before she could end her sentence, her phone rang a chirpy little tune, breaking the illusion. Dylan's name flashed across her phone screen…

Chapter 3

Shreds of lilac bridged across the sky as dusk began to emerge from a slow setting sun, for the final minutes of the day. But for Ines, the world around her had faded to black and her head filled with senseless noise. Luke took control of the situation without effort and she, drained and trembling as the adrenaline began to subside, accepted the support. The chaos of rush hour in Knightsbridge melted into the background as they stood, locked in a tight embrace.

Caressing her hair with tentative reassurances, he made the conscious decision to leave words unspoken until Ines was ready to talk about whatever had shaken her.

Scanning their surroundings, Luke spotted a little Italian restaurant further down the road. Sometimes, being six-foot-three had its advantages. 'Come on, I think I've found your perfect food haven.' Ines approved of the suggestion and took comfort being in Luke's capable hands.

The restaurant was a perfect setting for a quiet meal, away from the hubbub of London life. Settled in a discreet corner, the two companions eyed the menu with frayed enthusiasm.

A steaming bowl of spaghetti alle vongole for Ines and a risotto frutti di mare for Luke, reminded Ines of how much she missed Italy. It had been three years since she last visited Capri. Her last holiday before she met Dylan.

'Bon appétit.' Hungry, Luke swept the glutinous rice and a rather large clam away from the centre of the generous portion. Smiling demurely, Ines reciprocated the salutation with a nod and a softly spoken 'Bon Appétit,' and she began to twist spaghetti around her fork.

Feeling more and more relaxed as time passed, she had almost forgotten the reason why they had found themselves in a quaint Italian restaurant instead of drinking rum and chatting in Fordhams. Eating in relaxed silence, they stayed this way, small talk immaterial to their mood.

Unwelcome recollections of what she had experienced earlier, began to covertly seep to the front of her mind. Ines could feel herself sink into a dark melancholy, the deep cavity of her chest tugging at conflicting emotions.

Noticing her changing mood, Luke began bobbing his head in pigeon-like motion for humorous effect. Fanning the palm of a large hand ostentatiously across his plate, mimicking a shopping channel salesman, he was now laughing at his own comedic ingenuity. 'Look at us. Anyone watching would be having a field day. There's you trying to eat spaghetti and picking at these pesky clams with finesse and here's me wrestling the head off of a langoustine with a knife!' Luke threw back his head, his infectious laughter booming across the restaurant.

Now on a roll, he gulped his wine, and proceeded with anecdotes. 'I mean don't tell me that if you were at home now, you wouldn't be winding spaghetti on your fork to the size of a salami and sucking the clams out with gusto! Me? I would be twisting and tearing the heads off these crustaceans with my bare hands like a Neanderthal. Grrr haaar yaaa!' Taking his impression of a caveman a little too far, Ines puckered her mouth, making shushing noises. Her prim demeanour was futile when Luke projected the kind of face that can only be seen in front of a carnival mirror, prompting a burst of appreciative laughter, squeaking with each deep inhale. Resting the spoon and fork in the bowl, a prudish hand smacked her mouth frightened of spitting out her food across the table.

'Let's be honest huh chérie? You're part Latina, part Caribbean. Eating is a pleasure for you, it's not all about etiquette— unlike with us Frenchies.'

Accentuating his native vernacular, Luke mimicked a French sophisticate declaring a challenge. '*WE* do not use our hands, my dear. *WE* do not eat like peasants. *WE* will challenge anyone to eat a chicken wing with a knife and fork— even if it means certain death by starvation. Vive la France!' He ended his campaign speech with a haughty sniff of a twisted nostril, a patriotic salute and the rippling of a thick eyebrow. Ines, his sole adoring fan, giggled with delight. Content with the fact that he had lifted her spirits, he recommenced grappling with the langoustine, blissfully unaware of the effect his comical sketch had on the amused diners watching on.

'So, how did the viewing go? Are you and the charming Courtney going to be residents of W11?' asked Ines, in between chewing an over cooked clam. Watching Luke squirm gave her the impression that he wasn't enamoured by the question.

Waiting for an answer, she began the task of dislodging a bothersome mollusc which had somehow embedded itself between her two back teeth. With discretion, she tried to remove the offending piece of food with her tongue, inadvertently depicting the wrong impression.

Mystified at her behaviour, Luke tried so very hard not to get distracted. 'I'm not interested in moving in with her, let alone moving out of my flat. She's too eager to settle down, and we barely know each other.'

Safe in the knowledge that although the mollusc was still stuck between her teeth, it wasn't on show, Ines began to speak. 'Well, she may just be Miss Right and you're not open to it. You should maybe be a little less guarded about it.'

Feeling a pang of jealousy as she said this, Ines knew it was the correct way to behave, regardless. However, the idea of Luke being cosy with another woman was still not one she embraced. Rolling her tongue over her teeth, Ines was oblivious that she had once again begun trying to dig this clam out. Leaning in closer, Luke spoke in theatrical whispers across the table. 'What's with the tongue thing you're doing?'

Two eyebrows merged into a deep notch in response to Luke's bizarre comment. 'What are you going on about? What tongue thing?' Discombobulated, Ines wasn't aware of what she had been doing, making her naiveté more endearing than she already was.

'That thing when your tongue goes in and out from under your cheek…like this…' Luke gave a demonstration of Ines' tongue action.

Suddenly grasping the implication, she returned her tongue to its rightful place, mortified at how she appeared to onlookers.

Beaming back at her from under his nose, Luke raised his eyebrows, thanked her for the show and continued with their conversation. 'Anyway, Courtney is more "Miss for the Moment". I'm not interested in settling down with anyone. I'm too young.'

'You're twenty-eight.' 'Exactly.'

Taking another mouthful of his now lukewarm dinner, he changed the subject, defying his initial plan to say nothing. 'So. Want to talk about what happened in Fordhams earlier?'

Touched that Luke had managed to refrain from asking the question for so long, she began her dialogue. At first, it was an "in a nutshell" synopsis outlining the upshot of it all, but as her feelings spilled over like a boiling pan of water, she elaborated with more detail and her eyes began to sting.

Luke searched for a tissue inside his jacket pocket and handed it to a now very tearful Ines. She looked at the tissue with distaste as he held out the tattered white rag. 'It's clean,' he encouraged, waving it in front of her face. Not entirely convinced that it was, but not caring at this point, Ines wiped her eyes and blew her nose, before electing to tell him everything. Listening with an intensity that fuelled his anger, Luke's hands balled into fists every few seconds as Ines relayed her story.

'He's a tool through and through, my little butterfly. Do you want unbiased straight talk?' Intense eyes darted from side to side and then focused on Ines's face, which was now etched with misery. She looked so helpless, and it saddened him to see her this way. Ines nodded with acquiesce in response to his question.

'He's taking the piss out of you,' Luke stressed. 'He lives in a flat in the heart of Earl's Court and makes pitiful contributions like he's shacked up in the YMCA. He comes and goes as he pleases and screws around. He has no respect for you. But…' Luke was prodding the air with a wilful finger towards his friend. 'If you're allowing him to behave like this, then he will continue. He's like a feral cat.' Pausing for breath, he was about to go on ranting, but had suddenly become aware of something more pressing he had to address. 'You have a little fleck of bogey on your nostril.'

'Are you serious!?' Delivering a nervous laugh, Ines blushed. 'That just tops it all off, about me. 'It's not surprising he's looking elsewhere.'

Impassioned by Ines' self-deprecating outburst, Luke blurted his words. 'Hey, listen! You are beautiful, inside and out. You have class, sometimes a little scatty but you have many qualities that people admire. Him? He's insecure. Passive aggressive. A sociopath. A bully. These sorts of cretins need to make people feel like shit about themselves in order to live.'

Pinching the young woman's nostril clean and ignoring her wincing like a five-year old, Luke continued wiping her nose with diligence. 'People like him thrive on being adored, but without making it a two-way thing.' He felt bad for being so blunt but it needed to be said. 'It's your life and I can't tell you how to live it, but I understand the hurt and anger that you feel every day. Y'know, it's like holding a scorching piece of charcoal. The only person you're hurting is yourself. You're lost. You're not the girl I met three years ago, with dreams of happiness in her new home. You're existing, not living.'

Ines nodded, and nodded some more. It made sense and he was right. Deep down she knew this. But what to do? Dylan had succeeded in sapping all her self-confidence. She believed without a doubt that she didn't deserve better than him, that nobody would ever want her.

'One more thing. Has he suggested that you see a doctor?' 'What for? I'm fine.'

'Really? You truly feel fine? Really truly, Ines?' Luke was now challenging her in a way she'd never seen him do before. Waggling two fingers at his eyes, he concluded his observation. 'Because I see everything, and I can tell that you need to see someone soon.'

A little perplexed by his ambiguous remark, Ines pushed the subject further. 'What do you mean? See what?'

'Your clumsiness, walking like you've had a few too many drinks at times. This isn't normal.'

Squinting as daylight struggled to stream through the shuttered white slats, Ines began to wake up, opening one bleary eye first, the other lazily following suit. Groggy, she rolled over towards the walnut '30s nightstand, reaching for her phone. One message from Zara and two from Luke sent in the middle of the night. What was Luke doing awake at 03:23 am?

She didn't want to know. Sometimes it was better to be in blissful ignorance.

There was still nothing from Dylan. Hardly surprising seeing as he was 'sealing the deal in Manchester' and 'working so hard, babe', she mocked with bitterness.

Considering the possibility that her "beloved" could be waking up to Jenna, proving to him that her mouth wasn't just for pouting or incessant chatter, left an acidic feeling in the pit of her stomach. Throwing back the duvet, Ines grunted with the awkward effort it required to pull herself up to the edge of the bed. With outstretched arms, she scrambled for yesterday's discarded garments. Lurching like a zombie, the young woman cradled the bundle of clothes and shuffled across the checker tiled hall, dropping the pile into the laundry bin without ceremony, as she passed the bathroom.

Sitting on the bar stool in the kitchen, nursing a steaming mug of black coffee, Ines looked out of the window, admiring the tranquillity of the square outside as a new day emerged. It looked so pretty— an example of quintessential privileged London life, the lawns, littered with petals plucked away in the breeze from blossom trees and spring flowers.

Numb with exhaustion, Ines was unable to think straight. Her sense of dejection had now turned to anger. Taking one last drag of her cigarette, she snatched up the phone and dialled Dylan's number. She didn't see why she should be the only one who couldn't rest, and even if he wasn't going to answer, she could at least keep calling and disturbing him from whatever he was doing. Ines knew deep down that Dylan's phone was likely to be on silent, but conceded he would eventually see how many missed calls there were, and hoped that it would prick his conscience. It seemed to be that her brain was in a perpetual battle between logic and her heart.

'Who's calling you all the time?' groaned Jenna, trailing the contours on Dylan's taut abs with a long-manicured finger. 'It's too bloody early!'

'Ah ignore it, babe,' mumbled Dylan, pulling her on top of him.

Doing exactly that, Jenna set about enticing a reaction from Dylan, resting her fingers gently over his chest, and slowly kissed her way down, lazily tweaking the trail of tiny copper red hairs to his naval.

Dylan murmured, succumbing into blissful stupor as he sunk his head back onto the pillow. 'I could get used to this.'

With a knowing smirk, his latest mistress began to snake her way back up. Sweeping her long locks over a bony shoulder, she began to kiss his mouth in short, hard bursts.

Dylan's phone began vibrating across the bedside table, a tinny screech pulsating through their ears.

'Ugh, just tell them you're busy!' she whined, throwing her hands up in frustration.

In an act of sheer insolence, Dylan switched the phone off and threw it across the room. 'They can wait. Now. Where were we?'

Lying helpless on the bathroom floor, bewildered by what had just happened, Ines battled to remain calm as she tried to figure out what to do next. Try as she might, her leg was being held down by a force so strong that panic and confusion engulfed her like a tidal wave.

Unable to feel anything, she pinched her legs, desperate to find even the lightest sensation. Whimpering, she dropped her head back onto the cold tiles, overcome by a terrifying thought—was she paralysed? Had she lost her balance and knocked herself out on the floor, causing irreversible damage? Questions about the absurd situation she found herself to be in, bombarded her foggy brain as she struggled to retrace her steps.

Horrified as she looked down at her ankles, Ines had noticed that they were bleeding. Swinging her head around, searching the bathroom for an answer to the cause of her affliction, she decided to undertake the mammoth task of dragging herself towards the door, using her elbows as props. The effort, too onerous for her feeble body, forced her to opt for the closest wall instead. Resting against the harshness of cold ceramic tiles, she was unable to see anything which could explain the alarming situation she found herself in.

With an iron grip clutching at her lungs, breathing came in short wheezes. Giddiness whipped her brain with ruthless vigour. This was all too much to fathom and to add insult to injury, Dylan hadn't answered the numerous voicemails she had left him, begging for his help. Feeling trepidation rise from the pit of her stomach, tears of angst threatened to escape. Ines began to tremble, knowing she had to take stock through the woozy haze of vertigo and find a way out of this situation. Gosh, she felt ragged. Taking long breaths, the panic began to dissipate. Ines was now able to get a closer look at her wounded ankles. Appalled to see that they were in fact nail lacerations sent shivers down her spine, concluding that she had scratched herself hard enough to bleed and had done so unwittingly! Unnerved by a sensation that an army of ants were crawling under her skin, Ines began to claw at her flesh, first in long hard strokes and then with manic intention. It was like scratching a mosquito bite getting itchier with every scrape.

Looking through fuzzy eyes, Ines began to scan the space around her. Aha! There on the dark wood vanity unit, she spotted her phone, and after quick deliberation of 'do I? don't I?', with determination, she began to pull her frail body along the floor like a caterpillar, fighting the nausea and drunken sensation with what little strength she had.

Spaghetti arms extended, Ines puffed a heavy moan with all the exertion it took, uttering chastising words of discourse. 'Ugh. I need to get fit! As of tomorrow? I'm signing up for some weight training or something,' although she was about as interested in doing these classes as an arachnophobe would be in sharing a room with spiders. Realising the absurdity, Ines stopped with the nonsensical talk.

Even though she knew deep down it was pointless calling, Ines nonetheless phoned Dylan, on the off chance that he might do the decent thing for once and pick up. Predictably, it went to voicemail, his rumbling voice, promising that he will get back to the caller.

'LIAR!!'

Shaking from head to toe with anger and anxiety, she hung up, took a momentary pause and pressed redial. Recognising that it was a useless deed, there was still the sliver of a chance that he would come running to be by her side. With a tiny voice, she left Dylan a heartfelt message imploring him to call because of what had happened. Dropping the phone down by her side and feeling utterly spent, Ines wept. At first small sobs eased their way out, but the tiny drops of emotion rapidly evolved into a soul-destroying outpouring.

The phone rang! In one mad and encouraging split-second, Ines stopped crying and flipped it over to see if Dylan cared enough to call as soon as he heard her pain.

'Bonjour, my little butterfly. Did you manage to sleep last night?' Luke. Always there.

Hearing his genuine concern for her wellbeing, Ines burst into uncontrollable tears once more, unable to articulate her words. All that Luke could deduce between the long, sharp gasps of her forcible dialogue, was that she had fallen and was in the bathroom. 'Ok, I'm coming now.'

Her tears had eased and now she was breathing in short rapid breaths, sticky ropes of mucus hung from her crimson nose. Disgusted at the sight of the grotesque figure slumped against the wooden unit, scabby legs set apart, her shining eyes now listless and streaks of snot smeared across her face, Ines snarled in despair at the crude vision staring back at her from the mirror.

Luke couldn't see her like this. She still had some dignity, as fleeting as it might be. The mottled flesh on her thighs under the starkness of halogen lighting added to the shame of it all. No, there wasn't a hope in hell that Luke was coming over. Whatever the quandary, she was certain it would pass.

'Luke, I'm okay, I'm just having a bad morning. Honestly, I'm fine.'

'Don't be ridiculous. You are hurt and you need help.' Luke's tone was assertive and composed. 'I'll be with you as soon as I can.'

Resigned to the fact that she did indeed need help and it didn't matter how she looked, Ines finally agreed. 'You have a spare key. Remember I gave it to you after I locked myself out a few months ago?'

Luke mumbled something about a booty call at Courtney's, and he had to go back home and find them. Perturbed and wondering if everyone was at it apart from her, Ines assured her pal that she wasn't going anywhere anytime soon.

Her limbs began to feel rigid as the cold crept through her body. Shivering, the goosebumps emerged beneath her skin, spreading rampantly along her slim arms. Feeling a gentle brush against the nape of her neck, Ines looked up to find a towel strewn over the sink.

With a pincer grasp, she began tugging at the unfurling bath sheet. Admonishing herself for not thinking of it in the first instance, she wrapped herself in the thick, plush towel, revelling in the immediate warmth it gave her. 'God bless John Lewis for their high-quality products.' Snuggled down, she waited for Luke's arrival— which could be a long while yet given that he has to travel from Putney to Earls Court before even getting to her. 'All in the name of a booty call,' muttered Ines, tightening the towel around her body, cursing.

'Good morning, my little butterfly! Tis moi!' A voice bellowed through the hallway, way too cheerily for Ines's liking. Luke had arrived. Hearing the squeaking footsteps his Converse sneakers were making down the hallway, Ines suddenly began to feel an overwhelming sense of emotion. She was relieved that he'd arrived before her anticipated time but sad it hadn't been her supposed boyfriend who'd come to her aid.

'Knock knock' he called as he rapped the wall outside the bathroom and eased the door open a crack. Unsettled at the sight of a broken Ines slouched against the unit as he stepped across the threshold, Luke masked his shock.

'You could have made an effort if you knew I was coming.' Chiding with affection, he kneeled down beside her and stroked clumps of damp hair away from her clammy cheeks.

'I didn't have enough time. You came too quick,' smiled Ines. 'Not a complaint I'm accustomed to hearing, my little butterfly,' replied Luke evenly as he assessed the situation Ines was in. 'Right then, I'm going to lift you and your bum, and deposit you both in your bedroom,' decided Luke.

Alarmed that she was going to be carried, in what was essentially all her naked glory, by Luke to her bedroom, she began to speak in quick succession.

'No, no it's fine. Just help me up,' she insisted, pulling her bath sheet back around her, preserving her modesty.

Grinning, Luke replied, mocking her reluctance. 'Methinks the lady doth protest too much. Anyway, I don't see that you have much choice in the matter, do you, hmmm? Your prick of a boyfriend is probably getting blown by his mistress as you sit here struggling, so he won't be returning anytime soon which means you are not going anywhere. Or you can suck it up and allow me to carry you to safety.'

The words stung like salt in a freshly open wound, but Luke was right and nodded with reluctance. 'Shut up and help me, and this is not the time to be quoting Hamlet,' she ordered, reaching for his waiting hand.

Now lying on her bed in a pretty embroidered chemise (Luke chose well) with a soft, red blanket draped over her legs, Luke sat himself beside his ailing friend. Watching him drink his coffee made her feel content and grateful that he was in her life. As if reading her mind, Luke responded by sticking his tongue out and going boss eyed.

'There's no need for all this fuss,' protested Ines, at the smiling trio. She was being ganged up on by Luke, Zara and Sally standing in the kitchen with a look behind their smug grins that would brook no argument. Luke had called the girls when she had been taking a much-needed nap, and they had arrived as soon as they heard the news.

Pouring them all a glass of Crozes-Hermitage, Zara smiled with satisfaction as she watched the velvety red liquid, fill glasses that had been spaced out in symmetrical perfection. Being conscious about her appearance wasn't the only thing in her life she was O.C.D about; it spilled over to daily matters. After she performed the ritual in self-indulgent delight, Zara flashed a toothy smile. She loved the silent tension she was creating with her elaborate execution of pouring out wine. All her friends wanted, was a drink.

'Here's to good health and good friends,' toasted Sally.

'Santé,' countered Luke, Ines and Zara, clinking their glasses together.

'So, where's that idiot boyfriend of yours? Any news from him?' asked Zara with such hostility, it even surprised Luke.

'Probably doing the same shit as Nick,' Luke piped up.

Blushing, Zara's mouth clattered shut in an instant. Noticing her embarrassment, Sally frowned at Luke for being so tactless.

'That was uncalled-for,' she admonished, looking at Zara's saddened demeanour and scolding Luke. 'We can't help who we fall for.'

Empathising wholeheartedly with Zara's predicament, Sally curled her fingers over her friend's plump hand in a show of solidarity.

Knowing it was a fruitless endeavour trying to argue his case when he was outnumbered 3-1, Luke said nothing more.

Distracted, Ines began scratching at her shredded ankle and squeezing her right eye intermittently, unaware she was being watched by all three friends.

Willing her vision to focus clearly on Sally who was by now speaking about Ryan's potential as a rehabilitated citizen, Ines tried to catch up with the topic.

' … you have got to be shitting me,' snorted Zara, wiping a rogue drop of wine from her chin.

Luke, torn between watching Zara and Sally discussing Ryan and studying Ines's peculiar behaviour, he settled on watching the entire spectacle before him from a distance. Taking another sip of wine and looking on in bewilderment, he likened the scenario to being in a scene on One Flew Over the Cuckoo's Nest and wondered how he found himself to be caught up in the throng of it all. Right now, he could be swaddled in Courtney's doughy bosom. But he wasn't. Instead, he was sitting in Ines' kitchen watching her like a hawk as she continued to cast her eyes at every angle periodically and scratching her leg.

By now, Zara and Sally were in full discussion about the homeless situation in the city, folk who are less fortunate than them, who do and don't deserve a second chance. The kitchen had suddenly turned into a political arena and Luke found himself making a mental list of all the places he would rather be, right now, as he gazed at the bars of peach and coral stream through the tall kitchen windows.

'So, what are you saying? Give Ryan a job and then ask him out?' Tipsy, Zara's voice was now reaching a high pitch, at some points breaking into a gargle, as she became more incredulous at Sally's idea that Ryan should join the rat race and could become a potential love interest for her. Zara could be a tactless snob, sometimes.

Looking over the edge of their wine glasses at each other, Ines squeezed her eyes in mock exasperation at Luke. Responding with a long stare and an imperceptible smile, he understood what Ines was implying. He liked the fact that they didn't need to speak to know what the other was thinking.

Ines's vision began to blur, and the sensation of ants crawling beneath her skin was relentless. Scratching at her lacerated calves, her inebriated friends watched with curiosity as their friend seemed to regress from being mildly fidgety to behaving like a restless toddler. Sally correlated Ines' strange behaviour to the days when as a little girl, her mum would make her wear "itchy" tights and was expected to sit still and behave, when in public. With an involuntary shudder at the recollection, Sally reverted to the present. She moved her glass away, taking Ines' hand into her baby-soft palm. 'Sweetie, what are going to do about this?' her eyes, as light as the first mist of a winter's day glistened with sisterly concern. Circling a pale finger over Ines' legs, to highlight the point, she waited for an explanation.

'Huh? Oh, um, well ...' Lost for words, the truth was that not even Ines knew what she was doing. Releasing her hand from Sally's gentle hold, she mused aloud while she squeezed each eye, comparing the sight out of both. 'I think I'm going to make an appointment to see the optician.'

Zara placed her wine glass on the counter. 'Maybe it's time to make that appointment at the doctor as well, heh?'

Staring into her glass, Ines nodded the slightest affirmation. The room fell silent as all eyes settled upon the feisty pint size Latina who was now looking vulnerable. Reaching down, she began to scratch again.

'Stop it! You're tearing up your skin!' Sally had now leapt to the other side of the island and was batting Ines's hand away from her red raw leg. The look of alarm on Luke's face was enough to make her stop. 'I think, my little butterfly, that maybe you should go tomorrow, no?'

Just as she opened her mouth to reply, her mobile pinged an alert. Looking expectantly down at the screen, Ines unlocked the phone and read. Then again. And again.

'W…what's happened?' Asking with a rare show of empathy, Zara bit her lip.

Rolling her shoulders and throwing her head back in vexation, Ines remained wordless.

Always on hand for support and important tasks such as lighting a cigarette or pouring the drink, Luke passed Ines the cigarette he had subsequently lit for himself as well as his coffee. 'I bet your fancy barista doesn't do this for you,' he teased, watching the cup slide from his grip towards quiet hands. Grateful, she also took the lighted smoke from an outstretched hand, a gradual crescent forming beneath her nose, before taking an indulgent drag. Twisting her head, Ines exhaled a steady stream of smoke. 'That was Dylan. He's working away all of next week. Some bullshit about needing to meet target.' Entranced by the glowing embers dwindling in the Fordhams ashtray, Ines let out a long sigh.

'Prick. He doesn't exist in my eyes,' proclaimed Sally. 'We all know what he's doing, just not who with,' she continued, her flat blonde hair swishing with every impassioned word. 'You need to focus on your health and your well-being and just forget about him. Kick him out. Move on. He's using you, sweetie. He only wants the exclusivity of this address and your money.' Pausing for a moment to consider whether or not she'd gone too far, Sally decided that what she'd said was not inappropriate, given that nobody was interrupting her. This gave her even more confidence to say what she thought. 'He's a chancer, Ini. He couldn't afford to live in a place like this or in the area —— unless he shacked up with Ryan in the doorway of the café. He's got no respect for you, but why would he?'

Realising she was teetering on fragile territory, Sally softened her countenance. 'I know you love him, but do you *really*? Can you *really* love a man who you have allowed to take the piss, to walk all over you and treat you like a doormat? Huh? He should be here by your side, supporting you. But no. Where's the slimy git? You let shit that matters slide. Like you're accepting of his behaviour.'

Thrusting both hands out to express the conviction of her words, Sally was to all intents and purposes, unstoppable. 'You know what I think? I think you hope he will change, like BOOM!! You're hoping he'll have some kind of epiphany and stop his no- good, cheating ways.' Sally was now knocking her temple. 'But in reality, he never will, and he knows that you'll never kick him out. He's arrogant enough to believe this … and you are letting him get away with it!'

Sally was now on a roll, hot and upset. Her bottled-up feelings of her best friend's boyfriend spewed out like lava, leaving her friends speechless.

Ines's mind flicked through the catalogue of events over the last two years of her relationship with Dylan, and felt her stomach ache with sadness, whilst Sally gathered herself together after her rousing speech.

'Go Sally!' Zara caught her breath, stunned at Sally's outburst. 'I didn't think you had it in you, girl!' applauding Sally with enthusiasm, Zara's cheeks glowed with the combination of delight and the warming sensation of the wine. 'Crikey, don't hold back will you, love?'

Flushed and fanning her eyes by way of stopping herself from crying, Sally began to apologise. 'I'm so sorry.'

'It's fine, honestly… Oh no, don't get upset, Sal,' Ines croaked, morose that her friend thought of the situation this way. 'What you're saying is the truth and it needs to be said. I just didn't know that you felt like this. I hadn't realised that it was so obvious I was in the wrong situation in your eyes.'

'Babe, everyone feels that way,' added Zara curtly. 'Although … ' She eyed Luke through narrow eyes and tight lips. 'Luke, would you like a cushion, because it can't be very comfortable sitting on that fence?'

Stubbing his cigarette in slow deliberate measures into the ashtray, Luke watched the remnants smouldering, without answering. Unnerved by his silence and the heavy atmosphere, Zara reached for the open packet of Marlboro and pulled one out with her mouth. Ines and Sally exchanged skittish glances at each other, unsure of what to say or do next. Ines knew Luke well enough to know that when he's quiet, it's either because he's analysing a situation or he's using every bit of self-control to stop himself from losing it. His poker face is something nobody could read. After a pause of what seemed like an age, Luke spoke. 'I'm quite fine as I am thanks, Zara. From my view up on the fence, I see two sad and lonely young ladies. Both of whom have men they have to share with other women, even though they kid themselves into believing that they're in an exclusive relationship.' Coolly taking a drink of his freshly brewed coffee, his eyes searched out Ines who was by now rubbing her legs with her hand wrapped in a mitten fashioned out of a microfibre dishcloth.

Rattled, by the sense that she was under Luke's scrutiny, Ines felt like she'd been caught pinching from the sweet jar. Responding with a guilty smile, she tucked her hands under her bottom, away from view.

Conscious of Zara's livid glare aimed at Luke, the go-between supposed that if Zara's eyes were laser beams, he'd be a pile of cinders by now.

Feigning a cheery disposition, Ines climbed down from the bar stool and clumsily sauntered over to the window-sill where the lifeless Bluetooth speaker sat. 'Time for some music I reckon,' Scrolling through the music library on her phone, 'any preferences, name it now.'

In unison, everyone shrugged, impassive to the prospect of making playlist decisions. 'Something mellow. Chill out music,' suggested Sally.

'Yeah, something to lighten the mood … and I'll cook something for us all. It's getting late,' declared Luke as he opened the American style fridge and speculated what to make with the fare available.

Zara sat nursing her bruised ego, seething at Luke as he spoke. His candour was often cutting for a sensitive soul like Zara. 'I don't want anything to eat,' she said, folding her arms across her chest. 'I'm waiting for Nick to get in contact. We're going out.' This occasioned a sheepish tone, knowing full well what everyone thought of her love interest.

Shaking his head slowly at her childish behaviour, Luke began to speak from within the safety of the fridge, avoiding Zara's death stare—although fleeting, the thought that he was a perfect target for a knife to be flung into his back, had crossed his mind. Feeling brave enough to open dialogue with her, his voice resonated from the hollow space inside. 'Nick? Aha. The elusive Nick. How the devil is he? Will he be picking you up from Chez Garcia? I must say it would be great to have a drink with him before you head out.' Dumbfounded at the audacity, Zara's face contorted into what looked like a snarling beast 'Fuck off,' she mouthed, striking her arm out and flipping him off.

Sally's eyes widened like saucers at the spunky attitude of her friend who was a bit of an air-head at times, albeit a well-meaning one. However, Sally had secretly hoped to see him too, given that the only time they met was when Nick had been intoxicated on alcohol and cocaine. Piqued at how the events between Luke and Zara in the last hour had culminated into this ill feeling between them, Ines attempted to walk over to the butcher's console on the other side of the kitchen, where Luke was now standing, having had, by this time, removed his head from the security of the fridge and was chopping and slicing an aubergine and cloves of garlic with expertise.

A stilted conversation carried on between the three friends, but Ines was too distracted by the tingling sensation in her legs to pay much attention. Frustrated and determined to regain normal feeling, she took cautious steps, looking pained as she spoke. 'Can you both just be nice to each other? For goodness sake Zara, Luke included me as one of the sad and lonely women in his talk as well you know!' By now, Ines' leg was dragging with the sluggish steps of having a ball and chain clasped around her ankle. Clinging onto the central island for support, she fought to stay upright, her leg now buckling.

Horrified at the sight of their friend struggling to stand, Zara, Sally and Luke simultaneously demanded that she sit down. Not being left with much scope for argument, she sat on a chair that Sally had snatched from the bistro table nearby, gingerly placing it behind her.

'I'll definitely make an appointment with the doctor tomorrow morning,' she promised, looking around at her frightened audience, as if reading their minds.

Zara's phone started buzzing, bringing a smile to her face. Trying to conceal her delight upon reading the message, she began gathering her belongings with haste, bidding a breezy farewell to everyone.

'I'll see you all tomorrow. Don't wait up.' Winking as she scooted between Sally and Ines, Zara planted sticky lip-gloss kisses on their bemused faces. As quickly as she had received the green light, Zara shimmered out of sight, the tick-ticking of her stilettos fading down the hallway. 'More food for us then,' gloated Luke as he began to sauté the ingredients.

Chapter 4

Taking laboured steps through the office on Monday morning, Ines was becoming increasingly aware of her gait as she neared the group of buying assistants.

'Ooooh good morning to you, Ini,' shrilled Echo, holding a cup of steaming hot tea, her bleached white teeth dazzling under the LEDs. 'Looks like you've had a good weekend. How is Dylan?' Her eyes danced with implication.

Through gritted teeth, Ines smiled back. 'If you don't mind Echo, can you not call me Ini? And no, I didn't have a good weekend with Dylan.' Regarding Echo with an imperceptible curve of her mouth, Ines continued walking to her desk leaving Echo and her fellow co-workers to deliberate as to why she hadn't been with Dylan and who the mystery man was to have caused her to walk like John Wayne.

Watching them huddled around their desks, Ines could think of nothing worse than being amongst them. Hearing their frantic murmurs reminded her of a brood of hens contending to be the best in the pecking order. Allowing herself to indulge in the satisfaction of knowing she had their gossiping tongues in a furore, Ines couldn't help but smile to herself.

Settling into the chair behind her desk, Ines powered up the computer, an image of a grinning Sid James and Barbara Windsor materialising on the monitor.

Pinggg! Ines looked down at her phone and saw a message had come through. Confident that it couldn't possibly be Dylan reaching out to her, she opened the phone and saw that there were two unread messages:

-Hola chica, have you made an appointment yet? Had an AMAZING night last night. I truly think Nick has turned a new leaf. Exciting times!! Kisses.

Zara, always effervescent, rarely flat. Nobody could be peeved with her for long. Her heart was in the right place. 'I'll answer when I have time, otherwise she's going to chat and chat,' muttered Ines, scrolling to the next message, the one she'd conscientiously saved for last.

-Bonjour my little butterfly How are you feeling today? Have you booked an appointment to see Dr Cantrememberhisname?

She smiled. Her heart brimming with warmth, Ines always had time for Luke. She replied without hesitation.

-Hey you, you can't remember his name because you didn't know it in the first place! I'm calling in a minute, sir x

'Iniiii!' What sounded like a thunderous canter coming down the aisle and heading her way, Ines was not only peeved at the familiarity with which Echo was calling her out through the office, but also having to brace herself for a mind-numbing exchange of words.

Coming to a breathy halt, she was greeted with a look of displeasure and a stern face that jolted her into remembering that 'Ini' was a name only a few could use, and she was definitely not in that club.

'Iines! Ines! Guess what?' Out of breath with the exertion, she was unable to contain herself anymore. Blurting her news out with as much sophistication as an overzealous four year old, Ines supposed that she had better put the phone down and speak with the woman before she imploded.

'Yes, Echo? What could be so enthralling that you risked twisting your ankle to reach me?'

Giddy with excitement, she clapped her hands, and began to explain how Serena, the glamorous buying assistant had asked if her two cherubic looking kids would be ushers at her wedding, to be held at The Mountjoy.

'A joy to be mounted,' snickered Ines, taking a swig of water. Seeing a crestfallen Echo before her, Ines gave a coy giggle and backtracked with impressive speed. 'Sorry,' she smiled with apology. 'I didn't sleep great. So, what are Balthasar and Titus going to wear?'

Looking like a little girl seated in an enormous dark grey checked grandfather chair, Ines nodded resignedly as her doctor explained how he believed that the problem was an episode of acute sciatica and it would pass within a few weeks. Watching him as he began tapping on the keyboard, Ines wasn't convinced. Having challenged the doctor, who was barely out of nappies himself, she couldn't see how he was qualified to be in a position of diagnosing people, nor did Ines think that coming away with painkillers strong enough to knock a horse out was the solution that she had been seeking. She did however manage to get the referral for the CT Scan Zara had insisted that she have. If Ines was honest, this minor feat was more to stop Zara nagging her than it was for her own benefit. Being at the brunt of her friend's displeasure didn't bare thinking about. Struggling to not make it obvious that walking was becoming increasingly difficult, Ines wasn't sure how much longer she could put on a front. On the outside, to her friends in particular, she was calm and unperturbed by the unknown. But inside, she was confused, frustrated and wanted an answer so that she could move on with her life.

Feeling as though she was dragging her leg through quicksand and looking through an eye that seemed to have been smeared with Vaseline, Ines wasn't convinced that the doctor was on the right path in his suspicion that her troubles boiled down to an irritated nerve.

Somewhat distracted as she walked through the entrance of her office building, Ines hadn't noticed Michael having what appeared to be an in-depth conversation with Luke. Wait. What? Doing a double take at the unexpected appearance of the lovable rogue she wondered what the hell he was doing here? Predicting her reaction, Luke looked up and gave her a sly grin.

'Good morning, Miss Garcia,' greeted Michael, with a flamboyant bow. Saluting, Luke clicked his heels together, the sly grin, transforming into a smile that stretched across his unshaven face.

'Good morning, Michael.' Sceptical, Ines studied the pair of them with shrewd eyes. 'Is everything okay?'

'Quite alright, Miss,' Michael assured her. 'Mr Benoit is here acting as my advisor,' he added, feeling compelled to end the awkward pause which hung over them. Casting her gaze at Luke, Ines narrowed her eyes once again, suspecting there was more to their tête à tête than they were letting on.

Nonchalant as he lounged against the smooth, curved reception station, Luke crossed his arms. 'Well, my little butterfly, I wondered if you'd like to meet for lunch.' Guiding her with expert discretion, towards the waiting area within the foyer, Luke signaled for Ines to take a seat in the black leather chair. 'So, how did you get on at the doctor?'

'Fine. I've been approved for a CT scan. He thinks it's acute sciatica … oh and I've been given painkillers strong enough to knock a horse out.'

It was Luke's turn to narrow his light green eyes.

Michael stood behind his station feigning indifference, noisily brandishing a purple bag of his beloved chocolate éclair sweets from across the floor, offering them by way of alleviating the tension. Maybe he was wrong, but he found that sucking on a sweet was always a good diversion in these situations. He would often find himself focused so much on trying to catch the gooey chocolate which oozed out from the centre of the sweet, that he'd forget the topic of discussion.

Unwrapping the crunchy foil paper that covered his sweet, Luke popped the delicious caramel into his mouth, struggling with his natural instinct not to bite through. 'Hmmm, but you don't agree with him?'

'Well, no,' she admitted, rubbing her eyes in frustration.

Politely interrupting with a cough, Michael contributed to the discussion. 'Excuse me, I couldn't help but overhear. Maybe you should consider an eye test as well, Miss Garcia.' With that bold statement, he threw yet another of the moreish sweets into his mouth in conclusion.

'See? Everyone's saying the same thing. Did you make the appointment at the optician?' asked Luke, who by now had succeeded in breaking through to the chocolate.

Ines pulled her bag closer. 'He's a doctor, I'd like to think he knows what he's doing to some extent.'

'Well, Miss Garcia …'

'Ines. Please call me Ines.'

'Ok. Well Ines, doctors aren't always right. Look how many people are misdiagnosed. Maybe a second opinion would be wise.' Luke nodded in agreement, luxuriating in the remainder of his sweet. 'Michael is correct. You need further investigation. Your next stop should be a visit to the optician. It may be something linked to your physical symptoms or something completely separate. How is the eye, by the way?'

'Worse,' replied Ines, closing the bad eye, comparing the vision between both. 'All colours have just faded into wishy washy tones, and they both hurt like hell.' Pressing an offending eye, she winced for extra affirmation. 'Anyway, why are you here?'

'I had a viewing nearby, so I thought I'd drop in to see if you wanted to meet for lunch.'

'Ah, ok. For you and Courtney?' she assumed, immediately regretting that she asked, but not wanting to seem displeased for his newfound relationship progressing. Ines felt as though she had swallowed sand.

'No. For a client.'

Satisfied with his answer, she agreed to the lunch date with Luke and with that, made a Herculean effort in returning to the office.

'So, when do you have to head out to your next appointment?' purred Jenna, brushing her lips gently over Dylan's relaxed mouth.

Pondering the question and figuring that he'd have to go back to Montague Square at some point, Dylan considered the amount of phone calls his girlfriend had made to his phone, and the reception he'd receive on his return.

Ugh. She's a nagging pain in the arse.

Feeling a titillating sensation as Jenna stroked him, he looked down at her grinning face. 'Ooh that frown!' she teased in mock horror. 'I hope that's not the effect I'm having on you already.'

Aware of how his thoughts were presenting themselves, Dylan cupped her face in his hands and kissed her slowly, speaking in between each delectable one. 'I'm sorry, baby, I thought about work and it pissed me off. I don't want to leave you. I'll be going tomorrow morning but will be back in the evening, I promise.'

Sitting by the window at Café Café, Luke appeared agitated as he stabbed his way through a steaming bowl of pasta. Irritated, Ines placed her cutlery with purpose beside her bowl, leaning towards Luke. 'Okay, just for the record, for me, listening to the consistent tink tink sound of you prodding the food on your plate is on a par with sitting at a table with someone chewing with their mouth open. So, you're on a fast-track route to having yours truly poke you in the eye.' She was now wielding the fork at him. 'And you're being about as sociable as a tree stump. Pausing for dramatic effect as well as to give him a chance to reply, Ines shovelled a mouthful of risotto into her mouth, taking advantage of the short lull.

Looking at the shadows of his long sweeping eyelashes flickering across his cheekbones, she remained silent, sensing that something was askew. Letting out a heavy sigh, Luke continued to chew...with his mouth shut.

Not comfortable with the silence between them, she took the plunge and cracked the atmosphere with the finesse of a hellion. 'Anyway, I digress What's up? You've had a face like a slapped arse since I saw you earlier with Michael.'

'I shagged a girl I'd met last week at Fordhams, in a client's empty apartment.'

'And? That's not exactly new or unusual of you.'

'And I've just had sex with a potential buyer who'd viewed the same apartment earlier.'

Unimpressed by his behaviour, Ines stayed mute, her full mouth now a thin line until Luke had finished speaking.

'So, you're like a dog on heat. We all know this. What you're telling me is nothing new or surprising. Do you actually use protection during these spontaneous moments of passion with a stranger?'

'Sometimes yes, sometimes no. I don't plan on these things happening … they just, umm well, y'know, they just happen.' Raising his shoulders to his ears in a show of abashed resignation, Luke had nothing else to say.

'So, what you're essentially saying is that aside from behaving like a dog on heat, you could be impregnating these women or contracting some nasty STD from them, and passing it on to Courtney?' Ines was not happy with her friend's shenanigans.

Irked by his confession, Ines may not be a fan of Courtney, but the poor woman didn't deserve this. 'You know what? Dylan is an ass, and you don't condone his behaviour in any way shape or form. But you're exactly the same piece of shit. Playing away while the poor besotted cow is house hunting for the two of you is wrong. I don't like Courtney much, and honestly, I think you can do better … but no one deserves this.'

Ines was hot with anger now. All her feelings and emotions towards Dylan, Luke and her undiagnosed condition were culminating into one big hodgepodge. 'It's pathetic. Either stop playing the maggot or end it with Courtney once and for all.'

'We're not in a relationship. We're seeing each other. Nothing has been discussed about exclusivity.' Luke was now snarling through gritted teeth. Clenching his jaw, he made a bold attempt to fight his corner. 'We're not engaged or even girlfriend and boyfriend.'

'Oh, Luke,' Ines laughed, exasperated. 'For God sake, she's looking at places for the two of you, you must have given her some reason to think you're both committed.'

'I have done nothing!' he insisted. 'I never told her we were exclusive.'

'You didn't tell her you didn't want to move in,' she reminded him, her patience with Luke was waning. 'Look, if you don't want to be with her, end it. That's all I'm saying on the subject. And I have no clue why you're telling me about the women you're sleeping with. It doesn't paint you in a better light.'

Luke sank back in his chair, his jaw set in anger. 'I'm telling you this because I thought you would be sympathetic.'

'About what, your great sex life? Oh yeah, must be awful.'

His face darkening, he leant forward again and beckoned for her to do the same. 'Sympathetic because a girl I was "dealing" with passed something onto me.'

Ines froze momentarily before bursting into a fit of angry laughter. 'Oh, you twat!' she seethed. 'You are exactly like Dylan. You're cut from the same cloth.'

'Dylan is in a relationship with you! Courtney and I are not in a relationship, we're free to see other people.'

'In your world maybe… so, what is the purpose of your telling me this?'

'I need to get to a sexual health clinic and tell Courtney, but I don't know how to tell her. I'm nervous about going.'

'If you play with fire, you're going to get burned.'

Luke chose to ignore Ines' self-righteous quote. 'So? Will you come with me?'

Seeing how anxious he was, Ines couldn't help but feel a pang of sympathy for him. 'Yes, I'd be happy to watch you squirm while they assess you. As for Courtney, that's your call. I can't help you. You'll just have to give her your estate agent spiel and be upfront about it all.'

Luke nodded in acquiesce and grabbed a hold of her hand, stroking her knuckles with his thumb, preoccupied in his thoughts. For a few brief minutes, the two friends remained in quietude. Luke was the first to break the silence.

'Thank you,' he said with genuine gratitude, trying to meet her gaze. I appreciate your help. The appointment is this evening at six.' The moment was killed.

Ines jolted back, snatching her hand away from Luke's hold. 'Blimey. You don't mess about do you? Ooh no, sorry yes, yes you do mess around which is why you're in this shit show.'

Getting up to leave, Luke smiled. 'Lunch is on me. See you in the lobby of your office?'

Resigned to his pluckiness, Ines nodded slowly, watching her incorrigible friend disappear out of sight. Letting out a long groan, she pushed her chair back, making her clumsy exit out of the café. Back at her desk, Ines logged in to her computer, aware of the witterings of the buying assistants. There was a flurry of excitement amongst them, centred around Serena's impending wedding and the plans for the roles of the cherubic little darlings, Balthasar and Titus. Mumbling obscenities under her breath, Ines casually typed into the search bar for STDs in men; symptoms and prognosis, scrolling with fervour through the options for her to read.

Deep in research mode (she had five minutes left of her lunch break), Ines was oblivious to the outside world as she delved deeper into the WWW ether.

'Oooooh, what's this?' The owner of the grating voice came from

Martha. Bloody Martha. Mouth almighty Martha who was, by now peering over Ines's shoulder like a parrot.

Startled and knocking water over her hand, Ines turned to Martha. 'For God's sake, Martha, don't you believe in personal space?'

Recoiling from Ines' barbed reaction, Martha barely spluttered her response with the eloquence she was renowned for. Smoothing down her emerald green dress, Martha's hazel eyes fixed themselves on Ines, but not without stealing a quick glance at the open page on sexually transmitted diseases.

'Well, I hope the weekend antics were worth it.'

Bitch. Trying hard to contain her red-hot temperament, Ines could only reply with words and not a slap. 'Not that it's any of your business, but I'm looking into something my girlfriends and I were talking about… you know what it's like when girls get together and talk about their great lay, the conversation goes off the rails.'

Giving Martha a caustic smile, she continued, relishing every uncomfortable shift of her size 4 wedge heels, itching to leave. 'You know how it is.' Ines ended her sentence with a raise of her eyebrows and returned to her reading. Upbraided by the cutting remark, Martha sucked in her teeth and slithered away leaving a smug Ines to her own devices.

It was 5 pm. Never had a Monday been as surreal as this one in the whole of Ines's working life. Gathering her bag and coat, she made her way through the office to the lift, exhausted from the day. She'd been to see the doctor, made an appointment at the optician, lunch with Luke which turned into a terse exchange of heated words because of his sexual antics, she told Martha to effectively take a run and jump, is now as good as qualified in sexual health advice, and now she was going to a clinic with Luke to find out if he had caught something. To top it all off, in all of this, today's working day was productive. Bonkers.

Exiting the lift, Ines looked out ahead and spotted Luke loitering around the reception station, swigging water out of a bottle and unwrapping a sweet he presumably took from Michael's secret stash. Typical Luke.

Incredible. This man is about to find out what's eating his dick away and then drop the bombshell on his unsuspecting "non- exclusive girlfriend" afterwards and you'd think he was going for a drink with his mates. Catching her glowering at him, Luke tucked the bottle into his jacket pocket and swaggered over, with a ready smile on his face. The self-assuredness would be almost admirable if she wasn't so cross with him. 'Hello, my little butterfly.' Pulling her unyielding body closer to him and planting two lingering kisses on each cheek, Luke's hands rested comfortably on her waist.

Just as she opened her mouth to scold him, the entire buying team emerged from the lift, babbling and laughing demonically at something they were talking about. The cacophony receded as Martha spotted Ines first, in Luke's embrace.

Nodding across the foyer at them, Luke broke into his irresistible smile. 'Have a good evening, ladies.'

It was very funny to watch these supposedly cool, demure women regress into a bunch of giggling school girls, barely able to muster a small wave and coquettish show of acknowledgement between them.

Ines, revelled in the farce. Close enough to feel the day's stubble on his chin against her face, she was well aware that they were being surveyed. To anyone watching, they were new lovers in the first flush of dating.

Nobody had to know the scathing words coming out of her smiling mouth as she uttered them. 'For someone in so much shit, with a gammy dick and about to dump his girlfriend, you look like you're going out to have fun. Your arrogance is incredible and not in a good way.'

Smiling down, Luke kissed her forehead and threw an arm across her shoulders. 'A man is entitled to his last rites before his execution, non? I choose dicing with you, chérie. Come on, let's go.'

Still holding each other close as they left the building, Michael smiled on as he watched them leave. Sauntering past the group of women, Ines allowed herself to be engulfed in Luke's strong embrace as she smiled and bid them farewell one last time. This was something for her co-workers to chew on and dissect over their skinny blonde lattes. Smiling to herself, she did her happy little lamb skip as best she could and continued to walk with the charming scoundrel.

Entering the clinic, Ines looked around at the ultra-modern décor and couldn't help but feel that she was in a boutique hotel rather than a sexual health practice. Private care. What money can buy you. Reading her mind, Luke grinned as they walked across the white marble floor towards the receptionist with pink, glossy lips. 'It's very swish here, maybe we can ask for a room for the night,' he joked.

Rolling her eyes, Ines took a deep breath. 'You don't ever learn, do you?'

Ines watched every step she was making. Her kitten heels may be to die for but she wasn't ready to die just yet, and certainly not in this place. Her imagination running away at top speed, she envisaged slipping to the ground, splitting her head open and dying of internal head injuries. *Ines Garcia, died tragically in a sexual health clinic, granted a chic one.* Balking at the indignity of it all, she welcomed a distraction; a cheerful greeting coming from the shiny lipped woman behind her desk.

'Good evening. How can I help you?'

I know exactly how Luke would like you to help him, Ines thought, giving her friend a grim sideways glimpse.

'Ahem, yes. I have an appointment at six with Doctor Francescotti.'

Directing them to the waiting room, the mood became sombre for the friends. The early evening light squeezed through the narrow strip of clear glass atop the frosted covered window, a dazzling spectrum of colour creating a spectacle of light as a backdrop.

'Behave yourself when you go in there and keep it clean— no pun intended. And no flirting with the doctor.'

'What do you take me for?'

Ines could see the veins pulsating in Luke's temples, no doubt with anger.

A fire flared in her cool composure. 'Do you really want me to answer that question?'

Right on cue, a heavy oak door swung open. There she was, a raven-haired, green-eyed petite lady with a disarming smile. She was not that dissimilar to Ines. Trying to conceal her disappointment, Ines delivered a generous smile towards the alluring doctor standing at the entrance to her office.

Finding it difficult to conceal his delight at having to present his nether regions to this beautiful woman, Luke dropped his bottle of water onto Ines's lap and strode into the doctor's office.

Dickhead.

With an overly cheerful 'goodbye', the kind that's laced with joy, Luke left the office with a spring in his step as he laughed at some private joke shared between doctor and patient. 'Thanks again, doctor!'

Ines tilted her head. 'Thanks again doctor, mena mena meeeer,' ridiculed Ines, her arms folded, sounding more like a catty girl than a professional young woman.

Swooping down to retrieve his bottle of water from her lap, Luke took a massive glug. 'Ooh, I say, it's rather cold. Has it been between your legs all this time, chérie?'

'Ugh, you're so bloody predictable at times, it drives me insane. Can we just get out of here please?' grumbled Ines, wobbling as she stood up.

Reaching out intuitively, Luke caught her elbow 'Woah. Easy there. Have you been concealing a little bottle of Venezuela's finest in your bra, sipping on the sly?'

'No I have not.'

'Are you sure my little butterfly? I know you're partial to a little rum,' asked Luke, making a glugging motion with his thumb.

'Can you please just shut up? I don't know what's got into you. Well, I do but psychologically, you're behaving like a prize twit. Let's go.'

Placing one foot on the step, Ines paused for a split second and indicated to Luke that he should lead.

'No no, I cannot let you stagger up the stairs behind me. What if you get dizzy and fall? Who would catch you? Hmmm? I was taught by my grandfather that a gentleman stays behind a lady walking up the stairs and in front of her when descending them. So, up you go. Alley-oop.' Snapping his head in upward motions, indicating that she should proceed and that he was not budging, Ines accepted defeat, and grabbed the hand rail, conscious of the fact that a) his face was going to be level with her bottom and b) she was unsteady.

Luke grinned to himself as he watched on in mesmerising glory, the gentle jiggle of two voluptuous buttocks beneath her dress, the soft fabric clinging on to every curvy contour of her body, its hemline rippling below her knees like a waterfall tumbling lazily, with every step she took.

'I hope you're not perving.'

Huh, merde. She killed the moment. 'No no, I'm just focusing on your footing.'

'The way you've been behaving, as much as I'd like to believe you, I don't.' Pausing to regain balance, Ines looked down behind her as if she were searching for a mark on the back of her dress. 'So?' Tipping her head, Ines stared, psyching her friend out. She knew this man so well.

Incredulous but knowing full well his claim to innocence was debunked, Luke began to justify his actions. 'I'm a man walking behind a beautiful woman, with her bum in my face. I was contemplating how compact you are, although your butt is rather large compared to the rest of your body.' Luke's eyes shone with mischief, hinting that she should proceed to walk up the stairs.

'Careful, I can kick you in the teeth from here.' 'This I have no doubt, my little butterfly.'

Standing outside the clinic, Ines yanked Luke away from the entrance. Puzzled, he frowned and then the penny dropped. 'Aha! You're ashamed to be seen near this place. This is a place where only depraved people go. Their penance for carnal pleasures.'

'Carnal? The way you're behaving I'd say it's more hedonistic,' came Ines' dry reply.

'Well, either way I need to get to a chemist before we go anywhere else.'

Weaving niftily between clusters of grey wool suits congregating outside bourgeoisie pubs, Luke and Ines arrived at the pharmacy.

Handing over the prescription to an affable chap in thick rimmed glasses, Ines stepped away from Luke, to clarify that she was not the reason he needed medication for his willy. Minutes later, the pharmacist handed Luke the innocuous looking paper bag. Snatching the bag before he could open it, Ines victoriously made her way outside and found a quiet place to read the boxes. Flabbergasted at her nerve, Luke bumbled close behind. Coming to an abrupt halt behind Ines when she had stopped, Luke took a deep breath to prevent himself from saying something that he would later come to regret. Oh, he was very, very peeved.

'Fungal infection cream and tablets!?' Ines heckled. 'Seriously? What the actual hellfire?' At that, she began to laugh. And laugh. And laugh some more. Partly out of relief and partly because she's never known a guy with fungal issues. 'Pahahaha! That explains why you've been such an irritating prick lately! Hahaha.'

Mortified, he snatched the medicine back, blushing at the whole shameful saga.

Feeling the ugliness of the green-eyed monster rearing its head, Ines couldn't stop her mouth from spewing out scornful words. 'So, let me guess. You found yourself a girl in skin-tight jeans or a pair of faux leather skinny trousers. Things had warmed up down there.' Giggling, Ines's voice changed into dark, condescending tones, poking the air in the direction of his groin. 'And the teeny tiny iddy biddy spools of cottage cheese fungi grew and spread…and then your winkie caught it too. Before you knew it, you were growing a little cottage cheese farm.' Holding her arms out in a "et voila" pose, she spluttered a final burst of hilarity.

'Stop it!! Enough. That's enough. Yes, that is exactly what happened, and yes, she was a fan of faux leather jeans,' stormed Luke.

Furious at Ines's reaction and unsure of what to do next, he pulled out a packet of cigarettes and lit one. The silence between them an awkward reminder of the chemistry between them that both refuse to accept exists. Ines was now beginning to feel guilty for her behaviour. Taking a long drag and waiting until he had calmed down before speaking, she deemed it prudent to say nothing until Luke made the first move. This could take a while, but she had to remain subdued for as long as it took.

At last, Luke broke the hush. 'I'm a twat, yes. It could have been much worse, and it would've been my own fault for not being more careful. I have to consider my actions and their repercussions.'

Seeing how embarrassed he was, Ines gave a gentle smile. 'I'm sorry. I didn't mean to laugh at you. I was bang out of order.' Dreading the next question, she hated herself for being so curious even to the detriment of her mind. 'On a serious note though, did you do anything else? Orally I mean, because if you did you might need your mouth seeing to.' *Why do I do this to myself?*

Luke shook his head. 'No, not at all. We just screwed and then went our separate ways.'

Classy.

Ines nodded thoughtfully. 'And what will you do about Courtney? Are you still breaking up with her?'

'Yep. It's the right thing to do for both of us. I can't live like this. I'm lying to myself and to her.'

Chapter 5

As Ines opened her front door, a familiar scent bombarded her senses. Aftershave, and not just any aftershave.

Dylan's. He was back. Today was the strangest day. And there he was, sitting in the kitchen, unflinching while drinking *her* coffee and eating *her* chocolate. Regarding him with hostility, she dropped her bag with a loud "clonk" on the worktop, and walked guardedly over to the central island. Sitting on the bar stool, she flicked the lighter and lit a cigarette. Looking out on a silvery crescent moon, it had crossed her mind that she hadn't yet acknowledged Dylan.

'Alright babe? How are you?' Strutting over to where Ines was seated and kissing her on the mouth, he moved her hair out of her eyes, playing the ever-doting boyfriend.

Dismissing the greeting with a sweep of her thumb, she began to speak, trying to remain calm and collected. 'So, how was work? Did you manage to meet your target?'

No answer.

'Why didn't you call me when I left you voicemails and messages? You didn't even call to see if I was okay after my fall. I'm talking to you, Dylan. Wait. Where're you going? Can we please talk?'

Sauntering down the hallway like a surly man-child seeking respite, Dylan shirked the interrogation, indifferent to the questions raining down on him like hailstones. Finally, gracing Ines' pleas for a response, his deep voice reverberated through the walls. 'Aah yeah, well reception is a nightmare up there. I spent most of my days in an office below ground level, but I figured one of your witches and bitches would inform me if it was urgent. Anyway, I sent you a message and you said you were safe and resting.'

'Umm can you not talk about my friends like that? It's disrespectful, and they don't deserve it. They've been looking after me while you've been away,' called out Ines, tottering down the hallway after him.

'Whatever…so yeah babe, the trip went smoothly, and we wrapped up earlier than planned.'

Lie. Lie. Lie.

'The company's so pleased that they want me to do the same for the other branch,' he continued, predictably about to announce another departure. 'Bad news is, I'm off to Bristol tonight to meet their South West Regional Management first thing tomorrow morning to see if I can cut a good deal with them too. I'll probably be gone a week or so 'cause Head Office are likely to ask me to cover the South East as well. It's all about targets, babe.'

Arrogant pig!

Ines had caught up with Dylan, who was by now rifling through his drawers and wardrobe, packing whatever he could find into his Mulberry hold-all. Dispirited, she watched on, kneeling beside the bed. 'We've barely seen each other,' she whimpered, disappointed with herself for sounding so needy.

'Well to be fair babe, I got here early, hoping we'd spend some time together before I leave.' Staring through salacious eyes, he began peeling off his suit trousers and boxers. 'It's not too late to give me some love, I've missed you darlin'.' Slowly tugging himself, Dylan's free hand brought Ines's head towards him, tapping her half open mouth with the edge of his hardness. Stroking her hair, Dylan uttered sensual words of encouragement, her willpower melting away. Knowing that all of this was going against everything her friends warned her about, she was unable to refuse. Allowing him to undress her, she didn't care at that moment…

'But why? I don't understand!' Pleading for a more eloquent answer than 'we're not right for each other', Courtney was now hanging on by a thread.

Losing his patience but reasoning with himself that she had every right, Luke sat calmly on the striped sofa, with his head hung low staring at a speck of lint on the rug. 'First of all, I don't feel ready to move in with you, you have just assumed it to be the next step forward. Second, I can't imagine me being with you long term. We're not compatible. You're a lovely woman…but I don't love you and I won't ever.'

Courtney was now looking like a crazed banshee as her flailing arms swung down in protest. Her immaculate, newly coiffed hair had fallen out of place, strands whipped around her face, the back of her head resembling a nest of thorns. Flicking the solitary tresses hanging down the nape of her neck as if they were an irritant, she was now a dishevelled mess. 'Ugh!' Trying to compose herself, Courtney thought that she'd adopt another approach. 'You said we could look at moving in together if we were going to move forward in the next few months. You said...' Wailing and thumping the cushions, her behaviour was more like a belligerent love-struck teen than an ice cool siren.

Covering his face with the palm of his hands, Luke's voice sounded muffled as he spoke. '*If* Courtney. But it's not going to happen because I don't want this, and *if* you take a step back and look at what we have, it's actually not that special. I'm not what you need or want. You deserve so much better than this. I don't even want kids. You do.' His tone had now softened when he realised that she was nodding. She was in agreement.

Phew!

Decidedly alarmed at seeing Courtney's initial reaction, but feeling optimistic, Luke was dubious about asking his next question. Throwing caution to the wind he did anyhow. 'So, can we still be friends?'

'I'll see you soon, babe,' Dylan kissed Ines before he left her once again.

'Message me, yeah?' Her request was not going to be honoured, this she knew, but the deluded young woman lived in hope that maybe he would. She watched him from the tall sash windows in her bedroom, as he strutted through the pretty square, resplendent in glorious spring blooms. Downcast she watched Dylan disappear out of view, leaving only stragglers of dog walkers in sight as the sun sunk into the horizon.

Tomorrow's a new day. Pondering the toxic situation she found herself to be in, Ines began rubbing her bad eye and stretching out her leg which now felt as though liquid metal had been poured into her bones. Struggling to walk down the hallway into the kitchen, she could only equate the sensations she was experiencing to the feeling you get in a bad dream when you're unable to move because you're stuck in quicksand. The sense of dragging your limbs in slow motion, heavy and cumbersome.

Opening the fridge to consider what to eat for supper, she began a conversation— with herself. 'Usual table for one, madam? Ooh yes please, and I'll have a glass of the Chateauneuf-du-Pape while I'm deciding what to have. Thank you.' Pursing her lips and staring blankly at the void inside the fridge, Ines hoped that if she stared long enough, its contents would be transformed by a chef into a culinary extravaganza. 'I need to get a life. I'm talking to myself and laughing at my own humour. Right. Pâte with sourdough bread it is for me, then.'

Settling down in front of the TV, Ines began to eat her dinner for one. With one hand on the remote control, she surfed through the channels at speed. 'Nope, nope, God no, no, nope, hmmm, no, ooh.' Deciding on Dinner Date, Ines discarded the remote atop the dark wood coffee table, she had shipped over from Vietnam during her time globetrotting.

Mum calling! Mum calling! the alert shrilled from Ines's mobile phone like a warning, LED lights demanding ANSWER ME! Resigned to the fact that she had nothing better to do, she answered. 'Hi, Mum.'

'Hello darling, how are you? We haven't spoken in, well, it seems like forever.'

That's not a bad thing. 'Yes, I know. I've just been busy. Work and life seems to take over. Sorry.'

'So, any news? How's that handsome boyfriend of yours?' Not even waiting for an answer, and barely taking a breath for the next onslaught of chatter, her mother carried on. Ines continued eating, leaving her mum to witter on, only speaking to correlate a fitting response, while she watched the show. After all, knowing how the dates were going, was by far more important than listening to how wonderful her mother's husband was doing, blah blah blah.

'…he's a wally. Honestly, Brian's a law unto himself.'

Ines hated how her mum sang Brian's praises at every opportunity, as if the sun shone because of him. It was a crude reminder that her mum was not at ease in her relationship. It was like listening to a lovesick girl, over compensating for her bad romance, with dumb stories nobody had any concern for, by trying to justify his existence. It wound her up. But was she any better? Ines mulled over the question. Was she destined to follow her in her mother's footsteps?

Now not wanting to listen anymore, her disinterest resonated down the phone line.

'Listen Mum, it was great chatting, but I need to get ready for bed. It's been a long day.'

'Bed? What time is it? Oh my, it's nearly half-eight. We've been chatting for over an hour now.' *No. You've been chatting for over an hour.*

'Alright, well I'll speak to you soon, Mum. Take care, byeee.' 'Bye bye, take care.' Click. Just like that. Conversation over.

Taking a moment to gather her thoughts and energy, Ines looked around the lounge. She still took pleasure out of looking around her home. Throughout the apartment, were trinkets, soft furnishings and furniture which reflected her journey so far. It told an eclectic story of travel, experiences and people she's known along the way. Her home was her life journal. Puffing out the embroidered raw silk cushions she'd bought in Shanghai, when she was en route to Japan, Ines smiled to herself as she remembered meeting Jared in Yuyuan Old Street market. They had both been perusing the artisanal wares of the craft folk, sitting in their brightly painted wooden huts, diligently creating and perfecting pieces that would sell for ridiculous prices in the West, yet sell for a meagre yield there.

Jared was a young Spanish guy, with dark brown wavy hair and eyes the colour of mahogany. He was gorgeous. Their relationship began while haggling over a beautiful hand painted wooden box they had both spotted and wanted. A combination of Ines's broad smile, her charm and an impeccable execution of her femininity, helped her win. Pleased with her bargaining skills, she squeezed the box lovingly into her backpack. 'So, as the victor and you, the loser, I feel it's my duty to offer you a feast of pork bun and jasmine tea. Fancy a little break from the chaos?' The audacious confidence Ines oozed was infectious. Jared hung his head low in feigned melancholia at being defeated. 'Well, if my consolation prize is a pork bun and a drink with a beautiful hustler, I'll graciously accept.'

'I didn't say a drink. I said a jasmine tea.'

Blowing out his cheeks as if to throw up, he replied in earnest. 'I'd rather have a Tsingtao dark beer.'

'Okay, well how about we take a stroll around the pond in the botanical garden, and then head to a bar,' suggested Ines, with the diplomacy of a sage.

'Sounds like a plan.'

Meandering through the tranquil gardens of Yu Yuan, the companions had been enjoying their food as they came to a beautiful spot which warranted a pause to appreciate the view. Oblivious to Ines admiring him from afar, Jared had been standing close to the lotus pond, taking hungry bites out of his pork bun.

'We can sit in a bar and grab a beer, if you want,' offered Ines. Grateful at the perceptive gesture, Jared nodded with enthusiasm, as he chewed the remainder of the delicious warm bun. The pair continued walking in comfortable silence, munching and stopping to look closer at the beauty of the lotus flowers.

'Stunning, just look at how it blooms with every perfect petal in tact. Did you know that the lotus is sacred amongst Asian and South East Asian cultures? It's a symbol of rebirth and the life cycle.' Looking at Jared who appeared to be intrigued by the flower and the story behind it, she felt compelled to continue. 'And the reason it's so cherished is because at night, its bloom submerges beneath the murky surface of the pond, its roots growing within the mud and in the morning it emerges, unscathed by the dirty water, blooming in perfect natural beauty, later in the day.' Ines was passionate about learning, and her enthusiasm was infectious. Jared returned her enthusiasm with a smile. A large, warm smile.

However, although his patience was commendable, his attention had begun to waver. Ines beckoned him away from the peaceful haven and out into the bustling, craziness of Shanghai Old Street. The main streets were lined and crammed with brightly decorated wooden huts and buildings dating back from the Ming Dynasty to the present day, respecting the simplicity of Shanghai's style. Sloping black ornate tiles on the rooftops, lattice windows and tall swinging doors adorned the fronts of rickety buildings, standing like stoic elders, beside ornate, modern edifices.

Shuffling through the busy streets, Ines marvelled at how many people were in this one area alone. What was wondrous, was how the Shanghainese remain unperturbed by the manic style of daily life, going about their business, buying fresh ingredients, oblivious to old scooters, spluttering toxic pollution into the smoggy atmosphere, laden with what seemed like entire families carrying shopping bags. 'Blimey health and safety would be up in arms if they were here!' shouted Ines, above the cacophony. Winding through the market street, stalls selling piping hot cartons of noodles, dumplings and buns triggered hunger pangs. 'Shall we get some noodles?' proposed Jared.

'We can eat in the bar. The food is delicious. Trust me,' replied Ines, with confidence.

Easily convinced, he allowed her to lead the way to this elusive bar.

Reaching an old building, painted in gold and red, Ines melted through the doorway, the slatted doors creaking as they rebounded into their original position. The aromatic scent of incense rising from delicate ceramic holders placed at each table encompassed the spirit of Shanghai in a bygone era. Standing at the wrinkled leather bar, the parched young man was thankful to finally be there. Ordering a dark beer for Jared and a rum for herself, Ines looked completely at ease. Finding this trait endearing yet irresistible, before he could stop himself, Jared leaned down, placing a cautious peck on her cheek. Seizing the opportunity, Ines turned her face to meet his and stood on her tip toes, responding with a deep, warm, sensual kiss. It was a long-lasting memory that had been etched in her mind.

Ting ting!

Crashing back down to earth with a lousy thud, Ines's giddy trip down memory lane was rudely interrupted. The recently assigned ring tone belonged to Luke's number. 'Hello, you,' she smiled.

'Bonsoir, my little butterfly, what are you up to?'

'Well, I was reliving a most delicious memory of when my ex-boyfriend and I had our first kiss, until you rudely interrupted.'

'Ah. Sorry. But, the here and now is reality, I'm afraid. Can I come over?' So bloody forthright.

'I'm in my civvies!' Protesting, Ines glanced in the mirror and ran her fingers through her wavy hair by way of an attempt to tidy herself up.

'I've seen you naked on the bathroom floor looking like shit.' Ah Luke. There was no sugar coating with this guy. Anyone of a delicate disposition could be offended by his candour at times. Reconciled to his determination, Ines finally agreed.

Grinning from ear to ear, Luke stood brazenly with a bottle of wine and two glasses, at the mouth of the wide doorway to the lounge. His broad shadow danced a little jig along the expansive sage green walls, as he made his way over to the sofa. The merry little dance was short lived however, when his foot caught the underside of the antique Berber rug Ines had bought in the Kasbah, on a visit to Marrakesh. A lumbering struggle to keep himself from tumbling, ensued. Torn between the preservation of her rug and saving Luke and the glasses, Ines plumped for the rug. In blind faith, she yanked the corner away from Luke's precarious footing, jarring his back to form a magnificent arch worthy of an Olympic gold medal. With arms thrashing the air, the bottle, still with its cork firmly secured, catapulted through the room. In what seemed like triple slow motion, she watched on agog as the scene unfolded right before her eyes. It was comedy and chaos rolled into one.

Smash! The glasses shattered across the wooden floorboards,

sprinkles of glistening fragments, sparkled like snow under the moon's luminescent platinum light. The bottle continued to roll aimlessly across the floor, the wine, sloshing inside as it continued ambling along, bumping over small furrows in the wood.

Crashing into the two-seater sofa opposite Ines, Luke knocked the back of his head into the wall with a toe-curling whack. Boouff. Luke groaned as he rubbed his head, breathless as the adrenaline continued to race through his veins.

Uncertain of where to look first, Ines looked to her rug and then Luke. Her rug remained unscathed. Phew. A feeling of utter selfishness washed over her for checking on material possessions before her friend. Staring at him, she winced, feeling his pain. 'Well, that's what I call an entrance! Are you okay? I'll fetch you some arnica.'

Rubbing the back of his head, Luke examined the carnage on the floor. 'I'm fine, thanks to my lithe physique and cat-like reflexes.' A smile crept up one side of his face, amused at the look of disdain on his long suffering friend's face.

'I can see that thump didn't affect your modesty,' observed Ines. 'Nor did it seem to knock any sense of actuality into that thick skull of yours.'

'You're a hard woman, Miss Garcia,' sighed Luke.

Armed with the arnica, hoover and her bucket full of cleaning products, Ines returned to the scene of the crime and sat herself beside Luke. 'Come here and let me check you over.' Grabbing his face and turning him towards her, she checked for any wounds. Feeling her warm breath as she moved in for closer inspection, Luke found himself relaxed and willing to be at her mercy. The faint scent of amber and vanilla lingering on her skin filled him with a need to be in her arms. Fighting the urge to lean into that perfect mouth for a tender kiss and give in to every emotion he felt, was like quelling a a fire with a pipette. This moment, in this exact intoxicating moment, Luke was under Ines' spell and he didn't want it to end. Whether his actions would be reciprocated was still undetermined and this unnerved him.

Thwack!

'OUCH!! What was that for!?' Rubbing his cheek, Luke looked distraught.

'To wake you up from your reverie. Now, turn that wooden head of yours so I can check for bruising.'

Compliant, Luke shuffled round, still reeling from his harsh awakening. Blissfully running her fingers through his silky hair, Ines probed his skull, searching for any lesions. The smell of his hair was delicious. Was it apple? She could smell apples.

The efficient investigation soon led to gentle caresses as her fingers toyed in languid splendour with random locks on the top of his head, enjoying the luxury of being in such intimate proximity. Her heart beat so fast it felt like it would jump through her rib cage.

Stupefied by her relaxing touch, Luke didn't want it to stop. 'Am I wounded?' he muttered in mock weakness. 'Will I survive?'

Twisting tufts of hair around her fingers, Ines was still mooning and happy he couldn't see her reaction to his question.

'You'll be just fine.' Patting the crown of his head with a gentle touch, Ines swivelled herself around, bouncing along the sofa, faced with the grim reality of the devastation in front of her, a silver veil of sequins winking in the evening light. 'Bum. I forgot the reason I was checking your noggin ... I thought it was for nits in your hair.'

'You could be a great nit nurse, what with being so skillful and matronly.'

'Matronly!? Matronly?!' What a compliment! Ines was livid, and to think she had experienced moments of tenderness towards him. Fwit! Luke's hair burst into a feathery mess as Ines's hand swept the top of his head. Feeling as if he had all the energy sapped out of him, Luke slumped forward, unable to react with more than an "owww". Scruffing his hair back into shape, he continued with indifference. 'Well, the sooner we clear up, the sooner we can sit down and have that wine— if we can find it.'

Clapping her hands in conclusion, Ines rose and made headway for the hoover. 'Let's go! Come on. Then we can start on that elusive bottle of wine.'

Still feeling dazed after the cosy encounter with Ines, Luke got on his hands and knees and began spritzing and cleaning the floor, searching for debris and the bottle. Enthralled by the sight before her, she waved the nozzle around his head, delighting in watching his hair spiking towards its beak as the air sucked like a tempest. Fffft ffffwwwwft.

Ducking his head in nervous anticipation of being scalped by

the hoover, Luke blanched as Ines continued with sadistic glee at watching his angst.

In what sounded like a whimper, Luke placed his hands over his head — a natural reflex to protect himself. 'Enough. Play time is over now.'

Still waving the nozzle over him, Ines giggled. 'Awww, you scared?'

'No, but you're pissing me off.'

Realising that she was on the borderline and the joke was going to go one step too far, Ines retreated back to the task at hand. 'Oh, boo. You're no fun.'

Luke chose to ignore her retort, focusing instead, on crawling stealthily across the floor inch by inch, collecting large pieces of shrapnel.

Pulling a childish scowl behind his back, Ines fired up the hoover once again and began to sweep the wand briskly, back and forth, avoiding her moody but handsome friend, although the temptation to accidentally on purpose knock him with it was challenging her willpower.

Deep in thought, Luke was stumped by his behaviour towards the young woman. He got impatient with Ines, scolding her as if she was a nuisance, when all he wanted to do was play fight her to the ground and hold her close. Instead, he was berating himself for being confused about the mixed emotions whirling around in his head. The dynamics had changed in one fell swoop. The desire to kiss Ines had intensified, as he watched her move around the lounge, swishing back and forth with the utmost diligence, ensuring not a single piece of glass was left.

'Yaaay, here it is!' Bending down to reach for the rogue bottle of wine which had come to wedge itself beneath the tub chair by the bay window, Ines wriggled it out.

'Fantastic. Now let's put all this stuff away and do what we were meant to do in the first place.'

Not needing any convincing, Ines unplugged the hoover, pressing the "return" button with her toes, hopping out of the way to avoid the plug writhing like an angry cobra, as it reached the end of the line with a definitive clunk, nestling snugly into its cavity.

Flaked out on the sofa, the pair idly munched on tortilla chips, sipping wine, comfortable in each other's company.

'So, what's the purpose of your visit this evening? I thought Monday evenings were sacred to the recovery of your dog-like antics over the weekend.'

Throwing his head back in exasperation, Luke growled softly like a guard dog sending out a warning. 'Can you stop with this dog talk. I'm a free man. I'm not hurting anyone.'

'No, only Courtney… and you very nearly gave her an STD.' 'It's fungal.'

'Whatever. You still could have contracted one and passed it on!' Shooting a sideways glance to demonstrate her disapproval, Ines took a bite from her tortilla crisp as a defiant full stop.

Becoming increasingly frustrated, Luke slammed his glass down on to the table. 'What's with you? I came here to tell you my news and all you do is slag me off!' Looking at his dispirited face, Ines felt ashamed of herself for taking her frustrations out on him. What he did in his private life was his own business, and yes, he was well within his rights to be upset with her behaviour.

Chewing the inside of her bottom lip, Ines considered apologising. Deciding not to and instead opting for taking responsibility, she shrugged her shoulders. 'I don't know. No. I do know what's got into me. Bloody Dylan is doing my head in. I'm confused. It's driving me crazy.' With glazed eyes, Ines looked like she was about to cry.

'So, you're not done with him?'

With a meek 'no', Ines hung her head low, avoiding the disappointment in Luke's gaze.

'Has he been back? Where is he?'

'Yes, earlier this evening. We had sex, which I suppose was more like the patch up kind, and then he left. He's headed for Bristol.'

Tormented by the pang of jealousy in his chest, Luke caught his breath and began to speak, using every iota of self-control to curb his anger.

'W..why did you sleep with him, I thought the pep talk the other night that Sally gave you was the nail in the coffin? Your final decider. He's probably with his bit on the side, as we speak.'

Rolling the stem of her glass between her fingers, Ines considered Luke's comment. 'It's hard to break away. I know I should, but I think I should give it another chance. Better the devil you know and all that.'

'You think?'

Making a slow nodding motion, Ines continued. 'He works hard, he's very driven and determined to become a partner in the company. I believe he really is travelling around the country getting these deals.'

'And not ringing or sending messages to see how you are or to hear your voice? How's that okay?'

'Well, sometimes he's in a bad reception area.'

Cough cough. 'Bullshit' Luke spluttered. 'Come off it!' he roared, making her jump. 'You aren't that naïve.'

Ignoring his fury, and puerile reaction, she proceeded with her rationale of still being in a loveless relationship. 'And I'm sure when he has the time, he'll choose to spend it with me, and take me out.'

'As opposed to spending it with his mistress?' enquired Luke.

'No! Me! Me and only *me*! Stop scrutinising my relationship. I'm not comfortable with this inquisition,' glowered Ines, who had now dropped her gaze and focused on the dragon design painted on the dipping bowl in front of her. Caustic tears seared through her throat.

'And why were you thinking of your ex-boyfriend Javier when I called you?'

'Jared.'

'Jared. Why were you thinking of Jared when I called you? You know why? Because you, my little butterfly are NOT happy, and when we are not happy, we think of times, memories – that made us feel like we could never be miserable and we'd forever be in that place. That is why you were thinking of him and not Dildo. I am asking you these questions so you can open your eyes to the reality of what you're actually allowing to happen to you.'

Nodding in grim affirmation of what was being said, Ines rolled her tiny shoulders and mumbled something incoherent.

'What?'

'Nothing. I just said I know and I will.' 'Will what?'

Slamming her palms down on the sofa, Ines yelled. 'Will end it! I will end it…when I'm ready.

Unconvinced by her assertion but content that he was making a very fair point, Luke took the remote control, searching for an alternative to Dinner Date.

'Do you mind?' Whining like a child, Ines sulked. 'I was watching that.'

'Nope, I don't mind at all.' Flick flick. Luke's finger seemed to be glued to the buttons, much to her annoyance. 'Aaha. Casino Royale. Perfect,' grinning as he turned to a dumbfounded Ines, Luke stretched his long legs out and settled in to watch the film. Resigned to not watching her show, she took another chip and sat back to watch it.

'So, what was it you had to tell me?' she asked after some time had passed.

'Ooh bravo! You managed to say nothing for seventeen minutes.' Pompously glancing at his watch, Luke gave mock approval with two thumbs up.

Ines raised her hand, indicating that he should just shut up with his sarcasm and answer the question.

Motioning a shrug and, without taking his eyes off the screen, Luke remained unflappable. 'I broke up with Courtney. She took it well once she got over the initial shock. I made her see sense, that neither of us were truly satisfied with our match and that she deserved better.'

Searching his face, Ines struggled to fathom how everything went over him like water off a duck's back. Then it dawned on her. Of course it would, Eva Green is stating that "she's the money". Nothing can disturb that.

His eyes darting to the side, snatching a furtive glance at Ines's body language, Luke smiled to himself. 'She's French you know.'

'Ok. And Daniel Craig is English.' Bristling at his admiration for the pretty French brunette, Ines changed the subject before the catty side of her burst out like water from a broken dam.

'So, you're officially single?' she pressed. 'No one to answer to? Perfect.'

'Yep, and she sent me a message to say that I was right and went on to wish me the best for my future. A perfect break up.'

'Sold by the perfect salesman. You are truly jammie!' Tucking her legs beneath her, Ines reached for her wine and decided to play him at his own game, letting out appreciative sighs every time the debonair and rather handsome Mr Daniel Craig appeared on the screen.

Trying to hide his disapproval of her penchant for blond, blue eyed handsome Englishmen, Luke lit a cigarette.

Ping!

Exhaling a stream of curling smoke, Luke signalled that Ines had received a message. In a deft move, Ines swiped her phone off the table.

'You see? You're so lost in the world of Daniel Craig, you're not even noticing the world around you.'

Opening the message, she smiled. 'And what a gorgeous world it is.' Her good humour soon began to sag, a knitted frown taking its place. Cheerless, she flipped it across the table.

'Bad news?'

'Just your favourite person asking if I've washed his clothes from the trip to Manchester.'

'That's a strange question.'

On reflection, Ines decided that it was indeed a strange question. Re-reading the text, she found it unusual that Dylan should be contacting her so soon and with such a cryptic message. 'Well, maybe he has bought me a gift and wants to surprise me with it. I won't put his washing in until he gets home,' said Ines, full of empty optimism.

Seeing Luke pulling a long face, she felt an obligation to fight Dylan's corner. Ramrod, she glared at Luke. 'Hey, do you not think he is capable of such a thing?! You'd have him hung, drawn and quartered before a fair trial if you had your way!'

'No. I'd listen with great amusement to what he'd have to say. He's so full of the brown stuff, it's laughable. He's a joke.' Without even flinching, Luke continued regardless of Ines' death stare— or maybe it's one of hurt and disbelief that she was hearing the truth stripped bare. 'You know he's selfish and doesn't care about you or your wellbeing. He could have called you or any of us to see how you were after your fall. Don't tell me that Manchester doesn't have reception anywhere!' Stubbing out his cigarette, Luke looked impudent.

At no point did Ines divert her gaze. Fixated, she blinked twice, unable to utter a word. It was as if they had dried up in a solid mass and embedded themselves in her throat, scratching to escape. Her doe eyes shining like Murano glass, began to weep.

Alarmed primarily at the fact that he had upset Ines and secondly that he was about as useful as a silk saucepan where crying women were concerned, Luke found his stomach flapping, unsure of what to do. Trying to think back at the chick flicks guaranteed to make his date weep, which always ensured a win of brownie points for being "so in tune with women's emotions" and a night of naughtiness, Luke's brain scrambled through his memory bank trying to think of the acts of kindness that had won him so many bed partners…not that he was trying to bed Ines.

She was special and to see her so hurt saddened him. Feeling terrible, he wrapped his arms around a trembling shoulder and pulled her into him.

Recollections came flooding in, but none of it was relevant. Those girls didn't matter; Ines did. What he was doing right here, in this moment came naturally.

'Ohh la la la la, I'm so very sorry, chérie. My mouth sometimes engages before my brain and I speak like a buffoon. But what I'm saying is for your own good. This man doesn't deserve your loyalty or your heart.'

With her voice muffled as she sobbed into his chest, Ines nodded. 'I know. I know everything you are saying is true and correct, but I can't say it's over. Not yet.'

'Then when? What's it going to take, hmm? When you're beaten down over how many times he's lied to you?'

'I honestly don't know, but when it's time, I'll know.' Her sharp intakes of breath began to dissipate in the comfort of Luke's arms.

Encouraged by her answer, Luke kissed her head once more, and then rested his chin over her hair as they sat in silence for what seemed like an eternity. Easeful, Ines let out a big, contented sigh as the warmth from every breath and the rhythm of his gentle heartbeat lulled her into a sense of security.

The opalescent light of sundown had now shifted to a granite sky. Yawning, with misty eyes, Ines looked up at Luke and then at the blackness beyond the window. Realising that it must be late, she pulled herself away from his arms.

'You look tired, my little butterfly. Today has been draining to say the least.'

Smiling flimsily back at him, Ines patted his chest, agreeing with what he just said and began to rise from the sofa, leaving an impression of her bottom behind on the soft seat.

Luke's clomping reverberated through the hallway as he strode towards the front door. Reaching out for the brass lever, as he turned to say goodbye, he was faced with a disgruntled woman.

'Your boots. They're so loud! Can you remember to take them off when you come in and not when you're halfway through my flat, please?'

'Ah well, I cannot do anything about the sound, this is what happens when you buy quality leather sole boots.' Winking, his grin was as broad as his jawline. 'Maybe you can buy me some slipper-socks and I can pirouette through the rooms like a delicate ballerina.' Giving him a friendly push and following him out into the main entrance, Ines found herself unable to make a worthy come back. 'You're a twit, you know that? Maybe just maybe, you can take your posh boots off at the door,' she said in defiance, poking his chest with her finger.

'Yes boss,' laughed Luke as he sauntered down the white steps to the street below. Shaking her head with affection, Ines waved him off and closed the door behind.

Lying in bed, Ines scrolled through her phone, checking for any unanswered work-related messages. Nothing. Good. It meant that she could go to sleep without interruption. Tomorrow, she goes to the optician and will find out why her eyes hurt so much. Closing the left eye, the vision in the right eye was still bad. Bum. 'I probably need a new prescription for my glasses,' reasoned Ines as she settled down under her duvet. Peeping above the covers, she spotted Dylan's bag sitting unopened by the chest of drawers. Tempted, she considered getting out of bed to look inside the hold-all, and search for the elusive contents he was so anxious for her not to find.

Deciding that she was too cosy and couldn't be bothered to check at this time, Ines opted to investigate tomorrow. *Tomorrow's a new day*, she thought with optimism . Shutting her eyes and blocking out all thoughts of Dylan, she preferred to practice Luke's tried and tested yoga breathing to induce sleep. Ines swore blind it was just because you're concentrating so much on breathing and counting, it was just an adult alternative to counting sheep. Luke would beg to differ, but he would, wouldn't he? Smiling to herself, her heavy eyes began to close. Sleep wasn't far off.

Chapter 6

Through half open blinds, which once again Ines had forgotten to shut, she was woken by birdsong. Unwilling, Ines rose from the comfort of her bed, blinking her bleary eyes into what little focus she could muster and turned to put her feet on the floor. An electrical current seemed to be running through the same leg which she had been dragging along like a hulking weight, the same leg she had cut up from clawing at the imaginary ants crawling beneath her skin. The sensation soon dwindled, leaving Ines flummoxed at what she had just experienced. Sliding off the bed, she headed for the shower, making a mental note to take a look inside Dylan's hold-all on her return.

Standing underneath cascading water, it somehow didn't feel hot enough. Ines could feel patches of cold, even though the water was now steaming hot. Regardless of her skin turning an angry red from the heat, she was still feeling spots of cold over her limbs. It was as if someone had eaten a strong mint and breathed all over her. Unsatisfied with the morning shower, she stepped out, grabbed a bath sheet and enveloped her red raw body. Wrapping her tresses into a turban with the hand towel, she mumbled, 'must remember to put a fresh towel out.' For whose benefit, it wasn't clear, but somehow talking to herself verified her thoughts.

Trying hard to ignore the bag, Ines busied herself with getting ready for work. Deciding on black cigarette pants, her favourite black cashmere polo neck and snake print ballet pumps, she managed to get dressed regardless of the difficulty in trying to lift her dead leg to climb into her trousers. Sliding her feet into the shoes, her foot felt detached from its leg — as if she were wearing wire wool socks. No sensation at all. Grumbling, she came to the conclusion that maybe the young doctor was right, and she did in fact have an acute bout of sciatica.

Glancing over at the bag, Ines had been using all her willpower not to take a peek. Impressed at her disciplined behaviour, she began to apply her makeup at the Art Deco dresser she'd won on a car boot auction site for an absolute bargain price of thirty-two pounds— one man's junk is another man's treasure.

If she was ready, ahead of schedule, she could put on a load of washing. By coincidence, the dark wash needed to be done, meaning she'd have to add Dylan's clothes as well. Genius! Feeling duplicitous, she justified the motive behind it without issue on her conscience.

Giving herself one last check in front of the free-standing mirror positioned by the tall window, Ines twisted to get a view of her rear, and a sideways once over to ensure her little tummy looked cute and not paunchy. Satisfied, she turned back round, taking clumsy steps towards the bag, conscious of not "doing a Luke" and tripping on the tassels of the rug at the end of the bed. Grabbing hold of the handles, Ines dragged the hold-all through to the kitchen, plonking the hefty bag in front of the large grey washing machine. With the clothes spewed out onto the flagstone tiles, Ines began to separate them, hurriedly shoving them into the drum. A smell. No, a scent. She could smell something familiar. Sticking her head close to the pile of clothes, Ines located it. His jumper and boxers. They both smelled the same and it certainly wasn't aftershave she was detecting. It was heavy. Sweet. Floral. It smelled like one of the girls at work. Wracking her brain, Ines tried to recall the perfume. Like a bolt out of the blue, it struck her. Leila!! It wasn't her perfume. Obsessively smelling out the location of the scent, Ines determined that it was on the front of Dylan's jumper and the waistband of his boxers.

A ligature of cactus needles snaked around her throat as the blood pounded in her ears. All the signs of his indiscretions she'd naively dismissed as Dylan working hard, were right there in front of her. Peering into his boxers, her heart filled with dread at what she might find. Gasping at the sight before her, Ines held them up to the light to make sure she wasn't imagining it. A stain. A shiny, clear white stain on the crotch, glinting in the sunlight. Ugh. Insane with curiosity, Ines began foraging for other evidence in the depths of his bag. She found more clothes smelling of the same perfume, all of which had the same long blonde strands clinging to them like pieces of thread.

Beep beep! Damn, the alarm was telling her that it was time to leave. Ruthlessly, Ines crammed the remainder of Dylan's clothes into the drum and started the cycle. Leaving her washing for another day, she didn't want to combine her clothes with his nor did she want that tart's hair or perfume on her own clothes. She felt sick. Dylan had managed to make a fool of her once again, something her friends, especially Luke, had always warned her would happen and she consistently brushed it under the carpet.

Grabbing her beige swing mac, Ines made way to the front door, slamming it behind. Regardless of the lumbering gait, she walked with the conviction of a woman scorned. Ines tapped furiously on her phone, announcing what had happened, on the group chat Zara had set up, entitled 'Don't Trip. Keep Smiling'. Regardless of how she might be feeling, this always had the desired effect.

Two blue ticks indicated that everyone had read her message. Before answering any replies, she called Dylan.

Sleeping in the sumptuous bed, Jenna was blissfully unaware of the panic-fuelled conversation ensuing in the corridor outside the hotel room. After arriving in Bristol late at night, Dylan and Jenna had decided to eat dinner in their room, which led to dessert of their own making. Exhausted from the day before, his mistress lay deep in slumber, which left the coast clear for Dylan to deal with Ines on the phone.

'Babe, are you actually serious? What planet are you on?' Hissing down the phone, the cad sounded desperate.

Looking shifty as he spun round looking left and right for any nosy guests or worse still, Jenna, he continued fighting his case.

'I mean, seriously? You actually believe that I've got another girl on the side because of some evidence you think you have, which has a viable reason?' Sounding incredulous as if he were being unfairly accused of cheating, Ines immediately felt ashamed. Exactly the feeling he was hoping to create.

'Well, yes! Perfume all over the front of your clothes? Strands of long blonde hair all over your clothes? A stain on the crotch of your boxers?! Don't take me for an idiot, Dylan.' Standing in a shop doorway, adrenaline rushing through her body, Ines stood with ease, the issues her leg had been giving her for the last couple of weeks, gone.

'You're behaving like an idiot so I'm going to treat you like one!' he spat. 'I'm working my arse off here trying to make something of myself. I get no sleep. I'm stressed and all you can do is spout bollocks!' Suddenly becoming aware of a presence, Dylan stopped talking, pausing to smile weakly at the guy from room 267 passing by, nodding in acknowledgment.

Lighting up a cigarette she had retrieved from her coat pocket, Ines shook out the numb feeling in her foot, considering what to say next. 'So, how do you explain it then?' She was challenging him. Pacing up and down, Dylan's brain was working at lightning speed. Shit shit shit! 'Well Poirot, my jumper was hanging over the back of the passenger headrest in the boss's car. His wife's blonde.'

'And the perfume?'

'She reeks of it, babe. The smell rubs off everywhere, even on the seatbelt. Everywhere and I mean everywhere.' Dylan's heartbeat began to slow down as even he was believing his own spiel.

Yeah. Everywhere, thought Ines, drily. 'And the stain? Let me guess, they belong to your boss and you got them mixed up.'

Thinking fast on his feet, Dylan was beginning to feel the pressure. Jenna could come out looking for him any minute now, he had a meeting in half an hour and more and more people were starting to come out of their rooms. Leaning against the wall opposite his room door, wiping beads of sweat from his brow and combing his fingers through damp hair, the heat began to spread through his tense body. All of a sudden it came to him. A perfect excuse. Checking there wasn't anyone around within earshot to hear him, he cleared his throat and began to speak quickly in a hushed voice.

'Ahem, well you know I'm away from you a lot?'

Arousing a curiosity for what was next going to come out of his mouth, Ines encouraged him to continue.

'I started thinking about you and got horny. So, I leaked.' Cringing at what he'd just professed, Dylan held his breath, his eyes bouncing, as he looked around him for signs of his mistress making an appearance.

As if by magic, all her anxieties disappeared and Ines started to smile both with relief and for the sheer fact that she was flattered that her boyfriend still fancied her enough to have these lustful thoughts for her. 'Really?' purred Ines, her inner sex- goddess manifesting itself.

The feeling was definitely not reciprocated on Dylan's part. Shifting from side to side, he found it difficult to sound sincere when he replied. 'Yeah babe, I'll show you just how much I've missed you when I get back,' he lied.

Giggling as they said their goodbyes, Ines hung up and slid her phone into her pocket. With a jaunty little skip, she headed in the direction of the café, knowing that at some point she'd have to answer to her friends, who by now had left a million messages.

Walking back into the hotel room, Dylan caught a glimpse of himself in the mirror and blew out the air he'd been holding, relieved that the inquisition was over. Looking at Jenna stirring as she began to wake, he felt a yearning to hold her close.

Kissing her gently on the forehead, he squeezed himself onto the edge of the bed where she lay, trying not to slide off.

Still in a state of slumber, Jenna began to open her eyes. Smiling lazily up at Dylan, she stretched an arm out and rested a warm hand on his thighs.

'Morning, handsome.'

Dylan's beaming face peered down at her lined cheek, marked by the crumpled sheets. 'I've got to go to a meeting in less than half an hour. Will you be okay while I'm gone? It's only downstairs in the conference room. Once it's over, I'm all yours.' Whispering his words, as though he were in the presence of a sleeping baby, Dylan stroked her hair.

Nodding slowly, Jenna replied. 'Of course, I will, baby. I'm all yours all the time,' confirming the statement with a gentle squeeze of his hardness, the bounder's eyes lit up.

'Jenna Marden, you're a naughty girl,' he murmured as she began to unzip his trousers.

The street was now a bustling hive of commuters, already stressed and buggy pushing Yummy Mummies jogging along in their high-tech leggings, talking through Bluetooth earbuds and their protein packed smoothies firmly placed in eco-friendly cup holders. The morning sunlight promising a warm day, shone down like rays of gold.

Ines' joy was infectious to people rushing past as they caught her disarming grin, returning the gesture with affable smiles. Her mind was preoccupied with sublime thoughts of Dylan, unaware of her phone ringing from inside her coat. Coming to a grinding halt as she neared the café, she attempted in vain to conceal her surprise. Luke and Sally were waiting outside, chatting animatedly to Ryan. Bum. So much for divergence tactics.

Aware of the outrage at the news of "Laundrygate" that was about to ensue, Ines held her breath in apprehension. Like something that had been rehearsed, the three friends stopped talking right on cue, watching her advancing at a dubiously slow pace.

'Morning smiler, how ya doing today? Any better?' It didn't matter how bad life was for him, Ryan always had a charming demeanour. His smile warm and trusting.

'Hello, Ryan. 'I'm really well, thank you.' With two pairs of enquiring eyes upon her, Ines averted their stare, knowing she'd have to explain everything ... and she wasn't ready for a barrage of questions and lectures.

'And good morning to you,' greeted Sally, her head tilting to one side, vying for Ines' attention.

Laughing nervously, Ines' eyes darted between Luke and Sally. 'Mooorning guys! Sorry I'm running late, so I can't stop and chat.' Feeling rotten for fibbing, Ines re-directed the spotlight to Ryan. 'I'll be back later, and we can have a fag and a bitch about the world, then.'

Grinning back, he nodded in keen affirmation, concluding with a thumbs up as he chewed on his bacon roll.

Luke, steadfast and unconvinced with Ines' performance had no doubt this was a ruse to avoid cross examination. 'So, everything okay? You have your appointment at the optician at lunchtime, don't you?'

Squeezing her eyes shut as Luke spoke, Ines nodded. 'Yep, they'll probably tell me it's a severe migraine or something.' With that, a searing pain shot through her head as she applied more pressure. Flinching, she stopped right away.

'Must go. Bridget will deny me of any more treats from Patisserie Lydia if I'm late for the meeting. See you all later.' Waving like an over enthusiastic teen, relieved to get away from the clutches of the headmaster, Ines scuttled off in the direction of the underground.

'I'll call her later,' promised Sally, seeing the look of grave concern in Luke's eyes.

Fading into the distance, her tiny frame engulfed amongst the heaving crowd of commuters, Ines raised her arm, waving farewell in her final show of departure.

'And there she goes, slipping away and avoiding any questions like a pro,' Luke muttered soberly, shaking his head as he extinguished the cigarette into the ashtray atop the litter bin, which stood beside his and Ines' morning chat time bench. Luke predicted what had happened in the time between the group chat message and her arrival at the café.

Turning to speak to Sally, he was pleasantly surprised by the sight of both her and Ryan having a conversation so riveting that they'd hardly noticed Luke's eyes upon the pair of them. Bringing a balled fist to his mouth, Luke interrupted their flow.

'Ahem, excuse me for interjecting, but have you noticed the time?'

Amused, Ryan shrugged. 'What can I say, mate? The ladies love a cheeky chappie.'

The blood rushed to Sally's cheeks in an instant. Consulting her watch, her eyes widened in shock. 'Gosh. I'm going to be late!'

'You better go. Catch up with you soon.'

'Aaaargh I'm never late!' squealed Sally, grabbing her bag from beside Ryan's worldly belongings, bidding farewell and dashing off down the busy street leaving the two men in awkward silence. Expanding his chest, with his hands firmly in his trouser pockets of his navy suit, Luke made the first move to speak given that Ryan was now busying himself with counting his money donated by kind passers-by from this morning's rush hour.

'So, Ryan, how do you manage at night, out here in all weather?'

Taken aback by the question, Ryan arched his thick eyebrows, grinning a wide smile.

'It's not easy, especially when it's cold. Sometimes I get so cold I wish I could go to sleep and never wake up. If I'm lucky I get a bed for the night at a shelter or I pitch up my tent. It got knicked the other day, so I had to earn enough money to get another. Ines, bless her heart, gave me money towards another one. Keep the wind and rain off me, like.'

'How did it get stolen?'

'Someone had likely been watching me. You have to hide your stuff or you end up lugging it around with you which can be difficult, you see. I hid it behind these massive industrial bins and they helped themselves.' Raising a hand to shield his view from the sunlight, so that he could see Luke better, the lines at the outer edges of his eyes fanned like fine pleats. Ryan continued chatting as though he were talking about a tea party. 'So yeah, not easy living on the streets. Your stuff gets stolen, you get people fighting you, beating you, kicking you. They think you're scum and treat you like shit.'

'People beat you?' Luke was incredulous.

Ryan let out a deep throaty chuckle; 'Yeah mate. I've been beaten twice, once by other homeless guys for my money and once by a bunch of drunken city twats on their night out. I've been spat on, to add insult to injury. The wankers beat me, pissed all over me and threw my blankets while I was sleeping. That's why I got beat up. I had a go. And well, I got beaten black and blue.' Biting the inside of his cheek, Ryan's eyes began to glaze over at the memory.

Disgusted and mortified, Luke shook his head as he crouched down beside Ryan, by way of an egalitarian gesture.

'My friend, there has got to be a way out for you. What did you do before you found yourself in this shit situation?'

Watching two leggy brunettes teetering into the café, catching a sly glance of Luke, they were chatting away and oblivious to Ryan's existence. Lifting his chin in their direction as they entered the café, a smirk spread across his face.

'Trust fund-babes. You can spot them a mile away. Look down on anyone who earns less than 200k net a year.'

The smell of coffee floated to the outside, as the door swung open again, the delicious aroma of freshly baked bread and bakery goodies filled the air. Luke's stomach rumbled and he could only imagine how Ryan was feeling. 'Fancy a coffee and something else to eat? Then you can tell me what you used to do.'

'Aah mate, you're going to be late for work. The girls went ages ago and they were already running late.'

'The girls work in central London, I work 100 meters from here. I have time, don't worry.' Luke gave a curt nod as he got up and entered the café.

Plonking himself down next to Ryan, Luke handed over a large tea and a sausage and fried egg roll. Chewing hungrily, it was hard to believe he'd not long ago eaten a bacon roll.

The cold nights make you hungry, supposed Luke. 'So, what did you do before this situation?'

Gulping down a morsel of his roll, Ryan considered his reply for a moment.

'I used to have a café-bookshop in Brighton. One of the first of its kind in the 90s. It was a success and I was making a great living, had a partner and little girl. We lived a good life, never had financial problems. Nothing. Life was kind to us. Long story short, I lost my business as the mainstream cafes started to open up, offering free WiFi. Nobody was interested in reading a book and having a bite to eat anymore. It was all about the internet. Steph got fed up economising, found another bloke and shot off with him, taking my — sorry, our little girl. I got depressed, lonely and turned to alcohol. She wouldn't let me see my daughter and I gave up after losing everything to the bank— but losing my kid broke me the most. So, here I am. Homeless and wasting away outside someone else's café.'

Nodding sagely, reflecting on what he'd just heard, Luke looked at Ryan. He looked at him in a different light. He wasn't just Ryan the nice homeless guy, he was Ryan the homeless guy who had it all and lost it. Everybody has a story to tell.

'Ryan, I have to go to work now, I honestly could stay and talk to you all day. You're an interesting fellow.'

'No worries mate, chat soon,' waved Ryan as Luke gestured a salute.

Tapping her front tooth rhythmically with the end of the pen to the flow of her thoughts, Ines had immersed herself in a little bubble that nobody was able to break through. Glancing up from the pile of paperwork she had assigned herself to complete by lunch, Barbara Windsor and Sid James looked on at her in comedic mockery as her computer beeped and signalled that an email had been received.

The office was a network of activity and in the distance a deep hum resounded as staff seemed to speak in synchronisation. Apart from short outbursts of laughter, everything was calm. Even the buying assistants were relatively mellow. Everyone was working. Or was it like this every day, but for once Ines had opened her eyes and absorbed her environment. A peculiar morning indeed. Somehow Ines felt unnerved by the morning's events, although she had been reassured by Dylan that everything was genuinely misconstrued. Of course it was. When two people spend so much time apart, it's easy to let the devil's advocate wreak havoc when you miss them. However, things still weren't sitting right in her gut. Shaking the negative thoughts away, Ines leaned across and swiped the goats cheese and sun-dried tomato tart which had been sitting on her untidy desk all morning. She'd made a personal deal with herself to eat the savoury pastry before eating the large chocolate éclair she'd bought to complement her little treat, as opposed to the other way, which was often the case with her sweet tooth. Sweeping the crumbs meticulously over the edge of the desk and into the palm of her hand, Ines licked her finger and dabbed the remaining buttery tidbits.

'Heeeey Ines, how are you this morning?' Echo. 'Ooooh I say, being a little piggy. Butter pastry tart and a chocolate éclair.'

'It's goats cheese and tomato tart in a butter pastry,' corrected Ines.'… And yes a big fat chocolate éclair made with quality cacao and exquisite choux pastry. All from Patisserie Lydia.' It was unkind of her and she knew it, given that Echo was still desperate to shift the baby weight of her second child, born five years ago and she was a compressed, curves in all the right places, size 8. Echo looked at the crumpled paper bag, spotted with grease, the patisserie box where the éclair sat resplendent in pink lacy patterned paper, teasing her some kind of wicked. Following Echo's longing gaze, Ines felt a sudden pang of guilt.

'Would you like a slice? I can cut it up. My eyes are bigger than my tummy.' Flinching away, Echo's eyes widened in horror. 'I couldn't possibly, Ines! It's a sin.'

'What?' Laughing, Ines shook her head in confusion. 'Sorry. A sin, you say? Since when is eating a chocolate éclair a sin? It's not exactly up there with lust or gluttony, is it?' Wrinkling her nose, Ines was half amused and half alarmed that her co-worker deemed eating a patisserie oozing fresh cream and chocolate as a sin.

'It's a Slimmers Universe sin. If I put on any weight, I'll be given the cap of shame!' Echo seemed genuinely affected by this. Intrigued, Ines tried hard to process what she was hearing.

'Like a dunce cap for people trying to lose weight? Is this not a bit draconian?'

Echo looked away from the éclair coaxing her to take a share. 'Yes, except we're adults and all the ones who are successful in losing weight, look down on me for still battling the stubborn kilos of fat I have.' Pulling her jumper around her body in order to expose the doughy ring around her midriff , Echo dropped her eyes, desperately ashamed.

Ines felt bad for what seemed like an unduly confident, sniping woman on the outside. She was in fact, like any other woman who had her insecurities but concealed them well. Very well indeed.

'Crikey Echo, if doing this Slimmers Universe thing is making you feel like shit about yourself all the time, it's hardly beneficial to you. You're not exactly living, are you?' Leaning back in her chair, sliding away from the desk, Ines caught sight of her phone flashing message notifications like a silent beacon and then the pile of paperwork she had to complete by lunchtime. Bum.

Getting the distinct, uneasy feeling that they were being watched, Ines looked over Echo's shoulder, towards the back of the office. Realising that their interaction was being observed closely by the buying assistants, Ines spoke with an air of authority. 'Okay you know what?

Have a bit of cake, don't go back to this slimming club thing and just do things your way in your own time. Make the changes for Echo. Nobody will be judging you, then. Yes?'

Nodding her head with enthusiasm, Echo smiled with gratitude.

Ines rolled back to her desk and grabbed the patisserie box. Watching her every move with childlike fascination, Echo adjusted her jumper, plumping it out at the sides to conceal her much loathed mummy tummy.

'Right. Do me a favour, can you? Cut this bad boy in half. One for me and one for you. It's a two finger salute to your slimming malarkey. Life's too short. Take up the gym and eat sensibly. Small portions of WHATEVER you want without the guilt. Enough of this nonsense. With the money you save from paying these people, you can put it towards new clothes. Pushing the box into her hands, Ines smiled one last time and spun back round on her chair.

Filled with shock and gratification for Ines' generosity and kindness, Echo's heart skipped a few beats with joy. 'You're so right!' she exclaimed with renewed gusto, as she whisked off to the staff room to find a knife.

Choosing to ignore their messages of support and questions regarding "Laundrygate" for the time being, Ines threw herself into her paperwork. Catching Bridget's eye as she sped past Ines' chaotic looking desk, it was long enough for her hawk like stare to make a mental note of how much work was to be gotten through by lunchtime.

Taking a sneaky peek at her phone for the first time since she had begun ploughing through the order summaries for Autumn/Winter 2019, Ines saw that her friends had once again been on a texting tirade.

-Zara: What the hell is going on?

-Sally: Sweetie, you seemed really agitated when Luke and I saw you earlier.

-Luke: Wow, you left us at breakneck speed this morning. I may sue for whiplash lol.

-Zara: Inniiii!! what the hell's going on? Answer my calls!!! I'm dying to know if you've told him to pack his stuff and go!

-Sally: Yes!!! Even better, we can pack it for him and take it to the recycling centre!

-Zara: She's too quiet. Something isn't right.

-Luke: I agree. Ines, do not forget your appointment at lunchtime.

Five missed calls and a thread of messages from concerned friends and the one thing that gripped Ines' stomach was Luke's genuine concern for her and his calling her by her given name and not his nickname for her. She felt sad and confused. Deep down she knew her friends were right and only had her best interests at heart. Dylan had her like putty in his hands. Why were her hopes of them being wrong and Dylan being right still hanging by a very flimsy thread? And why, oh why, was she feeling sick at the thought of Luke being so upset with her? Ever the total opposite of Dylan, she thought, with fondness, yet now she sensed his discontent.

Despondent, Ines carried on with her work, trying to keep a level professional head as she tapped away at the keyboard, her eyes flicking to the corner of the monitor, intermittently checking the time. The combination of her workload and the appointment at the optician was a no brainer for Ines to opt for working through her lunch break to appease Bridget and stop the rumour mill of the entire Buying and merchandising department creating a 'why does Ines get paid for time off and we don't?' support group. Checking her phone one last time before dropping it into her bag (Luke's mobile phone slot suggestion didn't last long), Ines saw she'd missed more calls from Zara and Sally, but none from Luke and none from Dylan. Dylan was probably in a long meeting and Luke was more than likely brooding. The time flickered to 12:41. Her appointment was at 13.10, she still had time to walk carefully and slowly to the optician.

Walking down the wide aisle which separated the desks, she saw that a smattering of staff remained in the office eating their lunch. Hanging in the air, a concoction of aromas from takeaway containers sitting in front of computer monitors, taunted Ines' hunger pangs. Conscious of the rumbles and gurgling sounds coming from her stomach, Ines coughed loudly to avoid embarrassment, calling out aloud 'have a nice lunch' for added assurance. Much to her relief, her co-workers responded loud enough to drown out any sounds, eliminating any doubt, particularly from Will, the little guy with the baritone voice ensured this.

Ines squinted when she left the dimly lit elevator, trying to readjust to the glare of sunlight beaming through the glass doors in the lobby. An episode of vertigo disorientated Ines. Pausing to regain her balance, she felt a firm grip on her shoulders. Alarmed, she wheeled round to see whom the hands belonged to, her brain trying to catch up. Feeling as if she were drugged, everything was moving in slow motion. Blinking and grappling to find her composure, she took a wobbly step back, struggling to focus on the figure that had moved in front of her with such swiftness. She hadn't felt this disoriented and giddy since the night she and Jared spent the night in a Shanghai bar downing Baijiu infused cocktails. Ines was led into a false sense of security as she guzzled Pineapple Smash like it was …well…like pineapple juice. 'Gotcha!' came the husky voice, accompanied by the sound of jangling metal and hollow wood.

Attempting to recover from the frightening experience, Ines

gratefully stayed in the grasp of her mysterious guardian. Regaining focus and balance, Ines was able to see the person before her, dressed in a coral coloured silk blouse embellished in fine gold thread, long milky white arms adorned in brightly decorated Indonesian bangles and the palest blonde poker straight hair. Bridget!

'You okay?' she asked, concerned. 'I thought you were going to pass out.'

Pulling herself together, Ines smiled with uncertainty as to how she should play this. Play it cool or laugh it off? Hmm.

'Hahahaaha yep, never drink alcohol under your desk!' Laugh it off it is, then. 'Haha haaar!'

Braying at the end of her sentences when she was over compensating for a dire situation was something she hated about herself. She could hear her inner donkey escaping before she could steer it into a demure giggle. Looking bemused through cornflower blue eyes, Ines could see how shocked Bridget was.

'It's a joke, Bridget. I don't really drink under my desk. I sneak it in my water bottle.' *Shut up, just.. shut..up!*

Unconvinced, Bridget squinted with scepticism and dropped her arms down at her side. 'Come on, I'll walk with you. I'm going that way anyway. I prefer Café TonTon's food to Violets, anyway.' Bridget's discretion was admirable. Ines, being Ines, hadn't even realised what was happening. She was more often than not, in a world of her own.

The street was filling up with workers on their lunch hour, seeking sustenance and time away from the confines of their job. Sidestepping and bumping into the onslaught of hungry food seekers, Ines could feel her stress levels increasing. Petrified of passing out or her leg giving way to a crashing fall, she felt an overwhelming need to cry. Seeing the world out of eyes which appeared to have had fat smeared over them — the one on the right in particular having had a vat of it smothered over, Ines was grateful for Bridget's considerate gesture of kindness towards her. Hanging onto Bridget's arm, Bridget was unaware of the shame Ines was battling within her. She squirmed at the thought of how catty she was when talking about co-workers to her friends, which added to her guilt. Swallowing her self-pity away with the ease of gulping razor blades, she focused on trying to stay upright.

Marching through the crowded streets with certitude, their arms still linked, Bridget led the way, slinking through the bustle like a sidewinder, her bangles making melodic tinkling sounds with every move. Ines likened the sound to an assemblage of fairies prancing around a mossy tree hollow, sprinkling happiness dust all around. Where she inherited a vivid childlike imagination from was a mystery, but Ines was convinced that she had White Witch tendencies. Snorting at the irony of being a "white witch", Ines' musings were snapped back to reality with a sudden halt, jarring her neck. 'Here we are. Just in time. Are you okay from here?'

'I'll be fine, thanks Bridget. I appreciate it.'

'You're welcome. If you need me, I'll be in Café Ton Ton. I'm sure you won't, but I'm just saying,' said Bridget, stumbling awkwardly over her words as she tried not to sound overbearing.

Acknowledging the kind offer, Ines thanked her and began her tentative walk through the doorway of the optician's.

Ambient tones shone down from meticulously placed spots in the ceiling, like thin iridescent strips onto spotlessly clean glass display cabinets and tan leather sofas.

The sparkling glass was a transient reminder for Ines that she'd neglected her cleaning duties these past few weeks. However, it was only fleeting. Thankful that the guilt of being a slacker passed, Ines settled into the buttery leather couch, pulling her phone out of her bag. Ha! So much for Luke's theory, that's twice she's retrieved it from the bottom of her bag without aggravation…Luke. Ines' stomach flipped, at the very thought of him being upset with her. Like a child who knew they had done wrong, she was afraid to contact him for fear of hearing the disappointment in his voice.

'Good afternoon, madam, are you being looked after?'

The audacity of the smiling young woman stood in front of Ines, interrupting her train of thought!

Returning the smile from the comfort of the sofa, Ines had almost forgotten the reason she was actually sitting there.

'Hello!' creaked Ines a little more loudly than she'd have liked. Why would she get a voice crack like a pubescent boy at the most conspicuous times?

Sinking into the seat, feeling like a dumpy sack of potatoes, Ines attempted to sit upright to a more beguiling position, breathing her Patisserie Lydia-overloaded stomach in. Resting one hand casually in front of her in an attempt to conceal her bloating, Ines continued to speak in her best telephone voice. Somehow, her intonations went from being a well-spoken Londoner who was inclined to drop the last letter of a word, to articulating every word spoken, with eloquence. Even she found her nuances strange at times.

'Ahem. Please excuse me. My throat is a little dry. No, I haven't been seen yet. I have an appointment at ten-past-one.'

'For an eye test?' smiled the young woman.

Being Ines

No, for my teeth. 'Yes,' nodded Ines.

'May I have your name, and I'll book you in.' 'It's Ines Garcia.'

With saccharine grace, the overly willing assistant promptly turned on her heels and escorted back to her station with the grace of a ballerina. Ines looked on, desperate to try and keep the green-eyed monster from rearing its ugly head. Regardless of how successful her career was, the beautiful Georgian flat she owned or how she was not short of admirers, Ines believed herself to be the all-round loser friend. Thinking back to her childhood, she was always the quiet one whom bullies loved. In their eyes, she was easy pickings. Pretty, quiet and the darkest skinned in a predominantly white school.

Her parents had made money in property development during the recession of 1991, investing in repossessed properties around London at ridiculously low prices, renovating and reselling once the UK hit economic expansion.

Her dad was always away on business trips, which were also a ruse for taking his latest mistress on expensive illicit trips— not unlike Dylan, but Ines failed to admit that. She hated the idea that the man she was in a relationship with was also like the man who should have been her mentor, setting the standards high for his daughter to use as an example of how a man should treat his woman.

Ines often felt like a disappointment to her father. Her little brother was put on a pedestal and could do no wrong. Plus, he didn't talk back. Ines did. In Guyanese culture, the girl's role was perceived as being one of subservience and her role was to become a homemaker. In modern times, this had obviously changed, but her father's mentality was still very much stuck in the dark ages. It was a classic case of double standards.

Her dad could come home when he pleased, have mistresses and behave as he wished because he was the breadwinner. His wife had to keep quiet. Ines couldn't and so the clashes became more frequent until she finally packed her bags and went travelling, never to return home. Soon after she had left, the family unit began to crumble. Her mother took up a new hobby of tennis to pass her time. After all, her 19-year-old daughter was off on an adventure and exploring the world, and her son was 17 and interested in doing his own thing which didn't involve his mother.

Alejandra Garcia could never find the right opportunity to leave her husband, Dario. True, they had wanted for nothing, took regular holidays and they lived in a large Tudor-style house with an expanse of land large enough to house stables and a dressage circle for their horses. A business idea born from an equestrian loving mistress Dario had, a relationship so brazenly indiscreet, it made a mockery out of Alejandra when they flaunted their affair in public. Remembering these years and what she had put up with, fuelled her decision to call it a day. Divorce proceedings began and an acrimonious settlement deal had been thrashed out in court, resulting in generous funds being put aside for the Garcia children and a life of comfort for Alejandra.

Ines supported her mother wholeheartedly, but her brother felt compelled to remain diplomatic and support the womanising Dario. The dynamics shifted once again, the divide in the family growing bigger and bigger. This gave her father reason to target her as the whipping boy for his shattered life, incited by the devastation at his wife senselessly breaking up the family.

Ines had been accused of being equally responsible for the divorce due to the backing she gave her mother. Distancing herself from her father, she was reconciled to a life of a yawning void between her and the two men in her life. Time and experience would eventually change her brother's opinions. However, for now Ines had an adventure to embrace. Leaving England and leaving her family was easy. However, saying goodbye to her beloved grandparents wasn't so easy.

Buzz buzz!

On silent, a metallic vibration came from her phone, startling Ines back to the present as it growled across the glass table top. Grabbing at the phone to avert anymore curious stares in her direction, it seemed to turn into a slippery bar of soap, trying to escape her clutches. The more frantic the buzz, the more desperate she was to keep it still. Customers watched on in amusement as Ines wrestled with the phone to lessen the disturbance. Satisfied that she'd succeeded, she opened the message from Marco. It was a video of penguins huddled against winds of 124mph in temperatures of -48 degrees. Riveted, she watched with sympathetic eyes, feeling so bad for the cute, flightless birds. In a sudden bizarre twist, the sounds of arctic winds whistling in the background changed to the breathy sounds of a woman in the throes of passion!

'Oooh yesss!' Beyond mortified, it hopped between her hands and slipped through her fingers as she fought to mute the volume. Desperate to silence it, she only had the misfortune to increase the loudness. 'Aaah your dick is so…' Beads of sweat sprouted above her lip and the crevices of her nostrils as she became more and more flustered. Ines wanted to vomit. Oh, the shame! An entertained and captivated audience watched on as she grappled with the portable renegade, squeezing it under her bottom in a last-ditch attempt to salvage her dignity.

Squeezing her eyes tight, imploring the offending video to end, this had to be the most hideously embarrassing moment in the history of embarrassing moments. Stop, stop, stoppp! Please!! Marco you're deader than dead. I hate you right now!!!

Then silence fell upon the room. The ordeal had finally ended. The traumatic episode of pornography that played out loud enough for all to hear had finally stopped.

'Miss Garcia, would you like to go to room 3? Arjun is ready to see you now,' announced the young woman who had booked her in. This time, her sweet smile was replaced by a lopsided smirk. Ines swore she was taking full advantage of her discomfort. Witch!

Gathering her things together, Ines made a mental note to respond to her brother's message. Throwing the phone carelessly into her bag, Ines fed her coat through its straps. Fixing her eyes to the floor, flushed with embarrassment, she walked past a small audience and their fatuous snickering. In an attempt to recover what little composure she had remaining, Ines loftily swept rogue strands of hair behind her ear and sloped away.

Dazzled by the light while the lovely smelling Arjun was inspecting her eyes, his face close enough to touch hers, the ophthalmologist seemed to be taking his time. Peering into them with the fundoscope (which was NOT "fun" on this occasion), Ines held her breath in anticipation for the verdict. Maybe he was going to tell her she was as blind as a bat and needed eyewear as thick as a magnifying glass. The air was heavy with silent tension. The only thing that could be heard were Arjun's professional mutterings under his breath.

Without warning, Arjun leaned back on his chair. Swivelling to extend an arm for the light switch and flicking it on, he heaved a heavy exhale with the effort. The room gradually lit up and Ines blinked her vision back to its former blurry state.

Sitting back at his desk, the optician scribbled a brief letter and sealed it in an envelope. Watching closely and still none the wiser, Ines sat with admirable patience, waiting for him to finish. Like a croupier, he slid the envelope towards her.

'I'd like you to go straight to Moorfields Eye Hospital once you leave here.' Placing a stubby finger firmly over the brown envelope by way of confirmation, the optician continued to speak in a soothing tone. 'Enclosed is a note for the consultant on duty that you need to present him with when you get there. I shall send an email to notify them of your imminent arrival.'

'Wh..why is it so important that I go straight away?'

With clasped hands, his gentle eyes met Ines' imploring gaze. 'There's nothing wrong with your eyesight, Miss Garcia. The tests I've undertaken indicate that you need further examination. I tend to err on the side of caution and would rather you have it done now rather than later. Prevention being better than cure, as they say.'

Puzzled but feeling that now was not the time for refusing, judging by his impassiveness, Ines picked up the envelope and dropped it into her bag as she spoke.

'Righto. Well, thank you for your time. Do I need to come back to you at all?'

Arjun shook his head. 'That won't be necessary. You'll be in better hands from here on in.'

Ines thanked him, and left the room…still none the wiser and still mystified with what should have been a standard appointment.

Remembering the incident with Marco's message earlier, Ines hoped that the audience had all disappeared, with only the young woman at the desk left behind. Holding her head high and walking out of the office, she did a quick scan of the area to check nobody remained. Her concerns quenched when she didn't recognise anyone, she continued to walk towards the door. Reaching for the handle, a tiny derisive voice could be heard from a distance. 'Have a good afternoon, Miss Garcia.'

Looking over her shoulder to see to whom the voice belonged, Ines saw the young receptionist grinning her irritating lopsided smirk.

Filled with a compelling need to run and slap that stupid smile off her face, Ines took a deep breath, simply nodded in acknowledgment and left.

Chapter 7

Thundering down the street, fuelled by passionate feelings of wanting to have torn the young woman apart, Ines cussed herself for being so easily wound up.

'Silly little bitch,' she mumbled. 'You're lucky there're cameras in that place. Ugh. Shit. Oww!' Suddenly reminded that she was in no position to spoil for a fight nor walk at her usual fast pace, Ines slowed down to almost a halt as she realised that to anyone watching her, they'd be pardoned for thinking she was mentally unbalanced. Muttering furiously to yourself and walking like you're inebriated is not a forgiving look. Feeling the phone vibrating against her hip, Ines paused to reach into the dark chasm of her bag. Rummaging around, it seemed that her phone was on a technological mutiny today, determined to avoid her clutches. Huffing with frustration, she peered inside, the flashing LED light acting as a beacon for hapless mobile phone owners.

Zara was calling incessantly— to be that determined, she needed advice or a favour.

'Well, 'ello my loverrr!' Using her best West Country accent, Zara giggled at her own humour.

Shaking her head as she smiled down the phone, Ines found it difficult to be annoyed with her dipsy friend for the relentless phoning. In many ways she was shallow and self-absorbed, but when the chips were down, Zara always had her back.

'Awwright treacle, what can I do you for?' This could go on for a long stretch.

'Just calling to see how it went with Dildo.' Bum.

'Long story short, I got it all wrong and he explained everything to me.'

'Really. That's unlike him. So, how did he justify the hair and the stain? The perfume?'

'I can't go full story, but everything is fine now, I promise. The hair and scent were a result of his jumper being on the passenger seat of his boss's car. His wife is blonde and drenches herself in Leila. Very tacky, but y'know, money can't buy class.'

'And the stain?'

'Ooh well, it's a bit personal but, he was thinking about us and what he wants to do to me, and well he…ahem…got excited.'

Now walking through the street at a snail's pace, Ines was convinced it was the truth as she spoke it aloud.

Not as easily swayed by Dylan's story, Zara said nothing. The silence was deafening.

'Are you still there?' 'Yep.'

'So, you see, I was just being paranoid.' Cringing down the phone, Ines could hear how pathetic she sounded.

'Of course, you were,' replied Zara drily. Zara was frank, her filter usually non-existent, but on this occasion, she conceded to say nothing. Her friend was in a situation blinded by love and nothing could convince her otherwise. Ines would have to see it for herself, accept it was happening and she and only she can decide what to do. Only then will she be open to help.

'Anyway, I'm off to Moorfields for more eye tests, now.' 'Why?' asked Zara, concerned.

'I don't know,' admitted Ines. 'Apparently he wants to err on the safe side and have me checked properly. I'll keep you posted. Anyway, how's Nick? Are you still loved up?' Sidling against the window of a kid's clothing boutique, Ines succeeded in dodging a brigade of London's finest yummy mummies charging towards her with their state-of-the-art buggies. Passing in a flurry of energetic chatter, they nodded in appreciation. Fascinated by this impressive example of womanhood, she wondered if one day she'd be one of those women. Shuddering at the idea, she made a mental note that no, she wouldn't be. Ever. The irony of not practicing what she preached bore down on her conscience. Shamefully aware of the hypocrisy, Ines began peeling herself away from the shop front, switching her attention back to Zara.

'I think we're making real progress. Anyway, we have to be, now that I'm pregnant.' The latter part of her statement stopped Ines dead in her tracks. It was announced in such a cavalier manner, that she wasn't sure if she'd heard Zara correctly.

'You're pregnant!? Having a baby…really?'

Zara couldn't contain her excitement. 'Yes really! I'm 11 weeks. I just thought I missed my periods because of stress and not eating properly.

You're the only one who knows so far.'

'Ssso you're going to keep the baby?'

'Of course, I am. This will be the making of me and Nick,' gushed Zara.

'Lovely, you've barely been together eight months and that's not even been plain sailing. Plus you're twenty-seven going on seven.' Ines was starting to feel like the big sister giving advice. 'You haven't even told him yet; you've told me first. Doesn't that ring any alarm bells?'

The line was silent for a few moments. Ines could almost hear her friend's mental cogs whirring. Removing the phone from her ear to check the time, Ines let out a loud gasp. She'd been on the phone to Zara for 28 minutes, and was still no closer to reaching the eye hospital.

Moving towards the kerb, Ines stood patiently to hail a taxi. She'd been around London all her life and to this day, she still got confused about which was the indicator for an occupied cab. Orange light on or off? Which meant which? Frequently befuddled by this dilemma, she always put her arm out, regardless. If it was occupied, the driver would ignore her and the passenger would look smug, watching Ines retract her arm as they drove past. So, the cycle continued until she succeeded in hailing one. Someday she'd remember, but until that fine moment, she'd carry on as she always did. No skin off her nose.

Eventually answering, Zara began her quest to convince Ines that this was indeed a great life changing opportunity for her and Nick.

In a black cab at last, en route to Moorfields, Ines sat back in the black vinyl seat, the overpowering alpine smell emanating from the green tree air freshener dangling in the driver's cabin, making her eyes water.

'He'll be as excited as I am. It'll be wonderful.' Maintaining the same determination to convince Ines that everything would be fine, just as she had done with matters concerning Dylan, Zara paused, hoping to hear her friend's thoughts on the matter.

Bouncing around in the cab as it trundled through the busy streets of London, sliding into the window as the driver swerved to avoid pot holes the size of garden ponds, pedestrians and cyclists with a death wish jumping in front of the bonnet, Ines found her voice shook with the rhythm of the engine's chugging as she spoke down the phone. Texting Bridget an update while talking on loudspeaker to her excited friend proved to be challenging. After rewriting a long explanation of the ophthalmologist's instructions for a third time, Ines gave up and simply wrote:

-Hi, I've been referred to Moorfields immediately. Will keep you in the loop. Don't know what's going on. Ines x

'...so, what do you think?'

Bum. Caught off guard. Ines was so absorbed in typing her message to Bridget that she mentally removed herself from the conversation.

Whoosh. Message sent. Trying to decipher what she'd missed, Ines chose her words carefully. 'Do you think it's a good idea? Also, how can you be certain that Nick will want to embrace fatherhood at his stage in life? I'm concerned it'll go wrong.'

'How can an evening at The Samson with moi and glorious news go wrong?' Zara was adamant. There was no point in pursuing the discussion any further. The positive side of things was that Ines knew her friend well enough to ascertain the flow of her rhetoric, which in turn meant a Zara tantrum was avoided. Winning. Finally hanging up after assurances from Zara that all will be fine this evening, Ines let out a sigh of resignation and shook her head. Checking her phone, there was only one message from Sally wanting an update on this morning's "Laundrygate" and to see how she was. The other was a reply from Bridget: -Hope it goes well x

No message or missed call from Dylan nor Luke. Dylan was probably doing important stuff that regional managers do, and resolved that Luke was thoroughly peeved with her. Shoving the phone deep into her bag, she pulled out a bottle of water and a half eaten protein bar, remaining in a reflective mood until the journey ended.

***

Sitting in front of a variety of instruments used for measuring and examining the eyes, uncertainty crossed her face as the two doctors pulled their chairs and sat closer in order to explain the final step of the examination. The junior doctor remained quiet, observing her mentor and diligently writing notes as he spoke.

'So, Miss Garcia. We have one more eye examination to do. This is called an Undilated Eye Exam. It's not comfortable, and you will experience stinging and blurred vision. Given the current situation of your eyes, you may have a dramatic reduction in your sight. This can last up to six hours.' The doctor spoke softly and clearly to ensure he was conveying the information to Ines without causing her too much distress. 'Do you have anyone who can escort you safely back home?'

Ines' mind began to whir as she mentally scrolled through her list of contacts who'd be available to help. 'Willing' was not an issue, 'available' was a different story. Hmmm. Sally was snowed under with selling coffee contracted to gastro pubs; Zara would be happy to slope off work on a mercy dash; Dylan was away working; her mum was in Spain; and her dad would undoubtedly make an excuse not to leave the comfort of his house. Marco was away on a work trip. Luke? No. Her stubborn pride would rather see herself struggle than call him.

Fumbling in her bag, she retrieved her phone. 'Can I see if my friend can pick me up?'

The doctor nodded and indicated for her to go ahead and make the call. Rising from his chair, his hands deep inside the pockets of his navy-blue corduroy trousers, the grey-haired doctor wandered over to the other side of the room, giving Ines some degree of privacy. The student doctor followed suit, busying erself with the task of necessary note taking as she stood by the window opposite to where Ines was sitting.

'Ini, I can't darling. Today of all days, I'm attending a team meeting and I'm expected to make a presentation. I'm so sorry. I'm in enough trouble with them as it is. Shit. What about Luke?' Her voice quavered as she explained her predicament.

Being unable to help her friend was the last thing Zara wanted, however she was under another disciplinary. Her job was already hanging by a thread after her last warning. Why anyone would be affronted by Zara telling a lecherous old boy who had propositioned her at the annual conference, to 'go play with himself, because that's all he's ever going to get', was beyond her. The fact that it was the Chairman of the Board of Directors was irrelevant.

Sadly, Ines understood Zara's quandary. She knew about the incident in Geneva and although the old goat deserved it, Zara had gotten herself into a lot of trouble over it. Her friend was a liability at times. How she was going to bring a human being into this world and be responsible for it, was a complete mystery to Ines. 'No, it's ok. Luke's busy.'

'Busy or you're not talking?'

'Both.' Catching sight of the two doctors, Ines ended the call. 'All done?' asked the older doctor.

'Yes, I'll have to go it alone. I'm sure it'll be fine.'

'We shall try and do this as efficiently as possible, Miss Garcia. Ready?'

The process wasn't as long as she'd anticipated, however both her eyes stung terribly and her vision, impaired. She could hear the professional murmurs behind her, the frustration at identifying the incomprehensible vocabulary, increasing. All of a sudden, her ears picked up two words she had recognised from biology lessons. Optic nerve. Something was touching the optic nerve. One thing she was able to deduce from this, was that the optic nerve was close to the brain which meant that something was close enough to cause the symptoms she'd been experiencing.

'Right then, Miss Garcia,' the doctor said suddenly, pulling her out of her trance. 'We are going to send the examination off to the lab. We expect to have the results back in a couple of weeks, but I suspect they will return them sooner rather than later. We shall be in touch. Will you be okay? You can call a cab from the front desk.'

Blinking rapidly, Ines dabbed her red-rimmed eyes with the tissues she had been handed. Leading her to the door, the junior doctor walked at a slow pace as she adjusted to her surroundings.

'Would you like me to call you a cab?'

Shaking her head, Ines laughed nervously at her own discomfort. 'It's ok, thanks. I'll muddle through.'

Regardless of not having any idea of how she was getting home, Ines began making her way out onto the street. The City was bustling with people rushing in every direction, exacerbating her disoriented condition. Bumping along the tall buildings, unable to walk straight, Ines winced as pain shot through her body at being flung from every angle like a pinball. A longing for this nightmare walk to Moorgate station to end, bubbled on the surface like geysers, filling her with an overwhelming need to cry.

Clinging to the walls for guidance, petrified of falling to the ground, she didn't care that her beige mac was probably blackened by the dirt it was accumulating on the way. Her weakened legs became burdensome, no longer able to carry her tiny frame. Having no control over her body, it began to slowly sink into the ground. Like quicksand, the pavement sucked her further down as she fought to stay up. The battle was futile. Ines succumbed to the strength of gravity dragging her into the unforgiving cold grey surface.

Limp with depletion, she no longer cared what people thought— a young woman huddled into a ball, leaning against the granite wall of an office? It could easily be misconstrued as intoxication. Blinking away stinging tears rolling down her face, Ines whimpered like a small child, lost and hopeless amongst the chaos of the hordes of city workers brushing past her, ignorant of her plight. Ines felt so alone and scared.

'Are you okay, my dear? Can I help you?'

Looking up at the gracious, wide face with hooded, inquiring eyes of darkest brown, Ines attempted to smile, wiping wet cheeks with her sleeves. Trying to form an answer, all she could muster was the simultaneous roll of her shoulders and shake of her head.

'I'm having trouble. My legs don't work and I can't see properly.'

Stepping back in alarm, the good Samaritan went against the

unwritten rules of giving people personal space and crouched beside her. Jolted forward by a passer-by, the man splayed his hands out in front to avoid falling into Ines' lap.

'My dear, can you take a hold of my arm and I shall lead you slowly to the burger restaurant a few doors down, so you can rest? I will bear the weight. My wife has osteoarthritis, so I'm quite used to all this, you know,' confided the man. 'My name is Gerald. And you are?'

'Ines. Are you sure this is not too much for you? I can get a taxi and leave you to go on your way. It's fine, really.'

'Nonsense. What kind of a human do you think would pass an ailing young woman, when it's clear she's in need of help? I would like to believe that if my wife were struggling as you are now, that someone would do the same for her.' Gerald's voice was reassuring. He had a point, a valid reason for his chivalrous act. Ines nodded in acceptance and wove her arm through his.

As true to his word, Gerald bore her weight and lead her to the restaurant. It was crazy to think that she'd put her trust and faith in a complete stranger. Ines, always so cautious and the first to lecture her friends about the risk of accepting anything from strangers, especially from a guy. Gerald may well have been on day release from the psychiatric unit he resided at, for all she knew. However, at this point in time, she didn't care.

Sitting comfortably in the booth, Ines insisted on buying the coffee and some food for them both. They ate and chatted about their families. Gerald spoke about his wife with so much love and pride that she couldn't help but crave the same devotion to be bestowed on her, as well. A stab of longing twisted at her heart for that kind of love. Unconditional. Security. Loyalty. Her blood-shot eyes were watery with emotion, a serene smile flickered across her mouth as Gerald spoke with enthusiasm, unaware of her heartache.

Ines managed to catch a sneaky peek of Gerald's profile when he took a moment to answer a call. He had the faintest of webbed lines creeping within deep set jowls on cocoa colour skin, a slight upturn at the end of a slim nose and an archer's bow for a mouth. It was hard to figure out how old he was. He could be fifty, he could be seventy, she just couldn't tell.

Before she could stop herself, the words spilled out of her mouth. 'Gerald. How old are you?'

Startled by her boldness, Gerald let out an appreciative laugh. 'I'm sixty-three, my dear. I have a granddaughter probably around your age.'

'Wow! You were young when you started.'

'So was my daughter, I'm afraid, but Saffy— our granddaughter is a blessing to the family. Life is full of unexpected surprises. Some good, some bad,'

***

As quickly as the incident struck, it had dispersed. Ines regained the feeling in her legs. What had happened was a complete mystery, which concerned her as much as it frightened her. Why go through an episode of some kind of paralysis, only for it to pass as though nothing had occurred?

'I think I'll make a move now, Gerald. I'm feeling better. I can't thank you enough for your kindness.'

'It's nothing, my dear. I'm just glad that you've improved somewhat. Shall I hail a cab for you?' Getting up as Ines rose from the table, Gerald took her coat and placed it over shoulders.

Pausing for thought, Ines remembered her difficulty with the orange light indicator on black cabs. 'If you wouldn't mind, I'd appreciate it. Thank you so very much.'

'Think nothing of it.'

Gerald stood by the kerb, squinting as the sun shone through the clouds. His tweed blazer and chinos seemed befitting for the mature man standing beside her. He reminded Ines of the men from a by-gone era where people dressed well and took pride in their appearance, regardless of social status. Watching the black cab coming to a gradual stop, Gerald turned to Ines. 'Your chariot awaits, my dear.' Opening the door, he swept his arm wide, gesturing for her to climb in, taking a smart step aside.

Moving towards the cab, an overpowering sense of gratitude coursed through her veins. Emotion surged ahead and this time, she couldn't conceal it. Her face contorted like crumpled paper. Bowing her head to avoid Gerald's gaze, he placed a tender hand on her back.

'Now, my dear, the sadness is unnecessary. I have merely helped you get a cab.'

Shaking her head, aware of the cab driver's discomfort in what he was witnessing, and no doubt waiting for Ines to get in and tell him where she'd like to go, she spoke through short bursts of breaths. 'You don't understand what your kindness means to me. I'm so grateful,' she sniffed.

'You are very welcome. One day, you may see someone in need and do the same thing. Now, in you get or the cabbie will most likely get impatient and drive away,' he whispered into her ear in conspiratorial tones. Nodding with renewed enthusiasm, Ines hugged the kind man, repeating a final 'thank you' and got into the cab.

'Where to love?'

Being Ines

Waving farewell to Gerald, Ines answered the cabbie. 'Montague Square please.'

***

'Oh my goodness, you'll never guess what?' Martha was beside herself with glee. Clapping her hands together, her bracelets rattled in unison as she teetered on her precariously high heels.

'What? What's going on?' asked Serena, desperate to know why Martha was in a tizz. The focus was now very much on Martha, and her excitement was infectious.

'Well…' Lapping up the attention, Martha dragged the moment out a little longer for dramatic effect. By now, the entire office was watching with fascination, including Ines who had been playing Doctor Google, investigating her symptoms on her break. According to the research, she could potentially have a multitude of illnesses which needed immediate attention. Written in bold red letters, it intensified the advice. Anyone of a weaker mental disposition could well become sick with worry, even if there was nothing wrong with them to begin with. Closing the page with irreverence in order to watch the farcical show coming from the other end of the office floor, she took a bite out of a cookie she'd helped herself to earlier.

Savouring every delicious moment, Martha took a deep breath. This had better be good; she now had the entire department as her captive audience. 'I've got none other than Louisa Crosby liking and commenting on my Instagram!'

'Who the heell is that?' jeered David, a senior merchandiser who had the confidence of a peacock and the etiquette of a buffoon.

Choosing to ignore him, Martha took her phone out and showed the evidence, which wasn't difficult to retrieve given the page was already open.

As if it were a proud mama moment, Martha held out the screen as though she were holding a prized trophy one of her beloved kids had brought home. There, before their winged lined eyes, was a "like" and a comment by @LouisaCrosby. Lovely.

'Haaaha whaaat? Yer kidding me right? Yee've actually nearly passed out for a bloody "like" and one word? Beam me up!' laughed David who had been peering over the group's shoulders. Ending her reply to @LouisaCrosby with a "thank you" and a #feelingblessed #lovinglife, Martha turned to a sniggering David and an enthralled audience.

Through a tilted head of firmly gritted teeth, Martha stared at her adversary. 'David, what small-minded people like you don't understand, is that for popular lifestyle influencers such as myself, to receive recognition from a famous Instagrammer such as Louisa, is an accolade to my efforts and is testament to the work I do. We are a community, so, #sorrynotsorry, #haters.'

His Scottish accent thick and his laugh, throaty, David shook his head in mock theatrical sympathy. 'Ah, okay, if ye say so Martha. Ye keep telling yeself that. If it makes ye happy, even if it is a load of #bollocks, then keep influencing these poor bastards.'

Scarlet with fury, Martha became aware of the small crowd around her, their undivided attention unfaltering.

Rise above it, thought Martha. Cupping her flushing red neck, the object of David's ridicule smirked at him with self- righteous indignation. Ines, in the meantime, continued to watch the furore from afar, transfixed by the corned beef effect spreading to Martha's petulant face.

'I don't expect an oaf like you to understand,' Martha continued. 'I mean ha, come on, if you can't eat it or get drunk on it, it's above your level of understanding.' Ouch.

Stevie and a cluster of male co-workers who were huddled together like a bunch of teenagers, winced at Martha's comeback, feeling sorry for the hapless Scot.

'Aye, I suppose ye need the recognition to come from somewhere heh?' Touché.

Buzz buzz!

Ines's phone began flashing and vibrating, interrupting the spectacle she had been enjoying from a respectable distance. No Caller ID. Hmm. Faced with the conundrum of "to pick up or not to pick up/ important call or telesales?" she hesitated. On this occasion, Ines followed her instinct and answered. '

'Hello, is this Ines Garcia?'

Always weary of underhand fraudulent callers Ines replied with caution. 'Who's speaking?'

'Ah hello, Miss Garcia…'

'Excuse me, sorry I didn't say it was Miss Garcia. I asked who's speaking?'

Taken aback, the voice down the line stumbled over their words. 'Excuse me, my apologies. It's Doctor McCarthy calling from Moorfields Eye Hospital.'

'Ohhhwaa sorry, I thought you were trying to sell me something!' Ines sounded more light-hearted now that she knew to whom she was speaking.

Unsure of how to handle the rapid change in mood he'd just experienced, Doctor McCarthy erred on the side of caution and continued talking.

'So. We have your results back and I'm afraid you'll have to return to Moorfields as soon as possible.'

Pausing before replying, partly because she was distracted by the flurry of commotion up ahead in the office and partly because she wasn't expecting this phone call, Ines scrambled to process the information. Waiting for a response, the doctor interjected. With a polite cough, he asked, 'Miss Garcia, can you hear me okay?'

Breaking out of her daze, Ines answered with a nod and a 'yes'. Sounding relieved, the doctor began to speak. 'Good, well, shall we say tomorrow at 3 pm?'

Without even checking her calendar, Ines found the words spilling out of her mouth before she had time to think. It was her health after all. 'Yes, that's perfect. See you tomorrow.'

'Okay, good. See you then.'

Ending the call, Ines took a sip of mint tea and returned to her orders for the new Winter 2019 collection. Bored of the entertainment Martha and David were providing, it was easy to focus on her work.

***

Sitting in a small, dimly lit buttermilk yellow room, made all the more sombre with a narrow window providing a slither of a glimpse to the outside world, Ines looked for a distraction whilst waiting for Doctor McCarthy and a younger version of him to finish putting her medical notes in order. Fixing her sights on the Snellen eye chart, Ines tested her vision. According to her self- examination, she needed binoculars. That's that, then.

Doctor McCarthy was the first to speak. 'So. Miss Garcia. Hello. How have you been?' This was medical talk for "Tell me what's been happening with your symptoms since you were last seen?" 'Today, I am passing the baton to Doctor Starks. I shall be blending into the background.'

Doctor McCarthy's smiling replacement was a spritely, lean man with a genial but efficient demeanour. Shifting in the vinyl chair, aware of the fact that she was slouching, Ines corrected her posture, pulling herself up with the elusive, invisible Yoga & Pilates string. What would her instructor say if he were to see her now?

'Fine, thanks,' she began, with the universal reply to every "how are you?" The doctor waited for Ines to continue. 'In fact, no. My symptoms are weird. My eyesight is the same and my legs feel like they're not my own. I lost control and found myself sinking into the ground as I walked to Moorgate Station the other day. It's happened to me before. After an hour, it passed as if nothing had happened.' Waving her hands mystified by the phenomena, she concluded, 'and my GP has referred me for an MRI on my back to check for sciatica.' Phew. Ines surprised herself at how quick she was to reveal everything.

Sitting at the back of the room taking notes, Doctor McCarthy looked unconvinced as Ines spoke about the spinal MRI. Sensing his discomfort, she intuitively stopped talking.

'I think they're checking the wrong part of the body,' remarked the elder of the two doctors.

'What do you mean?' asked Ines, now feeling alarmed.

As if reading his mentor's mind, Doctor Starks pointed to his head, encircling it with an invisible halo.

'My head? My brain you mean?' The doctor nodded in slow accord.

Hearing these words, Ines gulped her heart back into its chest. Her suspicions that she'd been ignoring were rising to the surface. 'You think I have MS, don't you?' Her head was thumping, sick to the stomach with finally saying the words out loud as they tumbled from her trembling mouth. 'I've seen the posters all over the underground. The symptoms. I have most of them. It's MS, isn't it?'

Doctor Starks remained placid. Non-committal. 'Let's get you in for a brain scan and see what the results are. Then we can take it from there, once we have more information.'

He may as well have been speaking a different language. He made no sense to her. Everything he was saying merged into a melting pot of nonsensical words.

Wrapped in sandpaper, the words she tried to verbalise couldn't escape her throat. 'B..but Doctor McCarthy. I..I heard you mention the optic nerve last week. It's connected to the brain, no?' Like a fragile strand of silk thread, her voice was stretching under pressure, threatening to snap. She could no longer speak.

'Let's wait and see what the results say,' smiled the young doctor. 'You'll get a phone call with an appointment. Then we'll reconvene. Okay?' Still smiling, this was doctor speak for "conversation over".

Fighting back the tears, Ines stood up and squeaked an inaudible 'goodbye'. Wheeling round to leave, she staggered down the long corridor, her glazed eyes threatening to burst into floods of salty tears. Up ahead, stood a portly, stern faced cleaner hell bent on not moving for anyone. Looking up from buffing the parquet floor, he was stunned to see a young woman careening towards him, devastation stinging her face. Opting to move out of the way, the cleaner's sullen countenance quickly turned to pity when he realised that this was a grief-stricken person. 'Would you like a seat, miss?' His voice belying his testy demeanour, was as rich and soothing as a cup of cocoa on a winter's day.

Appreciative of the thoughtful gesture but shaking her head vehemently, Ines forced a 'no thank you', without pausing, for fear of breaking down in an unrecoverable heap.

Crashing through the same streets she had blindly made her way down a week ago, when the sweet and kindly Gerald came to her aid, Ines wept inconsolable tears, not caring what people thought. Her whole world was collapsing all around. The weight of utter despair crushed against her ribs. Adrenaline chased through her body, as the world passed by in a haze. Faces were unidentifiable, blending into one mass.

Standing in her path was a fresh-faced young man with perfect coiffed hair and shaped eyebrows. Handing out promotional leaflets of the über cool hair salon he worked at, he seemed to be happy with his lot— he was like a sprinkle of sunshine amongst the ominous tall grey buildings in the City. Waggling leaflets under unsuspecting passers-by noses, he shrilled his words with joviality. 'Twenty percent discount on your next hair appointment.' Anyone watching would see that he appeared to take great pleasure in disturbing their bubble.

Presenting a matt printed leaflet to Ines, she shook her head, rejecting his offer of a discounted hair-cut, her face by now twisted and wretched. Noticing her despair, the young man's mien changed dramatically. He looked determined. Enraged. Expanding his narrow chest and taking a large breath, with Spartan fortitude he bellowed after her, for all to hear with beautiful bravado. 'Sweetie, whoever he is, he's sooo not worth it!!!!' If only that were her reason for crying. Ines fanned her hand in wild response, her pace unfaltering, pushing through a deluge of office workers who had been soaking up the sunshine.

***

Broken, Ines entered the office building, her cheeks ruddy and stained with tears. A panicked Michael ran across the foyer and flung his arms over her quivering shoulders, ignoring protocol.

'Ines! What has happened? You look terrible!'

Ines felt rotten and knew that she probably did look as bad as she felt. Getting offended by Michael was not feasible. Spluttering her words, she found it hard to remain stoic. 'I can't explain right now, love, but I've a feeling I have MS and the doctors are all but confirming it straight out.'

Faced with a blank stare, Ines attempted to give her explanation more clarity. 'MS is Multiple Sclerosis.' Still met with bewilderment, an idea came to her. 'Umm hang on.' Scrolling through her translation app, she found the Portuguese definition. Holding her phone out in front of a pair of bulging eyes, she looked on expectantly.

'Esclerose múltipla!' Slapping his forehead in recognition of what he'd just been shown, Michael took a hold of her shoulders. 'Listen, you have no confirmation, so you can't be breaking yourself over what isn't definite. Okay?'

'Okay, thank you, Michael, I'll try. I better go up to the office. See you later.' Grateful for his kind words, Ines patted his arm and headed on.

***

Inside the lift, Ines felt alone and broken. A gaunt reflection she didn't recognise stared back at her in the tinted mirror. Unable to control the surging wave of months of pent-up emotion, Ines could feel acidic tears pushing their way up out of her gut. Watching her lip quivering, like a grief-stricken woman, the floodgates had opened and she was unable to contain herself. Making the slow ascent to the office floor, the doors began to slide open. Aware of being exposed, she tried and failed to compose herself. Sitting in their regular formation, the buying assistants caught sight of Ines. Aghast at seeing the feisty young woman, pathetic and staggering through the aisle towards her desk, they were unable to conceal their horror.

The first to react, with cat like reflexes was Serena. Leaping out of her seat with arms outstretched, she grabbed a hold of a precariously walking Ines.

'Ines! Oh my god what's happened? Have you been hurt?' Serena's sapphire blue eyes penetrated Ines' spiritless soul for the answer.

Without the intention of doing so, Ines blurted everything out, sobbing breathlessly in between sentences. 'I have to go for an MRI on my brain. I'm sure I have MS. I can feel it!' Ines' wailing had been making its steady climb to frenzied delirium. Her nose was now streaming threads of mucus, her face glistening wet with tears. Hot and flushed, she was desolate.

Guiding her to an available chair with certain adroitness, Serena sat the morose young woman down and shooed the others away. Stroking clumps of sopping hair away from Ines' face, desperate to calm her down, Serena cooed words of reassurance. 'It will be okay, lovely. You don't know this is the diagnosis for certain.'

'I do know, Serena. I feel it in my body. My symptoms tell me so. I've had these weird sensations for months and they won't go away.' Pausing to catch her breath, Ines was now howling her words. 'I'd rather be six feet under than in a wheelchair for the rest of my life!!'

Heartbroken to see Ines in this state, Serena tried once again to console her. 'Shush shush shhhh. You won't be, lovely. Everything will be fine. Whatever happens, EV-ERY- THING will be fine. I promise.' Taking a hold of her face, Serena implored Ines to calm down. 'Ines, breathe slow-ly. Take deep, slow breaths.' Inhaling and exhaling to demonstrate the momentum required to regain calm, Serena was heedful that Ines was following.

Her sobs beginning to abate into sporadic sharp in-takes of breath, Ines brushed her nose in upward strokes with the pad of her hand. With the agility of a cat and, out of nowhere, Echo whipped out a tissue, waving it in her face whilst encouraging her to drink some water. 'Take small sips every minute. I've added a few drops of homeopathic remedy.' Ines obeyed, mystified at how Echo managed to multi-task at an impressive speed.

'Do you have anyone who can take you home?' asked Serena, gently. Ines shook her head as she swallowed the peculiar tasting drink. Without hesitation, Stevie offered. 'I'll take Ines.'

Nodding her thanks, Serena continued. 'Someone will let Bridget know what's happening. She's in a meeting at the moment. Stevie will take you home.' Serena took a hold of the situation with expert discretion. There was no scope for deliberation. Allowing herself to be fussed over by her co- workers, they were happy to be at Ines' disposal. Stroking her back, Echo mouthed to Martha to fetch the pashmina hanging over the back of her chair. Frowning in response, Martha was not fully comprehending Echo's request. Like something out of charades, Echo flung an invisible wrap over her shoulders, poking her finger in the direction of her current favourite, "must have".

Nodding with enthusiasm, in recognition of what Echo had been trying to say, she scooted off to fetch the ochre silk pashmina. It was almost comedic to watch the two women communicate in silence.

Stevie took a protective stance beside Ines, as Martha styled their fragile co-worker in the wrap, the tiny crystal beads chinking a quiet melody, until she was happy with her work. This was a perfect photo opportunity.

'Voilà!' exclaimed Martha. 'If you didn't look so bad, I'd have taken a photo of you. Hmm, maybe I can keep your face out of it?' she mused out loud. Louder than she realised, in fact.

'Are ye for real? What planet are ye on?' asked David, incredulous at what he was witnessing.

Waving two jiggling arms out in front of her, Echo piped in. 'No no no, she's joking. Warped sense of humour. That's what having kids does to you!'

'Or there's something very "special" about Martha and she has no sense of empathy,' huffed David.

***

Once Stevie had left, Ines settled down for an evening of solitude and reflection. Remembering that Ryan had an interview earlier, which Sally had set up for him at her company, she perked up and called her friend.

'Alright darl, how did it go, today?'

'How did what go?' replied Sally sounding confused…which wasn't difficult at the best of times. 'The interview for Ryan, Brainiac.'

There was a long pause and Ines could almost hear Sally's brain cogs whirring at lightning speed as she processed the question.

'Oooooh oh yes, that interview. Yep, I think it went well. They liked him. He's full of surprises, you know? Talk about still waters running deep. Ryan has a Masters in Food Science. His main area of expertise is sustainable food. Cool, heh? Ooh and he scrubs up luverly,' gushed Sally. 'Hopefully they'll like him enough to employ him. Ryan can bring so much knowledge and experience to the company,' she sighed, sounding more like a love-struck teen than a professional twenty-seven year old woman.

'That's so good…so is this crush on Ryan moving to another level?'

'I do hope so,' came the coy reply. Ines could almost see her friend's image down the phone, shrinking into the seat with her geeky smile and crooked front tooth in full effect. 'Anyway, how did it go today at the follow up?'

Gulping in an attempt to soothe her dry throat, Ines began to share her news. By the end of the explanation, the two girls were sobbing. Hearing the sound of a foghorn, Ines smiled with affection at the rawness of her friend. There was a simplicity about her that was endearing. Allowing Sally time to finish blowing her nose, she took the opportunity to compose herself.

Clearing a parched throat, Ines squeaked. 'It will all be fine, Sal. Anyway, we're bawling like a couple of hysterical old women at a funeral and the results from the scan will probably be something irrelevant.' Assuring Sally was like trying to convince herself. It was comforting to hear these words spoken out loud, even though she wasn't quite persuaded by her convictions.

Her thoughts were interrupted by a loud ping. A message had come through and Ines could see it was from Dylan. Having Sally on loudspeaker as she read the message from her elusive boyfriend, she wondered why she even bothered.

Dylan: -Babe, hope you're alright? So, what did the optician say. Do you need glasses? You'd be my sexy geek, ha!

Ines: -No, I think I may have MS

Dylan: -Ah babe, no you haven't. You'll be fine. Will be back next Monday xx

That was it. It was as if she'd just told him she thinks she got outbid on the dress she had been watching all week. Asshat.

'Ini, I'm going to go now,' Sally said, pulling her back to the phone call. 'I'm here for you always, you know that, don't you? Whatever it is, remember that you are loved and we will all help you get through it. You hurt we hurt. Okay? I'll see you tomorrow at the café. I love you, my beautiful friend.'

'Where Ryan is, you mean?' Chuckling out loud, Ines still had the energy to tease her friend.

Responding with a hearty laugh, Sally tried fruitlessly to deny it. 'I'll see you tomorrow, missy. Shall I tell Luke?' Ines promptly declined.

Chapter 8

Walking barefoot through the hallway, Ines caught sight of herself in the floor length mirror. The morning shone its unforgiving light on two puffy, hollow eyes.

'Jesus, I look like a smack-head.' Poking and patting her face with the flats of her fingers, she groaned at the image staring back at her.

Flinching under the sunbeams falling across her face as she heaved the door wide, Ines considered calling in sick. Pulling black oversized sunglasses down over very tender eyes, she made her way across the square, the heady scent of hyacinths floating in the breeze lifting her spirits. The imposing magnolia tree in glorious bloom swayed lazily, its white spiky flowers like stars in the dappled shade. No matter how troubled her life could get, she never tired of the colours and smells each season brought with it. Ines never took for granted the organic evolution of nature.

Approaching the other side of the square, her serenity was scuppered when she looked ahead to the small parade of shops. There, bold and handsome in a light grey suit and electric blue shirt, stood Luke. Glossy hair with a halo of light bouncing off his head, her breath snatched for a split second. Hearing his explosive laugh all the way across from where she was standing, Sally could be seen giggling, swinging her green tote bag coquettishly against the back of her milky white legs. Sally could never grasp the concept of fake tan. For her, she is who she is and if people didn't like it, they could look away. She didn't care what people thought of her or her appearance. This was true self-confidence in Ines' opinion.

Ryan also seemed to have had a confidence makeover. He had an air of carefree abandon about him as he leaned against the bench, at ease with the company he was in.

Core. Check. Head high. Check. Fixed smile. Check.

Breathing deeply, Ines took awkward steps to where her friends were standing. Chatting. Laughing. With Luke. Feeling left out of the party, she put on a brave face and greeted them all with enthusiasm. 'Morning all.'

'Morning Ini, how are you today?' Sally was the first to greet her best friend.

Ryan gave his usual thumbs up and a 'Morning, love' with a silly grin, still on a high with the banter between him and Luke. Luke inclined his head, like the Gallic gentleman he was, muttering a polite acknowledgment. Ines truly believed he was of aristocratic breeding in a previous life. Dropping her head in subtle acknowledgment of his greeting, she succeeded in not having to look at him.

Watching the entire spectacle unfolding before them in puzzlement, Sally and Ryan felt a little uncomfortable. Neither was aware of the wordless spat between the pair, although they did find it odd that they seemed to have timed everything to perfection and kept "missing" each other. Ines turned towards the entrance of the café, asking if anyone wanted anything. An awkward 'no thanks' resonated from the small group of friends.

·|··|··|·

Picking up a bacon toastie for Ryan, with metal tongs, Ines felt a presence close enough to make her skin tingle. Smelling like a summer's day in Tuscany, swathes of bergamot and sandalwood clung to the air. A voice followed, bleeding deep into her core like beads of velvet. 'So. How's *Dylan*?' Luke. It had to be.

Dropping the snack into the paper bag, Ines feigned disinterest as she picked something out for herself. She also understood that Luke was not happy. He addressed Dylan by his proper name. This was a thing as rare as a five-legged fish. Eyeing the Emmental cheese and ham toastie, the contents, a gooey fondue oozing between two doorsteps of sourdough bread, resistance was futile and before she could change her mind, Ines grabbed the snack with the tongs. Plop. Dropping it into a separate paper bag, she looked over her shoulder at Luke. 'He's away in the West Country on business.'

Having a sudden change of heart, Ines turned to face him, detecting the faintest smell of coffee lingering on his unsmiling mouth. Her heart bore heavy in her chest on seeing this side of Luke. His expression was inscrutable. The atmosphere was gripped by a vice. She wanted it to be as it has always been. Ines missed him.

Luke's unrelenting eyes followed every flicker of her face, searching for a sign. Any sign, to tell him that she had finally seen the light— when would she stop kidding herself? Why was he so bothered? It's her life, after all. Finding the whole situation, crazy, Luke returned to considering her reply.

Ines knew Luke well enough to understand when he was struggling with refraining from saying something inappropriate or likely to cause offence. She could see a minuscule hint of a smirk. Sweeping the tongs up to his face with a flourish, she answered the question he was thinking, snapping them like a crocodile's mouth. 'And yes, I do believe him and yes, I have heard from him. He's home on Monday and I cannot wait, actually!' Feeling smug and finishing with a curt smile, Ines waited for a reaction.

Startled because there was a metal catering utensil in his face spitting crumbs in the air and because she was almost daring him to a challenge of words, Luke decided to choose his battles wisely and resisted answering back. He could tell she was raring for an argument, and it was a side of her he'd never seen before. Winded by this uncharacteristic behaviour, Luke remained impassive. He was also wounded by her words, though he had no intention of showing her that this was the case. 'I'm glad he's redeemed himself. The only way is up for you both.'

Bum. Ines was surprised, as she was expecting some kind of smart mouth retort she had grown accustomed to. Nonchalant, she brushed rogue particles of bread off of her brown leather pencil skirt, avoiding Luke's thick lashed green gaze. The sunlight gave them a hint of opalescent fern instead of the usual artichoke green, which she had noticed when she decided to snap the tongs with the insubordination of a stroppy thirteen-year-old.

This was a battle of two very strong-willed people— one fiery and red blooded, the other cool and enigmatically quiet.

Moving her head in every direction to avoid eye contact, Luke enjoyed watching her squirm. He knew her better than she gave him credit for, and he knew that she also believed things were askew where her relationship with Dylan was concerned. But, like with anything in life, to learn is to make mistakes first. 'Anyway, have you heard from Courtney?'

Grabbing the back of his neck in mock agony, Luke burst into that self-righteous laughter Ines hated. 'Woooah, you changed the subject so fast you've given me whiplash!'

Shaking her head in utter distaste to Luke's attempt at humour, she hissed, 'shut up!' and spun on her heels, to the beverages counter. Reaching for a sachet of mint tea, she tore it open and dropped it into her fuchsia pink thermos cup, watching the bag sink slowly into the boiling water.

Feeling like a chastised boy, Luke felt remorseful for upsetting what seemed to be an overly sensitive Ines. He edged towards her with caution (his experience of getting on the wrong side of Ines was limited but memorable). 'As far as I know, Courtney is well. She met someone else, so she's happy and grateful that my powers of perception were right in breaking up.'

Expressing her approval with a pithy nod, she then shuffled along the counter that threaded towards the till, catching sight of Luke reaching for his wallet inside his jacket, ready to pay for her purchases as they reached the pay point.

'I've got this. Thank you, though,' with a priggish cock of an arched eyebrow, her hand delved into her bag in search of her wallet.

'It's fine, don't be silly. My treat for you and Ryan.'

'I said *no*. Thank you.' Ines was now speaking through gritted teeth.

Beckoning to the confused cashier standing at the till, Luke handed his card before Ines could get to hers. Irritated at his insistence, Ines pushed Luke's arm away as she handed her bank card over. 'No, I said it's fine. If I say it's fine, then it is fine!'

Alarmed at the altercation between the pair, the girl didn't know which way to look or from whom she should take the card. The barista's eyes widened with apology. 'I'm sorry, sir but I will have to take the lady's card.'

Satisfied that she'd beaten the giant Frenchman, Ines smiled indulgently. Shaking his head in sheer frustration at how obstinate this impish young woman could be, Luke resigned himself to the fact that Ines was a breeze when she was calm but a fierce tornado when she wasn't. Today, she was the latter.

Patting himself down with vigour as they walked out the door, Sally watched Luke with interest. 'What are you doing?'

'Just verifying that I still have my balls and my pride in-tact.'

Ryan let out a roaring laugh, whilst a bemused Sally switched between looking at Luke and then Ines.

'Ines, Ines, Ines. What have you done to the poor man?' Ryan asked, looking on at the disgruntled pair before him.

'Nothing,' she grumbled. 'Luke's behaving like a prize twit and I'm not in the mood for any crap.'

'No shit,' sideswiped Luke.

Ines snarled back. Her top lip curling like the crest of a wave.

Sally, still none the wiser, took a sip of her coffee and concluded that she'd ask her later.

Handing over the brown paper bag containing Ryan's breakfast and a steaming cup of tea, Ines smiled generously at him as he took the bag of goodies. 'You're a star. If I get this gig, I'll repay you for your kindness.'

'Ahem,' coughed Luke

'My apologies, everyone's kindness,' corrected Ryan. 'Not *if*, *when* you get the job,' interjected Sally.

'Yes, I agree. *When* you get this job,' added Luke.

Raising her flask, the sun caught the metallic pink, momentarily blinding Luke, which tickled Ines, somewhat. Ha!

Today was not the best of days for those two. Ignoring his affliction as he blanched, Ines toasted Ryan's future good fortune. 'To Ryan.'

All eyes and smiles were on Ryan, except for Luke's. His eyes bore into Ines with utter discontent.

***

Lunchtime for Ines was at Violets, she had no inclination to make the walk all the way to Café TonTon.

Taking another bite out of the crab terrine, she cast a fixed gaze out the window at the lunchtime rush. People scuttling and bumping into each other, apologies being made by way of a hand gesture or a grimace. Everybody had a story to tell. Hers was no more special than the rest of them. She was just another face in the crowd. Just another number.

Ines' mind was a meteor shower of thoughts flying in every direction. Dylan…Luke… an impending brain scan…a diagnosis. What will happen to her? Will anybody want to be with her if it is MS? Will she be able to have kids? Will she have her happily ever after?

So many questions with so few answers…although deep down, she knew what to do about Dylan. Her heart said 'give him the benefit of the doubt' but her gut said 'don't'. Pushing her lunch around the matte china plate, she had no appetite for food let alone for life itself. It felt as if someone had pressed the pause button and she was the only one on hold. Maybe Luke was right, he'd given Ines words of wisdom that night in the Italian restaurant when she'd heard Jenna and her sidekick discussing Dylan. He told her that the anger and hurt she was carrying daily because of her useless boyfriend is like holding a hot piece of charcoal. The only person she was hurting was herself. Dylan *was* taking her for a ride.

Drringg drringg!

Her phone on vibrate, hopped across the steel table-top, nudging her fork off the edge of the plate. In an attempt to replace it whilst aiming to answer the phone, her hand decided otherwise and flipped the fork into an impressive 180° back flip, watching helplessly as it clattered onto the white tiled floor. Crikey, why did calamity follow her everywhere she went?

Drringg drringg! Number withheld.

Oh no no no! Like a bomb disposal operator trying to diffuse an explosive, Ines flapped trying to answer the call before it stopped ringing.

Muttering obscenities as she handled the phone with an unsteady hand whilst simultaneously retrieving the culprit of this mayhem, Ines finally answered before the caller could hang up.

Her heart was racing and a deep flush of red glowed on her cheeks from the panic that had ensued. Clearing her throat and trying to regain equanimity, Ines encouraged the caller to introduce themselves.

'Good afternoon, may I speak to Miss Garcia, please?'

'Yes, speaking.' Feeling that erring on the side of caution regarding fraudster phone calls wasn't necessary during these contentious times, she took the risk of agreeing that she was indeed Miss Garcia, hoping that it was the hospital.

'Ah hello, this is the MRI Department at the National Hospital for Neurology and Neurosurgery. We've received an urgent referral from Doctor McCarthy regarding a brain scan.'

Bingo. 'Yup.'

'Would you like to come in tomorrow at 12:15?'

The braying started before she could stop herself. 'Hawhaw you make it sound like I'm being invited for afternoon tea! Hawhawhaw.' Right now, she actually hated herself. Cringing down the phone, there seemed to be silence for what seemed like a very long pause before the voice spoke again.

'Erm ha ha yes, I suppose it does. I can't offer you cake but I can offer you an appointment.'

Reflecting on the statement as if it were a choice, Ines accepted, with her posh telephone voice.

***

Things were moving fast. Tomorrow was Thursday. A week from that would be her birthday. So much had happened these past three weeks and Dylan had not been involved the entire time.

All of a sudden, it dawned on her that she hadn't returned the missed call from Zara. Her friend didn't have the courage to make the announcement to Nick that she was pregnant on their special night out. She was, however, going to 'tell him today, for sure'.

Scrolling through her list of favourite contacts, she pressed Zara's name. 'Calling Zara with lipstick and syringe emoji' announced the phone.

Two ringback tones and Zara had answered it.

'Blimey, were you watching your phone?' laughed Ines.

'Noooo. Oh Ini, it's all gone terribly wrong.' Whining was something Zara was good at, but this seemed like a genuine cry for help.

Putting aside her own problems, Ines began to listen to her other best friend's strife.

'...so, he wants me to have an abortion. If I don't, it'll be the ruin of us. He told me I can't expect to endear myself to him if I'm making him become a dad when he doesn't want to be.' Zara let out a sorrowful puff.

Thinking about how she was going to convey her thoughts, Ines finally replied. 'Sweetheart, can you not see that maybe he just doesn't like commitment of any kind? He can't even commit to a relationship, let alone a baby. He would never be around for either of you. You'd end up being on your own, although "technically" you'd still be in a relationship with him.'

'So, what do I do?' wailed Zara. 'I can't abort my baby. I can't.' 'Think about a life of having a baby without Nick's constancy. Can you live in effect as a single mum or as an actual single mum?' Ines reasoned. 'Consider everything. Either way you'll always have me and Sal. It's for you to decide whether you want to be alone or with a self-centred twit who does what he likes and likes what he does.'

'Like Dylan? They're the same pieces of shit,' came Zara's poignant counter-reply.

Leaving each other with food for thought, Ines hung up, discovered a renewed appetite, and started to eat her food once again.

***

Returning to her desk, Ines logged back into her computer feeling calm and taking in the lively scene around of her. The buying assistants were wittering away animatedly— no doubt about Serena's wedding, David and Stevie were looking shifty, ogling Marcelo's monitor, which, judging by their puerile snickering and the slack mouths, Ines assumed it was to do with a female. Feeling grateful to her improbable guardians for their enormous support on Tuesday, which was still continuing, she harboured an overwhelming desire to tell them she loved them all. Smiling as she walked slowly over to them, her co-workers' chatter came to a sudden halt as Ines leaned against a desk.

'I just want to say I truly appreciate you all for helping me yesterday. I honestly don't know how I would have managed without you.'

In unison, the small group let out an 'aaaaw'.

Echo was the first to speak. 'We are all so very worried about you, Ines. To be honest, you're always so reticent, it shocked us all to the core seeing you so broken.'

'We're here for you. Please don't stress about going through this alone,' added Serena, her dialogue, reassuring. The rest of the team uttered words of support and agreement.

'Aye, and next time ye need taking home, I'll do it gladly. Stevie told me about yer gorgeous neighbour upstairs.' Somehow, Ines knew although he was jesting, David was also curious about Vera in Flat 2. Squeezing her eyes shut and laughing, she couldn't help but like the brash Scotsman. 'I'll put in a good word for you.'

Happy with the pledge, David shifted towards Ines, unsure of how his own intentions would be received. Tipping forwards, David threw his clumsy arms around her and hugged her in a vice-like hold. 'Ach lass. Ye loved by us all.'

'I love you all too, although I'd love you even more if you could do some work. Wiping the corners of her eyes, the perfectly applied eyeliner became a smoky smudge of kohl. The countless times she tried and tried to achieve that sultry look in vain and in one dismissive stroke she succeeds. Typical.

Everybody in good spirits, the office was a hive of banter and positivity. Something told Ines that from here on in, she wouldn't be alone. She had her friends and a great team of colleagues.

Bring it on.

***

Turning the key to open the glossy ink blue door, Ines could not cross the threshold quick enough. Padding across the black and white checkered tiles like a cat, she was relieved to have gotten to her own door. The thought of a hot shower and getting into loungewear to do absolutely nothing for the rest of the evening, thrilled her.

The familiar scent of home was shrouded by another more citrusy aroma. Ines swung round to see if there was an oil diffuser somewhere. The elegant entrance didn't just smell of the fresh cut flowers on the console table. It was almost as if she could smell a summer's day in Tuscany. The distinctive scent of bergamot and sandalwood was present. Sniffing the air like a lion hunting its prey, Ines felt sure Luke was here but she couldn't see him. Shaking off the feeling, she figured that it was just her imagination.

Wriggling the key into the lock, she smelled the scent again, but this time it was stronger. Her palpitations began to pulse, a chill of anxiety mounting. With her heart lodged in her mouth, the panic, now a chokehold, effected Ines to shut the door behind, promptly. To lock out the machete wielding intruder.

'Ines.'

Yeet! They know my name! A strange gargled sound she didn't recognise left her throat.

Extending his arm, Luke caught Ines as she morphed into a flailing octopus. Livid from shock, Ines glared behind enraged eyes— that he'd caught her completely off guard. The impish face widened with fury, blood thrummed through her veins. Panicked at her reaction, Luke was unsure of whether he should make a hasty retreat or to face the screaming banshee before him. Making a brisk calculation of the pros and cons, in his infinite wisdom he opted to stay.

'Shit, Luke! What the hell do you think you're doing creeping up on me like that? Where were you even hiding, you weirdo?!'

Affronted at being accused of being a weirdo, Luke interjected. Raising his palms up as a warning to Ines that she'd gone too far, he fought his corner.

'Woah woah wooooah. First. I'm not a weirdo. Second, I wasn't hiding. I'm 6-foot-3. Where am I meant to hide? Think logically!' Tapping his temple with his index finger was like waving a red rag at a bull.

'I swear you've got a death wish!' She was incensed, yet relieved to see him.

Fanning his large hands out in a show of surrender, Luke spoke with calm in his voice. 'Okay okay, I'm sorry I startled you.

Vera upstairs let me in and when I realised you weren't yet home, I went outside for a cigarette in the square. When I saw you had come home and left the front door ajar, I came back in.' A faint smile began sliding across his face when he saw Ines' petulant look. Deeming it safe, Luke proceeded, practicing due care. 'You must have been in the zone, because you didn't hear my footsteps walking behind you…and now here we are.' Luke chose his words carefully, deciding that he'd said enough to keep himself out of the fire-pit Ines was ready to throw him into.

Turning back around to resume unlocking the door, she grumbled words to the effect of 'Are you coming in?' Complying, Luke followed.

Taking off her shoes at the entrance, Luke did the same (the mood his little butterfly was in, he wasn't taking chances) then made his way into the kitchen while Ines headed for the bathroom. Now at the coffee machine, Luke scooped a handful of coffee beans from the glass mason jar, dropping the pellets into the grinder and firing it up. Releasing a satisfying belch as it began to heat the water, followed by a crunching as it guzzled the beans, an intoxicating aroma drifted through the flat.

Lighting up a cigarette, Luke perched himself on the bar stool, noticing that Dylan's hold-all was still sagging open in front of the washing machine. Snarling at it, he went over and swept it out of his eye view with antipathy. 'Asshole.'

Wisps of vanilla and amber floating along the hallway was Luke's cue that Ines was almost ready to join him, which would mean that she too would like a coffee. He knew her habits so well, and he also thought he knew Ines well, but her recent behaviour was extraordinarily out of character. Still, he wasn't leaving until he'd gotten some answers to his questions.

Ambling into the kitchen, Luke had noticed that her gait had improved over the last week. 'Ines. You're walking better.' Luke continued to refrain from calling her by his nickname for her. He addressed Ines by her given name or nothing at all. She was still perturbed by this, but as was usual in her character, she also desisted in showing how she felt about it.

'I feel like I am,' replied Ines. 'Maybe it is just a trapped nerve after all.'

Sliding her favourite cup across the worktop, Luke gave a slight non-committal shoulder roll. Ines took a grateful, long sip and settled into the acrylic moulded bar stool. Sheepish, she peered into her coffee, chewing the corner of her mouth in thought. Now that she was relaxed, Luke gave her a few moments to reflect before he spoke. Sitting across the island from each other, he tried to make eye contact, but Ines was still boring a hole into her cup, avoiding any risk of being read. Twisting her damp hair around one shoulder she began to comb through the tangles with a forked hand, pulling out loose strands and collecting them in her lap.

'This is unhygienic,' observed Luke. 'The kitchen is where you should practice good cleanliness.'

Frowning as she pulled at a long thick strand, Ines rubbed her fingers together to remove the stubborn hair sticking to moisturised skin. 'It's my kitchen, my hair is clean and I don't mind. I think I'm allowed to do as I please.'

Smiling to himself, Luke could see what an obstinate child she would have been. Taking a moment, he considered the best ways to approach the subject of her recent strange behaviour. When she was in this kind of mood, it was advised to approach with caution. Hazarding a guess, he reckoned she was a top-secret government experiment and they forgot to add a health warning with her.

'So, fire-woman. What's up?' He went for the high risk, ball buster option.

Silence.

'Hello? Is anybody home?' Luke sang his words. Still silent.

'Okay, is it the coffee? You don't like the coffee?' Not even a whimper. 'Somebody grabbed the last must-have dress that can now only be bought on auction at triple the original price? Umm…ooh, I know. You've run out of smoke?' Luke's patience was wearing thin. 'Answer me please Ines, because you're not your usual self. You've got the face of a bulldog chewing a wasp lately.' Brave or kamikaze, he couldn't gauge it, but he got a reaction, either way.

'So, you're saying I'm ugly?'

Here we go. 'No.'

'So, what are you saying?' She was now spoiling for a fight. He had to think quick on his feet.

'I'm saying that you look very displeased with me of late, which hasn't been a very nice feeling.'

And so their conversation began, with Luke listening and occasionally making a contribution of his humble opinion.

'Well?' she asked as Luke stared at her agog, trying to digest what he'd been told. Ines bared her soul to him and left nothing out.

'Well, I think that you're a very silly girl for not telling me about anything you've been going through, and I think that you're stupid and stupidly stubborn for not calling on me to help you, is what I think.'

Yikes.

'I've told you why I didn't.'

'It's done. In future, I don't care what's going on with us, you ask me for help. It's been a long week without you in my life. Boring in fact.'

Ines took this as an indirect compliment and grinned right back at him.

'So, who's going with you tomorrow?' Luke resisted making a snide remark about it not being Dylan.

'Nobody. Everybody is at work.'

'I'll go. Mags can hold the fort tomorrow. I'm owed time off anyway. I could do with a trip to Queen Square. Might even see if I can get a phone number or three from a few sexy young nurses.'

Rolling her eyes in exasperation, she chose to ignore the last comment.

'Are you sure? It's not exactly Fordhams.'

Batting away the reply with his hand, Luke smirked. 'Listen, MRIs at the National Hospital for Neurology and Neurosurgery is the new place to be. The Hoxton Square Massive are all headed that way with their bearded selves and brown leather messenger bags.'

'And the girls with their modette haircuts,' Ines giggled with delight.

'Exactly. Now, what's for dinner?'

***

Sitting side by side on a bench in Queen Square, Ines and Luke sipped on pungent thick black coffee, munching on what was quite possibly the hardest sourdough bread sandwich known to man. Masticating painfully slow, Luke could take no more.

'You like this shit?' he asked accusingly as he turned to see Ines also struggling with her sandwich. Unable to chew fast enough to answer, Ines placed a hand over her mouth and shook her head to emphasise her opinion. Luke prised open the sorry excuse for a sandwich to check its contents.

'Five pounds for this? It's robbery!' he exclaimed as he prodded the solitary piece of lettuce embedded in butter. Lobbing his lunch into the bin, a flock of scavenging pigeons flew down and pecked at the broken pieces. 'Look at them, even they are struggling to eat it.' One thing Luke hated was bad food. He would rant about it until he turned blue in the face. Oh, and the terrible condition of the British road network. '*It's unheard of in France. The roads here are ridiculous and you Brits accept it,*' he could often be heard bemoaning. 'Throw it away. We'll get something after the scan.'

Unable to disagree, Ines attempted to hurl the sandwich into the bin, but only succeeded in watching the bread and its measly contents explode into the air. A frenzy of birds vying for scraps surrounded the area, leaving Ines and Luke with no alternative but to skirt around them.

Walking across the pretty tree lined square, Luke began unwrapping a cereal bar he'd found inside his jacket and splitting it in half, sharing it with Ines.

'Thanks.'

Nodding in acknowledgment, they left the square and headed for the grand hospital entrance.

'You ok?'

'I think so. I don't know what to expect.' 'I'll be in there with you, don't worry.'

***

Having found the department through the labyrinth of corridors, they sat in the waiting area to be called. Engrossed in filling out a safety questionnaire, she hadn't noticed her friend reading over her shoulder. Pointing to a couple of questions like:

a) Is there a possibility that you could be pregnant? b) Do you have any piercings or tattoos? Luke sniggered. 'I think there's more chance of piercings and tattoos than you being pregnant.'

'Sshh sshh. Oh my god, you can be so tactless at times.' Nudging him in the ribs, Ines continued ticking "no" all the way through the questionnaire.

'Miss Garcia?' The stocky radiographer in scrubs entered the room. Raising her arm as if she were called out in the school register, Luke snorted. Giving him one last poke in the ribs, she smiled at the chipper man and got up. Rubbing his side, Luke made a decision not to anger her in the future. Not if he valued his limbs.

They followed the man in scrubs through a corridor until they arrived at a small windowless room, lit by fluorescent bulbs.

'Do you have any metal on you? Jewellery? A belt buckle?' 'Yes, I do, should I remove them?'

'Please, if you could.'

'What about her metal leg?' Bloody Luke. Incorrigible! 'Do you have metal rods in your leg?'

'No no, it's just my friend's warped sense of humour.' A hard elbow in his stomach winded him. Looking over her shoulder, a spiteful quirk of her mouth concluded her thoughts on the quip he made and began to take her earrings out. In the meantime, the radiographer made a discreet retreat to the radiology room.

***

Leading them through yet another corridor, the radiographer made small talk to ease his patient's anxiety. Trailing behind, as the designated packhorse, Luke bumped into Ines when she came to a grinding halt. They had found themselves in a cool, dimly lit room and a sombre looking machine which resembled a cylindrical plastic coffin. 'So, where do you go? In there?' Luke stabbed the air with his finger in the direction of the tunnel.

'I..I suppose so, yes.'

Simon, the chipper radiographer re-entered the room, clapping his chubby hands together. 'So, are you ready? This won't take too long.'

The explanation was conducted with military precision, leaving Luke and Ines exhausted from trying to absorb the information. Bending the rules, Luke was permitted to sit at the end of the flat bed and cast a protective eye over his fiery butterfly.

Stroking her dainty ankles absently, Luke appeared to be lost in his own thoughts. Dipping her eyes to steal a glance of her friend, his facial expression was that of a man being lead to the gallows— although when he spoke, Luke masked it well with puerile comments. Bouncing his leg in rapid movements, she observed that his body language revealed his anxiety. Feeling a warm sense of affection, Ines waggled her fingers at him. Returning her gesture with a small smile, Luke brought his fist up and placed it over her soft, delicate hand, his touch sending a tingling sensation through her body. If Luke had any idea of the effect he had on her, it would ruin their friendship. Up close, she noted the tiny dark hairs standing on end over his knuckles.

'You've got hairy knuckles.'

Leaning back to get a better look at his hand, he contemplated his hairiness. 'It adds protection when I'm scraping them on the floor.' Ines giggled. 'Besides, have you seen your toe hair? You're in no position to comment, missy.'

Mortified that he should think her toes were hairy, Ines raised herself off the bed, bumping her head on the scanner. 'I bloody do not!'

'Easy tiger, get back in your cage. I was winding you up.'

Just as he ended his sentence, Simon and his assistant approached Ines. With expert speed, the pair inserted ear plugs and placed headphones over her ears, gently squeezing her head in between two foam blocks.

Smiling, the assistant asked, 'Are you okay?' 'I'm fine, thanks,' joked Luke.

Giving a half smile of apologetic resignation that her friend was a twit, Ines nodded in affirmation. Placing a buzzer on her stomach, the gangly limbed woman explained that should she panic, all Ines had to do was press it.

'You're entering a giant roll of toilet paper. What could be so scary?' winked Luke. The assistant made one last demure smile as she began to slide the bed into the tube.

'Allez, go. See you later.' Luke's nerves were shredded.

Ines closed her eyes as she disappeared into the cold, hostile looking tunnel. Her heart thudded so fast she was certain it was going to jump out of her chest.

Chapter 9

Sitting in the cosy Greek restaurant situated in the mews close to the hospital, Luke leaned back on his chair after ordering meze for two and a bottle of Greece's finest red wine. 'So, how was it?'

'Noisy, but it became strangely relaxing. I think I nodded off.' 'You did, you had dribble stains down the side of your chin when you came out.'

Mortified for the second time today, Ines covered her chin, wiping it briskly with her napkin. 'Has it gone?'

Luke's shoulders shook with laughter, content that he'd succeeded in winding her up once again. Realising that he was being his normal irritating self, Ines banged the table with her little fist, irritated with his childish antics. 'Can you STOP?! Oh my gosh, you're so annoying!'

His laughter increasing, Luke struggled to get his words out. 'I'm sorry. Sometimes it's too irresistible. All I need to do is throw out the line and you take the bait.' Depicting a fisherman reeling in a fish, his grin spread with ease across his face, forming cracked lines around his eyes. 'It's funny, no?'

'In your eyes, maybe.'

'But you love me all the same.'

Ines' stomach lurched at Luke's words, which were uttered with innocuous intent. Hoping her face didn't reveal any feelings, she took a sip of the dry wine, tangy flavours of dark berries skimming across her taste buds. 'You wish.'

'With a mad woman like you? No thanks, I value my balls,' grinned Luke, cocking one eyebrow. 'So, tell me about the wedding event of the year.'

Scooping out hoummus with a piece of warm pitta bread she'd torn off, Ines handed Luke the other part. 'Well, it's over the Easter bank holiday at The Mountjoy.'

'…in Devon?'

'Yes, that's the one. Anyway, Echo's kids are going to be ushers and Martha's going to promote the wedding on her social media platforms. It's all a bit pretentious, but it's horses for courses, I suppose,' shrugged Ines, taking a huge mouthful of the delicious dip and bread. She was famished.

Luke smiled inwardly at Ines' love for good food and her unconcern for people's opinion on women with a huge appetite. In an age where females were so body conscious, she was at the other end of the scale and didn't care. He loved this cavalier attitude. 'So, are Echo's kids named pretentious names to go with the pretentious extravaganza of the year?'

'I'd say it's up there. They're called Balthasar and Titus.'

Tapping his ear as though he didn't hear correctly, Luke spluttered his sentence. 'Titus and Balthasar? Were they high when they named them?' Luke's laugh, infectious as ever had her flushing with delight at his comment. 'Can those kids ever forgive them? They're going to be known as Tight Arse and Baz. What the hell?' Luke was, by now, guffawing, and Ines started braying, unable to stop. The waiters continued the momentum of bringing the plates of food, amused by their conversation and were soon chuckling along with the comical pair of diners.

'Will you be going?'

Mopping away tears of glee, Ines nodded. 'Well, I can't wait to see the pictures.'

Her heart sank when she heard these words. The cutting reminder that Dylan was still on the scene, even if it was by token appearances, and that she was still hanging in there for a miracle, was a kick in the teeth.

***

Along a quiet cove, on the Jurassic Coastline, Dylan and Jenna soaked up the warmth of the afternoon, strolling amongst a couple of dog walkers who were watching their pets woofing and bounding in delight at the sea, fuelled by excitement as the waves rolled in, crashing over their sodden fur. Buttermilk sand dunes nestled easily amongst a blanket of emerald velvet undulating hills, illuminated by the golden glow of the sun. Tall stalks of pampas grass sighed in the sea breeze. It had been perfect; the best business trip in Dylan's opinion.

As if she was reading his mind, Jenna whispered, 'I don't want this to end.' Stopping near the shoreline, she lowered herself into the sand. Letting his body sink down beside her, Dylan wove his arm around her shoulder and inhaled the salty air.

'What are you doing?' Bumping shoulders with Dylan playfully, Jenna gave him a goofy smile.

'I'm getting a lungful of clean O2 before we go back to polluted London.'

'Can I ask you something?'

Dylan nodded. 'Yep. Go for it.'

'Will we carry on seeing each other when we get back?' Jenna knew the rules of casual relationships, but she felt compelled to ask. Her feelings had grown deeper than if it were just a transient fling.

Looking out to sea, Dylan reflected on his life back home. He was living a crazy life and it was getting tiring; the duplicity in particular between Ines and Jenna was wearing him down, but he wasn't prepared to give up his cushy life in Montague Square. 'Let's take it one day at a time, enjoy the ride and see where it takes us. Yeah, babe?'

Happy with his reply, Jenna rested her head on his arm and enjoyed the sound of the waves murmuring as they melted into each other, the sea spray catching their faces.

***

Back at the flat, Ines had explained to Dylan what had been happening in her world during his absence. Sensing his indifference, she questioned his lack of empathy.

'Have you been diagnosed? No. Have you been hospitalised? No. Stop following me around like a lap dog vying for my attention.' He spat the words with venomous conviction, causing Ines to flinch. Visibly upset and lost for words, she went into the kitchen and lit a cigarette, leaving Dylan to make his phone calls. He didn't give a shit and Ines couldn't work out whether she was more upset that he didn't care or that she was upset with herself for still hanging in there, hoping he'd change. Exhaling a long stream of smoke, she focused on the world outside her window and tried to think straight.

The realisation that the flat was quiet struck her like a bolt out of the blue. Overwhelmed by curiosity, Ines found herself stubbing out her cigarette with urgency as she slid off the bar stool. Barefoot, she crept along the hallway towards the lounge, scared to cause any disturbance.

With measured inhales as she peered around the door, Ines saw that Dylan was fast asleep on the sofa, his mobile rising and falling as it lay upon his chest, rousing the temptation to take a look. Breathing slow and controlled, his lips slightly parted, this was Dylan in deep sleep. A bomb couldn't wake him, sleep. In a split second, she made the decision to unlock his phone. Crawling towards him in triple slow motion, her body ached with tension, her pulse beat like a snare drum. Reaching out for his limp hand, she pressed his finger onto the home button.

Stirring as he felt the brush of skin against his, Ines ducked down with expeditious reflexes, not risking the slightest of an exhale. His eyes bobbing open, Dylan was satisfied that he saw nothing but the weakening light as day turned to dusk. Stupefied with fatigue, he fell back into a deep slumber, the phone slipping off his chest with a dull thud on the rug. An opportunity as rare as fairy dust was within her grasp. A gift from above!

Something needed to be done about this leech of a man. The phone lay within centimetres of her face, still unlocked. Seizing the mobile, Ines opened his messages. Pulling her own phone out of her back pocket, she feverishly began taking photos of the entire message thread between him and Jenna, only too aware of the fury that would ensue if Dylan caught her reading his phone…oh the irony. He would be furious with her for reading messages between him and his lover.

Rising with prudence from the child's pose she had been in, Ines replaced his phone on the floor and slinked out of the room. Entering the bathroom, she'd noticed that Dylan hadn't washed the shower out after himself. Amongst the evaporating bubbles, lay two long strands of hair, glistening like threads of gold. Ines was no detective, but it didn't need the prowess of one to figure that this was not his or her own. Dylan had auburn curls and Ines…well Ines was of the darkest chocolate, curly hair. This was blonde, over coloured hair. Her body still shaking with unease, she decided to do nothing and see if Dylan would see the evidence he'd left behind for himself.

Locking the bathroom door, she tiptoed to the toilet, guiding the seat shut. Scrolling through the photos, her stomach began to churn and knot in dismay. Photo upon photo, graphic images of him, her, them together and video stills penetrated her vision. Like an addict she knew that looking wasn't conducive to her state of mind nor her current health issues, but still she continued, shivering at the sight. There were images so intimate that they could be mistaken for porn. It was porn…their porn. While she had been struggling, he had been living a hedonistic life in hotels…with *her*. What to do? Confront him or bide her time?

He was meeting *her* on Wednesday. The night before Ines' birthday. Wracked with confusion, like a deer in front of headlights, she had to think logically before broaching the subject. This was evidence that justified her paranoia. How much more could she handle? Her world was crumbling, she knew what to do for the sake of her sanity, but how? Dylan had reduced her to a fragment of her former self. Any confidence she had, had been stripped as he worked his insidious ways on his naïve girlfriend.

***

Explaining everything to Sally and Zara over coffee on Tuesday evening, the girls decided that between them they'd have their revenge on Dylan. Zara being hormonal and a loose cannon at the best of times was ready for a row.

Sally was angry but was able to practice more control. 'We need to exercise calm. The cooler we are, the more effective we'll be.'

'If I had my way, I'd tear him and her apart. I'm livid!' snarled Zara.

Nodding in unified agreement, Sally and Ines sat in silence.

'I don't even know how you can remain so placid.' Zara was picking crumbs off of her plate with a newly manicured fingernail, licking it off with the end of her tongue.

'If Luke was here, he'd have something to say about your eating habits out in public,' chided Ines.

'Well, he's not here so ner,' she replied, licking her fingers, adding to her defiance .

'You can be such a kid.' Shaking her head like a disapproving mother, Ines tittered at the idea of Luke's reaction.

'So, have you decided what you're going to do about the pregnancy?' asked Sally peering with keen eyes.

Zara's entire demeanour changed. Softening at the question posed by Sally, she patted her stomach with pride. 'I'm having the baby,' she announced.

'Nick's not going to be happy,' warned Ines.

'Ini, I do not give a fiddler's fart. I'm having this baby and I have never been so sure about anything as I am right now. Shall we go for celebration drinks tomorrow night?'

Chinking their cups together in salutation, the excitement was in abundance as the girls discussed babysitting duties and vowing not to discuss babies on their nights out. 'Yes, there's more to me than being a mum to be.'

Sitting in the red leather booth, the girls threw sly glances around the bar to see if they recognised anyone. 'Oh.My.God. Look over there. LOOOOK!' Sally jabbed her head to her right. 'Look look look!' she hissed in quick succession.

Turning their heads in unison, Zara and Ines followed Sally's direction. 'Oh shit, they look like a couple of hookers…young ones at that,' muttered Ines.

'They're every weirdo's fantasy,' Zara laughed wickedly, snorting her drink out of her nose. 'Legal jailbait,' she added, dabbing her spillage.

'Speaking of weirdos, where's Nick tonight?' asked Ines, circling the rim of her tumbler with her finger. 'Oiii, that's the father of my child!' exclaimed Zara in mock offence. 'He's out with his mates tonight. I think they've gone to Seven.'

As she got up, Zara smoothed down her rose print bias cut skirt, brushing off remnants of honey roasted cashews. Placing her hand on Zara's doughy arm, Sally stopped her from moving forward. 'Where are you going?'

'To get a drink. My round.' She had a mischievous glint in her eye, one that could mean trouble.

Standing on her tiptoes at the bar, Zara caught a glimpse of herself in the mirrors behind the barman. She was very pleased with the way she looked tonight. Her jade angora jumper and silk skirt, complemented her blue eyes. Feeling like a million dollars, she glowed inner beauty.

'What can I get you?' smiled the barman, wiping down the pumps in front of him. His boyish smile, wide cheekbones and hypnotic southern Irish accent always turned Zara to jelly.

'An espresso Martini, a dark rum—neat and a white wine spritzer, please.'

'The rum's for your Latina buddy?'

'Yes, she's so predictable. If anyone wanted to poison her they wouldn't have difficulty. Have you got a crush on her?' teased Zara, swaying a happy little dance.

Taken aback by her candour, the barman threw back his head with laughter. 'You're no wallflower, are you?'

'Stop skirting around the question.' Zara was feeling cheeky. 'Nah, she's nice but I like someone else.'

'Ooooh who? Does she come here? Is she here now?' So eager to get the gossip on his crush, she hadn't realised that the two girls they'd been mocking, had sidled up to her. 'What's your name by the way? We always chat but have never exchanged names.'

'Aiden. And yours?' 'Zara.'

'Pleased to put a name to the pretty face.' Nodding with geniality, Aiden gave a generous smile.

Zara smiled back, with a toothy grin, blushing, content at the compliment. Enjoying the flirty exchanges and probing for more information, the barman was happy to answer her questions.

Choosing to hang around the bar a tiny bit longer, Zara overheard the conversation the girls beside her were in the middle of, after having ordered their drinks, which Aiden was now pouring out.

'...so, he's got the hump because I wouldn't go out with him. He's asked me a few times now.' Tugging her long black ponytail apart, from the top of her head, the girl seemed to be enthralled with the chase of this desperate man.

'If you don't want to go out with him, put the poor guy out of his misery.'

Resting on the back of her elbows, against the bar, the girl looked smug. 'I might do, but for now I'm enjoying him begging.'

Her friend nodded back, taking a handful of complimentary popcorn.

'Oh ohhhh, he's here!' Two tall, casually dressed guys, both in jeans, accentuating their footballer's thighs and perfect rears swaggered in, oozing with confidence and sex appeal. One had blond hair, cropped close to his head and a godlike bone structure, while the other had hair as dark as ebony and eyes as black as coal. There was a flurry of melodramatic excitement as the girl spun around to face the bar and pretended to not have seen him. 'Shush, don't look. Do.Not.Make.It.Obvious.' She spat ostentatiously slow.

Following her friend's lead, the second girl stole a quick glance before she too spun back around. 'Is he the blond or the mysterious looking one in the black polo?'

'The black polo.' The girl was making whinnying sounds by this point. 'He's fit! They both are.'

Curiosity was getting the better of her, so Zara cast a furtive glance to see this elusive hunk of a man. It was Nick! Shocked at finding out that what she'd been hearing, had been about her boyfriend, Zara began to panic, her mind scrambling to make sense of everything. This was just too much. She thought she was going to pass out with anger and disbelief. Before she could stop herself, Zara moved in closer to the girls.

'Excuse me, are you talking about Nick?'

Taken by surprise, the girl replied in monosyllabic words. 'Yeah.'

'Are you going out with him?'

'No. Why?' The girl didn't look comfortable with the way the interrogation was going.

'He's my boyfriend and we're having a baby.' Bam. And just like that, Zara blurted the words out.

The girl, disturbed by what had just happened, bolted to Nick and his friend.

'Hello you, this is a nice surprise. Wasn't expecting to see you in here,' leered Nick as he eyed the girl up in her short, pleated skirt and knee length boots.

Her bosom jiggled like cupolas of jelly from beneath her tight fitting V neck top, as she spoke ardently. 'Me neither. In fact, I wasn't expecting to be accosted by your girlfriend, either! You know, the one you never told me about?' Nick's friend shuffled, sympathetic to his friend's critical situation.

Confused as to which girl in his harem would assume the privilege of calling herself his girlfriend, Nick mentally scrolled through the potential candidates. Lisa, Chantal, Anna, Maggie, Zara…hmmm. 'What's her name, babe?'

Swallowing back her nerves with a blank stare, the girl looked helpless. All at once, it dawned on her that she had seen Zara disappear to the back, like a spectre. Jumping up with excitement and poking the air with her thumb behind, her voluptuous breasts threatened to bounce out of her leopard print bra.

Arousing lascivious stares from both Nick and his friend, Nick smirked, trying to abstain from lewd thoughts. His friend, Matt meanwhile had to tear himself away from the alluring vision before him— after all, it was his friend's girl.

'She went over there by the booths!' Delighted with her observational skills, the girl was filled with a sense of self- importance.

Looking over her plump shoulders, Nick narrowed his eyes in order to focus better. He couldn't see anything.

'Shit, he's looking over!' Sniggering behind the red leather- bound wine list, Ines and the girls lowered their heads in an attempt to conceal themselves. Giggling nervously, Zara asked what she should do? 'Go and challenge the bastard. He's obviously to blame. That girl hasn't got a clue,' replied Sally, in earnest.

'Sally! I do love it when you're peeved. Your words are simple but effective,' said Zara, a crescent for a smile spreading across rosy cheeks.

Ines remained reticent. Not long ago, she had been sitting over at that same part of the bar, overhearing two bubbled headed bimbos talking about her boyfriend. Now, Zara was in a similar scenario and Ines was consumed by an urge to help her friend out of this dire situation.

'I'll come with you,' she said determinedly. 'In fact I'll go first, and you can catch up. I may be rubbish at dealing with my own troubles, but I'll help you sort yours out.'

Looking back at Ines, her newly filled lips, quivered. 'You're an angel.'

'I know,' blinked Ines, and slipped away from the booth making her way towards Nick.

Watching open-mouthed in anticipation of what was unravelling before them, Zara was the first to speak. 'Vain bastard hasn't even noticed Ini walking over because he won't wear his glasses.'

***

The slow realisation that it was Ines moving towards him somewhat confused Nick. The girl had stated that it was a woman claiming to be his girlfriend. Ines wouldn't do such a thing, this much he did know... so, what was going on? Organising his thoughts in logical order, he concluded that it was some female being catty towards this poor, dim-witted girl, whom Nick resorted to calling 'babe' because he couldn't remember her name. His poor memory didn't go as far as forgetting her body, though. Then again, he never forgot an unaccomplished conquest that's on his "to do" list.

Ines, approaching ever closer, projected a beguiling smile at Nick and the small group around him. Grinning back at her, Nick fell into a false sense of security when he thought that his philandering ways were undisclosed.

'Hello, Nick.' All eyes were now on Ines. Uncomfortable with an audience at the best of times, she focused her attention on Zara's lothario of a boyfriend. Matt, the girl with no name and the girl with no name's friend stared at her in expectation for what this new mysterious woman wanted.

'Hello, Ines. How the devil are you?' Eyeing her up and down, he was assessing the pretty, petite lady in front of him, trying to decide if she made an eight or a nine out of ten.

Feeling violated by his eyes boring through her, Ines bridled at his behaviour.

'Fine thanks, I see you're keeping well,' staring pointedly at him then to the clueless young woman. Trying to laugh off his discomfort, Nick spread out his arms. 'Yeah well, you know how it is. Work hard play hard.' Avoiding the subject of introduction, Nick babbled on about trivial matters which were of no interest to anyone but himself. Googly eyed with devout adoration, the girl with no name smiled on. It made Ines feel ill that someone could idolise another human as pathetic as he. In a disturbing flash of a reality check, Ines saw that she had more in common with this girl than she'd care to admit. 'Sorry, I haven't introduced myself. My name is Ines.' Smiling sympathetically at the dopey girl, she put her hand out to be cordial.

The girl took Ines' hand, shaking it with enthusiasm. 'Hello, I'm Molly and this is my friend Milly. She swept her hand out towards her friend.

Molly and Milly…you couldn't make it up, thought Ines. Feeling bad for these girls, it was like speaking to simple people who meant no malice, just fun. 'Nice to meet you. So, how do you know Nick?'

Kapow. Nick, fidgeting on the spot, began to change the subject. Beads of perspiration trickled over his brow.

'W..,well we know each other…' Nick stumbled over his lies.

'We met at my office. I work as a receptionist at Holders & Wiseman and Nick chatted me up,' giggled Molly.

Nick prayed to the gods for a divergence.

Nodding slowly and expectantly, Ines waited for the next sentence.

'…and he's been asking me out now for the last three months. I keep saying no because…well, I'm eighteen and he's nearly thirty. It's a bit weird and my parents wouldn't have been happy.'

It was as if Molly had been injected with truth serum and there was no stopping her. Nodding her head in encouragement, all the while revelling, as she watched Nick melt into the floor, Ines was enthralled by Molly's epic narrative.

Meanwhile, the girls watched on like conspirators. 'I don't know what Ines is doing, but Nick looks as if he's about to be shot!' clapped Zara, excited at what she was witnessing.

'She's literally making him sweat. She's in that "we both know what you're doing, but will I say something?" mode. I love it when she's like that. Toying with him!' gasped Sally, slapping the table rhythmically with exaggerated joy. 'Do you think we should go over there now?'

With a vehement shake of her head, Zara rejected that plan. 'Nah, let's wait a few more minutes. Watching Nick squirm is just the best!'

Back at the bar, Aiden was enjoying the show as he continued to serve customers, listening to the conversation intermittently.

Molly continued spilling the beans and neither Ines nor Nick could stop her.

'I was actually saying to Milly earlier that I'd make him sweat a little longer and finally agree to go out with him, especially now that my family have gotten used to the idea of the possibility that I will have an older boyfriend.' As Molly smiled, her cheeks glowed a deep shade of pink. 'But he looks a little sweaty now. Not sure if that's a good look babe,' she tittered.

Loving every minute of this, Ines' eyes bounced between looking at the girls and the guys. It was brilliant. Comedy gold. The girls had no idea, and the guys were floundering in this game of cat and mouse between Ines and Nick.

Molly took a sip of her vodka and cranberry juice. 'So, sorry. You didn't say how you know Nick and Matt. '

Ding ding ding! 'Ooh. Well. Funny you should ask.'

Nick was looking like he was about to pass out through loss of water, he'd been sweating so much. 'Nick is my best friend's boyfriend and she's having his baby in six months' time.' A devilish grin broke out underneath her nose. Clangggg! And that was the sound of a secret hitting the floor.

Molly and Milly exchanged horrified glances with Matt and Nick. Aiden carried on wiping the bar, amused at the drama unfolding like a soap opera.

'YOU COMPLETE AND UTTER BASTARD!' screamed Molly. Her sweet and innocent demeanour switched to utter anger and horror.

Milly held her friend back, while Nick took a cautionary step away.

'It's not how she says it is,' Nick insisted. 'Zara's just a girl I see from time to time.'

'Liar.' Ines' tone was ice cold.

Confounded, the two girls looked to Ines. 'I'm so so sorry. I had no idea,' sniffed Molly, through small tear filled, hazel eyes.

Ines placed a consoling hand on the young woman's shoulder. 'I know you didn't. You needed to be told and Zara can see what an ass the father of her baby is.'

'Yep,' chimed Zara who had been standing by the bar watching on with Aiden.

'YOU want this kid, I don't!' Nick insisted. 'Do you actually think I want to be tied to you for the next eighteen years?' His condescending approach cut through Zara like spiked steel.

Stung by his words, Zara found the strength to fight back. 'You and I are done. I don't want your money or any contact with you. We'll be just fine. Just stay away from us.' Circling a finger around her stomach, added conviction to the impassioned speech. 'Piss off, Nick. What makes you think Zara would still have you? You're delusional. I'm glad for both their sakes that you don't want to be in their lives.' Ines stood firm, simmering at the lothario.

Nick could do nothing but laugh at the situation, while Matt kept his eyes on the floor, unable to support his friend.

'I hope for the baby's sake you fulfill your promise of not wanting anything to do with it. A loser dad who's got nothing to offer to the world, let alone another human being is pointless. Useless. Worthless. I'm sure Zara can offer everything this child will need and more!' Molly found her voice and wow, she knew how to use it.

'...and I don't want your stinking money either.' Cupping the non-existent bump, Zara jeered with salty tears blurring her vision. 'We will be just fine. Now if you don't mind, I'm going to enjoy the rest of the evening.' Nick and Matt stood slack-jawed. 'You've made your mind up, so have I. You will never have contact with your child. Ever. I hope you never find happiness!' Zara spun a dynamic turn and walked back to the bar and ordered a fruit juice.

'It's on me,' offered Aiden, giving her a kind half-smile.

'Thank you.' Taking a large gulp, the cold sweet taste of pineapple sliding down her dry throat was achingly refreshing.

Sally had caught up with her friends at the bar. The four girls grouped around Zara, protective of the mum-to-be.

'Here's to single motherhood and stretch marks,' announced a dejected Zara.

'No, here's to unconditional love,' corrected Milly.

The evening wasn't quite how they expected it to be and they somehow made friends with two girls who were a mismatch to their trio, yet complemented them. Who knew?

Chapter 10

'Happy birthday to you. Happy birthday to you. Happy…' Zara and Sally had terrible singing voices. Ines laughed them into shutting up. Sitting in the kitchen, looking out ahead at the square, she had been drinking her morning coffee, pondering her impending visit to the hospital. The phone serenade was a welcome distraction.

'Twenty-five years old!' squealed Zara. 'You're catching up to me.'

Humouring her friend's optimism, Ines agreed to meet everyone at their usual spot en route to work.

Grinning at the fond recollection of the girls' efforts of a duet, Ines hadn't noticed Dylan had wandered over. Bleary eyed and sporting a scruffy head of curls sprouting in every direction, he leant down to kiss her on the head and placed a bouquet of sunflowers on her lap. He remembered that she loved sunflowers the most.

'Happy birthday,' he murmured.

Looking wondrously at her gift, Ines thanked him for the flowers and for remembering.

'How can I forget? I value my life,' he half joked.

'Are you around later?'

'Dunno, I'll see what work's saying. I'll let you know.'

Already knowing the answer, with a twinge of sadness, Ines made a decision to cross him off the list. He never seemed available at important events. Weddings, christenings, birthdays, family gatherings; work always seemed to come into the equation.

***

Walking across the sun drenched square, Ines noticed that her gait had improved. Maybe the doctors were being overly cautious and she was being neurotic. Anyway, at this point in time, she didn't care. Today was her birthday, glorious weather had been forecast and she had her best friends waiting at their usual spot before going to work. Dressed in her favourite black suede pencil skirt, a black Bardot top and a cropped denim jacket, Ines felt amazing, even if Dylan did suggest the contrary. According to him, wearing black fitted knee length boots gave the wrong signals out, especially as the suede skirt clung to her bottom. Whatever.

Waving with eagerness at her, all her friends' smiles and excitement warmed Ines' heart. 'Here she comes!' called out Sally, giving out a loud wolf whistle with her fingers.

Looking on in amazement, Luke let out a throaty laugh. 'Where did that come from?'

Grinning at how surprised everybody was, Sally shrugged. 'I have three brothers. I'm the youngest. It was a rite of passage in my formative years.' Ryan looked at her in admiration.

'Woweee, look at you, sexy lady!' cooed Zara.

Raising his eyebrows, a crescent for a smile flitted from his lips as he leaned down to kiss her on each cheek. 'Happy birthday, my little butterfly.'

The buzz amongst the friends was so vibrant that people passing them by couldn't help but reciprocate the feeling.

Ryan was dressed in a suit and tie. 'You look very dapper, mister. Are you going somewhere?' asked Ines, more out of curiosity than anything else. Ryan was wearing a dark grey suit which was a little too big for him, a white shirt and a tie that Ines recognised to be Luke's.

'I've got my third interview this morning and Luke's lent me his whistle.'

Luke looked puzzled. Ines interjected. 'It's cockney rhyming slang for suit. Whistle and flute.'

Perturbed, Luke shook his head. 'You British have a wide variety of diction in your language.'

'We do mate, it adds to our rich cultural tapestry,' remarked Ryan, placing one hand on his chest like an erudite.

***

Coming out with a paper bag full of hot drinks and breakfast, everyone followed Zara into the square, so they could enjoy a birthday breakfast alfresco. 'It's better here amongst the flowers and tranquillity than on a bench with every Tom, Dick and Harry passing by. Right, I'll be mother...'

'May as well start getting used to it,' chuckled Ryan.

'Oh ha bloody ha, Ryan!' squealed Zara, as she handed out everybody's order, shaking her long fringe away from her face as she immersed herself into dishing everything out.

'We saw Dildo scuttling through here earlier, pretending to be talking on his phone— to avoid speaking with us, no doubt.' Luke. Straight to the point, as always. 'Is he going with you today?'

Taking a bite out of her almond croissant, Ines faced the sun, her skin drinking in its warmth.

'Did you hear me?'

Ines nodded, smiling inanely.

'So?' Nettled, Luke wondered if she'd deign to answer any time soon.

'So, I don't give a shit. In fact, today is a perfect day and I know that life will get better.'

Taking the ominous reply as a hint that the situation she was in with Dylan was a separation in progress, her friends exchanged surreptitious glances over their breakfast. Somehow they knew that she was steering the helm and resigned themselves to remaining quiet…at least for today.

Chattering away, the happy group hadn't kept track of time.

'Oh my goodness, look at the time!' exclaimed Sally. It was nearly 8:30. A panic ensued as everybody gathered their litter, knocking back the remainder of their drinks and shovelling the last of their breakfast into their mouths. With a mouthful of bread tucked into the corner, her cheek looked fit to burst as Zara attempted to speak. Covering her mouth, conscious of the fact that nobody wanted to be sprayed with bread crumbs, she mumbled words that needed careful deciphering. 'Mmmph. Sshee yaa laycher.'

'What did she say?' Luke had a genuine look of bafflement.

'She said mmwah, see you later,' Sally translated, with the confidence of a parent to a small child who had just begun to learn to speak.

'Rrright. Okay. If you say so.' Leaning his head to the side, Luke directed his question with a sharp flick of his clean shaven jaw. 'So, fancy a date with a hot Frenchman at The National later?' 'With Olivier Martinez? You don't need to ask me twice.' Ines' tone was as lewd as it was serious.

'Ooh yes please!' enthused Sally. Ryan shot a hurt glance. 'I'm kidding, as if. I prefer my men with rose-blond hair and and hazel eyes.'

Ryan looked marginally appeased, even though he knew it was a little fib on Sally's part.

'Or, maybe I will do,' offered Luke. 'I'd like to think my company's fun and engaging. Anyway, he's too old for you.'

Twisting her mouth thoughtfully as she contemplated the offer, Ines answered. 'Hhmm yes, I suppose you'll do. One o'clock outside my office. Be there or be square.'

Another British idiom that Luke still couldn't comprehend.

Gulping the last morsel of her panini, Zara called out directives like a pro. 'Okay, so let's message the group chat and play the day by ear. Ini, keep us posted. Ryan, good luck with the interview. You've got this. Smiling encouragement and producing two thumbs up as a full stop, Zara ended with a, 'Love you guys. Gotta go!'

And then she was gone. Like a fairy sprinkling happiness glitter wherever she flits, nobody could accuse her of being dull. Watching her fade into the distance, the click clack of her wedge sandals resonating across the square, the rest of the group of friends gathered their litter and placed it into the bin on the way out. Sally and Ryan left together, given the interview was at her office. Ines and Luke stood like two proud parents watching their kids go off on their first day at school.

'They make a great couple, don't they?' sighed Ines.

With his hands deep in his trouser pockets, Luke smiled slightly at the vision before him. His eyes never leaving the lovestruck pair, he started to say something but changed his mind.

'What? What were you about to say?' demanded Ines.

Luke shook his head, preferring to remain silent until she swatted his chest with her hand. 'Ow!! 'What was that for?

'Tell me what you were going to say. You're not telling me the truth. That's what it's for,' she cackled, wagging an accusing finger.

'Merde, you can hit, huh?' 'Yup. Don't forget.'

Ines cocked her head towards the street. 'Come on, I've got to get to work.' Regardless of wearing heeled boots, she still needed to stand on tip-toes to reach up and kiss Luke on the cheek. Smacking his face, Luke squealed like a teenage girl who'd just been kissed by her idol. 'Oh my gaaad, I'm never gonna wash again!'

'Allez, go you fool. See you later.'

Sitting in the waiting area, Ines was rubbing her palm with tense, repetitive strokes in anticipation of the meeting with Doctor Palmer, and Luke's knee was bouncing up and down at a rate of knots. Casting a snide glance at his knee, she could feel herself becoming increasingly agitated by the motion.

Fixing her gaze ahead, she tried with every fibre in her body not to mention it. Seconds feel like hours when something irritates Ines. It was no good, she had to say it. With a voice as brittle as dry wood, the words escaped. 'You know, knee bouncing is on a par with loud chewing in my opinion. I can easily go to prison for both.'

'I'll stop when you stop burrowing your fingers through
your hand. I too can easily go to prison for annoying practices.'

Taken aback by his reply, Ines looked at the angry red blotch looking back from her palm. 'I've stopped.'

'So have I.' At that, Luke pulled out his phone from the inside of his purple lined jacket and began to play his cross word game in French, while Ines continued to stare at the wall. The silence and tension between them both was insufferable. An albatross had been chained around their neck.

As if the nurse had felt their foreboding, she came forward and called Ines' name out. 'Miss Ines Garcia, please.' Shooting her arm straight up as though she were still at school (another quirky habit she was unable to shake off), Ines made her

Oh god, this goes hand in hand with my braying laugh. Aware that this was the second time she'd done it in the presence of Luke, she added "raising her hand" as another definite *no* to her catalogue of how to act demure and cool. As ever, the list was endless and lessons were never heeded.

Acknowledging Ines, the nurse smiled and indicated for her to follow. Without needing prompting, Luke dropped his phone back into his pocket as he stood up and began his march towards the doctor's office, taking long easy strides down the corridor behind Ines' hasty footsteps, until they came to a sudden halt when the nurse turned to the anxious pair.

'If you can sit here please and wait until Doctor Palmer calls you in.' The nurse, a petite Asian lady, spoke with a voice as sweet as honey, her eyes sparkling as she began to explain. 'Drinks are available over at the hot beverages machine and water cooler over to your right at the end of the corridor.' Although fraught with nerves, their misgivings were allayed thanks to the empathetic lady with the calming aura and sweet smile. Showing their appreciation to the nurse, they sat down on the tough plastic chairs and waited. Remaining subdued like the new girl waiting to go into class, Ines was pensive as she looked around at how varied the MS patients were. Comparing in childlike wonderment, she noted they went from seemingly fit and healthy to those with walking canes, as well as some who were unable to communicate properly, needing supportive care. MS is as unique as your fingerprint, to everyone. It was apparent that no two people experienced the same symptoms or progression. It seemed to her that it didn't care who you were. Young or old. It was going to wrap its unforgiving arms around you like poison ivy in a velvet glove and lead you into an unpredictable rollercoaster of eternal doubt. Is this it, are you going to remain unscathed and live a normal life unaffected by relapses, or will you end up in a position where you will need care because your condition dictates it?

Sensing her silent anguish, Luke took hold of Ines' hand and stroked the top of it with his long thumb. With words unspoken, Ines gratefully accepted his act of reassurance and curled her slim fingers under his. The young man sitting across from them in his wheelchair could only have been in his very early twenties, yet he laughed and chatted with his female companion as if he didn't have a care in the world. In fact, they were very entertaining to watch.

Smiling back at them, Ines shuddered at what her life might be like from here on. Deciding that she had a dry throat, Ines made to get up.

'Where are you going?' demanded Luke. His voice had a hint of authority in it, which Ines had only ever heard when he addressed his staff.

'I need water. I feel like I've swallowed sand.'

'Stay where you are, I'll get it. They may call you in.'

'But the nurse said the doctor was running twenty minutes late. I have time.'

Ignoring her protests, he got up and strode to the water cooler around the corner.

Flicking the switch for ambient temperature, he watched with painstaking patience as the water trickled into the white plastic cup. Aware of a presence beside him, Luke turned his head to see who or what it was. The female companion of the young disabled man stood smiling back at him. 'Sorry, I'm in your way,' he apologised. 'No no, you're fine. These things can be sooo slow at times.' She made excuses for Luke's awkwardness with the water cooler. His mind was not on the beverage. 'Are you here to see Doctor Palmer?' Taken aback by her frankness, Luke nodded.

'Yes, my…erm…my friend is going in. I'm here to support her.'

'That's good of you. She's going to need lots of help going forward, if the diagnosis is MS.' Shifting her cup under the tap, the girl nudged the switch with casual know-how. 'It's going to be tough for her and her loved ones. Not gonna lie, it's unpredictable. It's shit for the patient and it's shit for the people that love them when they have to watch the change and struggle over time. But hey, MS affects everyone in different ways and hopefully, if your friend is diagnosed with it, she won't be too bad. She'll need your help either way. My boyfriend has mine, one hundred percent.' Removing the cup from the cooler, the girl took a long gulp.

Sidestepping from the cooler, Luke looked at the girl properly for the first time. She couldn't have been more than twenty years old. He was touched by her genuine concern for her boyfriend. 'So, have you been together long? Were you together before his diagnosis?'

'I met him late into his diagnosis. He's in his wheelchair because long distance walking tires him out. I tell him it's because he's a lazy so and so,' laughed the girl. 'We have to make allowances for his limitations, but I love him and I don't care about that stuff. I see Dan as Dan. Handsome, funny and lovely Dan. I saw him, not his condition.'

Humbled by the girl's dedication, Luke smiled on. 'Well, to be honest, I don't think my friend's boyfriend will have the same attitude.' Taking steps to return, the young girl walked along side him. 'In my opinion and from what I see, you have to make it part of your life, too. Your partner and their condition go hand-in-hand, like a hinge and bracket. You have to be in this one wholehearted or bail out from the off. It's definitely not for the faint-hearted or the selfish. It can be like a rollercoaster at times.' Sounding like a pro, she continued. 'If your friend's boyfriend is not going to be that person, he should do her a favour and go.'

Taking a deep breath and exhaling between gritted teeth, Luke remained pensive on hearing the reality being spoken. Walking beside the girl through the corridor back to their seats, he remained in contemplative silence until they reached their places. 'Well, let's see what the diagnosis is, if there is one at all. Thank you for your candid advice. It's been enlightening to speak with you.'

'You're welcome.' The girl's face beamed as she sat beside her beloved Dan.

Sitting back down, Luke returned the smile with genuine admiration. Handing the cup of water to Ines, he looked at her, concern stretched like gauze, across his thin smile.

'What's with the face? You look like someone's about to shave your nuts with a blunt blade.'

At a loss, Luke puffed his words. 'Nothing. Do you want me to go in with you?'

Welcoming the offer, Ines slapped his thigh. 'Yeah, it's not like we're visiting the STI clinic is it?' She couldn't help herself.

Bristling, Luke rolled his eyes. 'It was thrush.' Remaining impassive, he asked again, 'Do you want me in there or not?'

'Yes please.'

A heavy blanket of silence fell over them, snuffing out their words until they were called in.

Finding herself sitting primly before Doctor Palmer, clasped hands upon her lap, Ines was in the zone. Luke sat ramrod close to her, afraid to breathe.

Sensing their tension, the eccentric looking Doctor smiled to bolster the morale of the young handsome couple in front of him. 'So, Miss Garcia. You're here for the results of the MRI you had last Thursday, referred to by Doctor McCarthy, after a few episodes of neurological symptoms. You've had an extraordinary route before getting here.' His rimless glasses were perched at the end of his nose as he sifted through copious sheets of paper. Waiting for what seemed to be hours for him to divulge the results, Ines tried to determine his age, given there weren't too many wisps of grey in his thick brown hair and surmised that he was no older than forty-five judging by the lack of lines around his eyes— it was just the doctor's choice of clothes which added years to him; dressed in a tweed jacket over a red striped shirt and a pair of chinos. He was a chap whose only purpose for wearing clothes was because it was essential to daily living.

Clearing his throat, the natty doctor spoke, at last. 'Aha, here it is.' Pulling out a yellow sheet of paper, pleased with his orderly chaos, he grinned with self-satisfaction. He seemed to have skimmed through the document, focusing on the essential paragraphs. 'Well, it's as Doctor

McCarthy suggested it might be, when we spoke. You have lesions on your brain, relating to Multiple Sclerosis. Judging by the brain activity, you're at the end of a relapse.'

The air had been punched out of her. Ines took a moment to process the news she'd suspected for a while now. To have those suspicions confirmed however, was a serious blow. Composing herself, Ines inclined her head and spoke in a slow and steady manner. Luke gripped her clammy hands. 'What kind of MS do I have? How long have I had it?'

'Well, judging by the lesions, it's estimated that you had your first relapse three years ago. This is the second one you've been through.'

Struck dumb, Ines remained wordless, staring bleakly back at the doctor.

'So, can Ines start treatment, like a disease modifying drug?' Luke croaked, trying and failing to conceal his distress.

The doctor looked over his glasses, impressed that Luke had pre-empted the diagnosis and had already done his research. Luke knew she had it before Ines knew herself. 'Well yes, I think this is a prudent step to take in order to delay disease progress.'

Like tight wire, every sinew and muscle within her body tensed until it hurt. This was all too much to absorb. Trembling, beads of tears began to creep out of devastated eyes.

Luke took control of the matter, allowing Ines time to consider everything. At the end of the consultation, it was agreed that she would have a meeting with Doctor Palmer to discuss treatment options. Saying a cheerful goodbye as if they'd just shared a cream tea together, the doctor opened the door and showed them out. 'I'll see you soon, Miss Garcia.'

***

Walking towards the Greek restaurant they had visited the week before, Luke snaked his arm around Ines' shoulders. 'So, do you want to message everyone later or shall I do it?'

In a daze, Ines muttered her inaudible reply. 'Can you do it, please?' Squeezing her tiny shoulder, Luke accepted his mission for the day.

Savouring the flavours of oregano and lamb cooked over charcoal, Ines took her time to indulge in the silken tender meat as it fell off the bone. Chewing heavenly mouthfuls, she didn't want her food to end. 'This is divine. Want some?' Waving the fork in front of his mouth, it was more a "try it or get a slap" offer. Opening his mouth wide enough to take the generous morsel, he smiled with appreciation as he began to chew, forming the universal symbol for perfect with his finger and thumb.

'So, any news from your boyfriend?'

Ines shook her head, dismissing the question as a pointless ask. 'I'll tell him if he asks or when I think he should know.'

'And your family?'

'I'll call them over the next few days. For now, I just need time to myself and get to grips with what's happening to me.'

'You know, I will be behind you every step of the way, yes?' promised Luke, stabbing a crunchy roast potato. 'Mmm, these potatoes are delicious.'

'I know you will be. Thank you.' Ines smiled through her reply.

Overhearing Luke, a cheerful Greek waiter appeared out of nowhere at their table. 'These are Cyprus potatoes, sir. They grow in copper rich soil which gives them the unique flavour and colour.'

Both looked at the olive skinned waiter with genuine interest at what he had explained. Obsidian eyes lined with thick lunate eyelashes shone as he spoke. 'Would you like to try the house dessert, mahalepi?

It's refreshing for this time of year. This is made with cornstarch and rose syrup.' His captive audience nodded in agreement.

Finishing the cooling sweet, Ines decided she wanted more, so she stole a large scoop out of Luke's bowl. 'That's another irritating habit of yours.'

'It's my birthday, allow it,' announced Ines, pulling a fatuous face as the piece of corn starch, laden with rose syrup, slid down her throat. 'What a day. Well, I won't be forgetting my date of diagnosis, that's for sure.' Immersed in profound thoughts, Ines took another spoonful of mahalepi from Luke's bowl.

Looking gravely at his dessert shrinking before his eyes, Luke snatched his dish away. 'So, are your plans for tonight involving an evening of copious debauchery or a civilised meeting of minds with your best friends?'

Thinking on the question, licking her spoon back to front, Ines considered her answer. 'Weeeell, Olivier isn't available, so I thought I'd spend it with you and the others.'

'Ooh, my lady, I am honoured. I win over Olivier Martinez.'

Seeing her giggling was so lovely. Ines' laugh could illuminate the darkest room. She had the most bewitching smile he'd ever seen in a woman. 'So, shall we just slope off work and get drunk at Fordhams? I don't think Bridget's expecting me to come back.'

'Deal.' Looking sexily assertive as he sought the waiter's attention, Ines had to reroute her thoughts. Admiring the pencil etchings which had been hung in no apparent order on the whitewashed walls, the sketches, depicted scenes of simple Cypriot life, stunning sea views and the famous Troodos mountain range. Captivated, she made a discrete note of the name of the areas which had been scrawled beneath each piece of artwork in artistic perpetuity.

Scraping back the wooden chair, Ines was the first to stand. Appearing out of nowhere, a waiter appeared holding her jacket with open arms. Uttering a bashful 'thank you' she shrugged her arms into the sleeves. 'How do I say thank you in Greek?'

'Efcharisto,' replied the genial waiter.

Articulating the word with astuteness as she sounded it out, the waiter clapped appreciatively. 'Bravo! You'll be speaking Greek before you know it.'

Luke shook the waiter's hand with fondness and thanked them all for such wonderful food. 'We will be back again soon,' he promised as he steered Ines, with cunning deftness, towards the door. She loved to chat, this he was sure of and her goodbyes were legendary for being long. She could be standing for another hour at the threshold, chatting away before she or her guests left.

***

The afternoon was as sunny and warm as the morning had guaranteed. It was hard to believe that they were in the middle of April. It was the kind of weather that filled people with optimism that summer was going to be long and blissful.

Meandering through the busy street brimming with international students, their chatter filled the afternoon air as they strolled alongside each other. Ines revelled in hearing the melody of different languages merging into one as they passed her by.

'Isn't London the best place to be on a sunny day? A melting pot of diversity and culture.'

Admiring the architecture surrounding them, Luke had to agree. 'Yes, it's lovely. We take it for granted because we live here. I bet all these visitors have seen more of London than we have.'

Seeing a large, picturesque square ahead of them, Ines excitedly pointed it out. 'Let's get a bottle of champagne and sit on the lawns!' Dragging him along with childlike enthusiasm, Ines had almost forgotten she was diagnosed with Multiple Sclerosis no more than three hours ago. It was her birthday, the sun was out and she'd think about it tomorrow. Tomorrow is a new day. Happy to be lead astray, Luke grumbled, feigning reluctance.

Walking into the aptly named Wine Cellar, Ines and Luke felt like two wayward teens looking for illicit booze.

'It's empty' whispered Ines, stifling a giggle.

'Sshh, they're going to think we're alcoholics with you behaving so shady.'

The sommelier surveyed them with dubious recognition. He'd seen their type before: city workers having an affair and seeking alcohol to heighten their passion. He was a short, wiry chap with a beaky nose and narrow lips. His beady eyes followed the now over excited pair, guffawing in the corner by the bottles of champagne. Losing his patience with the two imbeciles, the sommelier wandered over to them, assuming a need to clean the bottles of wine along the way.

'May I help you with anything?'

Choking back a laugh, Luke was the first to reply. 'Hi, umm yes… no…maybe. In fact, yes. Yes please!'

The little man looked up at Luke who stood eighteen centimetres taller than him. 'Is that a yes or a no, sir?'

'It's a yes!' Ines piped up. 'Yes please! *We* that is *us*,' waggling her finger between them both, 'would like some help *please.*'

Nodding stiffly, the little man smoothed his apron down and folded the microfibre cloth into three neat folds, before slipping the square piece down the generous front pocket. 'Is it a special occasion or are we being indulgent?' The little man was a patronising worm whom Luke found galling, most of all because Ines was being so nice, even though she didn't see that he was being an ass to her.

'It is a special occasion. My friend here is a quarter of a century old today.'

This induced a reaction in Ines when she heard an alternative way of saying twenty-five years old. 'You just made me sound old!' she pouted, batting his arm with the back of her hand.

'Very well, would you like to follow me?' The little man indicated with his palm in the direction of chilled special champagne. The two trailed behind him like mischievous children, poking one another, coaxing a reaction which had to be stifled. Their puerile behaviour hadn't gone unnoticed, but the uptight little man decided to ignore them. He found them tiresome.

Confident he'd picked champagne befitting of Ines' special day, Luke moved to the till where the pompous sommelier was waiting . Detecting a Bordelais accent in the man earlier in their encounter, Luke opened dialogue in his native tongue.

Not having detected so much as a lilt in Luke when he spoke English, the man was taken aback. Furthermore, he was not expecting the polite but ambiguous overtones coming from a stony looking fellow countryman. Bidding a terse farewell to a now po- faced sommelier, his paper-thin lips pursed in chagrin as he watched Luke march out with the bag in one hand and Ines hanging on to the other.

Convinced that she was skimming the air with the speed Luke was walking, alarm began to raise her heart rate when her little legs made every effort to keep up with the momentum.

'Can you slow down, please?' she puffed. 'What's happened?'

'Nothing. The man is an arse and there're times when speaking my mother tongue is more effective when another French person is involved.' Luke's tone was sullen. Ines rarely saw this side of her friend and assumed that he was mighty peeved.

Feeling more like a kite being dragged before its launch than a glamorous birthday girl, Ines tried to catch her breath. Oblivious, Luke continued with his furious pace, jostling through knots of crowds stopping to read their guides or to admire the views. Managing to wriggle her hand free from his firm grip, Ines took on a defiant stance, leaving Luke to march on alone. Realising that something was amiss, he looked over his shoulder to find her flushed with umbrage.

Taking pigeon steps towards him to emphasise her fragility, Luke slapped his forehead. 'Mon Dieu, I'm so sorry! I was so pissed with that prick at The Wine Cellar, I forgot I was holding your hand.'

'Dragging me, you mean,' corrected Ines. 'I don't know what this man did, but it's pretty obvious that he got on the wrong side of you.'

'I'm sorry, I was lost in thought. I promise to walk slooowly.' Offering an outstretched arm, Ines curled her fingers around Luke's hand, before they began walking at what was comfortable for her. Two minutes of dawdling and he was finding it a difficult task to keep to her snail's pace. 'Any slower and we'll be going backwards.'

'Shut it.'

'Okay.' Smiling to himself, Luke let Ines take the lead. It was her day after all.

***

Sitting on the freshly cut lawns, under an oak tree, the leathery rounded lobes provided a canopy of shade from the sun. Gazing up at its magnificence, Luke pointed out the strings of furry beads, dangling from its gnarled branches.

'They're catkins,' smiled Ines. 'Have you never seen these before?'

'Yes, but many years ago. When I was a kid I used to use them to tease the cat with…no pun intended.'

'No pun was noticed,' retorted Ines, fluttering her eyelashes. 'That's why I meditate, it makes me more aware and conscious of everything. Speaking of which, let's crack open the champagne.'

Ingots of shade danced across her legs as rays of sunlight peeked through the branches. Scrawling outlines around them with her finger, Ines hummed in tranquil gladness whilst she waited for Luke to pop the cork and pour the fizzing golden liquid into their plastic flutes. Raising his glass, he gave an enigmatic smile, making a toast to Ines. 'To being a quarter of a century. Happy birthday, you.' Clink. The plastic made a dull sound as the pair of friends saluted her being twenty-five. Savouring the bubbles as the drink trickled down her throat, Ines wrinkled her nose in delight. The sublime feeling was interrupted when her phone began to ring.

'Alright babe, you having a nice day?'

His face thunderous when Dylan's voice resonated through the phone; watching Ines speaking in the sweet manner that she always did, to that oaf, had Luke's stomach knotting in a ball of fury.

Flicking ringlets that danced in the breeze like ribbon streamers away from her face, Luke was unable to bear to listen or watch anymore. Getting up to remove himself from the dispiriting situation, he sloped away from earshot of the conversation and wandered across the lawns.

'...yeah, so I'm gonna be working late tonight. Important client to take out. I don't know what time I'm coming back, sorry about that.'

Ines had already written off an evening with Dylan which is why she'd made plans to be with her friends. 'Yes, that's okay. I understand your job's pretty heavy at the moment.' Mug.

'Thanks, babe. See you later, maybe. Yeah?'

Nodding down the phone, she was conscious of the fact that Luke had walked away, his disappointment evident in his body language. Keen to get Dylan off the phone, Ines said goodbye and flipped her phone back into her multicoloured shoulder bag.

Sensing that a leaden grey lid had drifted over them, threatening to end a dreamy afternoon, Ines waved across to Luke with unease. Damn Dylan and damn this ridiculous situation.

Taking his time to saunter across to where they were seated before being rudely interrupted, Ines figured that this was Luke's attempt at a protest walk. Smiling with affection, but tainted with guilt, she felt responsible for the glitch. Wincing in apology, a quiet hand beckoned for him to sit beside her.

'I'm so sorry, I wasn't expecting him to call. As it was, he only called to confirm what I already knew. He's not going to be joining me tonight.'

Raising his eyebrows suggesting that that was a given where Dylan was concerned, Luke took another swig from his glass. 'Beautiful. Truly excellent champagne. Anyway, today is your day, let's make it great.' He was peeved but had no intention of ruining Ines' birthday. She's not had the greatest day, all things considered. 'Thanks. You really are the best friend anyone can ask for.'

Ouch. That stung. Fer-rend. Friend.

'No problem, you deserve the best.'

***

In her favourite restaurant, situated near Camden Town, Ines was in her element. The Hummingbird specialised in Colombian food. It wasn't an upmarket eatery but the simple décor consisting of wooden tables and chairs, and brightly painted crockery added to its charm. The exposed walls were adorned with reclaimed oak shelves displaying colourful clay pots and plates. Along with the warm "home away from home" welcome, it reminded Ines of her grandparents. The food was like the food her abuela used to make. This was comfort food at its finest.

Shooting furtive glances over the chalked menu board in his hand at the small group of friends studying their food options, Luke found it hard to focus on the gastronomic offerings. His mind was on high alert while it ran across every possible eventuality that could occur this evening. Everyone had been categorically told *not* to mention the diagnosis until Ines was prepared to speak about it. Only she should bring the subject up.

Worrying for Luke, Zara looked fit to burst. Trying her hardest to practice restraint as instructed, she struggled to keep her mouth shut any longer.

'So, now you have the diagnosis, will you be on treatment ASAP? How are you feeling? We're all so worried about you, Ini,' she blurted the words before anyone could stop her.

Smacking the palm of his hand over a contorted face, Luke shook his head in dismay.

Ryan, dressed casually in a polo shirt and jeans smirked back at Luke; receiving a sharp poke, square in the hip from Sally. 'Sorry,' he whispered from the corner of his mouth.

Warmed by their efforts at being discrete, Ines placed her glass down. 'Guys, it's okay. You don't need to tread on eggshells around me. I need to talk about it openly anyway or I'll go nuts. If I'm honest, I'm scared. From my understanding, it's unpredictable. I'll have good days and bad days, relapses I can get through and others that may affect me for life. All I can do is take care of my mental and physical health and be surrounded by a good support network…which I already have.' Ines' smile was filled with genuine love as she looked around the table at four adoring faces.

'Oh Ini, you know that you are loved. We will always be there for you, the four of us.' Squeezing her friend's hand, Sally's silver-grey eyes carried Ines' gaze.

'Ahem. I think you'll find it's the *five* of us,' corrected Zara as she cradled her invisible bump.

'…and kudos to Zara for keeping quiet for longer than two minutes,' Luke quipped. The friends omitted from mentioning Dylan, seeing as he was the negative element in the equation.

'So, Ryan. I hear there's news on your part.' Luke gave Ryan an encouraging nod, suggesting that he should divulge his news.

Placing his fork back down onto his plate, Ryan squirmed, unused to the attention. 'Well, I've been offered a room in a hostel under the Housing for the Homeless Scheme. I moved in this evening. Well, it's not exactly difficult, I only have a rucksack with all that I own.' he joked.

'Anddd?' urged Sally

'And…well, The Amazing Coffee Company has employed me as their Ethical Sourcing Purchaser.' Blushing furiously, Ryan began morphing into a rose-blond gnome, his pointy ears turning into fiery red pinnacles.

'Whoop whoop, that's fantastic news. I'm so happy for you!' exclaimed Ines. 'This is a definite cause for a celebration. Well done. Amazing.'

Luke and Zara took turns in congratulating Ryan with equal gusto, whose evident discomfort of being the focus of everyone's attention had by now, affected the poor fellow, as he wiped tiny pearls of sweat away from his top lip, unsure of where to look other than down at the dregs of beer inside his glass.

'So, does that mean you'll be working with Sally?' asked Zara, with a crafty tip of the head. Wide eyed, Luke stared at her, disbelieving her audacity.

No sooner had the reddening dwindled, the flushing erupted once again, shaking his head with fervour. 'Oh no no, I'll be searching for products while Sally is out pitching sales at various stores and bars or eateries.' Pausing for breath, Ryan took advantage of the moment to compose himself for his next sentence. Looking humbly into Sally's eyes, the words flowed with ease. 'If it wasn't for Sally, I'd still be on the street.'

The bond between Sally and Ryan was there for all to see. The pair suited each other so well. Placid and genuine people, they deserved to be together. After the disastrous marriage Sally had been in before, Ryan was a gentleman who'd treat her like nothing else mattered.

'Sally saw the potential in you, and she provided you with the key to unlock the door when opportunity knocked. You, my friend, are the one who turned that key and opened it. You got the job yourself. Don't undersell your abilities,' Luke pointed out.

'Well said, hear hear!' said Zara speaking in between mouthfuls of chorizo. 'I have to say I think this is an amazing story. What a turnaround.'

For a few minutes, the group of friends ate in comfortable silence, relishing the variety of aromatic flavours on their plates.

Zara was the one to break the easy-going vibe. Securing a chunk of succulent beef and plantain with a toothpick, ensuring ease of retrieval when she'd finished saying her bit, her pretty round face was awash with anguish.

She looked troubled. Very troubled. 'Now that I'm with child, does this mean I can't use fillers or highlight my hair?'

Ines burst out into loud appreciative laughter. 'Shit Zara, by the look on your face, I thought that you were going to say something serious!'

Looking hurt and affronted, Zara protested the gravity of her concern. 'Well, I need to maintain my appearance. I can't look like a waddling bag of poop. Can you imagine if I bumped into Nick and his latest flame?' The genuine worry fuelled the guffawing coming from her friends.

Snorting between words, Sally was brave enough to speak up first. 'You will be blooming in your pregnancy and you won't need chemicals to enhance your beauty, sweetness. You don't need highlights. You have blonde hair anyway— and don't forget that your hair will be naturally sun bleached during the summer anyway. You'll be fine. As long as you and baby are healthy, that's all that matters.'

Zara wanted to remark about the infamous British summertime but continued to remain in silent dissent instead. Inclining her head in resignation, she popped the chunk of meat that had been under her watchful eye, into her mouth, luxuriating in the flavours of Colombia.

Making eye contact with Ryan, Luke smiled sagely. 'Sally's the voice of reason in this motley group.'

'Yes, I can see that,' replied Ryan, looking on at her in admiration.

Chapter 11

Back at her flat, it all seemed eerily quiet. Walking into an empty home wasn't anything new, but this time it felt strange. She left this morning buzzing at the prospect of a day with Luke, an evening with her beloved friends and an answer to her burgeoning health issue. Now she had returned, another casualty to MS, a birthday girl without her philandering boyfriend by her side and a wonderful time spent with her best guy friend (whom she harboured feelings for).

Metaphorically slapping herself into check, Ines knew that she wasn't Luke's type…granted she had a pulse so that passed for something, but he deemed her to be a buddy and now…well now, she had a degenerative disease which could render her disabled at some point in her lifetime. In her mind, she wasn't fit for purpose as far as girlfriend/wife material went.

Letting out a huge sigh, Ines slid her tiny feet into her new purple diamanté flip flops— a birthday gift from Zara no less, because 'we all need a little bling in our life, Ini.'

Flip flapping into the kitchen, Ines washed her hands with her fancy artisanal soap she'd bought on Luke's recommendation from a French market, whilst on a shopping trip together. Smiling at the memory as the soap began to form tiny pearlescent bubbles, Ines was startled by a loud thud.

Whipping her head round to see what it was, she made a futile attempt at adjusting her sight to the dimly lit hall. With one eye working and the other, although better was still not great, Ines squeezed her eyes, willing them to see properly. The figure walked in an arrogant swagger, a silhouette of bouncing curls and a broad muscular body. Dylan. Ines' heart skipped a beat, unsure of how to feel. Looking at her watch as he approached the kitchen, she noticed it was early in Dylan time.

'Alright babe, how was your day?' The man was brazen, she would give him that.

Surprised at his appearance, her throat had dried up. Trying to find her voice, she managed a squeak. 'It was lovely, thanks. Client meal go well?'

Nodding in affirmation, he walked over to the fridge. Foraging for something to eat, he managed to find some Parma ham and olives. Shovelling rolls of the thinly sliced pork, Dylan looked starved.

Baffled at his hunger, Ines lit a cigarette. 'You look famished, do you want a sandwich?'

Throwing a shiny black olive into his mouth, Dylan shook his head as he licked his lips. 'Nah, I just needed to fill a gap. It's been a long day.'

'So long that you've got yourself a bout of amnesia?'

Looking dazed and tired— stoned even, Dylan didn't reply.

He assumed Ines was talking her usual cryptic nonsense. 'I thought you ate with your client this evening?' Shit.

Master of turning an argument round on its head, Dylan reared like a bear. 'So what? I come in, a little high after a dinner meeting with my client, searching for something to munch and, well, I must be lying?' Intimidation. This technique was often adopted by him when he had to worm his way out of a situation. He would frighten Ines by convincing her that she was wrong, forcing her to retreat into a corner. Her mien, timid, Ines replied. 'I didn't say you were lying.'

With his face looming centimetres away from her nose, she turned her head away in disgust. Nausea swelled from the pit of her stomach; the stench on his breath, a potent combination of brine, beer and *her*. Ines felt her gut flip, churning bile and leaving an acidic taste in her mouth as she gulped. The least he could have done was brush his teeth before leaving his mistress.

'You've got a fucking cheek,' Dylan spat, his face darkening with rage. 'You've been out all day and night with your mates, looking like a slut dressed in those clothes,' waving his hand up and down to emphasise her outfit, his words spewed with venom '...while I've been working my arse off. Nah mate. You've got it wrong. You're a joker.' Shaking his head in self-righteous indignation, copper curls bounced like electrified springs out of his head.

Ines knew there was no point in arguing. He would justify having a mistress to go to because he wasn't getting any love from her. She was aloof and made him feel like he should be grateful when he was granted the privilege. None of which was true, but it was his way of feeling good about himself for doing what he does.

'I'm going to bed,' uttered Ines flimsily.

'Is that what people with MS do then? Sleep and walk like they're pissed all the time?'

He was vile. Vile to the core and Ines didn't want anything to do with him. She had her shower and got into bed, crying herself into a fitful sleep.

***

Waking up with hollow eyes, Ines realised that Dylan hadn't slept in her bed. Feeling as if someone had carved out her insides, she lay still listening for any sound of life outside the bedroom. Thinking about last night's altercation with him, Ines began to feel guilty. Was she wrong for making the judgment last night? Had she really smelled *her* on his mouth or was it paranoia? Maybe he was a little stoned and had the munchies. It's feasible.

Reaching for the phone, the time on the clock displayed 05:33. It was the crack of dawn and she was awake with the chickens. Calculating how much sleep she'd had in total, Ines rounded the figure to a total of three and a half hours.

Closing her eyes, willing for slumber to find her, if only for another hour, Ines tried to fall asleep. Her body and brain wracked with fatigue, she finally began to drift off…

ZING! The little ManThing that often tapped into her brain at night when she needed to rest the most, made an appearance. Of course, it did. Why wouldn't it? Little ManThing doesn't care if you have an important day ahead of you. If he wants to paralyse you with fear while you sleep, he will. If he wants to remind you of all the things that are troubling you, he will. Like treacle, he'll latch on to your thoughts and won't let go until it's time to rise.

This moment was no exception. 'How can I be paranoid? Those messages. Those photos. Those videos!' Images of her boyfriend and *her*, of their sex, everything which left nothing to the imagination came to the fore. He had been with her last night. Dylan always managed to turn everything into making Ines think she was the neurotic girlfriend. Manipulative sociopath. Zara was right. He was a sociopath. A narcissist. Just like Nick. Thoughts spread through her brain like poison. 'Go away! Think of fruits from A-Z…apple, banana…'

Waking up, fuzzy brained and groggy, Ines felt worse than she did when she awoke at the ridiculous hour of the morning. 'Ugh, I feel like shit.' Grumbling as she attempted to sit up, she knew that she had to move straight away, or she'd be inclined to remain under her warm cosy duvet. Scratching at gritty eyes, struggling to adjust to the light, Ines reluctantly stretched her bare legs out in front. Even with limited vision, she could see there wasn't a single hint of Dylan having even crossed into the room. Frowning with an overwhelming sense of dread sinking through her, she slipped her flip flops on and made for the bathroom. Another shower will freshen up her thinking.

Functioning solely on auto-pilot, Ines gingerly stepped out of the shower, yanking the hand towel off its perch, wrapping her wet hair. Leaning her head back, tucking the tail of the towel close to the nape of her neck, she let out a blood curdling scream. 'What the hell? You frightened the life out of me!' Dylan stood in the doorway grinning the stupid smirk that attracted her to him in the first place— amongst other things. 'I believe I live here, too. Why so surprised, heh?'

'Well duh, you're never here. So, I'm in my right mind to think I was alone,' Ines sideswiped with renewed confidence.

'Ouch.' Dylan appeared shamefaced…for a moment.

'In fact, I'm so used to being alone that I've decided from now on I'm going to bolt the door for my security. Anyone can get in. I'm vulnerable being on my own as a young woman.'

A rage shot through his body. Looming close enough over Ines for her to see the pores along the crevices of his flared nostrils, a black look washed over his contorted face. With a menacing thrust of his body towards the petrified young woman, his lip snarled into a curl.'Don't fuck with me, Ines. If I can't get in, I swear I'll smash that fucking door down. I don't give a shit!' Baring his teeth through a frothing mouth, Ines feared for her life, watching her boyfriend go ballistic. You're out of control, mate. You're behaving like a spoiled brat not getting their own way! Fucking princess!' he bellowed.

Driing, driing! shrilled Ines' phone.

Exchanging desperate glances, Dylan was fighting to break out of the swathe of red mist that had consumed him. He was close to slapping his girlfriend. Distressed and ashamed at his violent behaviour, he hesitated before suggesting to make a coffee by way of a peace offering. Snapping her eyes shut and turning her back on him was all the confirmation he needed.

Dylan's lumbering figure receded down the hallway to make himself a coffee. Ever paranoid, he lurked close enough to be out of Ines' eye view but within earshot to eavesdrop on whether he'd be the main topic of conversation.

'Ini Panini, are you okay? Shall we meet for lunch? I have to be in the office early this morning so I can't see you all for our usual pre-work rendezvous.' It was Zara. 'And I'm worried about you. We haven't had the chance to speak about yesterday's diagnosis.' Although she could be self-absorbed at times, when her friends were in trouble, Zara always stepped up.

'Morning, preggers. How are you and beanie?' Ines sounded normal. She disguised her anguish superbly. Dylan breathed a sigh of relief.

'We're fine, we are thinking about you.'

'Well, I'm fine. It's cool, honest. Can you do one o' clock today at Violets?'

'It's a date. See you later.'

Hanging up, Ines was left with a smile on her face— that short phone call was a gentle reminder that she wasn't alone.

Slathering cocoa body butter on her skin, Ines watched the goosebumps appear. As her hand glided along her limbs, a deep melancholy washed over her. These limbs were now hostages to a relentless and incurable condition. She was at the mercy of Multiple Sclerosis. The battle had commenced. It was her versus it.

Sitting on the chaise longue by the window, wrapped in her thick fluffy robe, Ines looked at the contents of her wardrobe, trying to figure out what to wear. The weakened sun had been struggling to shine through cauliflower shaped clouds drifting across a steel grey sky. What a difference a day makes, pondered Ines. Turning her attention back to the wardrobe, she rested her chin on the pad of her small hand. Sighing, she wished the outfit could just climb out and dress her itself. Not quite the fairytale existence of a princess. Plumping for a black sleeveless polo neck jumper, black cigarette pants and snakeskin ballet pumps, Ines got herself ready. Her makeup, was, as always, minimal but effective. A slick of red lipstick the colour of cherries on her plump mouth, a little highlighter on sharp cheekbones— features she was thankful to her mother's genes for, and finishing with a dash of mascara completed the look. Done. Alejandra always gave advice on how to take care of her skin and to never put too much makeup on.

'You colour your eyes or your lips, but never both.' Thinking about her mother reminded Ines that she had yet to tell her parents of her condition.

Ugh, not looking forward to the drama or explanation.

Spritzing some of her favourite perfume behind her ears and giving herself one last check, Ines grabbed her black leather shoulder bag and walked in short quick steps to the coat-hooks. Standing up on tip-toes, wriggling her fingers at the coat, a shirtless muscular arm stretched over her head and took a hold of the raincoat she had been reaching for. Nervous, Ines glanced to the side, frightened to look at him. Thanking Dylan, she scuttled off towards the front door. Intent on making Ines look at him, Dylan spoke in hushed tones.

'You smell nice. In fact, you look great, too.' Dylan was looking at Ines with fresh eyes, as though he'd forgotten how naturally beautiful and classy his girlfriend was. 'Is this for anyone's benefit?'

An hour ago, this man was close to smacking her.

Perplexed, she turned to face Dylan. Averting her eyes from his taut stomach and the fine trail of copper hair leading to his groin, was difficult. Wrapped around his trim waist was a towel not leaving much to the imagination. Oozing self-confidence and sex appeal, he threw a lustful glance at her. Leaning nonchalantly against the wall, his left hip jutted in Ines' direction. At this very moment, she hoped his towel would not slip to the floor. Clearing her throat of stifled words, the demure young woman attempted to articulate her reply.

'No, it's not for anyone's benefit. You don't see it because you're away at "work" all the time.' She waggled both sets of fingers to quote unquote— being so close to the front door gave her courage to get feisty. Retorting with patronising sarcasm Dylan rolled his eyes, shaking bulbous droplets of water hanging at the ends of curls over his shoulders. 'Well, I can't help it if I have to earn a living, my love.'

Bridling, Ines chose to rise above his uncouth attitude. 'I have to get to work or I'll be late. Will you be here tonight?'

Winking with mischief, he cocked his shoulder. 'Dunno. I'll see if the client wants a follow up meeting. I'll let you know.'

***

Watching Ines close the door behind, he laughed to himself at how she was so easy to manipulate. She could never be angry or hold a grudge for long. Unlike Jenna. She could be a moody cow sometimes but was always so eager to please him if it meant being in his good books. She was needy and Dylan liked that because she was always grateful. He liked grateful girls.

Ines on the other hand was fiery when it was called for but generally a very sweet natured girl who always saw the good in people. Dylan often called her gullible. She is also not in need of money. At twenty-five years old, she worked as a senior buyer for a large department store and owned a Georgian flat in an exclusive part of London. She was also stunning and had a fit little body. A great package, all in all. However, she also had MS which could mean that there was potential for her to be reliant on him for emotional, physical and financial support. *Hmmm this is something I need to think about*, reflected Dylan, sauntering back to the shower.

Under the cascading water, Dylan's mind wandered to thoughts of he and Jenna yesterday afternoon. She knew what he liked and wasn't afraid to vocalise how much he turned her on, either. A lecherous smile crept across his face when he pictured how he'd often have to hush her groans of pleasure. Feeling flush with erotic recollection, he stepped out of the shower and grabbed his phone. Hungrily scrolling through his videos and images, he found one video they made yesterday. Pressing play with a damp thumb, his breathing became shorter and more desperate as the video of their sex was played in high-definition sound and vision. Becoming hotter as he stroked himself into frenzied pumping, Dylan was insatiable.

Chapter 12

Walking languidly through the square, Ines' head was filled with thoughts of Dylan as she tried to decipher the events leading to this morning's confrontation. True to her character, she set about piecing the clues together with meticulous precision: the preceding months of his behaviour merged into a huge complex knot; the hold-all, the texts and all the media she found. Images and videos she had seen as he slept on the sofa, leaving her shaken to the core. His trips away, dinners with clients, smelling *her* on his mouth.

Any sane person would say 'get rid of him' but then in her infinite wisdom, she chose to believe his lame excuses … because they were plausible. However, excuses are only conceivable, reasoned Ines, if they don't have solid proof of a mistress. The Little Man Thing was dogging her thoughts so much so that she hadn't realised she'd stepped into the road.

TINGALING TING TING TING!!!

'Watch where you're going, I could've knocked you over!' An

angry cyclist fully kitted out in Lycra and Hi-Vis attire stopped within millimetres of Ines' quaking legs.

Visibly shaken, Ines apologised profusely. 'I...I'm so sorry. I wasn't paying attention.'

The cyclist shook his head in aggressive disapproval and rode off not caring for her explanation.

'BELL-END!!' yelled Sally, from the other side of the road, who had witnessed everything with Luke and Ryan.

Like a smear of navy lightning streaking across the roadway, Luke was suddenly in front of Ines, holding onto her shoulders, his large arms accentuating her petite frame.

'Is life so bad that you choose to go kamikaze by a cyclist, my little butterfly? If you want to do this, may I suggest something more extravagant, like maybe the Aston Martin over there, hmm?' Laughing nervously, Ines took hold of his arm and allowed herself to be led to where Ryan and Sally were waiting. Disconcerted as he gazed up at the threatening slate grey sky, Ryan made a prudent suggestion: 'Let's go inside, it looks like rain is on the way.'

Together, the friends walked in, still rattled by what they had witnessed a few minutes ago.

The girl at the counter who'd been the mediator during the spat between Ines and Luke over whom was paying for the breakfast, greeted them both with a wary expression, upon seeing them following Ryan and Sally into the café.

Detecting her apprehension straight away, Ines pulled Luke closer, smiling broadly as they passed. It was an unspoken act of assurance that the young barista would not be a party to another dispute. Returning the gesture with a grateful smile, she nodded, acknowledging the silent confirmation of accord between her and the "tall, fit guy"—words Ines once overheard the barista use to describe Luke to her colleagues.

Seated in the far corner of the café away from the draft of the door, Luke poured coffee from a large steel pot. It was strange to have Ryan sitting at the table joining them for breakfast, as opposed to the bench close to where he spent his days hanging his head low in the vague hope that someone might contribute a few coins, thus enabling him to get a hot meal. Watching the animated discussion between the three friends, Luke reflected on how funny life was. Unpredictable and beautiful at times, tragic and unjust at others.

Looking at dear sweet Ines, life for her was tragic and unjust while Ryan fell into the unpredictable and beautiful category. Clicking back into reality after hearing dramatic gasps coming from Sally, his attention turned to the girls.

'Is he for real!? I can't believe he said that. What did you do?' Ryan remained typically quiet. Merely offering half a smile and raising his eyebrows at Luke with an 'I'm keeping out of this one' look, he took another bite of his breakfast.

'W…well, I said nothing. I just went to bed. This morning he was still there and made a comment about how nice I looked and was it for anybody's benefit?'

Luke analysed Ines' body language from over a hot cup of coffee, ribbons of steam licking his face. He watched her unflinchingly. Sally and Ines were too enthralled in their conversation to notice anything— in particular, Dylan walking at a brisk pace past the coffee shop, talking on the phone. He looked so shifty, so slimy that Luke had an insane urge to run out and smack him on his chiselled jaw line. Sense prevailed when Ines interrupted his violent fantasies of knocking the crap out of Dylan there and then. '…haven't you, Luke? … Luke?'

'Umm sorry I was in another world. What did you say?' Chewing at a snail's pace, Ryan gave Luke a knowing smile. 'I'm just telling Sal how wonderful you've been.'

Picking at the almonds with his finger (Zara would be impressed) and sucking them up, Luke shrugged in the easy-going style he was known for. 'It's no more than what Ines would have done for me, I'm sure.'

'You two, you're just so bloody cute together. You'd make a lovely couple,' swooned Sally.

Cough, cough, splutter. Ines almost choked on her coffee. Patting her back vigorously, Sally leaned forward to look at Ines' scarlet face. Her eyes watery from hacking so much, their table had now attracted the attention of other customers.

The young barista at the counter came rushing over with a glass of water. 'Here, take this. Sip it slooowly.' She emphasised the word for added effect. Unable to speak without exploding into another coughing fit, Ines could only nod her gratitude as she hung her head close to her chest. Torn between politesse and ensuring her friend didn't keel over, Sally's face broke into a gentle smile.

'Thanks, she'll be okay. I think the coffee went down the wrong way.'

'Are you sure, madam? If it's a reaction to anything you've purchased here, we need to log it.'

Shaking her head determinedly, Ines spluttered. 'It… it's fine.' Cough, cough. 'It just went down the wrong way.'

'Okay, if you're sure.'

Ines began mopping her eyes with the serviette Luke handed to her. 'It's actually the effect I have on her,' he said, grinning back at the concerned face on the barista.

Smiling at the handsome pair in front of her, she looked dreamy, 'I hope to have that same effect on my boyfriend one day.'

'What? Make him choke?' enquired Ryan, drily.

'No ha-ha. I mean, to find someone who can be so loving.' That. Was.It. As if someone had tasered them both, Luke and Ines whipped their heads round to face her. Having two stunned people denying the absurdity that they were a couple had confounded the poor young barista.

Clapping her hands as if in prayer, Ines exclaimed, 'oh my good God no! We're very good friends. THAT IS ALL!'

Rooted in his place, Luke reciprocated the emphatic statement. 'No no, we really are just good friends. I'm very much single. It was just our silly Sal getting ahead of herself, which lead to Ines spitting out her coffee.'

Her face a vision of pained conviction, Ines feigned enthusiasm in support of Luke's monologue.

Looking relieved at what she'd just heard, the barista smiled sweetly. 'I apologise for any provocation. It isn't that obvious.'

Regardless of her embarassment, the barista took a leap of faith. 'B…but if you are single, then maybe I can invite you out for a coffee.' There was a beat and neither spoke. Swallowing hard, she dared not meet his gaze. The spotlight was on Luke, who was now lapping up the attention. It wasn't often he got propositioned by a pretty young barista this early in the morning. Leaning back on his chair, he opened his kid leather wallet and pulled out a business card. 'I'll leave it up to you.' Watching her slip his card into the back of her skinny black jeans, he appeared satisfied with the brief exchange.

'I'll call you later, then.' The tone, loaded with ambiguous promise, made Ines squirm with jealousy at the thought of what could develop between the café worker and her friend.

'What's your name, by the way?'

Pointing to the badge on the lapel of her shirt, the girl laughed in huskier tones compared to the sweet intonation she had been using. 'Amelie.'

Familiarity swept across Luke's face at the mention of the coquettish young woman's name spoken with a French inflection. Unable to conceal his pleasure at meeting a fellow countrywoman, Luke's shining eyes danced. 'You're French? From where?'

And so, a French tête à tête between them unfolded, and all Ines could do was smile helplessly at the connection between Luke and Amelie. It was Ines' turn to feel like she was rooted down by a boulder. Amelie was pretty, French and single— and Luke was going to meet up with her.

***

As she waltzed into the empty foyer, Michael couldn't contain his enthusiasm in seeing that the ray of sunshine that was Ines, had returned and she was armed with two large cake boxes from Patisserie Lydia. 'Good morning, hello and welcome back!' he bellowed with arms wide open.

Falling into his big arms, Ines likened the embrace to a bear hug. He was larger than life. Michael was as tall as he was broad, engulfing her. 'Oomph,' puffed Ines as he brought her close to his armpit.

Conscious of the boxes being precariously balanced in her hands, she didn't fancy them toppling over. Withdrawing with an artful sidestep from his grip, Ines slid them onto the reception desk and twisted back round to Michael, attempting to encompass him with her spindle like arms.

'So, how have you been? Everyone has been worried about you. What's happening?' Michael had become serious in his tone, folds of concern stretched across his brow.

Not seeing the point in beating around the bush with what she had to say, Ines came straight out with it; 'Well, it was as I had suspected for a long time. I was diagnosed yesterday with Multiple Sclerosis…and it was my birthday. Yay, happy birthday to me.' A faint smile slid across her mouth, at the irony in what she'd said. 'So, today I bring cake for all and I start a new day adjusting to the new me.'

Upset for his favourite Smythe & Co. employee, Michael spoke quietly. 'You are strong and you will get through this. It is bad news but you have a lot of support, and you know, modern medicine is great.'

'Yep, well we shall see. What will be will be. Here, take some cake.' Swiftly flipping the lid of the patisserie box for Michael to have first dibs, Ines glowed with sisterly affection as she watched his face light up. Michael chose an enticing looking choux slice which guaranteed thick sheets of fresh cream to ooze out of the sides when he bit into it. Delicious. Smiling at his choice, Michael popped the pastry behind the desk. 'I'm going to have this with a tea, in a minute. Thank you.' Squeezing his eyes with delight, he blew her a kiss. 'Happy birthday, Ines.'

Laughing at his cheek, Ines thanked him and made her way to the elevator. Pressing the button to call it down, she gave Michael a little wave with her hands tucked beneath the boxes.

'Oh and Ines, I think your boyfriend is a merda and Luke is the man for you!'

Taken aback by his comment, Ines shook her head in bewilderment. Her broken Portuguese enabled her to understand that "merda" meant "shit". 'You're funny!' her laugh, louder than she intended.

Watching as she entered the lift, Michael called out, 'I wasn't trying to be funny!'

As the elevator ascended through the levels, looking at her reflection in the smoke tinted mirror, Ines contemplated Michael's words. *What did he mean? What does he know that I don't?*

'Fifth floor' The tinny voice resonated through the speaker, breaking her train of thought. *Oh well, too late to ponder anything more.* The door hissed as it glided open.

The familiar heady scent of lilies enveloped Ines like an old friend as she took small steps out of the elevator. Like eager children waiting for their parents to collect them from nursery, it seemed that the entire buying and merchandising team were waiting for Ines to arrive. First to greet her was Stevie, followed by David and the buying assistants, who were sitting around Serena's desk. Visions of the Pendle Witches were once again mustered when she clapped eyes on her colleagues. For a moment, she felt guilty but that contrition receded as quickly as it had appeared, on seeing them huddled close together with matching wing lined eyes and poker straight hair. Yes, it was a befitting nickname for them. 'Hello stranger, how are you feeling?' Stevie threw a complaisant arm around her. Delicate wisps of grapefruit and verbena piqued Ines' nose when she rested her face against his shirt front, allowing herself to be wrapped in Stevie's refuge.

A whiny squawk rang through the air, interrupting the warm fuzzy feeling between the two of them. 'Iiiiines we've been so worried about you.'

Oh well. It was good while it lasted. Groggy with contentment, Ines lifted her head off Stevie. 'Helloo,' Ines smiled lazily. 'That's very sweet of you, guys. I'm okay, really. Thank you. Let me just pop these on my desk and get sorted. I'll tell you all about it. Who's making tea?'

Echo couldn't help but seize an artful glance at the two large Patisserie Lydia boxes in Ines' arms. Feigning indifference yet hoping the goodies were for them and not for the hierarchy to have in a meeting, she tried valiantly to put them out of her mind.

Bumping her brusquely into the fore, Martha nominated a vacant looking Serena to make teas and coffees. Frowning and mumbling her disapproval at her co-worker's delegation technique, Serena announced that she'd need help for such a big task. 'Martha, you can help me carry them through. Come on. The sooner we do it, the sooner we can hear what Ines has to say.'

Martha shot back a piercing stare, her lips pursed like dried prunes.

Taking everyone's orders with military efficiency, Martha went to the staff kitchen and lined up all the cups, creating a lively burst of colour whilst Serena began to operate the coffee machine, her mind lost in the process of the job at hand.

'OOOH WAIT!!' exclaimed Martha, her hands splayed out in panic.

The jug of coffee beans fluttered in Serena's grip. 'Christ, you made me jump!' Serena had been concentrating on pouring the correct amount of beans into the grinder with such diligence that Martha had taken her by surprise.

'I just want to take a couple of pictures of the beans, the machine and then the cups,' added Martha hurriedly, sweeping her hand in an elaborate arc, along the row of cups. 'Like a step-by- step process of morning coffee ritual in the office, y'know?' she said, with a sense of self-importance.

'So, y…you make a story for everything, even making coffee?' 'Uh huh, yup #freshcoffee #worklife #winning.'

Opting to keep her mouth shut, Serena let Martha take her pictures as she proceeded with making the beverages.

Walking back on to the office floor, Serena indicated that the teas and coffees had arrived, and the first table she had reached was as far as she was going. 'If you want your drinks, come and get them.'

Gathered around Ines' desk, apprehension loomed above the small group like a storm filled cloud on the horizon. The sensual aroma of vanilla and amber drifted in tenuous swathes from Ines' silk neck-scarf with every skilful move she made around the desk, lifting the lids off the patisserie boxes. Like an apparition materialising out of nowhere, Bridget had appeared.

Frozen and dumbfounded with shame at the sudden realisation that nobody had thought to inform their boss of the cosy meeting, the team smiled their guilt at her. The unexpected guest peered with eager curiosity over Ines' shoulder, unaware of six pairs of eyes following her gaze, expectantly. Engaged in watching her, the co-workers had been rewarded with sheer drollery. You would think that their boss had discovered the holy grail. Bridget's face beamed like a pink light bulb in the reflection of the cerise foil casing, scrutinising the mouth-watering contents, her focus so intent on an éclair. David was certain that she was going to bore a hole into it. To be fair, all eyes were feasting on the magnificent sight.

'It was my birthday yesterday, so I thought I'd bring in some treats seeing as I wasn't here to share it with you…and I didn't have any cake yesterday,' announced Ines.

As if on cue, the sextet, broke into birthday song and cheers of adulation for the birthday girl.

Radiating a warm show of thanks as she did a little curtesy, Ines poked the box. 'Right, help yourselves.'

A hum of gratification resounded in the office as everyone took their choice of pastry before withdrawing to redundant desks.

Supping hot drinks and attempting to nibble their heavenly treats with decorum when really, they'd be smacking their lips and licking their fingers if they were alone. The atmosphere, although buoyant, was tainted with certain foreboding.

For what seemed like an eternity, the wait had begun to unnerve the patient group; the shuffling of restless feet could be heard scratching along polished laminate floors. Taking the initiative, Martha instigated an irrelevant conversation about planting lavender in the summer months, as they waited in painful civilised silence, waiting for Ines to wash down a morsel of pistachio macaron with her coffee. Observing her every move, her co-workers could be forgiven for not being distracted by Martha's inane witterings.

'Fookin' hell Ines. Can you chew any slower? The suspense is killing us, lassie.'

'Do shut up, David!' exclaimed Martha. 'Let the poor girl take her time. Not everyone shovels food down their gullet like you. Some people like to savour what they eat.' Martha's haughty chastising had visibly irked David.

Foreseeing another argument between two of the most hot-headed members of the team, Ines took a huge gulp, swallowing the last piece and clearing her throat. Disgusted, Martha threw a fearsome glare back at David for making Ines rush.

'Ye carry on with yer lips all squeezed up. Ye look like a balloon knot— an' aam not talkin' the kind that you inflate either.' A stifled chuckle came from behind Stevie's hand. Evidently unaware of the urban definition, Martha made a silent vow to research the term he used and spit in David's tea next time she was on beverage duty. How dare he belittle her! Martha could think of nothing better to retaliate with. Frustrated, she shot a middle finger up, in front of her angry red face, regretting the childish practice in an instant.

Delighted at having reduced her to such an uncharacteristic reprisal, David's laughter boomed across the office, the apples of his cheeks crawling to the corners of his eyes with a conceited wink, exacerbating Martha's irritation.

Predicting a row of epic proportions, Ines swiftly interjected. 'Ahem. 'So, I'm not going to make this long. You know me, straight to the point.'

The group collectively nodded and laughed knowing all too well what Ines was like.

'The last few months have been tough and the past couple of weeks more so. Yesterday, I was diagnosed with MS. I have no idea where I go from here and to say that I'm a little lost and scared is an understatement.' Swallowing hard on her words, Ines felt as if she'd eaten a handful of shattered glass. 'I'll work it out somehow, I just need you all to please bear with me.' Dipping her head low so that nobody could see the emotion in her eyes, she dabbed at them with a tissue she'd retrieved from her coat pocket.

A ghostly silence fell across the room. Not one person had expected this. Dumbfounded, nobody deigned to move.

Stepping forward first, was Bridget. 'Ines, the diagnosis is a shock, but not a surprise. Watching you over recent months, especially the last two, has told me that there is something very wrong. My best friend has it, so I've seen all these things before. Look, we can talk later if you want.'

Feeling brave enough to look up, Ines and Bridget's eyes met. 'Ooh I'm sorry to hear that. How is she?'

With a doleful tilt, Bridget shook her head slowly. 'She has bad days and good days, but the bad are currently more prevalent. Let's talk more in depth, later.' Smiling, she patted Ines on the arm and returned to her office.

'I think the best thing to do is carry on as normal and roll with the punches as and when they happen,' said Echo distractedly whilst dusting a speck of filo pastry from her chin. Echo had been so blasé about her statement, that she underestimated the effect her short but poignant words would have. Everyone seemed surprised by her psyche. Blissfully unaware of her team's judgement, she carried on munching her 'sinful' sweet, guiltless. The talking to that Ines gave her regarding draconian diets a few weeks ago apparently didn't fall on deaf ears. In fact, she had lost more weight through her co-worker's advice than ever before!

'Well aye, have to agree with ye, Echo. Take each day as it comes, start ye treatment and stay as healthy as ye can,' added David.

Echo nodded, happy that her view had been taken on board. 'Right, on that note, move these cakes away from me before I scoff the lot of them!' Marching over to Ines' desk, she slid the boxes aside determinedly. 'Ines, we are all here for you in some capacity. Please don't hesitate to ask for help. We can be sensible too, you know?' She gave Ines a long hug before returning to her work station.

'Echo is most definitely right in everything she has said. We are one big family. Remember, it's okay to not be okay.'

'For God's sake, Martha! Why is it that everything that comes out of yer mouth has to sound like it heralds from a mindfulness website?' groaned David.

'It's all part of the social media experience. Everything is about the mind, soul and spirit,' mocked Stevie, holding two fingers up in a peace sign.

'Oh, please shut up!' hissed Martha. 'You two nay sayers are ignorant to the core. Maybe if you practiced the art of meditation and self care, you'd understand.'

'#bekindtoyourself' teased Stevie.

'#kissmyhairyScottisharse!' David piped in.

The two churlish men roared with laughter, Stevie half spluttering out his cake, half wiping away the tears, ignited a further episode of hilarity.

'Bloody imbeciles,' sneered Martha as she flounced off back to her desk.

Chapter 13

Tucking her legs beneath her bottom, Ines had been unaware that she had been chewing her lip, thinking about nothing in particular as she gazed out of the French windows.

Looking out across the courtyard, she knew how lucky she was to have not only the freehold on this flat, but to own the space outside. It was a real find, thanks to Luke.

As with the inside of her home, the outside had been well thought out. From the brightly painted planters, to the jasmine lined walls and vibrant pink geraniums, it was her little piece of fragrant heaven. The afternoon sun radiated a warm glow over the enchanting little garden, creating a rosy tinted ambience in the lounge. Not however, cosy enough to warrant sitting on the phone and divulging her news to her parents. She needed a cigarette and coffee.

It had been three days since her diagnosis and Ines had yet to call her family with the news. It was Sunday afternoon, she was on her own (as usual) and she was not doing anything in particular. Having completed an hour of Pilates and meditation, the flat was clean and she had spoken to all her friends except for Luke. He was on a second date with the alluring Amelie. A *second* date, marvelled Ines. They obviously hit it off, she griped, begrudging of their new-found happiness. Consulting her phone for the time, she slapped it back down on the arm of the cracked leather sofa, angry at herself for even allowing her thoughts to be consumed by the "happyity happy" pair.

It was 16:23. They are probably walking through the park, and she is more than likely pretending to be a cool chick who's fine with their boyfriend going out with the boys, loves watching football, isn't possessive, blah blah blah. As for him, he would be feigning interest when actually, he would be trying to figure if she'd succumb to his advances on their second date. Ines didn't want to think about him or his French "copine" anymore. It would drive her crazy. It was bad enough having hard copy images of Dylan and *her* to contend with, let alone envisaging Luke and Amelie.

Turning the coffee machine on, Ines began to think about how she'd have to explain and reassure her parents that everything wasn't as bad as it might seem when she broke the news to them. Taking deep breaths and exhaling slowly, she focused on the clouds from the window. Watching puffs of cloud bumping each other out of the way as the afternoon sun vied for space, the coffee machine gurgled and spluttered the viscous liquid into her cup, the rich aroma inducing her thoughts. Deliberating with herself, Ines concluded that she'd have a cigarette first and then drink her coffee whilst speaking on the phone.

This was the best way forward. At least when she wanted to take her time to decide on a response, her stalling tactic would be to take a sip of coffee… or light up yet another cigarette, (which according to all the MS websites she'd researched, was discouraged for her condition, along with ingesting sugar, gluten, alcohol and dairy). She was prepared to live a healthy life, but she wasn't prepared to live life denying herself of the few pleasures she had. Everything in moderation would prevent gorging. Yes, that was her belief and that was how she was going to continue.

Stubbing out the cigarette in the Fordhams ashtray, Ines bit the bullet and unlocked her phone. It read; 17:01. Crikey, where did thirty-eight minutes go?! Double checking, she looked up at the clock. Bum. It was right.

Scrolling down to her mum's number first, it seemed that the butterflies in her chest had formed into one inflated mass, crushing from within. Hitting dial, Ines held her breath in anticipation.

'…so, what can you do? Is it because I didn't pay you enough attention, that it's caused so much stress and now it's triggered th…th… this response?'

Oh, great. Now for the melodrama.

'No Mum, nobody's to blame. It's just one of those mysterious things. It's okay, stop fretting. Everything will be fine, don't worry.' 'But I don't understand.' Alejandra began to break. Uh oh.

'Why you, why my daughter. My niñita!' And it started.

Ines found herself in a position of having to reassure and comfort, when she was the one in need of exactly that.

After a lengthy conversation of explaining to her mother as much as she knew herself, Ines hoped it would appease Alejandra. Finally conceding to respect Ines' request to not be harassed and that everything was still the same, Alejandra sniffled. 'Okay my darling. If you need me, I'll be there in a flash.'

By no means a pessimist, Ines was, however, realistic and knew not to rely on her mother's ability to turn up when needed. The well-intended promise wasn't plausible. Her mum couldn't possibly be here in a flash. 'Thanks Mum, I'll let you know, if that day should come.'

One phone call down, two more to go. Through experience, Ines knew it was better that she should call her dad before her brother as this has been known to cause upset on occasion, when it transpired that he was the last to know.

Pouring herself a glass of water, Ines already felt drained and had only spoken to her mother. In the forty- five minutes they spent talking, the sun fell behind bluish-grey clouds, surrendering to imminent rainfall. For a moment, she thought that she had caught a glimpse of Dylan on the far side of the square. The stature and confident strut resembled him but with impaired vision, she couldn't be certain. He had seemed to develop a routine of being back for a night every two to three days, was never home at weekends, only to return on Mondays to start the cycle again. *It's impressive how well planned his hectic work schedule is*, she mused.

Speaking to her father was a test of her patience at the best of times, but having his girlfriend chirruping in the background, Ines found it hard to convey her reason for calling. His girlfriend was a Lithuanian "model" half his age. In fact, she was three years older than Ines, which was all a bit weird for her to fathom. Her step mum was pretty much the same age as her best friends.

'...so, what's this illness, then?' asked her dad who seemed distracted. 'I mean are they even sure?'

Sighing with resignation, Ines replied. 'Yes Dad, I had an MRI and it's been confirmed.'

'Ouch! Hun, be careful! Sorry, Lina's massaging my back… carry on.'

Ines cringed at the thought of her dad being massaged and she abhorred the word hun. Hun. Hun as in Atilla? Ugh. Even more weird was how his young girlfriend could even be intimate with him. Momentarily, her stomach turned at the nauseous image. Her dad's deluded belief that this girl was with him for anything but his affluence was a bone of contention for Ines, but she had accepted this as an impasse and that she should just remain silent on the matter. Returning to the situation at hand, she became agitated by her dad's lack of interest. 'Are you really listening or are you just hearing me? Because right now, this conversation is about your back massage and what a wonderful masseuse your girlfriend is!'

'Of course, I'm listening, it's just that Lina doesn't like it when I don't relax during a massage. She says it spoils the chakras.'

Ines had heard it all now. 'You're getting a chakra massage?' Thwarted with the call, she was rapidly losing her patience. 'Look, I'll just go. I've done my duty and told you. If you're interested, read up on it. I'll speak to you when you're not busy.'

'Hmmmph aah, that's good. Yeah there… Okay, we'll speak soon. What's it called again…the illness?' Enough! That was the straw that broke the camel's back. Ines' throat tightened as she fought back the frustration that threatened to burst. 'Multiple Sclerosis!'

'Huh? What was that?' His muffled voice receded, as the phone that Ines had tossed, rattled across the floor, reflecting her disdain.

'Bloody pointless talking to him.' Wiping droplets from the corners of her eyes with the back of a sleeve marked with salty tears, they turned to large beads chasing every last one down the contours of her face into a relentless outpouring of emotion. It was then that she began to weep for her newly diagnosed self.

Lying with trembling knees pulled in, the cold flagstone provided relief as the temperature rose within her, recollections of the time she got overheated in the bathroom, a crude reminder of what can happen if she didn't take stock of the situation. Shuddering at the thought of history repeating itself, she decided to remain where she was and wait for the episode to pass. Curled into a wretched ball, Ines searched for an answer from above, her angst now imploring, as she chanted the same words over and over again. *Why me?* Her frenzy of highly charged emotion was broken when the phone began to ring a tinny shrill, vibrating over the stone floor.

Unable to find her voice or catch her breath, with the little strength her arms had, she pulled the phone towards her ear.

'Ini, it's me. Are you okay?'

The voice, heavy with sadness and barely recognisable to her, Ines mumbled. 'Who's speaking, please?'

'Ini it's me, Marco. Mum's just called and told me.' Of course, she did. 'Shall I come over?'

Never had Ines heard her brother so concerned. Her sobs rapidly became wails as she tried to explain everything to him. 'I'm scared, Marco. I'm scared of what's going to happen to me.'

Marco's voice creaked under the strain of trying not to break down. Hearing his big sister like this seared through him like a hot knife. 'Mum said that your boss will talk to you…her best friend has it? She'd be a good source of information.'

Agreeing and making tiny whinnying noises as her brother spoke,

Ines somehow felt that it was she who was the younger sibling, clinging on to every word he was saying.

Without warning, she heard the sound of footsteps creeping through the hallway. Weary, she hauled herself away from the steel base of the island, managing to bring her body onto all fours, and began to crawl towards the door.

'Ini, are you still there?'

'Yes, yes I am,' she whispered quickly. Sliding the phone down her sports bra, she began inching closer to the kitchen door.

Arriving to face a pair of faded jeans, Ines raised her head to see who the owner of the legs blocking her way, was.

'Well, that's just the welcome I like to come home to.' Dylan. Her cheeks now suffused with a deep flush of red, the dishevelled young woman sat back on her heels. 'Ooh it's you.' Her relief soon turned acerbic. 'I wasn't expecting you to come back until tomorrow night. That's your usual set up.' Ines sounded as dour as her words. 'You're never here at weekends.'

Forgetting that her brother was still on the line, she started the onerous task of getting to her feet. Looking him in the eyes, Ines continued, brazenly. 'I was going to double lock the door. Just as well you did walk in.'

His eyes flashed with menace. 'I told you, Ines, don't fuck with me. I'd have broken the door down.' The tone, intimidatingly calm, spooked Ines into retreat.

By now, she had completely forgotten to end her call to Marco. He could hear every word being spoken. Seething, her brother made a promise. 'One day mate, you're going to come unstuck, you wait.'

'What's with the puffy face?' Dylan sneered. 'You look like you've done a round with Tyson.'

Sweeping frays of loose curls, Ines became self-conscious of the fact that she looked wrecked.

Licking dehydrated lips and smoothing her eyebrows into shape, she stumbled over her words. 'I've been on the phone to my family.'

'Well, that's enough to send anyone over the edge, I suppose.' Insouciant, Dylan started walking back to the lounge with a slice of buttered spice bread and cheese he'd found on the work-top. He hadn't even asked if Ines was going to eat it.

Ignoring his snipe about her family, Ines continued talking as she followed him down the hall, like a lamb following its mother. '...and it got me realising the seriousness of my condition. S...so, I had a meltdown, then Marco called.'

Marco! She forgot to end her call. Hoping he'd hung up earlier, Ines pulled the phone out and checked. Phew. He'd hung up.

In the lounge, Ines had made a point of sitting in the arm chair positioned near the French doors and more importantly, away from Dylan.

'So, where do you stand now on how you feel about it?' Dylan sounded as if he had an ulterior motive for the question.

'What do you mean?'

'Well, about your future. About us, our life together. That kind of thing.'

The question posed had thrown Ines off kilter. She wasn't expecting him to want to discuss their future. Her emotions twisted like knotted snakes, Ines battled with the logical and the sentimental as she tried to construct an answer. 'Well, erm, I don't know. I have no idea what will happen to me in the long-term. The same goes for us.'

Dylan was by now laying on the sofa, his long, lean legs stretched over its arm, munching on Ines' snack. 'Well, I suppose we'll just wait and see what happens. I mean, I might decide I'm not cut out to be your carer and you might need more commitment, know what I mean, babe?'

Unsure of what to make of the response she'd just heard, Ines frowned and rubbed her chin solemnly, reflecting on everything in her life. In a trance, her eyes drifted across to the haphazard row of painted miniature pots hanging against the bamboo fence in the courtyard. Looking at the mint leaves weighed down by rain, she observed how they drooped with laborious misery. The sun would, however, dry up all the rain and they would spring back to life once more. Just as she would. Every time.

Looking over at Dylan, heedless of the mess he was making on the sofa, Ines knew what she should do but wasn't sure how or when to. Would she ever have the strength to say that it's over?

Placing his plate on the floor, Dylan looked up at Ines. 'So?'

You've not given me an answer.'

She could do nothing more than drop her head. 'I...I'm not sure, anymore.'

A lascivious grin spread across his face. 'Well, how about you come over here and I'll help you decide.'

Hearing the unmistakable sound of her boyfriend's intentions, Ines remained steadfast, in her seat, resisting the cad. Shaking her head in a show of refusal, her fascination with the herbs that grew out of the miniature pots, intensified.

One by one, Dylan began to unbutton his jeans. Clink. The unmistakable sound of his belt being thrown open, shook her.

Wriggling his boxers over his thighs, he began to work himself, closing his eyes in hedonistic reverie. Stealing a peek at what she had suspected he was doing, Ines felt the tiny hairs on the back of her neck prickle.

Hating the fact that she was so inept at standing up to him, a hesitant Ines found herself crossing the floor on all fours towards Dylan. *He loves me, I know he does. He wouldn't be here otherwise.*

Exuding a confident lopsided smile, he knew she could never say no to him…

What appeared to be nylon entwined, tugged on Ines' tongue.

Retching at the sensation, she began to rise to her feet… 'I just need to go to the bathroom. Stay sexy for me.'

Nodding, Dylan carried on pulling at himself in long sensual strokes.

Switching on the light above the sink, Ines leaned closer into the mirror as she tried to remove what was caught on her tongue. Unravelling what she hoped was thread from his boxers couldn't have been further from the truth.

Gasping in silent horror, a long bleached blonde strand of hair loosened its grip. Gagging with repulsion, Ines dangled the wiry strand in front of her, examining it thoroughly. It was definitely a hair, the same hair *she* had. In her mind, Ines replayed the images she'd seen of *her* and Dylan. Wracking her brain trying to remember *her* specific features, Ines froze, remembering that Jenna's hair matched the strand she now held in her hand. *That* nasty hair belonged to *that* slut!

All at once, Ines made her decision. He'd taken the piss for too long and now was the time to deal with it. She had a high tolerance level, but this was the final step that took her to the point of no return. Calmly walking back in to the lounge, Ines looked at Dylan with utter contempt.

He lay on the sofa, with his hands resting over his groin, his dick, flaccid.

'I couldn't hold back any longer.' His head sunken in the velvet cushion had turned to face a sullen Ines.

'Woah, what's with the face, babe? We can always go for part two later if you're that pissed.' His tone, breezy, only fuelled the anger in Ines.

Holding the damned hair at arm's length with utter disgust, Ines hissed her words with so much conviction, it had startled Dylan into changing his demeanour. 'Do me a favour, tell your bitch to at least tie her hair back when she's going down on you— better still, have a fucking shower after you've been with her.' At that, she placed the stray hair on the cushion he had been resting on with such finesse, that it had unnerved him. He had never seen her like this. Ever. In the two years they'd been together, she had been crazy mad at times, but never had he seen her in quiet anger. He watched on, struck mute as she walked out of the door. Feeling stupid with his dick flopped out on his thigh and boxers halfway down his legs, Dylan lifted his hip, struggling to pull his shorts and jeans back up. Collecting the tissues he'd used to clean himself up with, from the floor, he felt strangely debauched. What was she doing? What was her plan of action? Bugger.

What if she kicked him out? *Think, for God's sake! What excuse can I tell her?* He was a desperate man.

Sitting in the kitchen, Ines gazed at the sky, streaked with tatters of silvery blue as dusk began to turn to night. It was nearly eight o' clock and her stomach began to rumble, but adrenaline was still coursing through her veins. Coffee and another cigarette would curb her hunger… although some chocolate would also be nice.

She sought her sneaky stash of goodies which she not only hid from Dylan, but also from herself, acting as a preventative measure against bingeing.

Crouching into the cupboard, Ines stretched her arm out, fumbling for the distinctive crunching sound of foil wrappers. The ability to distinguish between the sounds of plastic and foil packets had become an art form she'd honed to perfection. Gotcha! Feeling ever so pleased with herself and her find, she pulled out a bag of mini crème eggs. Yummy!

Unravelling the multi-coloured foil, Ines revelled in how the calorific sweet always took her back to secondary school days where she'd go to the sweet shop and buy a quarter of cola cubes, a tablet of honeycomb and a chocolate crème egg when Easter was approaching. She always knew it was coming up to her birthday and Easter, when the coveted eggs appeared in TV adverts.

Every year, around January, Ines would ask Mrs Berry, the village sweet shop owner if she'd had delivery of the much anticipated sweet, yet. 'No dear,' she would chuckle, 'they won't be here until February time.'

And so, Ines would appear at the entrance every day with the same look of hope on her face. With a sober shake of her head, Mrs Berry would signal that a delivery was yet to be had. Words were never needed.

Then, when that magical day would arrive, Ines could hardly contain herself, and she'd buy a half dozen of them. 'My goodness, dearie, how you still have teeth in that head of yours and remain so skinny is beyond me.'

Grinning with fondness at the memory, she took a bite out of the gooey treat, staring into her past life. From where she stood, Ines could see the magnolia tree, its rubbery stars, luminescent under the moonlight; the spring flowers were bobbing as if they were in the midst of an amusing conversation, deep into the night. It seemed that all of nature's inhabitants in Montague Square came alive when no one was around, like an enchanted garden. Smiling at the idea, she finished chewing the last morsel of chocolate. Craning her head out of the window, she sucked in a deep breath, attempting to unscramble her thoughts. Right now, she felt confined, and didn't want her head to be clogged with bad thoughts anymore. Holding her breath and releasing it in a gradual flow of air, Ines closed her eyes momentarily, enjoying the solitude. 'So, have you calmed down now? Can I explain myself before you cut my balls off?'

Fluttering her eyes open, Ines brought her head back in through the window. This was going to be interesting. Indicating with the faintest twitch of her mouth and a curt nod, Dylan acknowledged this as confirmation that he could give her his side of the "story".

'I stayed at the boss's house on Saturday and slept in his wife's studio… Antonia's a photographer. There were wigs and outfits everywhere. I must have slept on wig hair and it got caught up on my dick.' Clearing his throat like the guilty man he was, Dylan shifted his stance.

Sneering at him through squinted eyes, Ines laughed, mocking his excuse. 'Ahem. Let me get this right. You stayed at your boss's house on Saturday night, slept naked on his wife's studio sofa where she often places wigs, and a cheeky strand of hair found its way onto that?' Her finger pointed accusingly at Dylan's groin. Combing his hair with his fingers, Dylan reared himself into an offensive position. 'Well, yeah. It can happen and it did to me!' His tone was incredulous, shocked that she wouldn't believe him.

'So, you slept naked, without a sheet to protect you from germs or vice-versa and didn't shower today either?' Ines laughed so hard it chilled Dylan. She looked like she was going to implode. 'Well, nar, I wanted to come home. I didn't feel comfortable.'

He was good.

'...but you're comfortable enough to sleep naked on someone's work sofa where God knows who and what sits on it, without even a sheet?' she was laughing on hysteria mode now.

'...well yeah'

'You're good.' Enraged and wagging a slim index finger at him, Ines was now spitting her words out with venom. 'You're consistent, I'll give you that.'

Stomping out of the kitchen, the scorned young woman snatched her keys from the rubber wood console table and headed for the door.

Scrambling after Ines, Dylan, by now a desperate man, called after her. 'Where're you going?'

'For a smoke and a think.'

***

Sitting on the bench under the magnolia tree, its heady perfume filled the air. Ines rested her head on her knees, hugging them close to her chest, stretching the long sloppy sweater over her legs. She was so numb, her thoughts didn't make any sense to her at all. What to do, what to think. Think. Aargh! Her brain was a mass of jumbled short-circuiting wires.

Ting ting!

A message from Luke. Anyone else and she'd have ignored it, but Luke was different. Ines delved into the baggy front pocket of her hoodie and retrieved the phone.

Unlocking it with one hand as she lit a cigarette, she looked the epitome of a brooding teen— her hood hanging over a gloomy face, smoking and texting at the same time was quite impressive.

-Hello my little butterfly, how are you feeling?

Ines' heart skipped a beat reading those simple words. His concern meant so much, and yet he had no idea the effect it— and he had on her.

-Not great. Sitting in the square making some decisions about my life. How's your new luuurve interest?

She actually didn't care if he was happy with his new conquest or if Amelie was "the one".

No response. *Pah, she's probably whipping up an amazing meal for them and he's singing her praises.* She was always so unusually bitter where Luke and his love life was concerned.

The square was peaceful now. Lifting her head to face the stars, Ines looked on in wonder. The moon in the still of the night, veiled by a gauze of cloud created a calming sanctuary which seemed to muffle the sound of the traffic coming from beyond the gates, the sweet smell of damp soil and flowers in warm air, caressed her with a peaceful feeling deep within her soul. She knew what she had to do. Seeking validation from the photo album in her phone wasn't necessary. It was time to say goodbye and make a fresh start.

Climbing the sweeping steps towards the shaft of light shining down from the lantern, Ines drew a deep breath as she reached the door and pushed it open. Finding him spread out on the sofa, his legs stretched out in front of him, Dylan looked confident with that arrogant, crooked grin.

'You've made your point. Now what? Bed and start a new day?'

Ines shook her head, asserting her response. 'We're done. It's over. I suggest you get your things and go to her.'

Wide eyed and disbelieving at what he'd just heard, Dylan sat up straight. 'What planet are you on? You actually believe your neurotic thoughts?!' He was tapping his temples, implying it was all in her head. 'I actually believe you're going cuckoo, love. You sure they didn't check for schizophrenia as well, during that brain scan?'

Defiant, Ines stood her ground, her arms folded and listening to his defensive spiel. She almost yielded to his bargaining but stood strong. 'I know who she is, and I know you're with her when you're not here.'

He rolled his eyes. 'What are you going on about now?'

Ines took out her phone once again from the pocket of her sweater. Dylan watched on, puzzled by her behaviour. Taking care not to miss anything out, her quivering fingers scrolled through every screen shot she had taken from his phone. The only sounds that could be heard were of Dylan's heavy breathing and Ines' nails tapping on the screen as she browsed through the gallery.

Satisfied with her work, she pressed "send" to Dylan's phone. Ping!

Dylan opened the message Ines had sent him to find an emoji of the one finger salute.

Laughing with relief, his eyes shone like polished glass. 'Very funny. Sick joke, but very...'

Ping!

He opened the next one. Dylan turned a flushed shade of crimson. Ping. Ping. Ping...and so they continued coming in, thick and fast. The blood had drained from his face. When they finally stopped coming through, Dylan looked as though he was going to be hit by a careering train.

Still poker faced and standing before him, Ines nodded her head to the vulgar image on his screen. 'Give her a call and tell her you'll be over soon.'

Like a chastised child who knew there was no way out of the sticky situation he'd got himself into, Dylan rose from the comfort of the sofa and limped his way to the bedroom, unable to look Ines in the eye. 'I'll help you pack,' she suggested. 'It will be quicker.'

'No ta, I can manage.'

Shrugging her shoulders and pulling her mouth in the nonchalant Gallic style which she'd adopted from Luke, Ines left him to pack.

In the bedroom, Dylan sat on the chaise longue with hold-alls around his feet and began to type his message to Jenna.

-Hey baby, I'm leaving her. I've had enough, I can't be without you.

She replied faster than he anticipated: -OMG baby I can't

believe it. I've been hoping for this day to come. I love you!!

A broad smile filled his face, Dylan knew there was always the dippy Jenna to fall back on.

-Love you too, babe. I'll be over in a couple of hours max xxx

Standing with his belongings at the door, Dylan waited for the cab to arrive. Looking around at the luxurious flat and spotting Ines sitting calmly at her favourite place in the kitchen, she looked beautiful even though she'd been distressed all evening. Serenity had washed over her, and he had to catch his breath before he said something he'd regret.

BEEP BEEP!

The cab had arrived. With his entire life packed in bags, Dylan picked them up and glanced at Ines one more time. 'I'm going now. I'll be round to collect my speakers another time. I'll call you when I'm going to come by.'

'Fine. Leave your keys on the table please.'

Hearing the clatter of keys being placed in the dish, Ines' heart pounded so hard she thought it was going to spew out of her mouth.

This was it. This was the end of the road. No more uncertainty, no more insecurities. No more lies. She was at the helm of her future.

BLAM!

The door slammed shut. He was gone. Just like that, he disappeared into the night and into the welcoming arms of his mistress. Like a dormant volcano that had been waiting to wake up, Ines exploded into tears. The emotion poured out like molten lava. She was emotionally charged. Crying because she was about to embark on a new life on her terms, crying because she was brave enough to break free, crying because she had MS and crying because she was so frightened.

This moment deserved a crème egg… and a glass of rum.

Settling into the squishy velvet cushions on the sofa, Ines looked around her. The flat felt empty all of a sudden. Although Dylan was never home, from this moment on, she really was on her own. She could bolt her door every night and invite whoever she wanted over. Ines could live life for herself. Her life had been reclaimed. He was gone for good. The strange feeling of emptiness would dissipate. Taking a large sip of her rum, Ines began to make mental notes of plans for the summer. Having BBQs with friends and neighbours was a definite. She could even get David and Vera together. Molly and Milly could provide the entertainment and Martha would no doubt find them a fascinating subject for her Instagram stories.

Ting ting!

Luke had finally replied.

-Yes, all going ok with Amelie. She's a lovely girl etc but I get the impression she's demanding… all of my time and attention has to be for her. A little bit like Courtney. Anyway, all's good for now, wink wink.

Ugh!' Huffed Ines as she flipped her phone to the other end of the sofa without replying. He'd see the two blue ticks as a read message but wouldn't see a response. Not even a 'can't be bothered to type so I'll show a thumbs up emoji'. Nothing. Ines had had enough for one day and she felt empowered. It was her time to shine.

Chapter 14

Like a shy child hiding, the sun peeked behind cotton wool clouds as they idly floated by, coaxing Ines out of slumber. Waking up on Monday morning was strange. It was a feeling of a loss but a loss you're happy about. It hurt but it was a good hurt. Today marked the first day of her new life. Peeping over her duvet, she rubbed her eyes and blinked repeatedly to see if there was any improvement in her vision. She noticed that in fact, yes, she was seeing colour and objects with better clarity.

Deciding she had time for a few stretches and meditation before her day started, Ines slid off the bed and took tentative steps towards the chair beside her wardrobe and searched for a pair of shorts and vest in the pile of clean washing which had been there a few days. It was a job that was always last on her "to do" list. Leafing through the neatly folded clothes, she came across Dylan's boxers and hoodies. Her tummy made an involuntary flip, but as quickly it came, she was quick to tuck the feeling away into a little box in the further most part of her brain. *Yuk, snap out of any sentimental thoughts of him.*

Gathering her mat and resistance band, she padded into the lounge and lay them carefully on the floor. Looking up at the 1930s cinema clock above the French doors, it was twenty-five past six. She had an hour or so before she had to leave.

Standing at the end of her mat, Ines began her morning routine.

***

Connecting her tablet to the Bluetooth speaker, she cranked up the volume high and stepped into the shower. Singing loud to the thundering sound of 'Born to Run', she felt invincible. Between the water tumbling over her head and the high decibels of her tone- deaf singing, Ines missed a call from her brother.

Parading around her room like the women in the feminine hygiene adverts, Ines noticed her phone on the bed flashing missed call notifications. Snatching it up, she opened it as her heart pounded in anticipation. 'Oh yikes. Five missed calls. Marco and Luke, what do they want?' she muttered.

Luke could wait because she would no doubt see him at the café—and his new love interest. Grrr.

Slathering body butter all over herself, Ines placed the phone beside her and put it on loudspeaker. The phone rang twice before Marco answered it.

'Blimey, were you sitting on your phone? You're as bad as Zara.'

'I've been worried about you. You forgot to hang up when that idiot got back to your place. I heard pretty much everything.' Marco sighed down the phone. 'Ini, what's going on? I know he wouldn't hit you but the way he spoke to you was out of order!'

'It's fine. I kicked him out. He left last night.'

'What happened to make you change your mindset?' 'Let's just say I had an epiphany.'

And so, Ines began to relay the entire story, keeping the intimate details as discreet as possible whilst she rubbed thick body butter into her legs and decided on what to wear. Multitasking was something she could do without incident.

Marco was silent the entire time his sister was speaking. No interruption, no sounds of exasperation. Nothing. He listened intently apart from occasional grunts when she would ask if he was still there.

'So, that's it. I'm single and happy,' she sang. 'It's okay. Honest. He left without issue and will come back to collect his speakers at some point.'

'Let me know when he decides to pick them up. I don't want you being alone with him at any point.' Marco was fiercely protective of his big sister and didn't trust Dylan in the slightest.

Ines hesitated before answering. She wasn't comfortable with her brother being so engaged in her private life, but he was a welcome source of support when she needed him and right now, he was all she had as far as reliable family was concerned.

'Okay, if and when I hear from him, I'll let you know. I doubt it'll be any time soon though, seeing as he's playing house with *her*,' Ines pronounced *her* sourly. 'Look, I need to get cracking, I'm meeting everybody at seven-thirty.'

'Yeah, sure. Keep me posted, Ini. Love you.'

Smiling down the phone as she sat on the floor, struggling to pull her skinny jeans over her warm tacky skin, Ines mumbled her words like a hostage, bound and gagged. Humph. Hummph. 'Love you too.'

Hearing the strange noise coming from Ines, switched Marco's brain into a whirlpool of confusion. 'Ini, what's going on, are you alright?'

'Hmph mmmuph grrr.' Beads of sweat sprouted above her lip as she became hot and bothered with the effort. 'I'm…hmmm I'm fine! Ohh, for chrissake!'

'Seriously, Ini, what are you doing ? You sound like you're giving birth,' laughed her brother.

'Ugh. Done it!' Feeling accomplished, she turned her attentions back to Marco. 'Sorry, I put body butter on after I came out of the shower, so when I tried to get my jeans on, they stuck to my legs like papier mâché.'

'Err that's nasty. I'm going to wash that vision out of my head. See ya.'

'Oh, shush you!' Ines was now laughing. 'Smell ya laters stinky pants,'

'Oi, now you're getting personal about my hygiene. That's libel.'

'Go! Speak soon. Byeee.'

Ending the call with a swift flick of her thumb, she pulled herself up from the floor with the grace of a hippopotamus. A quick time check told her she had ten minutes to apply makeup and leave the house.

***

Ines walked across the square, taking in the scenery with wonderment. It was hard to fathom that a few hours ago, she had been sitting under the moonlight contemplating her life and future on the very bench under the magnolia tree she'd just strolled past. Last night was full of dread and tears, this morning was filled with overwhelming excitement— a promise of happier days ahead of her. She felt liberated. The emotional shackles that bound her to Dylan were broken.

'Oiiii, you! Yeah you, sexy wench in the tight jeans!' hollered Zara from across the road, with the fervour of a horny teenager. Sometimes that woman seriously lacked decorum.

'Swit swoo!' Oh jeez, Sally was wolf-whistling with her fingers. 'Check out that booty!'

Choosing to bury her face deep into her jacket, Ines scurried across the same road where she nearly got hit by a cyclist. Reaching the small, excitable group, she tried to speak through incredulous laughter.

'Bloody hell, can you two be any louder or embarrassing?'

Sally slapped Ines' bottom appreciatively. 'Be proud of the curves, girlfriend.'

Startled and jolting forward by the slap she had just received, Ines mumbled with bonhomie for them to stop.

'Yea maaain, you're a sort,' chimed in Zara, her cheeks pink with glee. 'In fact, if I was gay, I would, but I'm not so I won't. Don't you think she's a fittie, Ryan?'

Coughing to hide his embarrassment at being put on the spot, Ryan spluttered his words. Talk about being in a double jeopardy situation—*and* in front of the girl he wants to make his girlfriend. 'Yes, yes she's beautiful,' agreed Ryan, compliantly.

'Oh my God, can you give it up now?'

'Yes. Yes, we could, but we have dry throats and empty stomachs. Beverage and food are calling us,' said Sally, patting her flat stomach.

'I don't know what's got into you two, you're behaving like a couple of adolescents on a cocktail of Alcopop and high energy drinks.' Ines observed them both with the eyes of a disapproving mother. 'Who's going in to get the orders? Where's Luke, will he be joining us?'

'Yes, I will be joining you.' The silky tone was unmistakable.

Luke.

Ines spun round to find him leaning against the café front window, his arms folded in amusement.

A fresh excitement had kindled within as Ines tried to remain impassive meeting his stare. Clearing her airways to avoid squeaking the words, she stared into Luke's beguiling green eyes. Holding each other's gaze with unabashed magnetism, the headstrong pair appeared to forget that they were amongst others. In their own world, it was just the two of them, a tense undercurrent of desire and need, bubbling beneath a very thin veneer. The chemistry they refused to recognise as anything more than just being platonic was there for all to see.

Ines was the first to break the silence. 'Morning. Did you have a good weekend?'

Luke shifted from one leg to the other as he greeted her. 'Good morning to you, too. My weekend was good.' His mouth twitched at Ines' unease. 'I have to agree with your friends that you do indeed look very nice today.'

'How long have you been here? I didn't see you when I arrived.' Checking herself for how it must have sounded, Ines revised her wording. 'I…I mean you weren't in the group.'

'Long enough to hear your fan club welcoming you. I concur, from a humble man's point of view, that these jeans are very flattering on your figure. They umm … sit well in all the right places.' A smile formed across his face and he gave her a nod of approval as he traced his hands over the contours of her hips from a respectable distance.

The small audience watched on, enthralled. There were three pairs of eyes bouncing between Luke and Ines until Zara finally had enough. 'You two peeve me off.'

'Why?' asked the frustrating pair in unison.

Seeing the baffled expressions of the irksome pair had Zara shaking her head in irritation, muttering ambiguities under her breath about how everyone knows they should be together.

Deciding that she was hungry, Zara changed the subject to food, patting her tummy. 'Come on guys, my baby and I are starving. Who's on the breakfast run?'

It was decided for them— they had no choice. Ryan and Luke were going in.

Tearing a paper bag from the hot food counter, Ryan vigorously shook it open, ready to receive the warmed breakfasts that Luke was picking with tongs.

Plop. Plop. Plop. The last one made a satisfying sound as it fell into the bag.

'So, have you settled into the bedsit, well? It's your first day at work today isn't it?' Plop. In went another croissant.

'It's comfortable and I'm grateful. When it rained yesterday, I thought about where I'd be trying to keep dry. Yep, back to the salt mines today,' smiled Ryan. 'I can't wait to start feeling like a hard-working man, again. I've got so much gratitude for Sal. If it weren't for her, I'd still be on the streets begging for money and getting beaten up on the regular.'

'She's an angel,' said Luke, simply. 'Can you get another bag for the toasties? If Ines saw me mixing croissants with toasties, she'd batter me.'

Ryan laughed at the comment. 'Ha! Yeah, can imagine she's got a lot of gusto in her slaps.'

Creeping along the warm display cabinet to the self-serve hot beverages, Luke picked out a sachet of mint tea. Ines drank mint tea in the morning and coffee once she got to work.

'Have you got madame's flask there?'

Juggling the paper bag in order to retrieve the flask out of his jacket pocket, Ryan passed it to Luke. 'Is this her routine?'

'Yes,' nodded Luke, gravely. 'She's special like that. I'm sure she says that about me, too,' he blinked, dropping the tea bag into the thermos beaker.

'She'd smack you down for sure if she heard how you referred to her,' warned Ryan with fond recollection of her reaction to Luke's audacious behaviour a few months ago. Ines had been wearing black leather jeans and he associated her bottom moving with watching two seal pups fighting to get out of a black bin liner. 'Two words, mate. Bin. Liner.'

Luke pondered the correlation of the two words with Ines' furious slaps. Like a thunderbolt, the memory hit him. 'Ohh, yes. How can I forget?' He began to laugh as it all came flooding back to him. 'My arm will never be the same again. It's not often I get attacked by an angry dwarf.'

Ryan and Luke doubled over back and forth as they chuckled at Ines' expense. Grumpy morning customers either found their good humour a welcome distraction and would snicker along with them or tut and frown. Either way, the two men didn't care; they were too busy laughing at the vision of one of Snow White's seven dwarves, grabbing and jumping up at Luke.

Standing in line to pay, the merry pair had been struggling to gather themselves together, neither recognising the barista.

'Nice to see so much cheer on a Monday morning,' she remarked, pressing the lid with force over a cup of Americano.

Stopping to answer the barista, Luke was taken aback when he saw the sour glare boring into him. Sobering up in an instant, he smiled 'Good morning, Amelie. Long time, no see,' he joked.

As she slammed the handle down and fired up the machine for the next order, the switch clicked into momentum and seemed to mirror her mood, hissing out steam and coughing out boiling coffee. 'That's not entirely true, now is it? Your girlfriend leaves you in bed yesterday evening and this morning you're making suggestive remarks to your fat bottomed friend over there.' With a haughty cock of her chin in Ines' direction, Amelie continued. 'What can I get you?'

Ryan looked on in surprise at the vexed barista and at an even more vexed Luke. This was all very impressive for an early Monday morning. For a split second, he pondered on how many eventful moments he had missed, sitting outside in his sleeping bag.

Luke wisely opted for flight and not fight given that they were in a busy café with a line of commuters wanting their coffees— and that Amelie was at work. 'Three macchiatos and a decaf latte, please.'

'Please pay at the front and your coffees will be with you shortly, sir,' chirped Amelie, barely looking at him before moving onto the next customer, beaming a dazzling smile.

The two men stood in cheerless silence, their demeanour the polar opposite of what they were prior to Amelie's outburst. Ryan was the first to break the subdued atmosphere. 'Is Amelie your girlfriend, already?'

Luke's face remained glum. 'She's not. I screwed her and she thinks I'm her boyfriend now.' He glanced sideways at Ryan. 'I'd appreciate it if you didn't mention this to anybody, especially not the girls.'

'I wouldn't have anyway, matey. There's some things that are better left unsaid.'

Luke gave a knowing nod at Ryan. He was a good, honest man and they were fast developing a close bond. He was not happy with Amelie's churlish behaviour or how rude she was about Ines, especially when Ines had been nothing short of lovely to and about Amelie.

Once they were outside, the five moved across to the square and sat beneath the magnolia tree, Ines' favourite spot in Montague Square.

'So, how's Dildo?' Luke asked casually, wincing as the coffee burned his tongue.

'I don't know. Ask him or his mistress.'

Luke choked his words, the hot drink scalding his throat. 'Ouff aargh. What? What do you mean?'

Equally aghast at the news, four pairs of wide eyes stared back at her.

'Iniii, what the hell's happened?' screeched Zara.

'Are you okay? Why didn't you call us?' implored Sally, devastated that her friend had gone through a major event such as this on her own. 'I think I speak for everyone when I say if *ever* there's a time you need help, we are here for you.'

'Ini, sweetheart, why didn't you call any of us?' Zara asked, appalled.

Chewing on her almond croissant, Ines remained taciturn listening to everyone. In an act to avert the onslaught of a parent/child style lecture, she dropped her head to seek out and glean the rogue flakes of buttery pastry with her index finger.

'Are you listening?' Exasperated, Luke glared back at her.

'Yeah, alright dad!' Still dabbing at the remaining crumbs of croissant, Ines acknowledged their speeches. 'It was all in hand and it wasn't planned. Things developed organically.'

With bated breath, the group of friends listened to Ines' story. From the phone calls with her family announcing the diagnosis to the final click of the door shutting behind Dylan, she left nothing out.

'Your dad's with a girl close to Zara and Sal's age?' gasped Ryan in disbelief. 'Ouch!' Sally delivered a sharp blow to Ryan. 'Can you be a little more tactful?' she grumbled under her breath.

Nursing his ribs and catching a sly grin from Luke, Ryan pursed his mouth and winked.

'It's alright, Sal. Ryan's new to my weird world. Cut him some slack.'

'So, all the signs were there over the last year and a half, that Dylan was screwing around, and that he had a tart of a side chick these last few months.' Sally shot her head up, disapproving of Zara's bluntness, but Zara failed to see the look fired at her. 'And it then it takes a mouth hug and a strand of nasty peroxide hair for you to finally come to your senses? Phew, well at least you got there in the end.' Zara slumped into the bench and took a long gulp of her latte, signaling the end of her assertion.

With one hand slapped against her forehead, Sally despaired of Zara's candour at times. The two men remained gobsmacked and continued sipping their coffees, unsure of what to say or do.

'Well, yeah, I suppose that just about sums it up,' agreed Ines in typical good humour. Aaanyway, she's welcome to him. They deserve each other. That silly girl doesn't realise what a favour she's done me. Cheers, here's to better days.'

Raising their cups in the air, the four friends saluted Ines. In the distance, someone caught Luke's eye as they all smiled and laughed together.

Standing outside the café with her arms wrapped around herself, watching his every move was Amelie— a deep frown and tight mouth revealing her utter displeasure. Staring straight back, in equal measure, Luke made his feelings known which went unnoticed by the jovial friends but not the possessive young barista.

Chapter 15

Putting the phone down after a lengthy call with the manufacturer, Ines blew her hair away from her eyes and stretched out her arms and legs. The man she'd just spoken to was always happy to talk about the logistics of the orders, but then he'd chat about things that neither interested her nor inspired motivation to learn more— especially when she had analytics to assess for ladies wear. She would often feign commitment to her job, a hint which was about as subtle as a brick to his face. Exhaling a long breath, Ines made the executive decision that a coffee was well deserved.

Standing in the middle of the stark white and lime green staff kitchen, Ines continued shaking out her arms and legs, arching herself forward, a few times, to alleviate her fatigue, whilst the coffee machine chugged out the syrupy brown liquid.

'Ooh, just the person!' exclaimed Serena. 'Don't mind me, I just needed a word about the wedding.' Assuming an upright position, Ines smiled back at Serena. 'No no, you're fine. Coffee is ready and I just needed to stretch. Had a long discussion about golfing irons with one of the manufacturers and managed to convince him that golf isn't my thing, unless I could carry a hip-flask of rum, ha-ha.'

'Ooh, I know the man you mean. Yes, he's a chatterbox,' agreed Serena. 'So, umm about my wedding. You are still coming, aren't you? I wondered if you're bringing anyone with you and if you want me to book you a room at the hotel?' Serena wasn't comfortable asking, especially given the recent traumas Ines had been through. 'I feel bad asking you, it's just that we need numbers.' She was sounding apologetic now. Ines let out a reassuring laugh at the blithering woman standing in front.

'It's absolutely fine, please don't feel bad. Crikey, you're getting married, it's only natural you want everything to run smoothly. Yes I'll be going; yes, I'll be needing a room; and yes, I will be bringing a plus one.' She actually had no idea who would be attending this wedding with her, but she was confident that one of her sidekicks from the motley crew would go.

Clapping her hands, Serena squealed with delight. 'Perfect. This is going to be A-MAZING!!' Dancing a little jig, she hadn't seen Bridget walk in and somehow managed to collide with her boss. 'Oomph. Oh sorry, Bridget!' Serena blustered.

Looking impassive, Bridget accepted the excitable young woman's apology with aplomb. 'Not a problem, Selena.'

'Serena. My name is Serena, Bridget.'

'Oh. My apologies, SeRRena. I was on another planet.'

Accepting the apology, Serena headed for the door. Looking over her shoulder, she grinned gaily at Ines. 'I'll book you in for the whole shebang…and incidentally, why do you make coffee in here when there's the machine outside?'

Being Ines

Laughing at Serena's apathy to Bridget's presence, Ines stuck two little thumbs up at the proposal. 'The coffee in here is better than the machine, but don't tell anyone.'

Once Serena left the kitchen, Bridget took small steps toward Ines. 'I hope I'm not disturbing you. I know how you like your peace, especially when it's coffee time.'

'Oh no, no. It's fine.' It was always fine. Never would she say 'actually, it's not fine'. 'I was just grabbing a cup of Costa Rica's finest.' Ines pointed at the steaming milk-less coffee. 'Black, no sugar and strong.' She indicated with a little gesture of the head, at the purple glazed cup.

'Can't see the attraction myself, but as you British say, it's "horses for courses", I guess.' Raising both eyebrows and showing an awkward smile, she continued. 'So, I was wondering how you are coping and if you'd like a chat with Ciara, my friend who has MS.' Her tone was gentle and quiet.

'I'm okay, Bridget. I'm getting used to the idea of having it, but I would love to meet your friend, that would be helpful. I do feel in need of some guidance.'

'Fine. I'll call her and see when she's free. Do you have any preferences for days and times?'

Ines shook her head with certainty. 'No, no preferences. I can work around you guys.'

Bridget spoke with the self-assuredness she was renowned for. 'I shall return to you with a day and time. Until then.'

Ines half expected Bridget to goose step out of the kitchen. She was a funny soul. Awkward but well meaning. Luke would call her "special". That was his word to describe somebody with quirky nuances. Ines giggled to herself at the idea. Her train of thought was making rapid headway to coming off the tracks, as regard for Luke whipped around inside her mind. Shaking them out of her head, she swiped a biscuit out of the jar and held it between her teeth, in an attempt to carry both the coffee and biscuit back to her desk.

Quick stepping down the aisle, Ines resembled an ostrich on the run. With her bottom thrust out and her neck jutting forward, an overwhelming need to gag arose as the back of her throat began to swell. The rationale of securing said biscuit between her teeth versus dropping it was strong. Spit it out or tough it out? *Think! Quick!*

Coming to her rescue, Stevie stood in her way, extending his hands to catch the crumbling remnants. 'Haha, easy there, girl. You're going to choke on that.'

Dropping her jaw with unintentional haste, Stevie was able to seize the now half moist biscuit from his hapless co-worker's mouth. Holding her throat, Ines took small gulps in quick succession, offering her saviour a weak smile. Finding her voice after a few attempts at clearing it, she spoke with relief. 'Gosh, thanks Stevie. The biscuit nearly had to go.' Spluttering the last of her words out, Ines looked as if she'd completed a hundred-metre sprint.

'Well, we can't have you keeling over before you've eaten your treat, can we?' Walking Ines, the cup of coffee and softened biscuit back to her desk, he placed them beside the monitor, practicing absolute prudence not to break the accountable sweet treat.

'Thanks Stevie, you're a star.'

Gliding across the office floor, her bangles jingling as she moved, Bridget came to an abrupt stop at Ines' desk. 'Hi, well I spoke with Ciara. How does Wednesday straight after work sound? We can go to The Phoenix.'

'Perfect. I look forward to it. Thanks Bridget.' A grateful smile crept across Ines' face. Nodding once to acknowledge the sentiment, Bridget returned to her office as quickly as she had arrived.

⁂

The week had been uneventful, which was very much needed after the tumultuous few months she'd had. Ines welcomed the respite and the opportunity to reorganise her headspace. Dylan, for one, had been unceremoniously relegated to the furthermost part of her brain. The spell of beautiful weather had changed somewhat, and London had become a dank, grey and sombre place to be. The last two days had seen incessant rain. Monday held so much promise and then the slate grey skies the UK was associated with, reappeared by lunchtime. People's smiling faces had been replaced with unfriendly and grumpy exchanges.

Sitting in The Phoenix pub with Bridget and Ciara was a strange concept. In the three years she had worked with Bridget, she could not recall them ever having a drink by themselves.

'So, how have you been, Ines?' Ciara asked, a kindness in her voice that put her at ease straight away. 'Any follow up appointments with the neurologist?' Straight to the point. Ciara was attractive in an unconventional way: a tall woman with eyes like pebbles of tiger stone, gilded with tiny flecks of gold.

Swallowing the rum she'd just taken a sip of, it stung Ines' throat as it slid down. Grimacing at the substandard spirit she'd just paid an extortionate amount for, she had a good mind to complain. However, looking at both Bridget and Ciara who were waiting expectantly for a response, Ines felt it'd be rude to leave the table.

Spinning the thick silver ring on her thumb, Ines considered the question. 'Hmm, how have I been? Well, I'm starting to feel more myself again…which I haven't been for a couple of months. Hopefully that means the relapse is well and truly over.'

The two women approved of Ines' relatable statement.

Ciara continued speaking. 'You will feel at times that you are dealing with an obstinate child and it's a battle of wills. There may be times when your body wants to do something as simple as sweeping the floor but your brain says "no".' Wagging her finger to emphasise the "no" and her gaze unwavering, Ciara took a sip of her white wine.

'If you don't mind me asking, how long have you had it and how does it affect you?' Ines was curious about the walking cane that was propped against the wall, and how old she was when she was diagnosed.

'I was twenty years old. MS was still relatively new and under researched. There were only three treatments available in 1999. Had I had someone like me advising a younger Ciara, I would have started treatment when I should have. Back then we didn't have the internet to hand. Mobile phones were just for talking and texting, and if you needed to look anything up online, you had to go to an Internet Café. If ever there's such a thing as a good time to be diagnosed, it's now. So much research and progress has been made, advancements are continuing to give hope and there's a plethora of choices for treatment now.' Ciara opened her arms wide to indicate the enormity of what she was saying.

Ines calculated Ciara's age. Looking at her intensely, she couldn't believe that Ciara was forty years old. 'Ciara, you look amazing for your age! Ohh Bridget, I'm not saying you don't, but…well, I wasn't expecting

Ciara to be forty!'

Laughing, Bridget and Ciara leaned into each other with an affinity that can only be measured by years of trust and love between friends.

'That's very sweet of you to say so!' Rerouting the subject with expert finesse, Ciara proceeded. 'I experienced two massive relapses. One rendered my hand useless, so my career as an illustrator took a hiatus because I couldn't hold a pencil, let alone draw the way I used to.' Looking down wistfully at her misfortune, the corner of Ciara's mouth crept up diminutively.

'And then another relapse affected my balance. Some days I walk straight, others like I've had a few too many glasses of wine. I use my stick so people don't assume I'm a drunk.' Chuckling at the idea, her smile stayed on her face. 'But it means I can't ride a bike or walk far at times. I am on a treatment now, which has been successful in slowing progression down.'

'Have you had many relapses in between the big ones?'

'I've had a few, yes. Some went without incident, others have left a bad taste in my mouth. I won't sugar coat things, there are times when I've found myself spiralling into blackness when I retrace my timeline and realise that I'm not the same person I was even five years ago.' Saddened by saying these words aloud, Ciara's smile promptly returned. 'Callum and the kids keep me grounded and ensure I don't sulk for too long.'

'Callum's your partner?' interjected Ines. 'And how many kids?'

'Yes, we've been together since I was eighteen. The twins, Anthony and Sophie, are ten.'

'Ciara has a beautiful and vibrant family. There's never a dull moment, to say the least,' laughed Bridget.

The conversation and laughter flowed naturally between the three women, giving Ines a sense of positivity. 'What made you decide to start treatment?'

'Ah, well.' Ciara took a crisp from the bowl Bridget was sharing around. 'After so many relapses, I still remained pretty much unaffected by the condition, so I refused the treatment that my neurologist kept suggesting I take. One appointment changed all that when one of my neurologist's junior doctors told me point blank that I'd be looking at being in a wheelchair within a year if I didn't start.' Ines' eyes widened at the awful things she was hearing. Shaking her head in dismay, Ines popped another crisp into her mouth, indicating to Ciara that she would like her to continue with the story.

'So, I cried, devastated at the news. Callum and I discussed everything at length, we researched all the pros and cons, then decided which would be my best option. I've been on treatment for five years now, and in hindsight, I wish I started when I was advised to…but hindsight is a beautiful thing. At least I'm on something now. Better late than never.'

It appeared to Ines that MS was an unpredictable monster that nobody could slay. It could, however, be kept at bay with the right attitude and treatment. 'So, symptoms can vary with every relapse, and I can either make a full recovery or it can damage me permanently. Is that correct? I suppose the moral of the story is, listen to the professionals.'

'Exactly,' beamed Ciara, her zeal shining like the brightest star.

***

Sprawled across the floor with Amelie beside him, Luke stared blankly at the television. He had no idea what he was watching, but if it stopped her from asking what he was thinking, then it was a successful diversion in his eyes.

Thinking about Ines, her diagnosis and her new found freedom, he wondered what she had planned to do with her life. Was she going to take a year off on sabbatical and travel the world (again), meet Mr Right and marry on a beach in Fiji? Maybe she'll just go wild and go out most nights and have lots of meaningless crazy sex with different guys? Or maybe (and most likely), she'll work on a new health regime and be happy seeing her friends as much as being in solitude.

Smiling to himself at thoughts of Ines over the last three years they'd known each other, he began to snicker at the times he'd wind her up. Catching sight of Amelie casting him a sly look, Luke choked his laughter back and feigned a cough. As much as he tried to stop the chuckles, it got worse with every failed attempt until he exploded into thunderous laughter. Burying his face in the cushion, he tried to smother his amusement, his broad back and shoulders shaking in uncontrollable spasms.

Amelie pulled the alpaca blanket around herself, and watched on in displeasure.

'What's so funny?' Growing agitated by Luke's antisocial behaviour, she pouted like a spoiled child.

'Nothing,' he chortled, still unable to stop laughing.

'Are you going to be like this all evening? I mean, I'm sooo sorry, am I encroaching on your personal space?' She sulked, not deigning to look at him but choosing instead, to search for clues to this sudden outburst of joviality.

Luke's rapturous laughter may have been exacerbated by the mere fact that he had been worrying about Ines, and his reaction was a product of sheer relief. He'd been so tense for months—— maybe more, about the state of affairs where Dylan was concerned and her mysterious symptoms, that he was overcome with elation. True, he wasn't elated about her diagnosis, but his little butterfly finally had answers and solutions.

Sobering up as quickly as when he had begun laughing, Luke twisted on his side to face a sullen Amelie. 'I'm laughing because a thought came into my mind and it just ran into other memories.' Her jaw set, Amelie looked contentious, rocking on her bottom. 'Oooh let me guess, it's got to be something to do with your fat arsed little friend.' Her tone was ice cold. 'Little Miss "I'm so loved by everyone because I'm just a ray of sparkles and sunshine",' she mocked, her voice quivering in childlike whinnying.

Luke's blood was bubbling beneath his cool exterior. Sitting up, and facing Amelie, he tried to not explode into anger. 'Well, maybe being a jolly, selfless person, is the reason why Ines is loved. People tend to see through saccharine sweet smiles and over the top cheer. Their masks tend to slip off easier.'

Amelie flinched at Luke's implication. His words stung. 'Well, seeing as you have her up on a pedestal, I suggest you go get her. She may even be happy to settle for being sloppy seconds.'

'She wouldn't be sloppy seconds. Saving the best for last would apply under these circumstances.' The words resonated in his head. He loved Ines. It wasn't just a fleeting thing. It was real. He loved her. Luke was in love. With his best friend. His little butterfly. Now what?

'I think you had better leave, Amelie. We're done here. We couldn't work.' Luke had remained calm and collected.

Amelie's face was as surly as her discourse. 'So, I'm not to be your girlfriend anymore, is that what you're saying? You're choosing her over me. Really? You will never find anyone as good as me, in and out of the bed— but then again girls like Ines are needy and grateful for what they can get, they'll do anything to please their man. It's a win-win situation. She gets you and you have an obedient pet. Be happy.'

Luke held up his hand, cutting her in an instant. 'First of all, four days of hanging out, with substandard sex thrown into the mix, doesn't warrant us being a couple. Second, Ines is faaar from being needy or grateful. She has enough class to decide whom she sleeps with. She doesn't jump into bed with a man in the hope he'll want to be with her, just like that!' Snapping his fingers in Amelie's face was his denouement to this exchange of words.

'Fine. I'm going.' Amelie rose from the dark wooden floor, the blanket a surge of alpaca waves entangled around her feet. Hopping over the scattered cushions, she kicked and tussled with the soft, grey wool muttering words of frustration in her anger at failing to leave in a dignified manner, that would somehow make Luke regret ending their short-lived dalliance.

'Mind you don't trip.' 'I won't!'

What felt like an eternity unravelling herself, the jilted barista escaped from the twisted heap around her skinny legs. 'Asshole,' she spat, and stormed out of the lounge.

Hoping to slam the heavy front door by way of an epic finale, it inched its way shut, in painfully slow motion, mocking her desperation to make a dramatic exit. *Bloody fireproof door!* Click. It was firmly closed. In her face.

Alerted by the distinct sound of slippered feet shuffling down the hallway, the desolate young woman kept a footing on the step beneath her, pausing mid-stride as she strained to listen to Luke's footsteps. He was approaching the entrance.

Excited, she brought her leg back up on to the landing with discreet agility. Not daring to breathe, in anticipation of Luke opening the cumbersome white door, looking remorseful and wanting a reconciliation, she was dizzy with glee. He was on the other side of the threshold! Barely able to contain herself, Amelie was about to burst.

Clunk clonk.

Luke's pace dwindled as he walked back down the hall and into the bathroom.

Puzzled, she stayed as still as a statue, waiting with bated breath to see what he was doing.

Whoosh. The toilet gargled. Her hopes of any kiss and make up were flushed down the pan. A crude but accurate euphemism. Dispirited, Amelie left the building for the last time.

***

'Morning. How are you today?' Michael greeted Ines with a new found familiarity.

Briskly walking through the foyer, Ines was unusually late. 'I'm perfect. Everything is just dandy. My ex is coming to collect the last of his stuff tonight which means it's a closed book, and I'm going for a drink with my friends to celebrate afterwards.'

'About bloody time...'scuse me for swearing but he was the wrong man for you.'

'I know he was, Michael and if I'm honest, I knew it a long time ago. Anyway, I must dash. See you later!'

And then she disappeared into the lift, leaving Michael smiling after her like a proud dad.

***

Humming "That's Amore" to herself, Ines continued to work diligently, immersed in data analytics and enjoying the various challenges it posed. She had to question her geeky ways at times. 'I'm sure someone will love me for it one day,' she mused. Her pep-talk came to a sudden end by a husky voice behind her.

'Hi, Ines. How are you?' Since sharing a treat box from Patisserie Lydia during a meeting, Ines saw Bridget in a new light. And in recent weeks? She now deemed Bridget a friend. Amazing what a box of patisseries and a diagnosis of MS can do.

'I'm good, thanks. Listen, I just wanted to say a big thanks for inviting me out yesterday. Ciara is a lovely lady.'

'She's a sweetheart,' added Bridget.

'She is. Her advice was to the point and very much needed. Thanks again.'

'Anytime.' Bridget smiled on. 'If you are uncertain of anything, you're not on your own. There's no need to figure this out alone. Promise you'll ask for help if you need it?'

'I promise.' Remembering her little tartlets she'd bought earlier, Ines opened her bag and pulled out a little box. 'Want one?'

'That's naughty but we deserve it,' cooed Bridget.

***

Pacing around the flat, double checking then triple checking, and starting the cycle again, Ines ensured everything of Dylan's was in a pile in the kitchen. The kitchen was closest to the front door so there would be no reason for him to wander anywhere else. Looking down at the pathetic pile of clothes and his speakers, she thought it may be courteous to place the clothes in a bag at the very least, although he didn't deserve an iota of consideration.

Looking at the clock, she realised he was due any minute. Lighting up a cigarette, Ines looked across the square and wondered how Dylan was going to carry everything onto the train. 'Oh well, not my problem.' Ines had also contacted her brother to let him know that Dylan was on his way over.

-Okay. Will be there x

His short messages could easily be misconstrued as curt.

A heavy bass line reverberated over the quiet street for a minute before it came to an abrupt stop. Peering discreetly out of the window, Ines hid amongst the waxy leaves of the orchid plant— a gift from Jared for her twenty-second birthday. It was then, that it dawned on her that she was at liberty to get back in touch with him, now Dylan 'do as I say, not as I do, because I have double standards' Sinclair was out of the picture.

Switching back to reality, Ines could hear the familiar baritone voice speaking with the squeaky, grating tones of Jenna. The curiosity was too tempting for any wronged woman and she had to take a look at her and the car she was driving. Leaning closer into the plant, Ines felt as if she were on a secret mission, spreading the lush green leaves apart, granting her just enough of a view without getting caught.

Jenna drove a pink Mini Cooper convertible. 'Predictable.'

Observing her hair, clothes and makeup, she also decided that Dylan had downgraded. Feeling content with what she'd just seen, Ines skipped into her bedroom for a quick once over of her lip gloss and outfit. Just enough to show off her slender legs and pert bottom— she wanted Dylan's last vision of her to be a sultry, lasting memory.

Buzzz.

The intercom sounded aggressive. Ines could almost picture Dylan holding the button down that much longer on purpose. Petty.

As she fixed her top, the buzzer blared one more time. This time it was a short burst, one that she interpreted as 'don't play games, I'm in no mood'. Feeling empowered, and not caring a damn about what he thought, Ines sashayed out of her room and headed for the front door. Pressing the button to answer the call, she could hear the tinny echoes of activity outside.

'Hello?'

'Yeah, hi. It's me.' Buzzz

Ines opened the door to find Dylan looking cocksure and ruggedly handsome. Bum. 'Hi, I've collected everything and put it in the kitchen,' she pointed with an explicit nod of her head in the direction of the pathetic remaining scraps of his life with Ines.

Dylan followed her into the kitchen, kicking the front door behind him with his heel. 'You look well,' he observed, eyeing up her compact figure in tight low-rise jeans and a three-quarter sleeve Bardot top. 'Is that one of them button down underneath tops?' He leered like a dog on heat.

'Figure it out for yourself, because that's something I'm not going to tell you and you'll never know.'

'For old times sake?' He was an audacious rogue and a sexual opportunist.

'No. No way.' Ines recoiled at his brazenness. Looking at her watch, she attempted to put an end to the visit and steer him to the unwanted heap of belongings. 'Anyway, I'm on my way out. So, if you don't mind...'

'Yeah, same. I've got Jenna waiting in the car. One more thing, we were looking up on my rights. I'm entitled to a lump sum because I contributed to the mortgage and bills.'

Just like that. There was a moment of silence because she wasn't sure whether she'd heard correctly. 'What?' Ines was struggling to process the gall of this man's statement.

'Yeah, Jenna and I were researching it.'

Bitch. That fucking bitch! The palpations were increasing by the millisecond. 'Was it in big writing and have lots of pictures?'

'She's not thick, so shut up with spouting your poison!'

Her body language deceptive of her shock, Ines leaned casually against the worktop, the curve of a hip thrust out, with a clammy hand in the back pocket of her jeans, and she responded with an impudent roll of the eyes. 'Oh puuurlease. You aren't entitled to anything. I actually don't have the time nor the inclination to discuss your delusions of entitlement.'

'According to the calculation we made on a website, I'm entitled to ten thousand pounds. I'll take this to court. I have my rights,' interrupted Dylan who was now beginning to glower beneath his cool exterior.

Ines' jaw dropped with incredulity, as she repeated the words in case her ears hadn't heard right the first time. 'Ten...thousand...pounds? You didn't pay bills or the mortgage, you cheeky sod! You bought food a couple of times in two years. And where's your proof of these bills you paid then, huh?'

Knowing he was in a corner and couldn't get out, he opted for his normal line of attack: threatening behaviour to intimidate Ines into cowering back down, as she always had. The set mouth on her face, however, showed him that the gloves had, without doubt, come off.

'You know what? Stick your money,' he spat.

'I hadn't actually offered it to you. However, I can have you charged for blackmail and threatening behaviour.' That was a red rag to a bull. Ines had waved the proverbial red sheet in front of him and then smothered his face with it for good measure. He was furious, spitting words out of his mouth with such ferocity that tiny droplets of spittle fell onto his chin.

'No one's going to want you now,' he sneered, his face turning a violent shade of purple. 'Who the hell's going to want to tie themselves down with a cripple at a young age? You're finished, love. No one and I mean no one is going to want you. You're a freak!'

Before he knew it, Dylan was wheeled round with so much force that he lost his balance, falling like a sack of potatoes on to the cold floor.

'Hmmmph.'

'GET.UP! GET THE FUCK UP, NOW!' The thunderous voice was deafening.

Ines' hand flew up to her mouth, a bloodcurdling scream escaping— a reaction that she had no control over.

Groaning in pain, Dylan clung onto the worktop and attempted to straighten up. Before he could even say another word, Luke drove his fist squarely into Dylan's cheekbone. Snapping back, his head hit the cupboard. That was going to be a magnificent black eye in the morning.

'Get your shit and go,' Luke growled, his breathing heavy with fury and adrenaline.

'I'm going to sue you,' spat Dylan.

'Let me know how that goes for you, mate. Make sure you have money because I'll counter sue. Now go!!' Grabbing Dylan's elbow with one hand

and his bag in the other, Luke dragged him across the hall. With gusto, he reared his back and threw Dylan and his belongings out of the flat.

The contents of the bag spilled out into the entrance hallway, leaving a dazed and wounded Dylan not knowing what to do next. 'My speakers. They're inside. I want them.'

Without hesitation, Luke retrieved the coveted speakers and dropped them beside an unexpecting Dylan. 'Now piss off!'

Ines had moved to the window for a view of the cacophony that could be heard outside. Witnessing Jenna and Dylan provided great entertainment. Luke walked coolly over to join her. They both watched the mayhem outside on the street, reeling by what had just happened.

'Awwww no, baby why did he do that to you?' Jenna cried. 'Oh my God, your eye! You've got a shiner coming on.' Jenna hopped around her injured man like a little sparrow. Patting his bruises with tentative fingers, Dylan flinched where his doting girlfriend had touched a tender spot.

'Oww'

'I'm so sorry, baby. I can't believe he did this to you. Why would he want to hurt you?'

Cradling his face, Dylan snarled back at the dipsy young woman. 'They're just psychos.'

'Did you talk to her about getting the money?' Jenna's voice cut through the quiet street, slicing through the cool April air, like a badly tuned violin.

Loading the bag and speakers into the car, Dylan sensed that they were being watched. Glancing up at the window he found two victorious faces beaming back. Perturbed, he stared directly at the joyous pair relishing the comedy on the street below. Dylan shook his head in resignation. 'Nah, I can't be arsed. Let's just leave it.'

And with a boom of dance music as the engine was fired up, they disappeared into a haze of bubble gum pink, hurtling through the quiet roads of Montague Square.

Looking up at Luke with newfound respect and admiration for him, Ines marvelled at the tall, dark and extremely handsome man with the artichoke green eyes. 'Wow. Just wow. I mean what the hell was that?! I've never seen you so angry. You were like a wild animal unleashed.'

'Trust me,' Luke replied, grabbing ice from the freezer for his hand. 'That was a long time coming. The prick is just lucky he got away with it for so long.'

Leaning over the worktop and tapping her two front teeth with her fingernail in sync with the music playing in the background, Ines was lost in thought.

'Don't zone out on me,' Luke warned, wrapping his hand in a towel.

Twisting around to face him, Ines looked up and smiled, still tapping her teeth. 'Just thinking.'

'Careful.' 'Shut it.'

'Yes, boss.'

'How did you get in?' she asked, retracing the timeline of events. 'I didn't hear the lock. And in fact, why are *you* here and not my brother?'

Leaning into the counter to join Ines, Luke tapped his nose. 'I'm a secret agent. If I told you, I'd have to kill you afterwards.'

Laughing at his silliness, Ines punched her chivalrous friend on the shoulder. 'Oh, shush you, seriously. Tell me.'

'Your brother was stuck at work with clients, so he rang me and asked if I could check on you. I told him not to worry because you'd have probably knocked Dildo out with your iron pan and be masking up the body as we speak. To reassure him, I agreed to go.' Luke playfully nudged her. 'As for the door, well it was ajar, it was saying: "Welcome Luke, come in and smack the red headed imbecile. I know you want to". So, I did.' He gave a perfunctory roll of his shoulders. 'And hearing him talking to you like that was adding fuel to a fire that was already alight.'

'How long were you listening for?' Ines sounded surprised. She needed to be careful about the monitoring of her conversations. It was starting to become a habit.

'From when he propositioned you for old times sake. I don't like the man as a person, and I've wanted to hit him for a long time now. Listening to him speak to you the way he did tipped me over the edge.'

Fluttering her hand upon her heart, Ines feigned a damsel in distress. 'My knight in shining armour, my...my hero!' And with that, she spread her arms in theatrical bravado before reaching to lay a hand on his chest. 'Joking apart, I'm very grateful for your help. You're a good man.'

Luke didn't dare to move, scared the moment would vanish, never to be experienced again. He could feel Ines in a way he'd never felt her before.

Looking deep into each other's eyes, neither ventured to speak. Feeling Luke's warm breath against her face sent tingles down her spine. A hundred butterflies glittered in her chest as she took one step closer to Luke's expectant mouth...

Driiiing driiiing

Snapping out of their intense reverie, Luke cleared his throat. 'Best answer that or Nappy Brain will keep calling.'

Giggling at the new nickname Luke had for Zara, Ines answered the phone. 'Hello you, you okay?'

'Where is everyone, have you even left yet?'

'Yes, we're on our way. Give us fifteen minutes.' 'Us? Who's us?' quizzed Zara.

'Luke and I.'

'Oh.My.God. Are you two…y'know…together now?'

Shocked at Zara's directness, Ines denied the implication vehemently. 'Nooo! Oh my God. No. Get your head out of Cloud Zara Land.'

'Oh, boo. You two. Bor-ing,' drawled Zara. Ines coughed to conceal Zara's disapproval.

'Sorry to disappoint,' Ines smiled, covertly looking over her shoulder at Luke who was fidgeting with the towel around his fist. She couldn't help but notice how fit he looked, just sitting there nursing his bruised hand.

'What's the matter? Are you okay?' Zara was taking advantage of Ines' predicament.

'I'm fine. See you soon.'

'Okay. Anyway, I'm being looked after by the dishy Aiden,' whispered Zara, 'he's loverly.'

Shaking her head with fondness after hanging up, Luke grinned back at Ines. 'So, what was that look and the coughing fit about?'

Abashed that he noticed her checking him out, Ines brushed it off.

'Oh nothing, Zara made me laugh as usual. Come on, let's get going.'

Saluting, Luke stepped out of the way, following Ines compliantly. 'Yes, ma'am.'

***

Sitting in their favourite booth in Fordhams, the group of friends had listened intently as Luke and Ines recounted the fiasco earlier in the evening.

'What an absolute arrogant bastard. He got what he deserved,' cheeped Zara.

Sucking in her cheeks, demonstrating her bitterness, Sally interjected. 'What he and her both deserve, is an incurable STD.' Ines almost choked on her drink as she remembered Luke's trip to the clinic, a reaction that gave Luke cause to watch her with sharp eyes. Sometimes, Sally lacked the ability to be allusive. This remark was no exception.

'Don't hold back will you, lovely?' teased Ryan, patting Sally's knee.

'Well, I could say more and worse, but I won't.' Pulling herself together primly, Sally took a glug of her cider.

'That's the influence of having older brothers,' Zara explained with the flippancy that was habitual with her. 'It comes out around this time of the day.'

'I'll bear that in mind, thanks for the tip, Zara.'

Feeling audacious, Zara waggled her eyebrows and stole a cheeky glance over at Aiden. Catching his eye, he winked back at her and she giggled into her glass like a giddy teenager.

'Wooo, things are getting hot in here.' Highly amused at observing the flirtatious pair, Luke welcomed the distraction.

'So, next weekend is Serena's wedding,' Ines reminded them. 'It's a whole weekend away in Devon at The Mountjoy— spa included. I need a plus one. Any takers?'

There was a hum of enthusiasm amongst the small group.

'I would love to but I already have plans. I'm going on a date this weekend with Aiden.' Zara replied, jerking her head in Aiden's direction.

'It's next weekend'

'As I was saying, before you butted in, it may be that we see each next weekend,' said Zara, loftily.

'And Ryan and I are going to be viewing flats,' Sally told them. 'Luke has very kindly put forward some nice flats for Ryan to view.'

'Have you?' Ryan whipped his head round to look at Luke in surprise. 'Oww!' Leaning down to rub his leg, his eyes pierced into Sally who seemed remorseless in her actions. The unspoken words between them said that it was intentional. 'Have you lined them up already, matey? Cheers, I appreciate it.'

Luke leaned back into the soft red velvet chair, shredding the black coaster that sat beneath his glass, into tiny pieces. Shaking his head, uncertain of what to say, he erred on the side of caution. 'It's no problem. If I can help you find a decent home, I will.' Cocking his eyebrow in affirmation, Luke felt bad for fibbing. 'Erm, I've a few in mind, Sal.'

'What about Luke?!' exclaimed Ryan. 'You can go, can't you? It's not like you've got Amelie to think about anymore.'

Determined to tear the minuscule remaining piece, Luke's mouth contorted as he focused hard, avoiding answering. 'Yes, that's a good idea!' applauded Zara.

Ines shrunk further down her seat as the excitable chatter continued around her. Her eyes began to wander, detaching herself from the subject of Luke being the plus one. Lifting the glass of rum, she was tapped a little too hard by Zara, splashing the amber liquid over her hands. 'Ugh! Zara, what was that for?' whined Ines, snatching the red and black serviette out of her friend's clutches, frantically mopping up the alcohol off of her hands and top.

'I'm so sorry, Ini. I don't know my own strength, sometimes. I was only trying to snap you out of your trance. We were just sitting here suggesting that Luke go in our place if none of us can go.'

'Well, weekends are the busiest times for estate agents. If neither of you can go, I'll just go on my own.' Ines was preoccupied with cleaning herself up and finding every excuse to not go with Luke. 'I'm going to the loo to try and dry off.'

The other two girls stepped away from the booth, so that their friend could go to the ladies'. With expert manoeuvring, Ines threaded along the narrow gap between the table and the bench and promptly left.

'If I give you my card, could you get madam another rum please?' Waving her debit card at Luke, Zara also asked if anyone else wanted another drink.

'Put your card away, I'll get these,' offered Luke, and with that he strode off to the bar.

Fordhams was buzzing with workers who hadn't quite made it home yet after going in for 'one drink'. The days were longer, and nightfall wasn't until seven o'clock in the evening, now. Streaked with soft peachy marbling hanging in the sky, there was a definite feeling of summertime vibes in the air.

***

In conspiratorial hurried tones, Zara explained to Ryan and Sally that Mission "Meant-To-Be" must succeed. 'So. I love how we are all on the same page and fibbed our excuses…without even discussing it first. This is going to pan out beautifully!' Zara clasped her hands in delight. 'You are both viewing apartments, my date with Aiden *will* progress to

Easter weekend, so Ines will have to go with Luke because heaven forbid anything should happen, he'll be there to look after her. See? I've set up a little group chat between us three.'

'Roger, over and out.' Speaking in clipped Received Pronunciation, Ryan gave a thumbs up.

'Okay, shush now, she's coming back.'

***

Relaxed in each other's company, Ines and Luke walked along, forgetting that behind them, Sally and Ryan were lagging as they chatted in amiable contentment.

'So, Sal. Seeing as we're on a mission to get Ines and Luke together, Zara is going on a date with Aiden…I…I…was wondering…' Ryan was painfully shy and lacked confidence where women were concerned, and justifiably so.

Feeling as though her stomach was filled with feathers, Sally held her breath, dreading that she may start blabbing and ruin the moment.

'I was wondering if you would like to go out with me. Alone I mean. Not with anyone else, I mean obviously not anyone else because I'm asking you, but…' Ryan stopped dawdling and turned to look at Sally instead of the pavement.

He was rambling and he knew it. 'What I'm trying to say is, do you fancy going out alone? With me, I mean. For something to eat or a picnic this Saturday?'

Feeling joyous, Sally took a hold of Ryan's arm. 'I would love to! It's a yes from me.' Smiling broadly, her cheeks ached.

Ryan was so relieved he looked as if he were going to pass out. Hearing a chorus of laughter, Ines and Luke stopped to see where their friends were. They were a fair few meters behind and looking very pleased with themselves.

'They look like they have something to tell us,' Ines smiled on at the two of them.

Luke wanted to use the opportunity to say the one thing he's been trying to for weeks but couldn't. Instead, he opted for Plan B. 'Listen, if nobody is available to escort you to the wedding next weekend, I'll be happy to go. I promise I'll be a gentleman.' He bumped Ines a little too hard and she jolted two steps to the side. Grabbing her, Luke sniggered. 'Easy, girl, I think that rum was a little too strong for you.' Grinning roguishly at her, Ines responded with a shake of her shiny hair and laughter. 'I know you will, and I'll bear it in mind. Thank you…and thank you for all your help this evening.'

'Always here to help a lady,' he bowed, looking over his thick black eyelashes.

'That's what always gets you in trouble. Your willingness to "help" the ladies,' replied Ines.

'I'm turning over a new leaf. I keep meeting the wrong girls.'

Flicking her eyes upwards, Ines was well familiarised with this chat. 'We'll see how long it lasts. Your dick has a mind of its own.' Standing with her bag pulled close to her side, Ines refused to acknowledge the look of feigned hurt on Luke's face.

Cupping his hands around his mouth, Luke called out to Ryan and Sally. 'Come on! Merde, any slower and you'll be stopping!'

With a cheerful wave, the buoyant couple mimicked an elderly couple shuffling towards the two friends. Finally reaching them, Ryan had his arms around Sally's neat little waist.

'Well, I don't know. We leave at the same time and you rock up a few minutes later, cosy with each other. Ryan, you dark horse. I need to get a few tips from you.'

Feeling rather pleased with himself, Ryan pulled Sally closer to his hip. 'I asked Sal out and she said yes.'

'That's fantastic. Finally!' clapped Ines, with enthusiasm.

Smiling in agreement, Luke stood beside Ines, conflicting emotions running amok. He was genuinely happy for Ryan and Sally but there was a small part of him that was envious. The events of the last two weeks had confirmed his true feelings for the elfin woman standing next to him, but he was still in the dark about how she felt for him.

'So, new job, potentially a new home in the pipeline and you get the girl. Life is good for you. At last things have turned around. I'm happy for you, buddy.'

The girls were already walking ahead, leaving Luke and Ryan to talk alone.

Humbled as Luke reeled off the good things in his life, Ryan nodded. 'Thanks, matey. I never thought this day would ever come.' Holding it together, he coughed to clear away any possibility of an outpouring of emotion. 'When you're in the gutter, you believe that you're not worthy of anything better. Sal and all of you, saw I hadn't finished with life, yet. Cheers.'

Responding with a slap on the back, Luke gave him a gentle push of encouragement, and they began to walk together. 'You're a good person. People like you are rare. Come on. Let's catch up with the girls. Where are they?'

'I can hear squealing by the tube station. They're probably down there,' pointed Ryan with a quick nod of his head in the direction of the excitable nattering.

'It's hard to lose them,' observed Luke wryly. 'Come on, before they get cautioned for raucous behaviour.'

Chapter 16

Sunday afternoon and Ines was dressed in her favourite comfort clothes she wore to slob around in. Donning an oversized hoodie and soft feel lounge pants, she sat in the garden on a large purple bean bag with the lap-top sitting across her thighs. She loved Sunday afternoons. They were lazy and indulgent, and she felt completely justified in being busy doing nothing. After a workout, she'd get comfortable for the rest of the day and decide who'd she'd answer the phone to. Sometimes she would go an entire day of not speaking to anyone apart from herself, simply because she was enjoying her solitude. More often than not, Ines was equally as happy on her own as she was being in the company of others.

Having written a list of questions she had regarding MS, she sipped on a flask of a healthy concoction of super greens she had made earlier, yet was still bingeing on two crème eggs in succession. So far, she had discovered that it was advised that MS patients abstain from saturated fats, dairy and gluten. Smoking also contributed to exacerbate symptoms, old and new. It was also noted that the indications could vary from mild to extreme; some people went through life almost unaffected whilst others slowly or dramatically degenerated to severe disability. It truly was a fickle disease and and as unique as a thumbprint. No two cases were the same. Stumbling (in the virtual sense), across MS forums and reading different people's experiences, somehow gave Ines a sense of grim fascination. She knew that she shouldn't be reading them, but like watching bad TV, she couldn't stop herself.

Ping! Ines jumped at the unexpected interruption coming from her phone. Zara.

-Hello, my sweet! How are you? I went on the date with Aiden yesterday. We met during the day and he left this morning!! He's scrummy. He behaved like a gentleman even though I tried to get naughty with him … thinking about it, OMG maybe he finds me undesirable because I'm pregnant and it's not even his baby!

Smiling sagely back at the screen, Ines understood her friend's fears but also where Aiden's thoughts might be.

-Ines: Give it time. You've only just gone on one date. He's probably as confused as you are on this subject. How many guys have you known or dated, that get sexy with a pregnant woman, AND it's not his?

-Zara: Yeah, but he probably thought about it and wants to be in the friend zone.

-Ines: Well, ask him straight out. When are you seeing him *again*?

-Zara: The whole of Easter weekend. He told me to visit him at work so we can chat some more in the meantime.

-Ines: Well duh that sounds like someone who's interested in getting to know you.

-Zara: Hmm, maybe. By the way, I definitely won't be able to be your plus one at the wedding if we do see each other. I'm so sorry. Kisses.

-Ines: Don't apologise, silly! This is more important. I'll ask Sal. Failing that I'll go on my own xx

Zara reread the last message before determining how to handle this. That wasn't the response she was hoping for. Deciding on sending a quick message to Ryan and Sally informing them of Ines' intention to go alone, they both replied in an instant with a unanimous decision.

-Ryan: We can tell her we're definitely going on the viewings.

Sal said she'd have a word with Serena. Ryan :)

-Sally: Don't worry. I'll ask Serena to emphasise to Ini that the tables, meal settings and rooms have all been arranged and guests are all accounted for. It has to tally. Love you, Sal xx

Satisfied with Sally's master plan, Zara snuggled into her sofa, the scent of Aiden still on the cushions. Tearing open a bag of chocolate covered rice crackers, she nuzzled the side of her face into where he had been resting and switched the TV on.

***

The polystyrene beads crunched and rustled as Ines leaned over, placing the laptop on the decking.

Lighting a cigarette, she leaned back into the huge bean bag and read Zara's last message which simply consisted of three love hearts and kisses.

Having read through everything, Ines decided that she would steer clear of all forums. The negativity and wittering of the audience was draining; if someone had been through a bad relapse, the other person had been near death and come through it.

'No, thank you. I'll do everything in moderation and live my life. I'm not cut out for living the life of a Buddhist Monk. That's enough research for one day. I can only do so much.'

Sparking her second cigarette, she exhaled and delighted in watching the plumes of smoke spiralling into the air.

She felt relaxed in herself and with life. Stubbing the remainder of the cigarette into the heavy frosted glass ashtray, Ines considered it to be a great weapon in self-defence. Rubbing the tip of her nose in reflection, she marvelled at how her brain ticked. What the correlation between relaxing with a cigarette and clouting an intruder around the head with an ashtray was, was a mystery to her. Her thought process could, at times be a candidate for unsolved mysteries.

Wriggling down, Ines tilted her face towards the sky, soaking up the comforting rays of the sun. Her body tingled with bliss, her eyes drifting as languor began to wash over her like a wave of anaesthesia she had no control over. MS fatigue. Her eyelids, weighed down by lethargic stupor, began to close, like curtains to the world.

Thwack!

Suddenly bolting up, Ines slapped a mosquito to its death.

With one expert wallop of her magazine, she'd squashed the cretin who was now spread over the dark wood. Looking at the offending creature in disgust, with pinched fingers and a paper towel she had been using as a book-mark she picked up the splattered remains. Curling her lip in repugnance, she held her arm out and placed the tissue into the compost bin.

'Ugh.' Slamming the lid shut, Ines jauntily skipped back towards the

French doors, remembering to collect her laptop and cigarettes on her way. Shutting the door behind her, she decided that tonight, she didn't fancy being a mosquito's dinner.

Feeling revived after her siesta, Ines remembered reading about MS fatigue and that it can be all encompassing, leaving many people listless until they take a rest. She had been able to make an educated guess and figure out that the stress she'd been under, which had now dissipated, contributed to these symptoms.

'Note to self, avoid stressful situations where possible.'

This time, she spoke out loud as she always did when she was not in danger of being caught having conversations with herself.

Padding through the hallway, Ines swung into her bedroom and threw herself on to the king size bed, arms and legs splayed like an angel against the crisp white cover. Luxuriating in the soft feel of cool cotton against her skin, she writhed around the bed feeling energised. She was as happy as a dog with two tails. This feeling was incredible. Dylan was no longer in her life, her flat was no longer charged with emotional negativity, and most importantly, she was free! She was almost tempted to call Luke and ask him over for food and banter…

***

Sitting in her freshly mowed garden, Serena leaned back on the wooden deck chair, twirling her loosely plaited ponytail with her fingers as she listened half-heartedly to Sally's cunning plan. Her mind had wandered to the impending wedding, thoughts about the weather and hopes that it would bless them with beautiful sunshine, like they were experiencing.

Hypnotised by the orange flames dancing atop the bamboo torches under the mauve light of dusk, she had lost track of Sally's plotting.

Oh balls.

Her eyes darting from side to side, Serena tried in vain to recollect hints of the conversation. Popping a juicy looking cherry into her mouth, Serena wrinkled her nose as she bit into the tart fruit. Feeling robbed of what she thought was going to be a sweet sensation on her palate, Serena snatched up the glass of sparkling mineral water and quaffed away the taste.

'Umm, Serena are you still there?' enquired Sally, worried she'd been talking to herself for the last twenty minutes.

Clearing her throat and running a pointy tongue across perfect straight teeth, Serena squeaked a response to confirm that yes, indeed she was listening. 'Sorry.' Harf. 'Yes, I'm still…' Harf!

Concerned about the frenzy of coughing down the phone,

Sally spoke with hesitation. 'Are you sure you're okay?'

'Yes, yes absolutely.' Coughing once more, Serena began to splutter her words. 'The water went down the wrong way.'

Sally's reluctance to continue the conversation was evident, however Serena assured her it wasn't a medical issue. In fact, she

thought that taking advantage of Sally's uneasiness, although slightly underhand, was beneficial to the confab because she could get a recap regarding the purpose of the phone call. Serena liked Sally, she warmed to her straight away when they had met at a Christmas party Ines had brought her along to. A transient feeling of guilt arose, and Serena was close to confessing that she'd barely listened to any of the one-sided conversation, but thought better of it.

'Ahem, right, where were we? All that coughing and spluttering has made me lose track of what you were saying. Can you remind me again? My brain's turned to mush, sorry to be a pain, Sally.' Feeling cunning as she smiled sweetly down the phone in the hope it could be heard in her voice, Serena threw hopeful gazes around the garden whilst a pregnant pause hung in the air on Sally's end.

Finally, she spoke, as her memory retraced the conversation and what it had alluded to. 'Of course, I don't mind, silly. Blimey, I had enough trouble trying to remember, so I totally understand!

Goodness knows what I'll be like in twenty years from now.' Laughing at her own joke, Sally let out a little snort.

Serena laughed along with her, relieved that she hadn't upset Sally. Flicking a spider off the table, she sat comfortably, this time focusing on the subject with her undivided attention.

'So, basically, Zara had this idea to get Luke, a great mutual friend of ours, and Ini together because…well, they should be but they don't see it … or if they do, neither of them is doing anything about it. So, we have all said that we can't make it as her plus one and I thought that maybe…'

And so, Sally explained the idea and where Serena came into the equation. Squealing like an overexcited teen, Serena gushed with enthusiasm. 'That's a perfect strategy, I love it, it's all very complicit. Leave it to me!'

Chapter 17

Sitting at her desk, scrolling through her favourite clothing website, Ines searched intently for new outfits to wear for the wedding weekend of the year. If she was honest, she found herself pretty excited about it now that she had been freed of the shackles that bound her to Dylan. Harbouring fantasies about being the lone, enigmatic and alluring guest, Ines felt tingly all over, envisaging being the woman everyone either wanted to be or be with.

Driiiing driiiiing

Startled by the unexpected shrill coming from beside her, she seized the phone. 'Hello, Ines Garcia speaking.'

'Ah, hello Ines, it's Ralph from McGinnis textiles.'

Boring. It was as if she were being admonished by her elderly headmaster back at primary school. 'Hello there, how are you?'

Listening to Ralph droning on about his dilemma of being unable to honour the agreed date for delivery, Ines continued perusing the websites for her clothes whilst consulting all the data regarding the collection for the next cycle of spring/summer 2019.

'Yep, okay well, we have a tight schedule to stick to, Ralph.'

Expanding the images to get a better look at the clothes that piqued her interest, Ines either closed windows in rejection, or added items into the virtual basket. Getting as far as the checkout, she knew time was of the essence for both Smythe & Co. and her must have capsule wardrobe for this weekend. She couldn't risk messing up on either conundrums.

Click. *Thank you for your order.* Just like that, she'd spent £630 and completed her shopping for the upcoming events.

'...so, is that agreeable to you?'

Switching back to Ralph's dialogue, Ines removed all evidence of her viewing history and answered him in an uncharacteristically official manner. 'Yes Ralph, it's within the threshold, so it will be fine. However, if it's delayed further, we shall have to cancel the order, I'm afraid.' Bristling, Ines cut the call short. 'So, if you can email me confirmation and include Bridget Nyman in it, I'd appreciate it. Take care now, bye.'

'Uptight git,' grumbled Ines as she placed the receiver back on its cradle. Checking her order confirmation on her phone, Ines blanched when she reviewed the total once again. 'I need a new wardrobe anyway.' Scratching the doubts in her head, away, she returned to data analytics of the upcoming Easter promotion.

Ping!

A message from Zara in the group chat: Hi sweetie, I'm definitely not going to make the wedding, Aiden wants to see me for the entire weekend. Eek I'm so excited!!! You were right. Love you xx

Frowning at the screen, Ines felt her emotions swaying. A huge part of her was so happy for her friend, but a tiny part envied her joie de vivre. Being in a relationship at this moment in time was not what she wanted but she did hanker for a man who would love and adore her unconditionally at some point. Would such a man ever come into her life? Feeling despondent at the thought of drifting from one relationship to another and forever being Auntie Ini, she sent a reply and placed her phone face down on her desk.

Striding down the aisle towards Ines' desk, her bottle of water sloshing with every step she took, Serena came to a halt as she reached her.

'Afternoon my lovely, how are you? Just needed a quick chat.' Taking a large swig of water, Serena lowered herself onto the chair Ines had pushed across with her leg.

'You're going to turn into a fountain with the amount of water you're consuming.'

'I know but I need to make sure my skin is clear and I'm looking radiant. I don't want Damon to think he's marrying a sloppy bird. He can find that out in due course, hahaha!'

Ines giggled at Serena's zaniness. Looking at the clock, it was nearly time for a coffee break. 'I'm getting a coffee, want to join me? I know you're avoiding junk but there's no harm in getting a kick from the smell of coffee beans is there?' winked Ines.

Swooning at the coffee machine, Serena took another glug of water. 'So, I was wondering if you're sorted now for a plus one? It's just that Damon called the hotel and well, in a nutshell, everything is paid for, so you have to bring a plus one, otherwise we stand to lose out on a lot of money. Everything is already paid for. Everything.' Staring back with wide eyed solicitude, Serena waited for a response.

Ines pondered who she could ask, and knew that at such late notice, she was running thin on the ground for options. It was Wednesday afternoon and everyone was planning on arriving on Good Friday. Groaning louder than she intended to, Ines concluded that Luke was her last resort. 'Okay, I'll see if Luke can go. If not, I'll ask the delivery guy at my local Thai house. He's an absolute sweetheart.'

Serena looked uncertain about whether she should laugh it off or take it seriously, given Ines' reputation for her love of irony.

Wiping the worktop clean, in long, lazy strokes, Ines watched Serena squirm under her casual demeanour with impish delight. Grabbing a hold of her coffee and popping the peanut-butter cookie she swiped from the jar into her mouth, she could see poor Serena's patience beginning to wane.

Leading the way out of the kitchen, Ines chewed the doughy biscuit which was by now tucked into her cheek and being broken down, morsel by morsel.

'So? Have you decided yet?' If it was humanly possibly, Ines believed that Serena would internally combust. Gulping the last bit of yumminess, she followed it with a swift mouthful of coffee. Relishing the combination of flavours, she realised how rude she must seem. 'Yes, sorry.' Slurp—another artful sip. 'I'll ask Luke when I get back to my desk.'

Seeing her shoulders drop as the stress drained away from Serena, was quite endearing. Or alarming.

Ines wasn't quite sure which one it was. She got a mischievous kick out of winding people up and felt, at times, quite mean when other people were struggling to work out if Ines was serious or not. 'Fab!' Clapping her hand to her heart, Serena flushed with joy, smiling from ear to ear. Ines supposed, that much of this was down to the fact that the delivery guy wasn't going to be in attendance.

'On second thoughts, I may ask Gamon to come. I feel bad.'

Serena couldn't take it anymore. Tears sprung out of glassy eyes. Bad joke. Shit! 'Oh no, I'm only joking Serena. I'm so sorry. It's just my warped sense of humour. I promise you, I will ask Luke right now. Hell, you can even watch me.'

Now feeling melodramatic, Serena refused the offer. 'It's okay. I know you were teasing me. I'm just being over sensitive right now. Everything is getting to me.'

Ines put a comforting arm around her co-worker, feeling a pang of sympathy towards her.

'How about we get completely wasted when all this is over?' she suggested, with a wicked grin.

'Ooh yes, that sounds like a fantastic idea!' cheered Echo, from her desk.

Ears of a bat, that one, thought Ines.

'We can make it a post wedding session!' added David.

Anything to do with alcohol or food and it captured the attention of both men and women. Incredible.

Chapter 18

It was agreed that they would leave late on Thursday evening and pay for the extra night themselves. This was to avoid the chaos of Easter Bank Holiday traffic and save Luke's ears and head from any infliction of pain, served out by Ines.

Sitting in the oxblood red leather seat, Ines took in the plush interior. 'It's very swish, isn't it? What car is this?' she asked, pointing at all the buttons on the steering wheel in amazement. 'It's like being in a spaceship.'

Poking the touchscreen on the dashboard, Ines' childlike fascination with the gadgets in his car made Luke smile. Leaning into her shoulder, he whispered his words as if he didn't want to wake a sleeping child. 'It's an Audi RS5. Want to be the DJ for the journey?'

'Ooh yay, please!'

Syncing her Bluetooth with the car, Ines began to consider each playlist with studious intent.

'Okay. Simple rules. No moaning and no pee breaks every hour. Deal?'

'Yes sir, sergeant sir!'

'Keep calling me 'sir' and it could be a very interesting car ride.'

Ines tried hard not to blush as she considered just how interesting that particular scenario could be.

Firing up the engine, he gave a lascivious grin as it roared into life. 'Beautiful.'

Ines gazed back at Luke quizzically. 'Me?'

Luke turned to face her. 'No, my car,' and caressed the leather steering wheel as he put the transmission into "drive".

***

Sending a message to their covert group chat once they had received confirmation that Luke and Ines had left for Devon, Zara was able to relax : - So, it looks like "Mission Meant-To-Be" is coming together.'

Confident about their collusion, Sally mused resolutely:- Yep, and now hopefully they'll acknowledge the spark that everyone else has been seeing for God knows how long.

***

As the car purred up the long gravel driveway, Ines stared in awe at the imposing scenery unfolding before her. 'Oh Luke, isn't this beautiful?'

'It is, yes, my little butterfly. I'd imagine it would, however, look so much better in daylight rather than at two o'clock in the morning.'

Annoyed, Ines crumpled her face at him. 'Can you stop being so bloody pragmatic about things and appreciate the beauty, even if it is late.' Feeding her palms to the windscreen, emphasising what she wanted to convey, Ines blabbered on. 'Why can't you appreciate its magnificence under the moonlight and the lanterns? I swear you were a cold water fish in a previous life. There's no passion in you.'

Smirking, Luke shook his head. He'd lost count of how many times Ines would get over-enthusiastic about something and he would always remain impassive.

Reversing the car with skill, into a small parking bay, using only the palm of his hand, Ines inwardly admired his expertise in handling a car. The music came to a sudden stop as the engine dwindled to silence. The fan whirring was the only sound that could now be heard, until Luke broke the silence.

'Well, I don't know about you, but this cold-water fish needs to sleep. Are you staying in the car or will you sacrifice your reputation and stay at this magnificent hotel in its magnificent surroundings with a philistine like me?'

'Oh, shush with your sarcasm,' snarled Ines in pouty retaliation.

'Yes, dear.'

Glaring back at him, she fought the urge to slap him. Stepping down from the car, Luke could read her thoughts, which had him chuckling to himself, irritating Ines further. Arching back and stretching his legs, she couldn't keep herself from stealing glances at how good he looked in jeans. Grabbing his case out of the boot, he began to make his way to the imposing entrance of the Elizabethan manor.

Affronted by his nonchalance, a fire boiled up inside Ines which threatened to bubble over. Watching him climb the steps, the flame burst into an inferno. Uh oh.

'So, you're just going to leave me here then, are you?'

With one foot on the next step, Luke coolly turned back to find the scowling imp in the car, the interior light enhancing a set mouth.

Ha! *Hmm here we go*, thought Luke. 'Ding ding: round one.'

Ines got down, furiously, to impress her discontent. Marching towards the back of the car, she lost one of her flip flops. 'Owww! Shit!'

Watching with amusement, Luke rested his case on the step. 'You okay?'

Turning back to retrieve the rogue sandal, she wriggled her foot firmly back in. 'I'm fine!' Hissing in a loud whisper to avoid waking up other guests, Miss Garcia was not happy.

'So, are you coming in or not?'

Ines was, by now, rummaging in the car boot, tugging lamely at the luggage. Realising she needed help to get her cases out, she turned to find Luke with a smug countenance.

'Do you need any help with those?'

'Ugh! Yes please, if it's not too much to ask.'

Shaking his head, he obligingly descended the steps, swaggering back to the car. Leaning close enough for Ines to smell him, she took a sharp inhale of his cologne, the faint notes of sandalwood and bergamot evoking memories of balmy evenings in Italy.

Twisting to place the luggage by her feet, Luke cocked his chin at Ines. Mumbling words of thanks, she focused on her silver toe ring winking under the beam of light emanating from the hotel foyer.

'You're welcome, mademoiselle. Would you like your humble man servant to carry them into the magnificent hotel?'

'I swear, if you carry on, we'll be on round ten by the end of this weekend, unless I knock you out, beforehand.'

Twisting his mouth, Luke nodded in solemn acquiesce. 'Understood. No more humour at your expense.'

Beep. He locked the car and took a hold of each case.

Satisfied, Ines gave a haughty nod of approval of his oath to behave for the duration of the weekend.

***

'I'm afraid, madam it seems that the room booked by Miss Edwards on your behalf, is a double.'

Flustered, Ines slouched over the reception desk like a discarded coat. 'You mean it has two single beds, yes?'

Sympathising with his guest, the clerk shifted in unison with her. 'No, madam. It's a super-king-size bed. It does, however, have a double sofa.'

Having never seen Ines out of her comfort zone in this capacity, Luke found this all to be a revelation. 'It's okay,' he assured her. 'I will sleep on the sofa bed. I trust it's big enough to accommodate a man of my stature?'

Grateful for Luke's input, the clerk nodded, his burnished gold hair gleaming under the spotlights. 'Oh yes, of course, sir.'

Open mouthed and unable to articulate anything more than relief, Ines could only mutter words of gratitude as if on loop.

'I think you're tired, mademoiselle, you need to rest. You sound like you're giving an acceptance speech.' Taking hold of the handles, he began walking to the elevator, with a stupefied Ines trailing behind, bidding goodnight to the clerk.

***

Click.

The heavy door opened to what appeared to be a suite. The beech wood floor spilled out across the ultra-modern furnished room. 'Wowzers, it's boutique but on a grand scale. It's massive!'

'Why, thank you, ma'am. I am pretty proud of him.'

Ines spun a ninety-degree angle to face Luke and his twitching smile. 'You're so predictable.'

'Maybe, but it got your attention.'

Flinging her bag across the room, Ines followed and jumped onto the sumptuous bed, sinking into the plump pillows. Kicking off her flip flops, she stretched out her nimble body. 'Pfft. Don't flatter yourself, sunshine. By the way, you're sleeping over there.' Wriggling a freshly manicured foot in the direction of the leather sofa, she grinned with self-satisfaction, enjoying the lavish surroundings of their home for the next four days. Plonking his case beside the wardrobe, Luke unpacked and hung his clothes with care before heading to the shower. 'Are you going to have a shower?'

'That's generally the idea, when someone has taken a towel and searches for clean boxers, yes.'

'Well, what if I need to use the loo?'

'Hold it or squat over the bin.' Tipping his head over to where the steel basket stood, a wicked smile began to form across his face.

'I can't do that!' she insisted, horrified.

Bringing his finger to pursed lips, Luke held his laughter. 'Sshh, you'll wake our neighbours up. If you need to go, go as you would normally do. I'll be locked away in a steaming glass cubicle, safe from your roving eyes.' At that, he disappeared into the bathroom, leaving a dumbfounded Ines behind. The nerve of the man was legendary. She could swing for him if she could reach his beautiful face.

Watching Luke settling in his bed, from the squishy comfort of hers, Ines felt a little guilty that her tiny frame was lost in her bed whereas he looked like a bear laying in a cot.

'Do you want to swap?'

Shielding his eyes, as if he were searching for something in the distance, Luke paused when he spotted a mass of dark hair shrouded in a sea of white. 'Ahoy there, I couldn't see you in all that expanse.'

'I feel bad.' Looking forlorn, Ines started combing her fingers through the ends of her hair. 'Do you want to get in with me? No monkey business, just to share. The bed is big enough for at least four of us.'

Reflecting on the offer, Luke asked. 'Do you snore?' 'No.'

'Talk in your sleep?'

'Not that I'm aware of.' 'Fart?'

Puckering her brow, Ines laughed at the conversation she was having. 'I don't know. Maybe.' Patting the pillow beside her, she summoned him over.

Throwing back the duvet, Luke slowly stood up, half expecting Ines to laugh and say she was only kidding. But she didn't. Instead, she shuffled to the far end of the bed to allow room for him. As he stood, broad, tall and athletic in muscle tone, Ines' throat tightened at the sight of him. It was the closest to naked she'd ever seen him; an olive skinned Adonis in loose cotton boxers and just enough chest hair. She could feel her insides in disarray, between tearing her eyes away and seeking something to distract her. The most she'd ever seen of him, was in a pair of knee length cargo pants and a tee.

There were awkward chortles, concealing the fact that this was all very novel to them both, as friends and individuals. 'Promise not to fart?'

'I promise,' Ines snorted. 'The question is, can *you* promise not to fart?'

'No. I cannot.'

Sleeping within arms length of Ines was torturous. Luke struggled to fall asleep when his instincts told him to wrap his arms around her. Neither of them would have thought it strange if they were fully clothed. *No monkey business, no monkey business.* The mantra went round and round in his brain until slumber found him.

Keeping one eye open, Ines peeked covertly over the covers. Watching Luke sleeping was something she never imagined ever doing. His mouth relaxed, she traced the contours of his entire face with attentive eyes. Her chest, filled with fluttering wings, she had to pay extra attention to keep her breathing steady. Clasping it as though to silence what she was certain could be heard reverberating in the halcyon of night, Ines inhaled Luke with every breath he took. Three glorious days on their own, undisturbed and in beautiful Devon. *Perfect*, thought Ines dreamily as her eyes slowly began to close and sleep found her.

Chapter 19

Waking up to an empty bed, Ines panicked as she scanned the room for any signs of Luke and she couldn't see him.

With what felt like gauze over her eyes, she rubbed her hands over her tired face before grabbing her phone and checking the time.

'What! It's nearly eleven o' clock!' Flipping back the duvet, Ines stretched out her limbs before sliding off the bed.

'Do you always talk to yourself?'

Startled, Ines looked up to locate where the voice was coming from. The heavy drapes flapped softly across the balcony door, catching the sea breeze blowing in.

'Where are you?'

'Outside. I'm outside, my little butterfly.'

Frowning in bewilderment, she took tiny steps towards the voice. Looking through the crack of the door, she recoiled as the sunlight burst in. Rubbing her eyes with one hand and pulling back the damask curtain with the other, Ines adjusted to the brightness.

Stepping out onto the balcony, Ines found Luke lounging at the marble top table, lapping up the morning rays. The view ahead was breathtaking. Up ahead over the lush green hills, the sea could be seen, resplendent in rich hues of blue and turquoise, and the faint sound of waves crashing into rocky coves in the distance. Drifting her eyes over the backdrop beyond, Ines took a deep breath, filling her lungs with the pure salty air.

'Isn't this sublime?' she sighed.

'Mmm, it's rather magnificent, if I do say so.'

Thwack!!!

'Owww, what's that for?' Rubbing the top of his head, Luke mumbled something about never attacking a sleeping man because it's a sign of cowardice.

Plonking herself into the chair beside him, Ines poured some coffee from the pot.

'Help yourself.'

'Well, I'm not going to wait for you, am I? Anyway, when did you get this?'

Wincing in the sunlight as he lifted his sunglasses over his head, Luke pointed his thumb behind him. 'Room service— and before you ask, they didn't come in. The sight of you with your mouth all slack and eyes rolled back, scared them.'

Horrified, Ines stared back at Luke with eyes as big as golf balls. 'I wasn't. Oh my God, Luke, tell me I wasn't!'

'It's okay, I shielded them from the horror of witnessing a zombie lying in bed asleep. No harm done.'

Looking troubled, she wasn't sure whether to laugh it off or take it seriously. Sense prevailed. Ines chose not to fall prey to his provocation, instead opting to take a bite of the flaky apricot pastry.

Watching her enjoy the silence for a few minutes, Luke poked Ines on the cheekbone. 'You've got bed sheet creases down your face. It looks as if you've been folded up like a piece of paper.'

Jolting her head away from his probing finger, Ines groaned. 'Will you stop? You're not painting a very good picture of me this morning. According to you, I look like a sleeping zombie with a face that's been turned to origami.'

'My apologies. You look beautiful, even as a zombie. Shall we go for a picnic on the beach, today?' Looking up at the clear blue sky, he concluded that the day was going to be fine.

Contemplating the wedding and what she needed to do to get ready, Ines replied guardedly. 'Well, yes but not too long because I need to get myself sorted for tomorrow.'

Furrowing his brow, Luke's eyes swept over Ines from head to toe, searching for an answer, in an attempt to decipher the reply she had given him.

'Is there something I'm missing? Like what? What could you possibly need to do before the wedding?' Luke rubbed the whiskers along his face, in genuine confusion.

'Well, I need to get my hair done and shower, etc.'

Luke shook his head in the vain hope that he'd get a clearer understanding of Ines' world of preening. 'But the wedding is tomorrow. I'm talking about today.'

'Hmmm, well I suppose I can shower in the morning and then

have my hair done in the room.' Pinching her lips together, Ines looked deep in thought.

'Brilliant. Bloody wonderful idea!' Luke lauded. 'Now that the conundrum of the day is over, can we get on with enjoying it?'

***

Sitting on bath sheets they took from the hotel, Ines gratefully nibbled on treats they managed to buy at the local convenience store. The urban dwellers took it for granted that all shops remained open, even on Bank Holidays, in London. However, now they were neither in a city nor in a large town. Durston was a quintessential Devonshire village.

Feeling the sea spray on her face as the waves rolled and chased each other endlessly, the cove was a secluded sanctuary, perfect for the peace she craved so much on a daily basis, back home in London. Sucking in a handful of blueberries out of the palm of his hand like a vacuous boy, Luke coughed a couple back up, struggling to swallow them all at once.

Staring at him stolidly, Ines shook her head and returned to look out to sea.

Cough cough haaarf!

Unruffled, she waved a paper napkin under his aquiline nose, dropping it into his lap. 'You're too kind.'

'I know.'

Not feeling the need to fill the yawning void with small talk, the refuting pair continued to eat and drink, appreciating the stunning views surrounding them. The gleaming blue sea sparkled with foam that shimmered like scattered diamonds.

'I could stay like this forever,' murmured Ines, resting her chin upon her knees.

'Me too.' Without warning, Luke rose from his place. 'Let's go for a dip. Come on.' Peeling off his white tee, Ines looked on agog.

'No way! I haven't got my swimsuit.'

His trainers strewn across the sand, Luke began to unbutton his jeans. Grinning, he stopped as he got to the last button. Ines could feel a burning, spreading like wildfire inside her. 'Come on. Be spontaneous!' encouraged Luke. 'You can wear my tee shirt over your underwear if you're too shy.'

Not wanting to come across as a prude or a party pooper, Ines caved in. Lobbing the shirt across to her, Luke zig-zagged his way to the shore with a merry little jig.

Smiling at his childish antics, she pulled the tee over her head. Grateful that it swamped her petite frame, she yanked the hem over her thighs before following Luke to the shore. Unsteady on her feet, Ines crossed the warm, golden sand to a cheeky, smiling dreamboat in black fitted jersey boxers.

Oh God, thought Ines as she approached him. *He's gorgeous!*

Staggering back to their picnic, buzzing from having had so much fun, Ines and Luke threw themselves onto the towels. 'We're going to have to dry naturally. I only managed to bring these two from the hotel,' apologised Luke.

Plunking herself down, Ines turned away with indifference. 'It's okay. We'll be dry in no time.' Squeezing salty water out of her ponytail, she found the last share bag of crisps.

'Ooh, bagsy they're mine!' Ravenous, she stuffed two crisps the size of small countries, into her mouth, wincing as she bit the inside of her cheek.

'Serves you right for being greedy,' Luke teased. 'You're all heart.'

Sitting close, Luke accepted the crisps she was passing to his eagerly awaiting mouth. 'It's like feeding my mum's dog.'

'Woof.'

'Twit.'

Washing down the crisps with what was now hot water, Ines laughed at Luke's grimace when he took a swig. Flicking droplets of water in retaliation, she threw her head back in sheer delight, squeezing her eyes tight.

Her laughter was infectious as she squealed with hilarity. Pausing to watch her, Luke recognised an emotion soaring to the surface that he only ever felt with Ines. An intense, loving sensation surged with a compelling urge to kiss her.

Sensing a strange feeling, one of craving, Ines blinked her eyes open, searching for what, even she wasn't certain. Leaning in closer, Luke's eyelashes, cast a shadow over glacial pools of green, his face, hovering close to her salty warm skin, intoxicated by its scent.

His heart pounded like a drum. Thoughts whirled around in his head like a tornado— if he kissed her, would he be rejected?

Her chest tugging until it ached, Ines held her pulsating stomach in anticipation. Edging closer to meet Luke's mouth, her soft lips brushed against his.

Tasting her sweetness, Luke lingered long enough to feel the zing between them. Cupping her face in his hands, his mouth kissed Ines with gripping fervour as she succumbed, throwing two eager arms around his neck and pulling him closer.

Finally pulling away from each other, Ines smiled coyly, poking

Luke's chest. 'Whacha smiling at?'

'Do you know how long I've been wanting to do that?' Shaking her head in response, Luke spoke in a gentle tone.

'Since the day you got that promotion. You were just so happy and all I wanted to do was grab you right there and then, and kiss you. You were radiant. Delectable.'

Feigning giddiness, Ines crashed down. Looking up at a cloudless sky, everything in her world was perfect. Today really was Good Friday. It was a magnificent Friday. 'That's a long time.'

Luke agreed. 'Yep.'

Lying down beside her, the pair watched a buzzard soaring through the open skies. Circling the fields nearby, the bird of prey hovered before swooping out of sight. 'Looks like someone's hungry,' observed Luke, barely opening his mouth as he spoke.

Turning her head to see his profile, Ines tugged his chin and spoke like a ventriloquist. 'Hello, my name is Luke and I'm too lazy to talk.'

'Eh merde, I'm too relaxed.' Brushing her hand away, Luke snuggled into her. 'Let me sleep.'

'You can't sleep in your underwear!'

A broad smirk crept across his face forming small creases at the corners of his eyes. 'Because you don't trust yourself? It's okay, I'm a big boy, I can handle myself with a nymphet dwarf.'

Walking back into the hotel suite, Luke threw the sandy towels into the linen basket as he made his way to the balcony door. 'I'm going to have a coffee, a cigarette and watch the sun set. Then, I'm going to have a shower and we can grab dinner. We shall dine on fish … it is Holy Friday after all. What say you?'

Nodding her approval, Ines grabbed the phone and called room service, requesting a cafetière of coffee and sandwiches.

Sitting outside with their much needed coffee and cigarettes, Ines looked distressed.

'Are you okay?' he asked, panicked that she was regretting their kiss.

Peering over the cup, her mood had changed from euphoria to deep melancholy. 'I think so. I'm not sure. Ooh, I don't know.' 'The sandwiches are still wrapped up if you are concerned about food and hygiene safety.'

'Oh, ha bloody ha. No. It's not that.' Gazing over his shoulder, across the beautiful grounds, Ines watched the sun making its descent, the sky blazing in a spectacular show; slithers of lilac and orange filling the landscape.

'I'm wondering what will happen now that we've kissed. Was it just curiosity after all these years and will we go back to London as friends, or will it be more than that?'

Exhaling a long stream of cigarette smoke, Luke contemplated the question posed, longer than Ines anticipated. Her pulse raced at a rate of knots, waiting with bated breath for his answer. Trying to look the epitome of a cool chick, Ines took a sip of her coffee and continued to gaze at the sunset. Her eyes didn't meet Luke's once. Loose strands of hair whipped around her face as the evening breeze picked up and got to the point where she was looking more cavewoman than alluring sophisticate. 'Well, I'm not doing this to fulfill a goal on my conquest tally chart. I have feelings for you which, if you let me, I want to share them with you.'

Hearing this, filled her with terror. As deeply as she felt about Luke and as much as she wanted to be with him, she knew him all too well, and sadly, Ines knew way too much about his playboy antics. She couldn't be another anecdote, another girl to be pitied. The fragile young woman could handle Dylan doing it to her but not Luke. Never Luke.

Pushing her chair back, Ines stood up. 'I'm not sure. You're a player, a dog. I don't want to end up like the others.'

Determined not to cry, Ines walked back into the room, her throat arid and scratchy. Marching with purposeful strides, Luke followed close behind.

'Stop calling me a dog, Ines. It's different with you. I would never behave like that if we were together. Believe it or not, I'm loyal.'

'You're loyal to your balls and that's it. I've never heard you speaking of a serious relationship. Ever. At the age of twenty-eight you'd expect a guy to have had at least one long-term relationship.' 'I never met anyone I wanted to be with,' he explained, feeling aggrieved. 'So, shoot me. Am I a bad person for choosing not to be with someone just for the sake of it? What makes you better than me, huh? What makes you so bloody self-righteous to judge me for choosing to live my life the way I have? You think it's better to be with a man who's screwed everything with a pulse when he's got you? I didn't sponge from these girls and I certainly didn't treat them like a doormat, unlike Dildo!'

For once, Ines didn't have a sharp retort. Feeling faint with the highly charged emotion looming in the air, all that she could muster was a creak to acknowledge that she knew he was right— before tears sprouted out of her eyes.

Appalled, Luke reached out to her, waving his hands for her to stop. 'No no, please don't cry. I'm so sorry, chérie. I didn't want to do this to you, but you must trust me. I'm not a dog … Luke Dog, or anything like that ex of yours. My intentions are as true and sincere as can be. What do I have to do to prove to you that I'm not an asshole?'

Taking a cautious step closer towards her, Luke felt courageous enough to take another one. His eyes brimming with fear and compassion as they met Ines' distraught face, he lifted her chin with a steady finger, smiling nervously. Sighing in resignation, he shook his head as she looked back at him, chewing her lip. Leaning down, Luke caressed her sun-kissed face, tucking windswept locks away. 'Give me a chance, please,' he begged in a whisper. 'We have time. We can take it as slow as you want.'

Smiling meekly, Ines nodded. 'Thank you. It's going to take a while to learn to believe in me and believe in relationships again.'

Planting a kiss on the end of her nose, Luke turned her towards the bathroom door. 'Now, go have a shower, you can't be going out for dinner smelling like a fish wife.'

Taken aback, Luke looked at Ines with reverence when she came out of the bathroom a little while later, wearing a black dress, the Sabrina neckline and chignon emphasising her elegant décolletage. 'Wow. You look beautiful. Bye bye, fish lady. Hellooo stunning lady.' Checking her out from head to toe, he couldn't take his eyes off of her.

'May I say again how honoured I am to be your escort this entire weekend?' Bowing chivalrously, he took her hand and kissed it with a featherlight touch. 'Now, I better up my game, I don't want you to be embarrassed, being seen out with me.'

Sitting on the balcony to have a quick cigarette while Luke got ready, Ines checked her phone to see if anyone had called. Two missed calls from Echo and Serena.

As the phone clicked into life, she took a long drag and swiped open the messages. As is standard practice, a message always followed a failed attempt at a phone call.

-The eagle has landed!! I hope you're feeling well. We're having drinks in the bar at 7:30 if you're interested. If not see you tomorrow. Excited!!! Serena x

Smiling, Ines replied:

-Hey you, all good so far. We're going out for dinner at 8.30 but will sneak a couple of cheeky drinks beforehand. See you soon xx

She moved on to the next message from Echo:

-Hello lovely, how are you feeling? I hope you managed to get some rest today. Are you going to be at the drinks thingy, later? If so, see you there xx

-Echo, how are you, my sweet? I'm feeling good. Loving the sea air. It's beautiful here. Yes, will be down for drinks. See ya xx Looking at the time, Ines called out to Luke. 'Umm we need to go for drinks downstairs before we go out. Are you okay with that?'

There was a pregnant pause before Luke answered. His voice sounded strained as he lifted his chin up to spray aftershave. 'Yup, no problem. I'm done anyway.'

Loping onto the balcony with an air of magnetic cool, Luke reached for the packet of cigarettes.

'You look very dapper, Mr Benoit.'

His arms open wide, he smiled back. 'Will I do then, ma'am?' 'Yes, you certainly will. Shall we have a quick coffee and a smoke before we go downstairs?'

Never one to refuse a coffee and a smoke, Luke sat beside Ines and sparked their cigarettes while Ines poured the coffee.

After, having brushed the taste of coffee and nicotine away, Ines reapplied her favourite red lipstick and spritzed some perfume.

Sswit swiiit swiiit.

'It's smelling like a bordello in here. Allez, let's go.' Waving the perfume vapours away, Luke held the door open for Ines as they left.

Chapter 20

Meeting with Serena and the wedding guests was a great ice-breaker before the big day, and all in all, it was shaping up to be a classy affair. Ines stood in the middle of the room with her colleagues while Luke went to fetch their drinks.

'There's a time for rum and a time to be refined,' Luke lectured, as he had handed her the flute of the creamy sparkling drink. Ines had congratulated herself at refraining from falling prey to his implication that drinking rum was gauche, and instead chose to store that little gem of Luke's condescending wisdom in her memory bank.

'So Luke, let me introduce you to the little ushers of the day. With her hands draped lovingly over both boys, Echo beamed with pride as she inclined her head, pointing to each child. 'Meet Balthasar and Titus.' Having notified Luke of their names a while ago, Ines felt confident that the meeting would escape any sarcastic comments.

'Hello, Balthasar and Tit-uss.' Luke put his hand out to shake hands with the two smiling youngsters.

'It's Titus, pronounced Tight-us,' interjected Echo.

'My apologies. Sometimes I say things as they are pronounced in French.'

Ines squirmed in her faux zebra fur sling backs. *Please behave, please please please.* Diverting the subject, Ines managed to begin a banal conversation about the boys' exciting role as ushers, their schooling and their favourite subjects.

Luke looked bored, and like a child, when he was bored, he'd get puckish. He'd behave himself for Ines' sake but his love for satire and double entendres were legendary.

From the corner of her eye, Ines caught sight of Serena chatting and laughing with a young couple. Their bright white teeth and matching suntans being the main factors for noticing them.

Nodding and laughing politely with Luke at Echo's "hilarious" stories of her two sons' escapades, Ines spotted Serena, coming to the rescue along with the smiling couple. Ines surmised they had just had their teeth whitened and wanted to get their money's worth.

'Iiiines, you look stunning. But you always look stunning, even in joggers you look bloody gorgeous!!' she swooned. 'Ooh and you must be Luke. I've heard so much about you. Don't you think she looks a-mazing, heh?'

Luke smirked as he watched Serena, evidently a little sloshed, babbling away with the eagerness of an excited teenage girl. 'Thanks awfully for coming along, otherwise poor Ines would have had to couple up with one of Damon's lot. Aawkwaaard,' she giggled, her drink slopping over the rim of the glass.

Raising his shoulders, he replied in smooth dulcet tones. 'It's what a gentleman would do for a lady. Obviously, I make an exception for Ines.

She scrubs up well, so it's not been too arduous of a task.' Ines switched her gaze from Serena and the toothy couple to Luke. Biting her tongue, she chose not to react.

'I do, however, think you'll be a bride with an enormous hangover tomorrow.' Luke pointed to the champagne bottle hanging from two hooked fingers at the end of Serena's hand.

Throwing her head back, exposing perfectly straight teeth, Ines couldn't help but wonder if Serena and her friends got a special group discount. 'Oooh Luke you're so very funny. Let me introduce you to my utterly adorable dear friends, Felicia and Rupert.'

Twiddling her white opal earring, Ines stole a quick glimpse at Luke. *Oh. You can't make this up.* He shot her a furtive look as though he had heard her thoughts and agreed.

Shifting on her kitten heels, Ines checked her watch.

'Hello there, lovely to meet you. Isn't it just wonderful here?' gushed Felicia, her blonde curls bouncing with every bob of her head as she spoke.

'Yes, yes it is,' agreed Ines. 'Serena and Damon have done everything to perfection. It's truly magical.' Speaking in her perfect telephone voice, she wondered why she did this. It was as mysterious to her as her donkey brays.

'It's magnificent!' Rupert piped up.

Great. Catching the slightest pinch of Luke's mouth, Ines took that as her cue to speak. It was time to go, before he said something unforgettable.

'Luke, it's nearly eight o'clock. We better get going.' Ines spoke softly but with the assertiveness of a teacher. Tugging at the hem of his soft leather biker jacket, to reiterate her words, Luke looked down at her pleading eyes, reconciling that the boss had spoken.

'Well, it's been lovely putting faces to the names. I think I speak for both of us when I say we are looking forward to tomorrow. It's going to be wonderful!'

Nodding in concurrence, Luke opened his mouth to speak. 'It's going to be mag..'

A sharp, sly poke in the gut, supplied by Ines, ensured Luke would stop talking.

Spluttering as he gasped, it was all the indicator required that her deed had worked. Throwing a vexed look at her, Luke said his goodbyes to the small group.

'I hope your cough clears up!' Rupert called out after them.

Luke raised his arms and showed an amiable thumbs up as they left the bar.

***

Stretching the seat belt across his chest, Luke fiddled with the touchscreen, searching for suitable music. 'I'll be DJ,' announced Ines.

'Just don't put on any of your rock music. I don't need a headache,' warned Luke as he turned the ignition.

Smirking at a perturbed Ines, he steered the car out of the bay. 'So, we have Fellatio, Dildo and TightArse/Tit-Arse. Any other obscure names you have in your life I need to know about?'

'Only Hugh.'

'There's nothing wrong with that name.' 'Only when his surname is Jass.'

Laughing out loud, Luke looked sceptical. 'You've got to be joking?' The creases in the corners of his eyes splayed like sun rays, as his wide smile stretched across his face.

Giggling, Ines stared back at Luke, wrinkling her nose, the faint freckles folding into each other.

***

'Tock…tock…click…clicketty…click.' Mumbling to herself, Ines was walking precariously in her heels through the marbled hotel foyer, towards the elevator.

'Good evening,' greeted the reception clerk from behind the monitor, flashing a knowing smile at Luke while Ines focused on her steps, oblivious to the small talk around her.

'Good evening,' Luke grinned back, rolling his eyes in mock exasperation, indicating with his thumb that Ines had too much to drink.

Nodding, sage-like, the clerk returned to his work and spoke softly as he bid goodnight.

'What are you doing?'

'Well duh, I'm calling the lift…'

Pointing to the badge, Luke sighed. 'That's the company logo.'

'Oh. Well, it's been moved because earlier it was a call button.' His voice dripping with sarcasm, Luke nodded in agreement.

'Of course it has, my little butterfly.'

As they entered the lift, Luke brushed Ines' fingers away from the numbered buttons. 'I don't fancy going up and down every floor tonight.'

'You're no fun. In fact you're booooring.' Mimicking Luke, Ines found herself to be funny. Tipping back into the mirrored walls, Luke dived forward to grab her.

'Woah there.' Pulling her back up, Ines swayed into his chest.

'My hero. My shexshy, French knight in shining amore.' Puckering her lips ready to give him a kiss, Ines missed, streaking his jaw with cherry red lipstick. Holding her waist firmly, so she couldn't wriggle away or fall, she looked up at Luke with a glint in her eyes. 'So, now what?'

Amused at her emerging sexual prowess, Luke pushed her gently away, his eyes searching the vacant expression on her elfin face. He felt his heart would burst with love. 'Looking at the state of you, I'm going to help you get ready for bed and leave your inebriated self to sleep it off.'

'Oh boo. You're so pragmachick. You're no fun.'

'I don't see the enjoyment of taking advantage of a marinated woman.' Turning her towards the sliding doors, Luke ushered her out.

'Click…tick…cloppity cloppp.' Ines resumed concentrating on the sound her shoes made on the tiled floor. Feeling a sudden surge of being swept off her feet and flung over Luke's broad shoulder, Ines squealed with delight. 'Whoooeee!!'

Even in her drunken state, she could appreciate the lithe muscles beneath his clothes, which she'd caught sight of earlier that day. 'Luke…'

Striding down the corridor, Luke answered in between short sharp breaths, exhaling intermittently. 'Yes?'

'Am I too heavy for you?'

'No, but your bottom is obscuring my vision.' 'Is it big?'

'It's perfect. Just enough jiggle. I think I'll manage.' Slapping her buttock appreciatively, they continued in silence, smiling to themselves.

Tucking her into bed, Luke handed Ines a glass of water. 'Keep drinking. The more you drink, the less shitty you'll feel in the morning.'

'I'm not drunk, I'm just a leeetle tipsy,' protested Ines, her speech becoming sloppier by the minute.

'Okay, whatever. Just keep drinking the water.' Placing a kiss on her forehead, Luke swept the stray hair from her cheek. 'Goodnight, my little butterfly.'

Nestled deep into the duvet, Ines smiled, cosy in her cocoon. 'Nanight my handsommm fillet of French yumminess.'

Chapter 21

Leaning over the ornate iron balcony, Ines gazed through achy eyes at the scenery ahead. The hills cascading into a shimmering cerulean sea were very much a sight for sore eyes. Squinting up at the sky, it was set to be another beautiful, cloudless day.

Clutching a mug of coffee, she inhaled the fresh air, in an attempt to clear her fuzzy head. Although she nursed a slight headache, Luke's insistence of drinking water throughout the night worked wonders. She averted a hangover thanks to his theory.

'Good morning.'

Startled, Ines whipped her head around in search of where the voice was coming from. 'Down here.' Looking below, Ines saw Luke waving his arms out, jazz hands splayed.

'What are you doing down there?'

'Ran out of cigarettes and I thought you might fancy some breakfast.' Rattling a packet of nicotine's finest he had just pulled out of his pocket and a paper bag, as though they were maracas, Ines beckoned him up, smiling at Luke's cheerful morning demeanour. The weekend was turning into something so very special.

***

Dressed in a beige linen, slim fit suit and a crisp white shirt, Luke's French flair for dressing well was evident.

Buffing his tan brogues, Ines watched him with a hankering. He was handsome, there was no doubt, and right now, he ticked all the boxes on Ines' list of "must haves" in a man. Pulling himself back up, his eyes sparkled when he caught Ines staring at him.

'So, will I do as your plus one?'

Smoothing his open shirt collars down, Ines looked up at him, her eyes dancing. 'You'll do.'

Standing back, Luke held Ines at a distance. 'You look stunning. Wow.' Gesturing in awe, Luke shook his head. 'I mean you always look great, but right now, you are exquisite.'

Beaming with joy from within, Ines felt like a million dollars. Wearing a three-quarter length fuchsia pink Qipao, the gold thread brocade glinted in the sunlight with every move she made. Watching her wiggling across the room in oyster coloured sling backs, the dress clung on every curve, restricting her normally quick stride, her hips sweeping from side to side. A crooked smile began to slink across Luke's face in lascivious delight of the vision before him.

Grabbing her coat, Ines swung it over bare shoulders, luxuriated by the feel of the glassy lining, gliding down her body.

'Magnificent. You look like a fortune cookie in shimmering pink wrapping.' Luke blinked cheekily, raising his fists in anticipation of a smack.

Ines looked crestfallen. 'What's wrong with how I look? Do I look too much? It's the dress, isn't it? Do I not look nice? I can change it.' The poor thing was speaking like a condemned woman. Luke shook his head slowly. 'You don't look "nice". You look perfect. Just perfect.' Luke walked towards Ines and took her delicate hand in his. Bringing it to his lips, she felt Luke's whiskers tickling, as he bowed his head and placed a velvet kiss on the inside of her wrist. Although shy of the attention, she revelled at the sensuous gesture. Even if he was full of baloney, it was very flattering.

'So, which one is Tight Arse again?' Leaning mischievously into Ines' ear, Luke had discovered one of her erogenous zones earlier, when he whispered sexual references about Felicia's name and noticed the tiny hairs prickling along her neck.

'Ssshhh!'

'Or is it Tit Arse? I forget.'

Shooting a sharp glare in return to his puerile behaviour, Ines pinched his thigh as hard as she could. Bumping away from her vice like grip, Luke looked on, bored as he watched the women guffawing and cackling, flashing toothy smiles under layers of heavily glossed lips and false eyelashes.

Looking at Ines' understated chic and effortless class, he smiled with contentment to himself. She was a rarity in a world of filters and fakes. Thinking better than to critique the guests, Luke's mind wandered to thoughts about the French rugby league.

He was brought back to the present by the sudden change in music and the sounds of hundreds of guests getting to their feet. Looking over his shoulder, he could see a vision in white making her way towards them, beaming from ear to ear.

Watching Serena move with willowy grace down the aisle, glowing with happiness, she looked every bit the beautiful bride. If Luke was honest, the entire wedding was meticulously put together. Resting his hand upon Ines' quiet hands, Luke squeezed them gently. Smiling demurely up at him, she closed her eyes in acknowledgment of his unspoken thoughts.

***

The warm, sunny weather allowed for the reception to be outside in the marquee. Lit with twinkling fairy lights and flickering candles scattered across draped white table covers, the ambience was dreamy. Sharing a table with her co-workers, Ines and Luke's table seemed to be the most raucous. The fact that Stevie, David and Luke were sat within a meter of each other may have had something to do with it. The trio maintained a constant cycle of hilarity.

Intoxicated by the scent drifting from the posy of freesia and roses, Ines seemed to be in a state of ecstasy.

'Ye okay there, Ines? Seems like ye enjoying yerself,' winked David.

'You're filth. Get your mind out of the gutter.' Ines gave him a playful punch on the arm.

'Okay children, who's in need of fresh air or a smoke?' Moving his chair away from the table, Luke patted down his jacket in search of his cigarettes.

A cluster of guests had spilled out onto the lawns, laughing, chattering and dancing to the music resonating from the DJ's decks. A few drunken revellers passed Luke, Ines and the rest of the motley crew she worked with, singing with verve to the chorus of "Dancing Queen", overcompensating for not knowing the lyrics.

'So, did Serena's "mistake" work?' Martha. Never one for skirting around a subject, she knocked back the last of her gin and tonic, her keen eyes seeking for an answer.

'What mistake?' Puzzled, both Luke and Ines looked at each other before Stevie interjected.

'Nothing, there's no mistake. Martha's half-cut, ignore her.' Stevie was now speaking through gritted teeth. Dismissing the statement as though it were the most ridiculous idea, he took a long drag of his cigarette, his brain working overtime to figure out what his next move would be, should Martha not shut up, which was highly probable.

Affronted by his lack of support, Martha stared back at Stevie open mouthed. 'What? You know Serena had planned this after Ines' friends spoke with her! Obviously, Ines and Luke know about it. Look at them both. It's plain to see they're in the know now. Duh.'

Not actually knowing what to say or where to look, Stevie sought David's support.

'Martha, ye really don't know when ye meant to quit charging forth with ye mouth, huh?'

A petulant swipe of another glass of wine from the silver tray as the waiter sauntered past, Martha knocked back her drink. 'I'm not charging forth with my mouth for your information, David. I'm merely pointing out the obvious which Ines and Luke are by now aware of. God, I should be taking photos and going live on my profile. I promised Serena there'd be lots of great images. Instead, I'm justifying myself to a bumbling buffoon.'

Stepping in when Luke had seen David's complexion turn crimson with anger at being called a bumbling buffoon, Luke stubbed his cigarette into a tall ashtray.

'Okay, in David's defense, Ines and I have no idea what this is about. So, would anybody care to enlighten us, hmm?' Looking around the sheepish group who were now a united front of withholding information, Luke focused his attention on Echo who had been toying with her gold chain over her chin during the spat.

'Echo, please can you be the voice of sanity in all of this?'

Ines had remained quiet throughout, trying to decipher what was the underlying cause for Martha's revelation.

Taking a deep breath to prepare herself, Echo shooed away her boys when she saw them bowling towards her. Understanding the implication of the desperate gesture their mother had adopted, both boys retreated to the children's play area which had been specially organised by Serena as part of the meticulous plan for a wonderful day to be had by all.

Shuffling from one leg to the other, Echo took a sip of her drink to clear her throat. How was she supposed to explain this?

'Erm, well...' Echo took another sip for Dutch courage. 'So, your friend Zara had this thought...'

Zara. It was inevitable she'd be the mastermind behind whatever hair-brained idea this was going to be. 'Well. Sh...she thinks you two should be together. So, in her infinite wisdom, she made sure that none of your friends were available to be Ines' plus one. Then, Sally called Serena and told her the situation.' Looking apologetically at the shocked pair in front of her, Echo took yet another sip to moisten her dry throat which was cracking under the pressure.

Nodding in encouragement, Ines smiled. 'Okay, and then what?'

Gulping hard, Echo could feel her gullet closing in. 'So, then Serena's job was to explain that all the guests, rooms and food were accounted for and had to reiterate that you needed to bring someone along...namely Luke. When you confirmed that he was coming along, Serena then booked a double room for you. Now we're here. All of us. Together. Ta daa.'

Incredulous, Ines pieced everything together in the timeline. 'Which explains why my reservation which was going to be a twin room had inexplicably become a double suite upon our arrival on Thursday night.'

Luke laughed out loud, his voice booming above the music in the distance. 'Zara. Zara. Zara. The little minx. And everyone else, well done. Kudos to you all for being so cunning.'

Snaking his arm around her waist, Luke drew Ines closer to his side. 'Well, it's early days, but I think I speak for both of us when I say we're touched by everyone's involvement. Ines is very special to me.' Kissing her tenderly on the cheek, Ines bloomed. Her incandescence spoke a thousand words.

Exhaling a huge sigh of relief, Echo tipped her head back and demolished the remainder of her drink. Giving a thumbs up to Serena who'd been flinging herself around the marquee to the jovial sounds of Could It Be Magic, both women gave generous smiles, Serena's toothy grin radiating amongst the sea of people.

***

Ribbons of mauve and indigo hues floated across the sky as day gradually turned to dusk. Having danced until they cried with laughter at Luke's "dad dancing", Ines nimbly skipped across to the polite waiter with the fixed smile on his young face, standing firm behind a table enrobed in a crisp white cotton tablecloth, providing a variety of drinks and nibbles for guests, inebriated and sober alike.

'May I have two flutes of champagne?'

Relieved to hear that Ines was neither inebriated nor obnoxious, the young waiter relaxed a little as he handed her the fizzing drinks. 'Would you like anything to eat with those, madam?' Oh, the irony. The young man was probably the same age as Marco and he was addressing her with the same respect and charm, as if she were forty. Her eyes scanned the display of food. Plumping for a bowl of tidbits that both she and Luke could share.

Placing linen coasters underneath the glasses, the waiter handed the ornate rose painted tray across to Ines.

'Enjoy your evening.'

'Thank you, I'm sure I'll be back for another round.'

Ines walked back to where Luke was now sitting, cornered by a gaggle of shrieking young women. Catching his eye, Luke looked over the predatory girls' shoulders, his eyes glittering with amusement.

'Ah, there you are!' The relief and gratitude in his voice was comical, and Ines had half a mind to leave him to it.

'Hello, I thought you might like a drink.' Although finding the scene humorous, Ines felt her morale sinking rapidly as the potential for one of these young, flirtatious fillies to knock her off the leaderboard became apparent. Her insecurities washing over her like a tsunami, Ines tried to put on a brave face with remarkable effort.

'Ooh. Is there one for me too, Lukey?' A ruby red-haired vixen who had squeezed herself between Luke and her friend on the bench, was relishing the attention.

Casting her long wavy hair over a bare shoulder so that Luke could catch a whiff of her perfume, the coquettish young woman reached out to the tray Ines had been holding, curving her fingers around the stem.

'Eeeek!' The screeches were deafening as the glass tipped over, splashing the fruity scented drink all over the young vixen. The gaggle of girls that had been standing, jumped back in time to avoid ruining their outfits and the friend who'd been so dimly regarded, sitting next to her, slid aside in cunning anticipation. She, however, hadn't been so shrewd.

Sloughing away the debris of champagne clinging onto the iridescent green sequins, in dramatic sweeps, the young woman huffed, muttering obscenities at Ines. 'Bloody idiot. Can't she hold a tray? Piss head!'

Stung by her words, Ines struggled hard to fight back the humiliation she could feel rising out of her eyes. Her hand tremors caused the tray to shake the glasses off and onto the lap of the diva in front of her. Belittled and ashamed, she apologised.

Staring intently at Ines, it pained Luke to see her reduced to bowing down to a spoiled brat. Flinging the girl a napkin, Luke leaped to Ines' defence, taking her hand.

'You know, if we weren't amongst friends, I'd have put you in your place. Think yourself lucky, you haven't experienced my wrath. Apologise to the lady for your disgusting behaviour. Now.' When Luke spoke coldly, adopting an impassive face, he was scary. You didn't argue because you knew he meant business. It was his 'I'm in no mood for stupidity' look.

The girls watched on as their friend was put in her place. Curious to see whether she'd defy him or apologise, it was all too enticing for them to back her up.

The loathsome girl whipped a handful of hair over the other shoulder, shaking the ends loose. Small, hazel-coloured eyes narrowed, her mind calculating the pros and cons of the dilemma her ego was faced with. Tilting a bony chin, she stared Luke in the eyes. He was not amused nor was he bluffing. Cocking one eyebrow, his face unyielding, he glared right back.

Stroking Ines' thumb with a reassuring touch, Luke stood, in full protective mode, waiting for the girl to apologise. Her eyes darted between the couple, as she chewed her lip. The vexation was obvious in the tight line of her small mouth. Luke's eyes remained fixed, still saying nothing. Ines was calmer now, the tiny beads of sweat which had appeared under her nose at the time of the incident were gone and her heart, although still beating fast, was pounding more in anticipation than humiliation.

Finally, the girl broke. 'Sorry.'

Luke still remained impassive. With a steely face, he continued to remain unimpressed.

The small group were agog, watching for the final outcome to a dramatic turn of events. 'Just apologise properly, Tabitha,' a small whisper came; the voice of reasoning from within the circle.

The obnoxious, spoiled girl's lip curled at the corner as it became apparent to her that she had to apologise to Ines as well. In a huff and turning to face Ines, she clenched her jaw, snarling beneath a false smile. 'I'm sorry if I upset you. I was shocked and upset about my dress.' Pointing to the damp patches spreading across the sparkling fabric in dismay, Ines almost felt bad for her.

With a sympathetic smile, Ines replied. 'That's okay, I'd be gutted if it happened to me. If you take it to laundry service, they'll have it as good as new in no time. I'm sure you've back up outfits to wear, in the meantime.'

The girl accepted the suggestion and walked away with her little squad in tow.

'See? Trauma over. I did feel bad for her. The poor thing was bricking it. You can be very overbearing at times,' Ines teased, poking Luke's stomach.

'She was a little shit and deserved it. How are you feeling now?'

'I'm okay. I'll sit down for a few minutes and let the wobble pass.'

'Good idea. Drink? At least we've still got the bowl of nibbles in tact,' he snickered with ambiguity, his pale green eyes turning a deeper shade in the violet tones of twilight. Ines took a deep contented breath. She adored this man and how he protected her, although at times, uncompromising when he's convinced that it's justified.

'I'll have an espresso Martini and a glass of water.'

Watching Luke doing a comical sideways jump as he bounded off to fetch the drinks, she giggled to herself. Looking up at the heavens, she whispered a 'thank you,' to her grandparents.

***

Shimmering like diamond dust against the silken blue cloak of the night, the sky had become a blanket for thousands of stars. Ines closed her eyes, enraptured by the perfume of honeysuckle coming from the courtyard nearby.

Luke and Ines sat in sublime abstraction as they watched the revellers lingering, a low hum in the still of darkness. The marquee up ahead looked enchanted under dancing candlelight and webs of fairy lights strewn as far as the eye could see.

The disco lights twisted and turned in multicoloured synchronisation, as the music resounded through the air, silhouettes of figures dancing, arms flailing like floppy windmills. 'They look like they're all having a blast,' observed Luke, lying idly on his side, propped up on one arm whilst Ines teased his hair into a spiked bird's nest. The lawn was cool and spongy beneath them, providing a comfortable place to relax.

Hearing the first chords to a tune Ines loved, she rolled Luke away with gusto and stood up. Alarmed and confused at having been rudely shaken up, he ruffled his head into some sort of style. 'For someone so small, you sure have strength when it suits you!' Dragging him down the pathway towards the marquee, Luke feigned objection at being pulled along, his long legs struggling to stay within Ines' smaller strides. 'Come on, we'll miss the song!' she squealed with such excitement that Luke couldn't help but find endearing.

'Can't Take My Eyes Off You! I love this song so much. Oh Luke, this is from me to you.'

Serenading Luke with tone deaf notes, whilst he drew her back and forth towards him, dancing in an uncoordinated muddle of a jive and the twist, their happiness was there for all to see.

'You sing like a cat meowing, it's terrible.'

Stepping back, Ines broke into an energetic routine of her own, singing as loudly as she possibly could. Falling back into his arms, exhausted but high on euphoria, Luke gestured to on-lookers that she was a little crazy. As the DJ faded the song into the next, her eyes began to mist over in recognition of Last Request breaking in. Stepping as close as she could physically get, Ines wrapped her warm arms around Luke's neck, laying her head upon his chest. Feeling his heart beating and smelling the woody notes of his aftershave, Ines shut her eyes in a state of bliss. They could be the only people on the dance floor for all she knew.

Resting his chin on her head, Luke took a deep breath of her delicately scented hair. The pair moved slowly in circles, oblivious to their audience.

Chapter 22

With one eye open and the other seemingly welded shut, Ines struggled to focus as she tried to wake up. Pulling the covers back over her head, she sunk down into the pillow. 'What time is it?' Her voice, muffled under the duvet, was barely audible to even the sharpest of hearing.

'Argh, stop it, it's too early!' Slapping her hands over her eyes in protest to Luke whipping the cover from over her head, she sought to kick him with a violent thrash of her leg.

'It's eleven o'clock … and it's Easter. We have to get ready for church.'

Bolting upright in horror, Ines managed to prise the obstinate eye, wide open. 'Church? But we went yesterday for the wedding!'

'And today is Easter. We must celebrate the Resurrection.' 'Are you having a laugh? You can go, I'm not.'

'Heathen.'

'Pah! Whatever. I'm still not going.' Climbing off the bed, Ines stomped her way to the bathroom. Click. Locking the door behind her was a sign that the conversation was over.

Luke smirked, shaking his head at her stubbornness. 'Sheesh.'

***

'It's not even nine in the morning!' Shrieking from the bathroom, Luke ducked in time to avoid a hairbrush slicing through the air. 'What did you do that for?'

Laughing nervously at her morning anger, Luke cowered into his arms for protection against the onslaught of Fire Woman anger. Backing into the balcony doors, the frightened giant felt protected enough to talk. Holding his arms out in surrender, Ines stopped launching anything to hand.

'I ... well, I thought it'd be nice to enjoy our last day here, before heading back to London. No?' Dropping his bottom lip to help highlight his case, Luke looked delectable. 'I don't want this to end.'

'What about church?'

'I was joking. Just wanted to get you out of bed. I wasn't counting on your heathen ways being so strong.' Smiling a wry grin, Luke relaxed his arms.

Ines sauntered over towards where he was standing. Holding his breath, he was unsure what her next move would be— he could be kicked or kissed…he never knew with her.

Close enough to feel his breath, anticipation swelled inside, every fibre of her being, ready to burst like a dam.

Standing on her tiptoes, placing a soft lingering kiss on his mouth, Ines glided her hands beneath his t-shirt, feeling the taught muscles as she swept his back in long, sensual upward strokes.

Aroused, Luke's cupped hands slowly slipped away from her face, edging tenderly over her slender décolletage, tracing each move with featherlight kisses.

Exploring every inch of flesh beneath a flimsy swathe of silk, his hands crept expertly up smooth thighs. Wrapping a feverish hand around her buttock, captivated by the soft, doughy flesh, skin on skin, the heat rose with every trembling touch. Burying his face into the delicate hollows of her neck, Luke kissed them with fervour as Ines raked his hair with abandon.

Sliding the thin straps of her navy slip away from her shoulders, Luke stepped back as he felt the cool fabric fall across his feet. Taking a few seconds to appreciate her feminine curves, he snatched her back into his arms, his kisses intense with desire.

Drawing Ines in, her body had now succumbed, feeling him pressing against her.She ached with a powerful yearning.

Lifting his top over his head, Luke's breathing was heavy with longing. Pausing, he gazed into her eyes with intensity. 'Are you sure you want this?'

Pushing him back onto the bed, Ines looked from beneath ardent eyes, her full mouth breaking into a crooked smile.

***

Laying on her side, legs entwined with Luke's, Ines was the first to break the silence. 'I'm starving.'

'Hmm?' Luke was in a state of sublime bliss and not very responsive.

'I.Am.Starving.' Emphasising each word by poking him, Ines prodded the last word with extra conviction. 'Well. I can give you a nice response or a Luke special. The choice is yours.'

'Given the fact that I know the likely content of the Luke special, I'll go for the nice response.'

Puffing his cheeks out, Luke looked hurt. 'Well, that's not nice is it? Pshhh, people are so judgemental these days.' Slapping her bottom, he marvelled at the little jiggle. It was like watching jelly wobbling in slow motion. Raising his hand to repeat the motion, Ines swiftly put a stop to it.

Thwack. 'Oww!'

'Behave yourself. Come on, let's have a shower and go find a restaurant. If you're lucky, I'll let you scrub my back.'

Chapter 23

Curled up on the sofa with a large flask of water, Ines felt low in her mood. After the dizzy heights of a glorious weekend with Luke, it was like a drug that had worn off, leaving only the dregs of a come down, and Ines couldn't escape the desolation engulfing her. She couldn't understand why she felt so morose when there was a man who loved her and was willing to stay with her, no matter what. She had the perfect man for her and was having the best time of her life. Smiling sadly and reliving every delicious moment of their weekend together, Ines realised that she couldn't have a normal relationship with Luke. Maybe if they had gotten together before her diagnosis they might have stood a chance. But not now. Now, everything had changed. Her future had changed, and she couldn't subject Luke to the life that awaited her. Ever. A man like Luke was too good for her and she didn't deserve him … and he deserved better than a woman like her.

Like a chokehold, images danced across her mind's eye, threatening to consume her. It was as if the universe wanted to mock her: "Here have a taste of happiness, because that's all you're getting".

A man as classy and sexy as Luke could be reduced to being the carer in the relationship, when he could be with anyone he wanted? When he could be with someone strong and healthy? Ines shuddered at the very idea. Scrolling through messages from friends expressing their joy at the pair finally getting together, Ines' heart grew heavier by the second. This was going to be the hardest thing she'd ever have to do.

Pacing the lounge like a caged lion, Luke ran his fingers through dishevelled hair, desperately trying to process what Ines had just explained to him.

'I'm sorry,' she croaked, her bloodshot eyes stinging with the tears she had shed.

Pointing an accusing finger, Luke's voice trembled. 'Don't!' he snapped, unable to lift his head to look at her. 'Don't. Say. *Anything.*'

Knowing that he needed a minute, Ines obeyed his wishes. Wringing her hands, she searched in despair for an answer to this dire situation she had dragged Luke into.

'Ines, for God's sake, why? Have I said or done anything wrong? Have I upset you?'

'Of course not!' she cried.

'Then why?! You're ripping me apart and you're not even giving me a proper explanation.'

His eyes searched for a glimmer of emotion, a sign of what had compelled her to have this dramatic change of heart.

Seeing him so broken— funny, cheeky, cocksure Luke, had Ines in shreds. She couldn't bear to look him in the eye knowing how much she was hurting him. Her heart was beating so fast, Ines thought she was going to be sick.

'L…Luke. I'm so sorry. This is breaking my heart too, you know.' Her head hung low. 'But you deserve better and the life that's waiting for me is not a nice prospect. I don't deserve to have you.'

Crouching down, Luke rested his hands on her knees. Tear drops dotted her jeans, as they rolled silently from her eyes.

Speaking softly, Luke tried to reason with her one last time. 'From the first time I saw you, I knew you would be special to me. Over time, my feelings for you turned to love. I love you, Ines. I need you in my life.' Clearing his throat, he took Ines' hands in his.

'Your spirit, humour…even your slaps. I need this in my life. I can't see myself without you by my side, moving forward. I want children, a scruffy dog, your craziness. I want to share everything with you.'

Reaching out, Ines implored Luke to understand. 'You don't see it, but a year from now you'll realise I was right. I have MS. Do you know what that means?' With glazed eyes, Ines was now facing him. 'It's incurable. Fickle. It's degenerative. I may not be the Ines you fell in love with in a few years' time. There may come a day when I can't wear heels or dance. I don't know.' Holding her palms out in an impassioned act of desperation, she continued trying to hold back more tears. 'It's the unknown and the unpredictability that scares the shit out of me. Please try and imagine how it would be for you.' Pausing to take a long deep breath, her voice creaked. 'You're handsome, fit and, touch wood, healthy. You need to be with someone like you, not someone like *me*.'

His eyes filling with tears, Luke looked at Ines, pleading her to take heed. 'Anything can happen to anyone. Would you think anything less of me if I were in your shoes?'

Ines shook her head vehemently. 'Don't be ridiculous. I love you for who you are, no matter what.'

'So, why can't I love you for you? We will get through these testing times together, no?' Tucking the ponytail away from her perspiring neck, Luke passed her some water.

'I love you,' he insisted as she drank. 'I have never ever loved anyone the way I love you and I will never love again. Please do not do this. We belong together. If I can't be with you, I may as well continue life as I always have.'

'But you'll be free. You won't ever have a shortage of women.' 'They won't be you.'

Shaking her head in uncompromising refusal, Ines was not changing her mind. 'It's for the best. You'll see.' Smiling a thin smile, she buried her head in her knees and hugged them tight.

Luke understood Ines better than anyone. Her resolve was as tough as iron. It was like trying to bend stone. Standing up to leave, he rested his brow against her head, breathing her in for the last time. 'Goodbye, my little butterfly.'

Chapter 24

'What the hell? Why? I mean, I know why but, no no no. This can't happen.' Zara swung her legs nervously on the bar stool in Aiden's kitchen as she listened to Luke's devastating story.

'There's nothing I can do. God knows I've tried. But she's made her mind up and I have to accept her wishes.' Luke was crestfallen. Zara's heart, was leaden for the pair of them.

'I'll make her see sense. You two are perfect together, you're meant to be. I mean, I understand Ini's thinking. It isn't easy to deal with a diagnosis like this, let alone when the man of your dreams is thrown into the equation as well. Her brain must be fit to explode. But it isn't fair, you two have been years in the making. My poor friend. My poor you. This is truly wrong!'

'Listen, I'm leaving on Friday morning. I've taken sabbatical from work and I'm going to see if I can get any work out there. I'll stay with my family in Avignon first for a couple of months, though. I need head space.' Open mouthed, Zara couldn't believe what she was hearing. 'What about the flat?'

'Ryan will rent it from me. I spoke to him earlier.'

Zara was gobsmacked. How could something so beautiful come to a grinding end this way? Zara began to sob. 'Oh, Luke, no. I can't believe what I'm hearing. On Monday, everything was beautiful and now…well now it's all gone to pot— and you're leaving!'

'I will pass round to say goodbye to you, and obviously Sal and Ryan, on Thursday.'

As quick as a flash, Zara had called Sally who was equally as distraught by the news.

'What will we do?' Sniffing down the phone and listening to Zara, Sally appeared to be looking around for something. Knowingly, Ryan whipped a tissue out of the abstract patterned box, passing it across to a now sobbing wreck.

Sounding like a foghorn as she blew her nose between sentences, Sally stammered, 'I can't believe she's going through this on top of everything else. Her mind must be shot to pieces. How is she even going to cope with losing Luke? It can't be easy. Everything that's happened recently has winded her and wrecked her ability to think straight.'

'We have to act quickly, Sal,' Zara insisted. 'This is so screwed. We need to fix this! Talk in a bit. Think. Think.'

Numb, Ines sat looking out of the kitchen window, in the vain hope that she'd catch a glimpse of Luke walking to the café. It was Thursday evening and she'd had no news from him, even though she knew he was leaving tomorrow morning. Every ping, every driiing,… her heart skipped a beat in the hope that it would be Luke, but then why would he call? She had essentially told him to stay out of her life and find someone else.

Collapsing into a pathetic heap over the worktop, Ines sobbed uncontrollable tears at the irrational decision she had made. Her body wracked in jagged pain, hot and drenched with the deluge of emotion, as the idea that Luke would never be in her life, came to the fore once again, stinging every nerve in her body.

Buzz!

Somebody was at the entrance. Like a rabbit caught in headlights, Ines stared through the kitchen door at the intercom flashing a notification. Her heart in her throat, with hope, Ines couldn't breathe.

Croaking an incoherent 'hello' down the mouthpiece, she waited for what seemed an eternity for the caller to answer. Was Luke coming to convince her to change her mind but was too nervous to speak? She decided that she'd initiate the conversation.

'Luke?' A tiny voice whimpered from within Ines.

'No darling, it's us. Can we come in?' Sally looked at Zara with renewed optimism, crossing her fingers. As the door clicked open, Zara cast a sly conspiratorial wink before pushing the door open. 'She blatantly hoped it was Luke. All hope is not lost,' whispered Zara in a hurried whisper.

Entering the flat, the girls found their wilful friend, in a bedraggled, broken heap by the kitchen window.

To see her looking so frail and desolate, saddened them enormously. Throwing their bags down, the girls ran to their friend, cocooning her in their arms and assurances that everything would be okay. Scraping damp hair away from her face, Zara and Sally fussed around like mother hens, making her drink water and sitting at her favourite spot in the kitchen.

Thirsty, Ines gulped down the sweet, cool water. Grateful, she wiped her mouth with the back of her hand and managed a meek smile. 'Hey.'

'Hey yourself. So, want to talk? Or listen?' Zara looked at Ines through sharp-witted eyes. 'It's non-negotiable, take one or the other.' Signalling she meant business, Zara shuffled her bottom onto the stool. Sally pulled the other, closer, forming a tight-knit triangle.

Having explained everything to her friends without interruption, there was a gloomy silence hanging between them.

Sally spoke first. 'Sweetheart, I'm going to be frank with you. Why are you denying yourself of the opportunity to be with a man who clearly loves you? Luke has been mad about you for so long, in a way I've never seen before. And now he's broken in a way I've never seen before. Luke will cherish you from now until you're both dead, and some. He was destroyed when I spoke with him, much like how you are now. I just don't understand, if you both love each other, why can't you be together? Even Ryan said that this is crazy.'

'And now he's leaving because he's broken-hearted,' Zara continued. 'Ini, Luke's a grown man, he doesn't suffer fools gladly but last night when we spoke, he was a desperate and shattered man. He loves you and he needs you.' Pausing to take a sip of her smoothie, Zara spoke again, with more conviction; 'So let me get this right. You're concerned about him potentially having a disabled partner in the future. Yes?'

Morose, Ines agreed.

Zara continued with her speech. 'Well, my dear Ini Panini. You could be healthy, have your whole life sorted and one day, heaven forbid…' She was now tapping her head to indicate touching wood, '…be in a bad accident, then POW!' Slapping the island for added effect, she stared at Ines, waiting for a reaction. 'Are you going to kick him out? Will he leave you then? No. And you know why?'

Ines shook her head slightly.

'Because he loves you, Ini. He's a man of honour who doesn't piss off when the going gets tough. That's why darling. He's not like the Dylans and Nicks of this world. He's bloody rare, is what he is.'

Sally nodded in agreement. She was impressed with Zara's wisdom. It seemed all those nights of watching law shows had rubbed off. 'What would you say if it were me or Zara doing this?' Sally's tone was soft and encouraging.

Taking a sip of water to contemplate the question, Ines chewed her mouth in defeat. She was in a corner. Bum. 'I'd tell you not to worry until it's actually happened, if it happens at all. Then you deal with it. Stop stressing over things that might not happen.' 'Okay, can you see what we're trying to say to you?' Sally rested her hand on Ines' trembling fingers.

'Ini, when Aiden told me he didn't mind about the baby, I was expecting him to follow it with Ha! "Dream on!" Zara paused for effect. 'I wouldn't believe him. You know what? He was speaking the truth. His mum was pregnant when she met her husband. She too was left high and dry, but Colin didn't care. He loved Aiden's mum and when she gave birth, Colin adopted him straight away. Aiden has only ever known his adoptive dad. That's how he's been brought up. So, you see, out of my bad experiences, I could have lost a chance to be happy with a man who adores me and my unborn baby. Don't lose what is the most beautiful thing to happen to you both. Do you know what the trouble with you is? You just don't see in yourself what others do. You deserve this happiness. Embrace it darling. You won't be sorry.'

Twisting her hands as a welcome distraction, Ines muttered. 'I'll think about it.'

Disheartened, both friends looked at their friend in disbelief.

Massaging her forehead in frustration, Zara couldn't even bring herself to speak.

'You'll think. Hmm. Okay. You think about it, but remember this while you're "thinking": Luke's flight leaves British soil at 9:05 tomorrow morning. From Heathrow.' Sally raised her blonde thinly shaped eyebrows in affirmation.

Chapter 25

'Oh no! Oh my God, I'm going to be so late!' wailed Ines as she threw back her covers.

Hopping precariously into the legs of her jeans, chaos ensued in the effort to make up for lost time, snatching at what was laid out in preparation for the last minute flit. 'No, no, no. Oh nooo!'

Chastising herself for sleeping through the alarm, Ines calculated how much time she had to get herself to the airport. She didn't have a shot in hell of making it. 'Damn, shit and double shit. Idiot. I'm a bloody idiot!'

Doing a quick search of the flat ensuring everything was switched off, Ines grabbed her rucksack and keys, pulling the door shut behind her. She had to make it on time; she needed to talk to him. Darling Luke. Pain in the bum Luke. Her Luke.

Looking up at the monitors, the gate number flashed across the screen, bold and luminous green. Luke began to weave his way through the crowds with ease, heading for the designated area where he would get the flight and be away from London and away from the raw hurt of having Ines, only to lose her again. Joining the staggered queue of business-men, tired parents juggling their babies with all the luggage that accompanies parenthood travel and irritable kids trying to make their great escape from their parent's clutches, Luke's eyes remained lifeless as he watched the plane being prepared for take-off. People in high visibility vests and ear defenders, milled around, working diligently whilst laughing in animated conversation. Smiling at the sight, Luke appreciated the distractions.

These were short-lived however, as thoughts of Ines wormed their way from the little compartment at the back of his head to the front of his mind's eye. His heart ached, the longing for her disarming smile and low tolerance for his silliness was too much. Feeling his throat tighten, Luke took a gulp of water while he looked around for a welcome diversion.

Catching sight of the two pretty airline gate attendants, the tall blonde, flashed pearly white teeth and flirtatious glossy red lips at Luke. Returning half an awkward smile, he saw these women in a different light. They were meaningless. Irrelevant.

After experiencing the warmth, madness and sensuality of the impish woman he was truly madly deeply in love with, nothing could compare. Stepping forward to present his passport, Luke stood patiently, waiting for the attendant (who was taking a little too long inspecting his photo) to return it.

Slipping her business card in between the pages, the pretty blonde's wink was so discreet, as she wished him 'Bon Voyage', it could easily have been missed, had Luke not looked up to thank her.

Unimpressed with the brazenness of the woman, he slid his passport back into the inside pocket of his jacket, holding onto the card. Pulling the jacket zipper up, the distinctive smell of vanilla and amber wafting into his nostrils, struck him like a slap on a cold winter's day. The scent was so real, Ines could have been standing beside him. Her smell was in every pore of the leather. She had worn it during their evening stroll on Easter Sunday because she felt cold and didn't take heed of Luke's advice to dress warmer. Now, he was wearing her scent.

Seeing the business card fluttering to the ground, the lady behind him reached down to pick it up. 'Excuse me, you've dropped something.' Giving Luke the card, he took it out of politeness.

Looking at it momentarily, it dawned on him what it was. Ugh. 'Thank you.'

As the passengers shuffled along like cattle towards the aircraft, Luke tossed the gate attendant's card into the bin before stepping onto the plane.

Watching people shove cases determinedly into the overhead cabin only made Luke dislike human nature more than usual. Devoid of any feeling, he stared into emptiness. On better days, he'd spout a dry sarcastic comment, but his love for mischief had waned.

Waiting soberly behind the exhausted mum he'd seen earlier, struggling with her baggage and a small child who decided that he wanted to clamber his way over the seats, Luke felt bad for the woman. Placing his luggage between his knees, Luke reached out to her.

'Here, let me help.' Relieving her hands from the burden, the flustered woman looked at Luke, grateful for the help.

'Thanks so much.' The small boy tugged his mother towards him, pulling her hoodie over her shoulder revealing a white vest. 'Max can you stop pulling mummy, darling. The kind man is helping, so we can sit down and watch the plane go vroooom in a minute.'

Luke laughed to himself because he knew that had Ines been here, she'd have told the child that she was Santa's elf and would ensure he only got a piece of coal if he didn't shut up. Smiling at the thought, the woman assumed Luke thought her conversation with the child was entertaining.

'Thank you so much. Enjoy your trip.'

Acknowledging the sentiment, Luke reciprocated with a smile and a 'You're welcome. Take care,' before continuing up the aisle to find his seat.

Settling in, he hoped that the two empty chairs beside him would remain like that for the duration of his flight to Marseille. He was in no mood to make polite chit chat with anyone.

Resting his head against the window, Luke switched off from the buzz amongst the passengers and cabin crew, losing himself in his hopeless thoughts. Life as he knew it would never be the same.

A loud crackle came over the speakers as the captain attempted to speak.

Cruckkk

'Good morning ladies and gentlemen, this is Captain Turner speaking. We will be ready for take-off a few minutes later than scheduled.' A resounding groan of disapproval rippled through the plane. Luke, who hadn't been listening, caught the tail end of the announcement. 'Thank you for your patience and we will be up, up and away in no time. In the meantime, sit back, relax and think of the wonderful wine and gastronomic delights waiting for you.'

A hum of fervent laughter exploded into the atmosphere, leaving Luke grinning at the Captain's humorous anecdotes. Resigned to the fact that they were going to remain grounded for a while, he closed his eyes and tried to sleep. Images of Ines tore through his mind like ceaseless gunfire, but trying to squeeze away the visions that taunted him, was futile. Luke hurt so badly.

Feeling something or someone invade his space, Luke huffed under his breath. He struggled to find slumber and now sensed that he had another person sitting beside him. Great. Out of sheer pigheaded intentions, he decided that he was going to remain detached from his neighbour for the entire flight. The fact that his companion wasn't talkative either, was a good sign. By way of a non-verbal mutual agreement, neither wished to speak. Suited him just fine.

The engines began to wheeze and whir as the plane started taxiing down the runway.

Bing bong!

The familiar sound of 'fasten your seatbelt' indicator lights illuminating above, rang in his ears. He was heading back to France, leaving London and worse, leaving Ines.

A swathe of her perfume caught his breath. Like fragments of glass scratching his lungs, Luke was engulfed with a sorrow he never thought was humanly possible to feel. Ines was everywhere. Thoughts of her would continue to consume him, especially if he didn't get his jacket cleaned soon. Luke made a note to take it to the dry cleaner when he arrived at his mother's later today.

'So. You were going to leave without saying goodbye, heh?'

Was he dreaming? Not daring to open his eyes for fear that he was in fact, imagining it, they remained firmly shut. A light brush against his lips was soon met with a trail of teardrops wetting his face, every kiss as desperate as the last. Cautiously opening them, Luke's eyes rested on the elfin face before him. Filled with an insurmountable joy, his eyes glittered.

'Is it your fault the flight's delayed?'

Casting a sheepish sideways glance, Ines looked from beneath the moist crescents of her eyelashes. 'Is there room for a little person at your parents'?'

Considering the question with a thoughtful nod, he scratched his chin. 'I suppose we can shove you in somewhere.'

Replete with happiness, Ines watched the patchwork terrain below, melting away as the plane climbed steadily through the sky. She had done it. She had turned her life around.

Squeezing her hand, Luke closed his eyes— this was the start of life with his little butterfly.

Acknowledgements

This could essentially be written with a simple Thank you and a list of names, but I feel the people who've been a party to the completion of Being Ines, deserve a proper salute.

Being a debut author is no mean feat and I couldn't have gotten through this journey without the help of my writer friends. Kelly Evans, Dave Campbell, Rob Edmunds, Sharon Loeber and Deborah Anderson, you have all provided invaluable advice and constructive criticism. Thank you.

I am grateful to my beta-readers who critiqued and bolstered my writing. Your honesty is very much appreciated. Ellie-Marisa Laudriec, Dave Campbell, Sharon Loeber, Deborah Anderson, Kip, Victoria Rose, Nicola Gant and Michael Patrick, I thank you, all.

To the writing community, thanks for the laughs, the encouragement and the technical support (my struggles were real and prompted a couple of meltdowns). Nigel Baines, your patience for tech-dummies is admirable and David Strover for your graphic expertise.

Ginevra Giammatteo's perceptiveness of what I sought for the cover design made the task less stressful at a time when I needed to concentrate on other issues.

With enormous thanks to Rae Davennor at Stardust Book Services for the amazing formatting work in the eleventh hour.

The songs mentioned in the book are:
Born to Run by Bruce Springsteen
That's Amore by Dean Martin
Dancing Queen by ABBA
Could It Be Magic by Take That
Can't Take My Eyes Off You by Frankie Valli
Last Request by Paolo Nutini

And finally, to Christophe and Jean for the input you made, so I could fulfill my ambition to write in a professional capacity. Thank you.

Eva truly appreciates that you have purchased Being Ines and hopes that you enjoyed reading it as much as she has enjoyed writing it.

A small ask from the author is that you leave a review; that would make her a very happy lady.

Should you wish to connect with her, you can find Eva on: Twitter @laulauev or Email: info@evalauder.com

About the Author

Eva has lived with Multiple Sclerosis for twenty-five years. In that time research and treatment has advanced at a rate she never thought she'd ever see in her lifetime.

After a relapse compromised her mobility Eva worked from home as a comic illustrator and then went on to creating natural skincare. Another flare-up affected the dexterity of her hands. It was then, that she realised her aspirations to become a writer, could finally happen.

Born in London, Eva spent her youth living in the Hertfordshire countryside before returning to city life, studying fashion design and technology at the London College of Fashion. Having spent three years living in the Rhône Alpes, Eva returned to the UK. Now in East Sussex, Eva spends her time writing blogs and novels. Although she has written children's stories and a book on Multiple Sclerosis, Being Ines is her first published novel. When she's not writing, Eva can be heard laughing a lot, eating chocolate and reading.

evalauder.com